REMEMBRANCE OF THINGS PAST

" When to the sessions of sweet silent thought
I summon up remembrance of things past . . ."

VOLUME VII

CITIES
OF THE PLAIN

PART ONE

Of this special edition in twelve volumes of

REMEMBRANCE OF THINGS PAST

one hundred and sixty-five sets have
been printed of which one hundred
and sixty are for sale

No. 56

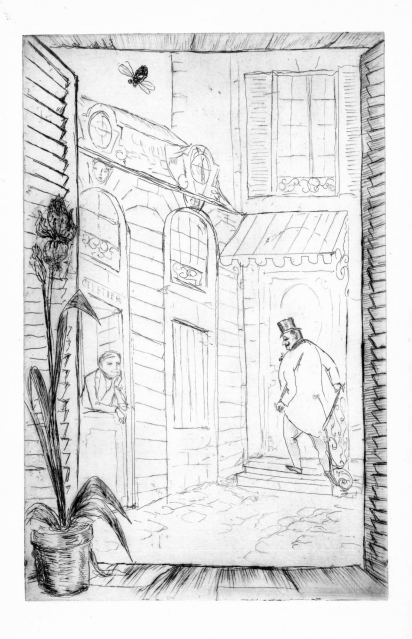

THE BARON DE CHARLUS ENCOUNTERS JUPIEN

MARCEL PROUST

CITIES
OF THE PLAIN

PART ONE

Translated by
C. K. Scott Moncrieff

ILLUSTRATED BY
PHILIPPE JULLIAN

1949
CHATTO & WINDUS
LONDON

First published in English (cr. 8vo) 1929
First issued in the Phoenix Library 1936
First issued in the Uniform Edition
(12 vols.) 1941
Reprinted 1943, 1949

CONTENTS

✻

CONTENTS

PART TWO (continued)

LIST OF ETCHINGS

*

CITIES OF THE PLAIN

PART I

Introducing the men-women, descendants of those of the inhabitants of
Sodom who were spared by the fire from heaven.

> *La femme aura Gomorrhe et l'homme aura*
> *Sodome.*   Alfred de Vigny.

THE reader will remember that, long before going
that day (on the evening of which the Princesse de
Guermantes was to give her party) to pay the Duke
and Duchess the visit which I have just described, I had
kept watch for their return and had made, in the course
of my vigil, a discovery which, albeit concerning M. de
Charlus in particular, was in itself so important that I
have until now, until the moment when I could give it the
prominence and treat it with the fulness that it demanded,
postponed giving any account of it. I had, as I have
said, left the marvellous point of vantage, so snugly contrived for me at the top of the house, commanding the
broken and irregular slopes leading up to the Hôtel de
Bréquigny, and gaily decorated in the Italian manner by
the rose-pink campanile of the Marquis de Frécourt's
stables. I had felt it to be more convenient, when I
thought that the Duke and Duchess were on the point
of returning, to post myself on the staircase. I regretted
somewhat the abandonment of my watch-tower. But at
that time of day, namely the hour immediately following
luncheon, I had less cause for regret, for I should not
then have seen, as in the morning, the footmen of the
Bréquigny-Tresmes household, converted by distance into

minute figures in a picture, make their leisurely ascent of the abrupt precipice, feather-brush in hand, behind the large, transparent flakes of mica which stood out so charmingly upon its ruddy bastions. Failing the geologist's field of contemplation, I had at least that of the botanist, and was peering through the shutters of the staircase window at the Duchess's little tree and at the precious plant, exposed in the courtyard with that insistence with which mothers "bring out" their marriageable offspring, and asking myself whether the unlikely insect would come, by a providential hazard, to visit the offered and neglected pistil. My curiosity emboldening me by degrees, I went down to the ground-floor window, which also stood open with its shutters ajar. I could hear distinctly, as he got ready to go out, Jupien who could not detect me behind my blind, where I stood perfectly still until the moment when I drew quickly aside in order not to be seen by M. de Charlus, who, on his way to call upon Mme. de Villeparisis, was slowly crossing the courtyard, a pursy figure, aged by the strong light, his hair visibly grey. Nothing short of an indisposition of Mme. de Villeparisis (consequent on the illness of the Marquis de Fierbois, with whom he personally was at daggers drawn) could have made M. de Charlus pay a call, perhaps for the first time in his life, at that hour of the day. For with that eccentricity of the Guermantes, who, instead of conforming to the ways of society, used to modify them to suit their own personal habits (habits not, they thought, social, and deserving in consequence the abasement before them of that thing of no value, Society—thus it was that Mme. de Marsantes had no regular "day," but was at home to her friends every morning

2

between ten o'clock and noon), the Baron, reserving those hours for reading, hunting for old curiosities and so forth, paid calls only between four and six in the afternoon. At six o'clock he went to the Jockey Club, or took a stroll in the Bois. A moment later, I again recoiled, in order not to be seen by Jupien. It was nearly time for him to start for the office, from which he would return only for dinner, and not even then always during the last week, his niece and her apprentices having gone to the country to finish a dress there for a customer. Then, realising that no one could see me, I decided not to let myself be disturbed again, for fear of missing, should the miracle be fated to occur, the arrival, almost beyond the possibility of hope (across so many obstacles of distance, of adverse risks, of dangers), of the insect sent from so far as ambassador to the virgin who had so long been waiting for him to appear. I knew that this expectancy was no more passive than in the male flower, whose stamens had spontaneously curved so that the insect might more easily receive their offering; similarly the female flower that stood here, if the insect came, would coquettishly arch her styles, and, to be more effectively penetrated by him, would imperceptibly advance, like a hypocritical but ardent damsel, to meet him half-way. The laws of the vegetable kingdom are themselves governed by other laws, increasingly exalted. If the visit of an insect, that is to say, the transportation of the seed of one flower is generally necessary for the fertilisation of another, that is because autofecundation, the fertilisation of a flower by itself, would lead, like a succession of intermarriages in the same family, to degeneracy and sterility, whereas the crossing effected by the insects gives to the subsequent generations

3

of the same species a vigour unknown to their forebears. This invigoration may, however, prove excessive, the species develop out of all proportion; then, as an anti-toxin protects us against disease, as the thyroid gland regulates our adiposity, as defeat comes to punish pride, fatigue indulgence, and as sleep in turn depends upon fatigue, so an exceptional act of autofecundation comes at a given point to apply its turn of the screw, its pull on the curb, brings back within normal limits the flower that has exaggerated its transgression of them. My reflexions had followed a tendency which I shall describe in due course, and I had already drawn from the visible stratagems of flowers a conclusion that bore upon a whole unconscious element of literary work, when I saw M. de Charlus coming away from the Marquise. Perhaps he had learned from his elderly relative herself, or merely from a servant, the great improvement, or rather her complete recovery from what had been nothing more than a slight indisposition. At this moment, when he did not suspect that anyone was watching him, his eyelids lowered as a screen against the sun, M. de Charlus had relaxed that tension in his face, deadened that artificial vitality, which the animation of his talk and the force of his will kept in evidence there as a rule. Pale as marble, his nose stood out firmly, his fine features no longer received from an expression deliberately assumed a different meaning which altered the beauty of their modelling; nothing more now than a Guermantes, he seemed already carved in stone, he Palamède the Fifteenth, in their chapel at Combray. These general features of a whole family took on, however, in the face of M. de Charlus a fineness more spiritualised, above all more gentle. I regretted for his sake that he

4

should habitually adulterate with so many acts of violence, offensive oddities, tale-bearings, with such harsh-
ness, susceptibility and arrogance, that he should conceal
beneath a false brutality the amenity, the kindness which,
at the moment of his emerging from Mme. de Villeparisis's, I could see displayed so innocently upon his face.
Blinking his eyes in the sunlight, he seemed almost to be
smiling, I found in his face seen thus in repose and, so to
speak, in its natural state something so affectionate, so
disarmed, that I could not help thinking how angry M.
de Charlus would have been could he have known that
he was being watched; for what was suggested to me by
the sight of this man who was so insistent, who prided
himself so upon his virility, to whom all other men seemed
odiously effeminate, what he made me suddenly think of,
so far had he momentarily assumed her features, expression, smile, was a woman.

I was about to change my position again, so that he
should not catch sight of me; I had neither the time nor
the need to do so. What did I see? Face to face, in that
courtyard where certainly they had never met before (M.
de Charlus coming to the Hôtel de Guermantes only in
the afternoon, during the time when Jupien was at his
office), the Baron, having suddenly opened wide his half-
shut eyes, was studying with unusual attention the ex-
tailor poised on the threshold of his shop, while the latter,
fastened suddenly to the ground before M. de Charlus,
taking root in it like a plant, was contemplating with a
look of amazement the plump form of the middle-aged
Baron. But, more astounding still, M. de Charlus's attitude having changed, Jupien's, as though in obedience to
the laws of an occult art, at once brought itself into har-

mony with it. The Baron, who was now seeking to conceal the impression that had been made on him, and yet, in spite of his affectation of indifference, seemed unable to move away without regret, went, came, looked vaguely into the distance in the way which, he felt, most enhanced the beauty of his eyes, assumed a complacent, careless, fatuous air. Meanwhile Jupien, shedding at once the humble, honest expression which I had always associated with him, had—in perfect symmetry with the Baron—thrown up his head, given a becoming tilt to his body, placed his hand with a grotesque impertinence on his hip, stuck out his behind, posed himself with the coquetry that the orchid might have adopted on the providential arrival of the bee. I had not supposed that he could appear so repellent. But I was equally unaware that he was capable of improvising his part in this sort of dumb charade, which (albeit he found himself for the first time in the presence of M. de Charlus) seemed to have been long and carefully rehearsed; one does not arrive spontaneously at that pitch of perfection except when one meets in a foreign country a compatriot with whom an understanding then grows up of itself, both parties speaking the same language, even although they have never seen one another before.

This scene was not, however, positively comic, it was stamped with a strangeness, or if you like a naturalness, the beauty of which steadily increased. M. de Charlus might indeed assume a detached air, indifferently let his eyelids droop; every now and then he raised them, and at such moments turned on Jupien an attentive gaze. But (doubtless because he felt that such a scene could not be prolonged indefinitely in this place, whether for

reasons which we shall learn later on, or possibly from
that feeling of the brevity of all things which makes us
determine that every blow must strike home, and renders
so moving the spectacle of every kind of love), each time
that M. de Charlus looked at Jupien, he took care that
his glance should be accompanied by a spoken word,
which made it infinitely unlike the glances we usually
direct at a person whom we do or do not know; he stared
at Jupien with the peculiar fixity of the person who is
about to say to us: "Excuse my taking the liberty, but
you have a long white thread hanging down your back,"
or else: "Surely I can't be mistaken, you come from Zurich too; I'm certain I must have seen you there often in
the curiosity shop." Thus, every other minute, the same
question seemed to be being intensely put to Jupien in
the stare of M. de Charlus, like those questioning phrases
of Beethoven indefinitely repeated at regular intervals,
and intended—with an exaggerated lavishness of preparation—to introduce a new theme, a change of tone, a " re-
entry." On the other hand, the beauty of the reciprocal
glances of M. de Charlus and Jupien arose precisely from
the fact that they did not, for the moment at least, seem
to be intended to lead to anything farther. This beauty,
it was the first time that I had seen the Baron and Jupien
display it. In the eyes of both of them, it was the sky
not of Zurich but of some Oriental city, the name of which
I had not yet divined, that I saw reflected. Whatever the
point might be that held M. de Charlus and the ex-tailor
thus arrested, their pact seemed concluded and these superfluous glances to be but ritual preliminaries, like the
parties that people give before a marriage which has been
definitely "arranged." Nearer still to nature—and the

multiplicity of these analogies is itself all the more natural in that the same man, if we examine him for a few minutes, appears in turn as a man, a man-bird or man-insect, and so forth—one would have called them a pair of birds, the male and the female, the male seeking to make advances, the female—Jupien—no longer giving any sign of response to these overtures, but regarding her new friend without surprise, with an inattentive fixity of gaze, which she doubtless felt to be more disturbing and the only effective method, once the male had taken the first steps, and had fallen back upon preening his feathers. At length Jupien's indifference seemed to suffice him no longer; from this certainty of having conquered, to making himself be pursued and desired was but the next stage, and Jupien, deciding to go off to his work, passed through the carriage gate. It was only, however, after turning his head two or three times that he escaped into the street towards which the Baron, trembling lest he should lose the trail (boldly humming a tune, not forgetting to fling a "Good day" to the porter, who, half-tipsy himself and engaged in treating a few friends in his back kitchen, did not even hear him), hurried briskly to overtake him. At the same instant, just as M. de Charlus disappeared through the gate humming like a great bumble-bee, another, a real bee this time, came into the courtyard. For all I knew this might be the one so long awaited by the orchid, which was coming to bring it that rare pollen without which it must die a virgin. But I was distracted from following the gyrations of the insect for, a few minutes later, engaging my attention afresh, Jupien (perhaps to pick up a parcel which he did take away with him ultimately and so, presumably, in the

8

emotion aroused by the apparition of M. de Charlus, had forgotten, perhaps simply for a more natural reason) returned, followed by the Baron. The latter, deciding to cut short the preliminaries, asked the tailor for a light, but at once observed: "I ask you for a light, but I find that I have left my cigars at home." The laws of hospitality prevailed over those of coquetry. "Come inside, you shall have everything you require," said the tailor, on whose features disdain now gave place to joy. The door of the shop closed behind them and I could hear no more. I had lost sight of the bee. I did not know whether he was the insect that the orchid needed, but I had no longer any doubt, in the case of an extremely rare insect and a captive flower, of the miraculous possibility of their conjunction when M. de Charlus (this is simply a comparison of providential hazards, whatever they may be, without the slightest scientific claim to establish a relation between certain botanical laws and what is sometimes, most ineptly, termed homosexuality), who for years past had never come to the house except at hours when Jupien was not there, by the mere accident of Mme. de Ville-parisis's illness had encountered the tailor, and with him the good fortune reserved for men of the type of the Baron by one of those fellow-creatures who may indeed be, as we shall see, infinitely younger than Jupien and better looking, the man predestined to exist in order that they may have their share of sensual pleasure on this earth; the man who cares only for elderly gentlemen.

All that I have just said, however, I was not to understand until several minutes had elapsed; so much is reality encumbered by those properties of invisibility until a chance occurrence has divested it of them. Anyhow, for the moment I was greatly annoyed at not being able to hear any more of the conversation between the ex-tailor and the Baron. I then bethought myself of the vacant shop, separated from Jupien's only by a partition that was extremely slender. I had, in order to get to it, merely to go up to our flat, pass through the kitchen, go down by the service stair to the cellars, make my way through them across the breadth of the courtyard above, and on coming to the right place underground, where the joiner had, a few months ago, still been storing his timber and where Jupien intended to keep his coal, climb the flight of steps which led to the interior of the shop. Thus the whole of my journey would be made under cover, I should not be seen by anyone. This was the most prudent method. It was not the one that I adopted, but, keeping close to the walls, I made a circuit in the open air of the courtyard, trying not to let myself be seen. If I was not, I owe it more, I am sure, to chance than to my own sagacity. And for the fact that I took so imprudent a course, when the way through the cellar was so safe, I can see three possible reasons, assuming that I had any reason at all. First of all, my impatience. Secondly, perhaps, a dim memory of the scene at Montjouvain, when I stood concealed outside Mlle. Vinteuil's window. Certainly, the affairs of this sort of which I have been a spectator have always been presented in a setting of the most imprudent and least probable character, as if such revelations were to be the reward of an action full of risk, though in part clandestine. Lastly, I hardly dare, so childish does it appear, to confess the third reason, which was, I am quite sure, unconsciously decisive. Since, in order to follow—and see controverted—the military prin-

ciples enunciated by Saint-Loup, I had followed in close
detail the course of the Boer war, I had been led on from
that to read again old accounts of explorations, narratives
of travel. These stories had excited me, and I applied
them to the events of my daily life to stimulate my courage. When attacks of illness had compelled me to remain for several days and nights on end not only without
sleep but without lying down, without tasting food or
drink, at the moment when my pain and exhaustion became so intense that I felt that I should never escape
from them, I would think of some traveller cast on the
beach, poisoned by noxious herbs, shivering with fever
in clothes drenched by the salt water, who nevertheless
in a day or two felt stronger, rose and went blindly upon
his way, in search of possible inhabitants who might,
when he came to them, prove cannibals. His example
acted on me as a tonic, restored my hope, and I felt
ashamed of my momentary discouragement. Thinking
of the Boers who, with British armies facing them, were
not afraid to expose themselves at the moment when they
had to cross, in order to reach a covered position, a tract
of open country: " It would be a fine thing," I thought to
myself, " if I were to shew less courage when the theatre
of operations is simply the human heart, and when the
only steel that I, who engaged in more than one duel
without fear at the time of the Dreyfus case, have to fear
is that of the eyes of the neighbours who have other
things to do besides looking into the courtyard."

But when I was inside the shop, taking care not to let
any plank in the floor make the slightest creak, as I found
that the least sound in Jupien's shop could be heard from
the other, I thought to myself how rash Jupien and M. de

Charlus had been, and how wonderfully fortune had favoured them.

I did not dare move. The Guermantes groom, taking advantage no doubt of his master's absence, had, as it happened, transferred to the shop in which I now stood a ladder which hitherto had been kept in the coach-house, and if I had climbed this I could have opened the ventilator above and heard as well as if I had been in Jupien's shop itself. But I was afraid of making a noise. Besides, it was unnecessary. I had not even cause to regret my not having arrived in the shop until several minutes had elapsed. For from what I heard at first in Jupien's shop, which was only a series of inarticulate sounds, I imagine that few words had been exchanged. It is true that these sounds were so violent that, if one set had not always been taken up an octave higher by a parallel plaint, I might have thought that one person was strangling another within a few feet of me, and that subsequently the murderer and his resuscitated victim were taking a bath to wash away the traces of the crime. I concluded from this later on that there is another thing as vociferous as pain, namely pleasure, especially when there is added to it—failing the fear of an eventual parturition, which could not be present in this case, despite the hardly convincing example in the *Golden Legend*— an immediate afterthought of cleanliness. Finally, after about half an hour (during which time I had climbed on tip-toe up my ladder so as to peep through the ventilator which I did not open), a conversation began. Jupien refused with insistence the money that M. de Charlus was pressing upon him.

"Why do you have your chin shaved like that," he

inquired of the Baron in a cajoling tone. "It's so becoming, a nice beard." "Ugh! It's disgusting," the
Baron replied. Meanwhile he still lingered upon the
threshold and plied Jupien with questions about the
neighbourhood. "You don't know anything about the
man who sells chestnuts at the corner, not the one on the
left, he's a horror, but the other way, a great, dark fellow?
And the chemist opposite, he has a charming cyclist who
delivers his parcels." These questions must have ruffled
Jupien, for, drawing himself up with the scorn of a great
courtesan who has been forsaken, he replied: "I can see
you are completely heartless." Uttered in a pained,
frigid, affected tone, this reproach must have made its
sting felt by M. de Charlus, who, to counteract the bad
impression made by his curiosity, addressed to Jupien,
in too low a tone for me to be able to make out his
words, a request the granting of which would doubtless necessitate their prolonging their sojourn in the shop,
and which moved the tailor sufficiently to make him forget his annoyance, for he studied the Baron's face, plump
and flushed beneath his grey hair, with the supremely
blissful air of a person whose self-esteem has just been
profoundly flattered, and, deciding to grant M. de Charlus
the favour that he had just asked of him, after various
remarks lacking in refinement such as: "Aren't you
naughty!" said to the Baron with a smiling, emotional,
superior and grateful air: "All right, you big baby, come
along!"

"If I hark back to the question of the tram conductor,"
M. de Charlus went on imperturbably, "it is because,
apart from anything else, he might offer me some enter-
tainment on my homeward journey. For it falls to my

lot, now and then, like the Caliph who used to roam the streets of Bagdad in the guise of a common merchant, to condescend to follow some curious little person whose profile may have taken my fancy." I made at this point the same observation that I had made on Bergotte. If he should ever have to plead before a bench, he would employ not the sentences calculated to convince his judges, but such Bergottesque sentences as his peculiar literary temperament suggested to him and made him find pleasure in using. Similarly M. de Charlus, in conversing with the tailor, made use of the same language that he would have used to fashionable people of his own set, even exaggerating its eccentricities, whether because the shyness which he was striving to overcome drove him to an excess of pride or, by preventing him from mastering himself (for we are always less at our ease in the company of some one who is not of our station), forced him to unveil, to lay bare his true nature, which was, in fact, arrogant and a trifle mad, as Mme. de Guermantes had remarked. "So as not to lose the trail," he went on, " I spring like a little usher, like a young and good-looking doctor, into the same car as the little person herself, of whom we speak in the feminine gender only so as to conform with the rules of grammar (as we say, in speaking of a Prince, 'Is His Highness enjoying *her* usual health'). If she changes her car, I take, with possibly the germs of the plague, that incredible thing called a ' transfer,' a number, and one which, albeit it is presented to *me,* is not always number one! I change ' carriages ' in this way as many as three or four times, I end up sometimes at eleven o'clock at night at the Orleans station and have to come home. Still, if it were only the

Orleans station! Once, I must tell you, not having managed to get into conversation sooner, I went all the way to Orleans itself, in one of those frightful compartments where one has, to rest one's eyes upon, between triangles of what is known as 'string-work,' photographs of the principal architectural features of the line. There was only one vacant seat; I had in front of me, as an historic edifice, a 'view' of the Cathedral of Orleans, quite the ugliest in France, and as tiring a thing to have to stare at in that way against my will as if somebody had forced me to focus its towers in the lens of one of those optical penholders which give one ophthalmia. I got out of the train at Les Aubrais together with my young person, for whom alas his family (when I had imagined him to possess every defect except that of having a family) were waiting on the platform! My sole consolation, as I waited for a train to take me back to Paris, was the house of Diane de Poitiers. She may indeed have charmed one of my royal ancestors, I should have preferred a more living beauty. That is why, as an antidote to the boredom of returning home by myself, I should rather like to make friends with a sleeping-car attendant or the conductor of an omnibus. Now, don't be shocked," the Baron wound up, "it is all a question of class. With what you would call 'young gentlemen,' for instance, I feel no desire actually to have them, but I am never satisfied until I have touched them, I don't mean physically, but touched a responsive chord. As soon as, instead of leaving my letters unanswered, a young man starts writing to me incessantly, when he is morally at my disposal, I grow calm again, or at least I should grow calm were I not immediately caught by the attraction of another. Rather curious, ain't it?—Speaking of 'young gentlemen,' those that come to the house here, do you know any of them?" "No, baby. Oh, yes, I do, a dark one, very tall, with an eyeglass, who keeps smiling and turning round." "I don't know who' you mean." Jupien filled in the portrait, but M. de Charlus could not succeed in identifying its subject, not knowing that the ex-tailor was one of those persons, more common than is generally supposed, who never remember the colour of the hair of people they do not know well. But to me, who was aware of this infirmity in Jupien and substituted "fair" for "dark," the portrait appeared to be an exact description of the Duc de Châtellerault. "To return to young men not of the lower orders," the Baron went on, "at the present moment my head has been turned by a strange little fellow, an intelligent little cit who shews with regard to myself a prodigious want of civility. He has absolutely no idea of the prodigious personage that I am, and of the microscopic animalcule that he is in comparison. After all, what does it matter, the little ass may bray his head off before my august bishop's mantle." "Bishop!" cried Jupien, who had understood nothing of M. de Charlus's concluding remarks, but was completely taken aback by the word bishop. "But that sort of thing doesn't go with religion," he said. "I have three Popes in my family," replied M. de Charlus, "and enjoy the right to mantle in gules by virtue of a cardinalatial title, the niece of the Cardinal, my great-uncle, having conveyed to my grandfather the title of Duke which was substituted for it. I see, though, that metaphor leaves you deaf and French history cold. Besides," he added, less perhaps by way of

16

conclusion than as a warning, "this attraction that I feel towards the young people who avoid me, from fear of course, for only their natural respect stops their mouths from crying out to me that they love me, requires in them an outstanding social position. And again, their feint of indifference may produce, in spite of that, the directly opposite effect. Fatuously prolonged, it sickens me. To take an example from a class with which you are more familiar, when they were doing up my Hôtel, so as not to create jealousies among all the duchesses who were vying with one another for the honour of being able to say that they had given me a lodging, I went for a few days to an 'hotel,' as they call inns nowadays. One of the bedroom valets I knew, I pointed out to him an interesting little page who used to open and shut the front door, and who remained refractory to my proposals. Finally, losing my temper, in order to prove to him that my intentions were pure, I made him an offer of a ridiculously high sum simply to come upstairs and talk to me for five minutes in my room. I waited for him in vain. I then took such a dislike to him that I used to go out by the service door so as not to see his villainous little mug at the other. I learned afterwards that he had never had any of my notes, which had been intercepted, the first by the bedroom valet, who was jealous, the next by the day porter, who was virtuous, the third by the night porter, who was in love with the little page, and used to couch with him at the hour when Dian rose. But my disgust persisted none the less, and were they to bring me the page, simply like a dish of venison on a silver platter, I should thrust him away with a retching stomach. But there's the unfortunate part of it, we have spoken· of serious matters, and now all is over between us, there can be no more question of what I hoped to secure. But you could render me great services, act as my agent; why no, the mere thought of such a thing restores my vigour, and I can see that all is by no means over."

From the beginning of this scene a revolution, in my unsealed eyes, had occurred in M. de Charlus, as complete, as immediate as if he had been touched by a magician's wand. Until then, because I had not understood, I had not seen. The vice (we use the word for convenience only), the vice of each of us accompanies him through life after the manner of the familiar genius who was invisible to men so long as they were unaware of his presence. Our goodness, our meanness, our name, our social relations do not disclose themselves to the eye, we carry them hidden within us. Even Ulysses did not at once recognise Athena. But the gods are immediately perceptible to one another, as quickly like to like, and so too had M. de Charlus been to Jupien. Until that moment I had been, in the presence of M. de Charlus, in the position of an unobservant man who, standing before a pregnant woman whose distended outline he has failed to remark, persists, while she smilingly reiterates: "Yes, I am a little tired just now," in asking her indiscreetly: "Why, what is the matter with you?" But let some one say to him: "She is expecting a child," suddenly he catches sight of her abdomen and ceases to see anything else. It is the explanation that opens our eyes; the dispelling of an error gives us an additional sense.

Those of my readers who do not care to refer, for examples of this law, to the Messieurs de Charlus of their acquaintance, whom for long years they had never suspected, until the day when, upon the smooth surface of the individual just like everyone else, there suddenly appeared, traced in an ink hitherto invisible, the characters that compose the word dear to the ancient Greeks, have only, in order to convince themselves that the world which surrounds them appears to them at first naked, bare of a thousand ornaments which it offers to the eyes of others better informed, to remind themselves how many times in the course of their lives they have found themselves on the point of making a blunder. Nothing upon the blank, undocumented face of this man or that could have led them to suppose that he was precisely the brother, or the intended husband, or the lover of a woman of whom they were just going to remark: "What a cow!" But then, fortunately, a word whispered to them by some one standing near arrests the fatal expression on their lips. At once there appear, like a *Mene, Tekel, Upharsin,* the words: "He is engaged to," or, "he is the brother of," or "he is the lover of the woman whom we ought not to describe, in his hearing, as a cow." And this one new conception will bring about an entire regrouping, thrusting some back, others forward, of the fractional conceptions, henceforward a complete whole, which we possessed of the rest of the family. In M. de Charlus another creature might indeed have coupled itself with him which made him as different from other men as the horse makes the centaur, this creature might indeed have incorporated itself in the Baron, I had never caught a glimpse of it. Now the abstraction had become materialised, the creature at last discerned had lost its power of remaining invisible, and the transformation of M. de Charlus into a new person was so complete that not only the contrasts of his face, of his voice, but, in retrospect, the very ups and downs of his relations with myself, everything that hitherto had seemed to my mind incoherent, became intelligible, brought itself into evidence, just as a sentence which presents no meaning so long as it remains broken up in letters scattered at random upon a table, expresses, if these letters be re-arranged in the proper order, a thought which one can never afterwards forget.

I now understood, moreover, how, earlier in the day, when I had seen him coming away from Mme. de Ville-parisis's, I had managed to arrive at the conclusion that M. de Charlus looked like a woman: he was one! He belonged to that race of beings, less paradoxical than they appear, whose ideal is manly simply because their temperament is feminine and who in their life resemble in appearance only the rest of men; there where each of us carries, inscribed in those eyes through which he be-holds everything in the universe, a human outline en-graved on the surface of the pupil, for them it is that not of a nymph but of a youth. Race upon which a curse weighs and which must live amid falsehood and perjury, because it knows the world to regard as a punishable and a scandalous, as an inadmissible thing, its desire, that which constitutes for every human creature the greatest happiness in life; which must deny its God, since even Christians, when at the bar of justice they appear and are arraigned, must before Christ and in His Name de-fend themselves, as from a calumny, from the charge of what to them is life itself; sons without a mother, to whom they are obliged to lie all her life long and even in the hour when they close her dying eyes; friends without friendships, despite all those which their charm, frequently recognised, inspires and their hearts, often generous, would gladly feel; but can we describe as friendship those relations which flourish only by virtue of a lie and from which the first outburst of confidence and sincerity in which they might be tempted to indulge would make them be expelled with disgust, unless they are dealing with an impartial, that is to say a sympathetic mind, which however in that case, misled with regard to them by a conventional psychology, will suppose to spring from the vice confessed the very affection that is most alien to it, just as certain judges assume and are more inclined to pardon murder in inverts and treason in Jews for reasons derived from original sin and racial predestination. And lastly—according at least to the first theory which I sketched in outline at the time and which we shall see subjected to some modification in the sequel, a theory by which this would have angered them above all things, had not the paradox been hidden from their eyes by the very illusion that made them see and live—lovers from whom is always precluded the possibility of that love the hope of which gives them the strength to endure so many risks and so much loneliness, since they fall in love with precisely that type of man who has nothing feminine about him, who is not an invert and consequently cannot love them in return; with the result that their desire would be for ever insatiable did not their money procure for them real men, and their imagination end by making them take for real men the inverts to whom they had prostituted themselves. Their honour precarious, their liberty provisional, lasting only until the discovery of their crime; their position unstable, like that of the poet who one day was feasted at every table, applauded in every theatre in London, and on the next was driven from every lodging, unable to find a pillow upon which to lay his head, turning the mill like Samson and saying like him: "The two sexes shall die, each in a place apart!"; excluded even, save on the days of general disaster when the majority rally round the victim as the Jews rallied round Dreyfus, from the sympathy— at times from the society—of their fellows, in whom they inspire only disgust at seeing themselves as they are, portrayed in a mirror which, ceasing to flatter them, accentuates every blemish that they have refused to observe in themselves, and makes them understand that what they have been calling their love (a thing to which, playing upon the word, they have by association annexed all that poetry, painting, music, chivalry, asceticism have contrived to add to love) springs not from an ideal of beauty which they have chosen but from an incurable malady; like the Jews again (save some who will associate only with others of their race and have always on their lips ritual words and consecrated pleasantries), shunning one another, seeking out those who are most directly their opposite, who do not desire their company, pardoning their rebuffs, moved to ecstasy by their condescension; but also brought into the company of their own kind by the ostracism that strikes them, the opprobrium under which they have fallen, having finally been invested, by a persecution similar to that of Israel, with the physical and moral characteristics of a race, sometimes beautiful, often hideous, finding (in spite of all the mockery with which he who, more closely blended with, better assimilated to the opposing race, is relatively, in appearance, the least inverted, heaps upon him who has remained more so) a relief in frequenting the society of their kind, and even some corroboration of their own life, so much so that, while steadfastly denying that they are a race (the name of which is the vilest of insults), those who succeed in concealing the fact that they belong to it they readily unmask, with a view less to injuring them, though they have no scruple about that, than to excusing themselves; and, going in search (as a doctor seeks cases of appendicitis) of cases of inversion in history, taking pleasure in recalling that Socrates was one of themselves, as the Israelites claim that Jesus was one of them, without reflecting that there were no abnormals when homosexuality was the norm, no anti-Christians before Christ, that the disgrace alone makes the crime because it has allowed to survive only those who remained obdurate to every warning, to every example, to every punishment, by virtue of an innate disposition so peculiar that it is more repugnant to other men (even although it may be accompanied by exalted moral qualities) than certain other vices which exclude those qualities, such as theft, cruelty, breach of faith, vices better understood and so more readily excused by the generality of men; forming a freemasonry far more extensive, more powerful and less suspected than that of the Lodges, for it rests upon an identity of tastes, needs, habits, dangers, apprenticeship, knowledge, traffic, glossary, and one in which the members themselves, who intend not to know one another, recognise one another immediately by natural or conventional, involuntary or deliberate signs which indicate one of his congeners to the beggar in the street, in the great nobleman whose carriage door he is shutting, to the father in the suitor for his daughter's hand, to him who has sought healing, absolution, defence, in the doctor, the priest, the barrister to whom he has had recourse; all of them obliged to protect their own secret but having their part in a secret shared with the others, which the rest of humanity does not suspect and which means that to them the most wildly improbable tales of adventure seem true, for in this romantic, anachronistic life the ambassador is a bosom friend of the felon, the prince, with a certain independence of action with which his aristocratic breeding has furnished him, and which the trembling little cit would lack, on leaving the duchess's party goes off to confer in private with the hooligan; a reprobate part of the human whole, but an important part, suspected where it does not exist, flaunting itself, insolent and unpunished, where its existence is never guessed; numbering its adherents everywhere, among the people, in the army, in the church, in the prison, on the throne; living, in short, at least to a great extent, in a playful and perilous intimacy with the men of the other race, provoking them, playing with them by speaking of its vice as of something alien to it; a game that is rendered easy by the blindness or duplicity of the others, a game that may be kept up for years until the day of the scandal, on which these lion-tamers are devoured; until then, obliged to make a secret of their lives, to turn away their eyes from the things on which they would naturally fasten them, to fasten them upon those from which they would naturally turn away, to change the gender of many of the words in their vocabulary, a social constraint, slight in comparison with the inward constraint which their vice, or what is improperly so called, imposes upon

24

them with regard not so much now to others as to themselves, and in such a way that to themselves it does not appear a vice. But certain among them, more practical, busier men who have not the time to go and drive their own bargains, or to dispense with the simplification of life and that saving of time which may result from co-operation, have formed two societies of which the second is composed exclusively of persons similar to themselves.

This is noticeable in those who are poor and have come up from the country, without friends, with nothing but their ambition to be some day a celebrated doctor or barrister, with a mind still barren of opinions, a person unadorned with manners, which they intend, as soon as possible, to decorate, just as they would buy furniture for their little attic in the Latin quarter, copying whatever they had observed in those who had already " arrived " in the useful and serious profession in which they also intend to establish themselves and to become famous; in these their special taste, unconsciously inherited like a weakness for drawing, for music, a weakness of vision, is perhaps the only living and despotic originality—which on certain evenings compels them to miss some meeting, advantageous to their career, with people whose ways, in other respects, of speaking, thinking, dressing, parting their hair, they have adopted. In their quarter, where otherwise they mix only with their brother students, their teachers or some fellow-provincial who has succeeded and can help them on, they have speedily discovered other young men whom the same peculiar taste attracts to them, as in a small town one sees an intimacy grow up between the assistant master and the lawyer, who are both interested in chamber music or mediaeval ivories; applying to the object of their distraction the same utilitarian instinct, the same professional spirit which guides them in their career, they meet these young men at gatherings to which no profane outsider is admitted any more than to those that bring together collectors of old snuff-boxes, Japanese prints or rare flowers, and at which, what with the pleasure of gaining information, the practical value of making exchanges and the fear of competition, there prevail simultaneously, as in a sale-room of postage stamps, the close cooperation of the specialists and the fierce rivalries of the collectors. No one moreover in the café where they have their table knows what the gathering is, whether it is that of an angling club, of an editorial staff, or of the " Sons of the Indre," so correct is their attire, so cold and reserved their manner, so modestly do they refrain from any-thing more than the most covert glances at the young men of fashion, the young " lions " who, a few feet away, are making a great clamour about their mistresses, and among whom those who are admiring them without ven-turing to raise their eyes will learn only twenty years later, when they themselves are on the eve of admission to the Academy, and the others are middle-aged gentle-men in club windows, that the most seductive among them, now a stout and grizzled Charlus, was in reality akin to themselves, but differently, in another world, beneath other external symbols, with foreign labels, the strangeness of which led them into error. But these groups are at varying stages of evolution ; and, just as the " Union of the Left " differs from the " Socialist Federation " or some Mendelssohnian musical club from the Schola Cantorum, on certain evenings, at another table, there are extremists who allow a bracelet to slip down from beneath a cuff, sometimes a necklace to gleam in the gap of a collar, who by their persistent stares, their cooings, their laughter, their mutual caresses, oblige a band of students to depart in hot haste, and are served with a civility beneath which indignation boils by a waiter who, as on the evenings when he has to serve Dreyfusards, would find pleasure in summoning the police did he not find profit in pocketing their gratuities.

It is with these professional organisations that the mind contrasts the taste of the solitaries, and in one respect without straining the points of difference, since it is doing no more than copy the solitaries themselves who imagine that nothing differs more widely from organised vice than what appears to them to be a misunderstood love, but with some strain nevertheless, for these different classes correspond, no less than to diverse physiological types, to successive stages in a pathological or merely social evolution. And it is, in fact, very rarely that, one day or another, it is not in some such organisation that the solitaries come to merge themselves, sometimes from simple weariness, or for convenience (just as the people who have been most strongly opposed to such innovations end by having the telephone installed, inviting the Iénas to their parties, or dealing with Potin). They meet there, for that matter, with none too friendly a reception as a rule, for, in their relatively pure lives, their want of experience, the saturation in dreams to which they have been reduced, have branded more strongly upon them those special marks of effeminacy which the professionals have sought to efface. And it must be admitted that, among certain of these newcomers, the woman is not only inwardly united to the man but hideously visible, agitated as one sees them by a hysterical spasm, by a shrill laugh which convulses their knees and hands, looking no more like the common run of men than those apes with melancholy, shadowed eyes and prehensile feet who dress up in dinner-jackets and black bow ties; so that these new recruits are judged by others, less chaste for all that themselves, to be compromising associates, and their admission is hedged with difficulties; they are accepted, nevertheless, and they benefit then by those facilities by which commerce, great undertakings have transformed the lives of individuals, and have brought within their reach commodities hitherto too costly to acquire and indeed hard to find, which now submerge them beneath the plethora of what by themselves they had never succeeded in discovering amid the densest crowds. But, even with these innumerable outlets, the burden of social constraint is still too heavy for some, recruited principally among those who have not made a practice of self-control, and who still take to be rarer than it actually is their way of love. Let us leave out of consideration for the moment those who, the exceptional character of their inclinations making them regard themselves as superior to the other sex, look down upon women, make homosexuality the privilege of great genius and of glorious epochs of history, and, when they seek to communicate their taste to others, approach not so much those who seem to them to be predisposed towards it (as the morphinomaniac does with his morphia) as those who seem to them to be worthy of it, from apostolic zeal, just as others preach Zionism, conscientious objection to military service, Saint-Simonism, vegetarianism or anarchy. Here is one who, should we intrude upon him in the morning, still in bed, will present to our gaze an admirable female head, so general is its expression and typical of the sex as a whole; his very hair affirms this, so feminine is its ripple; unbrushed, it falls so naturally in long curls over the cheek that one marvels how the young woman, the girl, the Galatea barely awakened to life, in the unconscious mass of this male body in which she is imprisoned, has contrived so ingeniously by herself, without instruction from anyone, to make use of the narrowest apertures in her prison wall to find what was necessary to her existence. No doubt the young man who sports this delicious head does not say: "I am a woman." Even if—for any of the countless possible reasons—he lives with a woman, he can deny to her that he is himself one, can swear to her that he has never had intercourse with men. But let her look at him as we have just revealed him, lying back in bed, in pyjamas, his arms bare, his throat and neck bare also beneath the darkness of his hair. The pyjama jacket becomes a woman's shift, the head that of a pretty Spanish girl. The mistress is astounded by these confidences offered to her gaze, truer than any spoken confidence could be, or indeed any action, which his actions, indeed, if they have not already done so, cannot fail later on to confirm, for every creature follows the line of his own pleasure, and if this creature is not too vicious he will seek it in a sex complementary to his own. And for the invert vice begins, not when he forms relations (for there are all sorts of reasons that may enjoin these), but when he takes his pleasure with women. The young man whom we have been attempting to portray was so evidently a

woman that the women who looked upon him with longing were doomed (failing a special taste on their part) to
the same disappointment as those who in Shakespeare's
comedies are taken in by a girl in disguise who passes as
a youth. The deception is mutual, the invert is himself
aware of it, he guesses the disillusionment which, once the
mask is removed, the woman will experience, and feels
to what an extent this mistake as to sex is a source of
poetical imaginings. Besides, even from his exacting
mistress, in vain does he keep back the admission (if
she, that is to say, be not herself a denizen of Gomorrah):
"I am a woman!" when all the time with what stratagems, what agility, what obstinacy as of a climbing plant
the unconscious but visible woman in him seeks the
masculine organ. We have only to look at that head of
curling hair on the white pillow to understand that if, in
the evening, this young man slips through his guardians'
fingers, in spite of anything that they, or he himself can
do to restrain him, it will not be to go in pursuit of
women. His mistress may chastise him, may lock him
up; next day, the man-woman will have found some way
of attaching himself to a man, as the convolvulus throws
out its tendrils wherever it finds a convenient post or
rake. Why, when we admire in the face of this person a
delicacy that touches our hearts, a gracefulness, a spontaneous affability such as men do not possess, should we
be dismayed to learn that this young man runs after
boxers? They are different aspects of an identical reality. And indeed, what repels us is the most touching
thing of all, more touching than any refinement of delicacy, for it represents an admirable though unconscious
effort on the part of nature: the recognition of his sex by

itself, in spite of the sexual deception, becomes apparent, the unconfessed attempt to escape from itself towards what an initial error on the part of society has segregated from it. Some, those no doubt who have been most timid in childhood, are scarcely concerned with the material kind of the pleasure they receive, provided that they can associate it with a masculine face. Whereas others, whose sensuality is doubtless more violent, imperiously restrict their material pleasure within certain definite limitations. These live perhaps less exclusively beneath the sway of Saturn's outrider, since for them women are not entirely barred, as for the former sort, in whose eyes women would have no existence apart from conversation, flirtation, loves not of the heart but of the head. But the second sort seek out those women who love other women; who can procure for them a young man, enhance the pleasure which they feel on finding themselves in his company; better still, they can, in the same fashion, enjoy with such women the same pleasure as with a man. Whence it arises that jealousy is kindled in those who love the first sort only by the pleasure which they may be enjoying with a man, which alone seems to their lovers a betrayal, since these do not participate in the love of women, have practised it only as a habit, and, so as to reserve for themselves the possibility of eventual marriage, representing to themselves so little the pleasure that it is capable of giving that they cannot be distressed by the thought that he whom they love is enjoying that pleasure; whereas the other sort often inspire jealousy by their love-affairs with women. For, in the relations which they have with her, they play, for the woman who loves her own sex, the part of another woman, and she

offers them at the same time more or less what they find
in other men, so that the jealous friend suffers from the
feeling that he whom he loves is riveted to her who is
to him almost a man, and at the same time feels his beloved almost escape him because, to these women, he is
something which the lover himself cannot conceive, a sort
of woman. We need not pause here to consider those
young fools who by a sort of arrested development, to
tease their friends or to shock their families, proceed with
a kind of frenzy to choose clothes that resemble women's
dress, to redden their lips and blacken their eyelashes;
we may leave them out of account, for they are those
whom we shall find later on, when they have suffered the
all too cruel penalty of their affectation, spending what
remains of their lifetime in vain attempts to repair by a
sternly protestant demeanour the wrong that they did to
themselves when they were carried away by the same
demon that urges young women of the Faubourg Saint-
Germain to live in a scandalous fashion, to set every con-
vention at defiance, to scoff at the entreaties of their
relatives, until the day when they set themselves with
perseverance but without success to reascend the slope
down which it had seemed to them that it would be so
amusing to glide, down which they had found it so
amusing, or rather had not been able to stop themselves
from gliding. Finally, let us leave to a later volume the
men who have sealed a pact with Gomorrah. We shall
deal with them when M. de Charlus comes to know them.
Let us leave out for the present all those, of one sort or
another, who will appear each in his turn, and, to conclude this first sketch of the subject, let us say a word
only of those whom we began to mention just now, the

solitary class. Supposing their vice to be more exceptional than it is, they have retired into solitude from the
day on which they discovered it, after having carried it
within themselves for a long time without knowing it,
for a longer time only than certain other men. For no
one can tell at first that he is an invert or a poet or a
snob or a scoundrel. The boy who has been reading
erotic poetry or looking at indecent pictures, if he then
presses his body against a schoolfellow's, imagines himself only to be communing with him in an identical desire
for a woman. How should he suppose that he is not like
everybody else when he recognises the substance of what
he feels on reading Mme. de Lafayette, Racine, Baude-
laire, Walter Scott, at a time when he is still too little
capable of observing himself to take into account what he
has added from his own store to the picture, and that if
the sentiment be the same the object differs, that what
he desires is Rob Roy, and not Diana Vernon? With
many, by a defensive prudence on the part of the instinct
that precedes the clearer vision of the intellect, the mirror
and walls of their bedroom vanish beneath a cloud of
coloured prints of actresses; they compose poetry such as:

> I love but Chloe in the world,
> For Chloe is divine;
> Her golden hair is sweetly curled,
> For her my heart doth pine.

Must we on that account attribute to the opening phase
of such lives a taste which we shall never find in them
later on, like those flaxen ringlets on the heads of children which are destined to change to the darkest brown?
Who can tell whether the photographs of women are not

I   33   D

a first sign of hypocrisy, a first sign also of horror at other inverts? But the solitary kind are precisely those to whom hypocrisy is painful. Possibly even the example of the Jews, of a different type of colony, is not strong enough to account for the frail hold that their upbringing has upon them, or for the artfulness with which they find their way back (perhaps not to anything so sheerly terrible as the suicide to which maniacs, whatever precautions one may take with them, return, and, pulled out of the river into which they have flung themselves, take poison, procure revolvers, and so forth; but) to a life of which the men of the other race not only do not understand, cannot imagine, abominate the essential pleasures but would be filled with horror by the thought of its frequent danger and everlasting shame. Perhaps, to form a picture of these, we ought to think, if not of the wild animals that never become domesticated, of the lion-cubs said to be tame but lions still at heart, then at least of the negroes whom the comfortable existence of the white man renders desperately unhappy and who prefer the risks of a life of savagery and its incomprehensible joys. When the day has dawned on which they have discovered themselves to be incapable at once of lying to others and of lying to themselves, they go away to live in the country, shunning the society of their own kind (whom they believe to be few in number) from horror of the monstrosity or fear of the temptation, and that of the rest of humanity from shame. Never having arrived at true maturity, plunged in a constant melancholy, now and again, some Sunday evening when there is no moon, they go for a solitary walk as far as a cross-roads where, although not a word has been said, there has come to meet them one of their boyhood's friends who is living in a house in the neighbourhood. And they begin again the pastimes of long ago, on the grass, in the night, neither uttering a word. During the week, they meet in their respective houses, talk of no matter what, without any allusion to what has occurred between them, exactly as though they had done nothing and were not to do anything again, save, in their relations, a trace of coldness, of irony, of irritability and rancour, at times of hatred. Then the neighbour sets out on a strenuous expedition on horseback, and, on a mule, climbs mountain peaks, sleeps in the snow; his friend, who identifies his own vice with a weakness of temperament, the cabined and timid life, realises that vice can no longer exist in his friend now emancipated, so many thousands of feet above sea-level. And, sure enough, the other takes a wife. And yet the abandoned one is not cured (in spite of the cases in which, as we shall see, inversion is curable). He insists upon going down himself every morning to the kitchen to receive the milk from the hands of the dairyman's boy, and on the evenings when desire is too strong for him will go out of his way to set a drunkard on the right road or to " adjust the dress " of a blind man. No doubt the life of certain inverts appears at times to change, their vice (as it is called) is no longer apparent in their habits; but nothing is ever lost; a missing jewel turns up again; when the quantity of a sick man's urine decreases, it is because he is perspiring more freely, but the excretion must invariably occur. One day this homosexual hears of the death of a young cousin, and from his inconsolable grief we learned that it was to this love, chaste possibly and aimed rather at retaining esteem than at obtaining possession, that his desires have passed by a sort of virement, as, in a budget, without any alteration in the total, certain expenditure is carried under another head. As is the case with invalids in whom a sudden attack of urticaria makes their chronic ailments temporarily disappear, this pure love for a young relative seems, in the invert, to have momentarily replaced, by metastasis, habits that will, one day or another, return to fill the place of the vicarious, cured malady.

Meanwhile the married neighbour of our recluse has returned; before the beauty of the young bride and the demonstrative affection of her husband, on the day when their friend is obliged to invite them to dinner, he feels ashamed of the past. Already in an interesting condition, she must return home early, leaving her husband behind; he, when the time has come for him to go home also, asks his host to accompany him for part of the way; at first, no suspicion enters his mind, but at the crossroads he finds himself thrown down on the grass, with not a word said, by the mountaineer who is shortly to become a father. And their meetings begin again, and continue until the day when there comes to live not far off a cousin of the young woman, with whom her husband is now constantly to be seen. And he, if the twice abandoned friend calls in the evening and endeavours to approach him, is furious, and repulses him with indignation that the other has not had the tact to foresee the disgust which he must henceforward inspire. Once, however, there appears a stranger, sent to him by his faithless friend; but being busy at the time, the abandoned one cannot see him, and only afterwards learns with what object his visitor came.

Then the solitary languishes alone. He has no other diversion than to go to the neighbouring watering-place to ask for some information or other from a certain railwayman there. But the latter has obtained promotion, has been transferred to the other end of the country; the solitary will no longer be able to go and ask him the times of the trains or the price of a first class ticket, and, before retiring to dream, Griselda-like, in his tower, loiters upon the beach, a strange Andromeda whom no Argonaut will come to free, a sterile Medusa that must perish upon the sand, or else he stands idly, until his train starts, upon the platform, casting over the crowd of passengers a gaze that will seem indifferent, contemptuous or distracted to those of another race, but, like the luminous glow with which certain insects bedeck themselves in order to attract others of their species, or like the nectar which certain flowers offer to attract the insects that will fertilise them, would not deceive the almost undiscoverable sharer of a pleasure too singular, too hard to place, which is offered him, the colleague with whom our specialist could converse in the half-forgotten tongue; in which last, at the most, some seedy loafer upon the platform will put up a show of interest, but for pecuniary gain alone, like those people who, at the Collège de France, in the room in which the Professor of Sanskrit lectures without an audience, attend his course but only because the room itself is heated. Medusa! Orchid! When I followed my instinct only, the medusa used to revolt me at Balbec; but if I had the eyes to regard it, like Michelet, from the standpoint of natural history, and aesthetic, I saw an exquisite wheel of azure flame. Are they not, with the transparent velvet of their petals, as it were the mauve

orchids of the sea? Like so many creatures of the animal
and vegetable kingdoms, like the plant which would produce vanilla but, because in its structure the male organ
is divided by a partition from the female, remains sterile
unless the humming-birds or certain tiny bees convey the
pollen from one to the other, or man fertilises them by
artificial means, M. de Charlus (and here the word fertilise must be understood in a moral sense, since in the
physical sense the union of male with male is and must
be sterile, but it is no small matter that a person may
encounter the sole pleasure which he is capable of enjoying, and that every " creature here below " can impart
to some other " his music, or his fragrance or his flame "),
M. de Charlus was one of those men who may be called
exceptional, because however many they may be, the
satisfaction, so easy in others, of their sexual require-
ments depends upon the coincidence of too many conditions, and of conditions too difficult to ensure. For men
like M. de Charlus (leaving out of account the compro-
mises which will appear in the course of this story and
which the reader may already have foreseen, enforced by
the need of pleasure which resigns itself to partial accep-
tations), mutual love, apart from the difficulties, so great
as to be almost insurmountable, which it meets in the
ordinary man, adds to these others so exceptional that
what is always extremely rare for everyone becomes in
their case well nigh impossible, and, if there should befall
them an encounter which is really fortunate, or which
nature makes appear so to them, their good fortune, far
more than that of the normal lover, has about it something extraordinary, selective, profoundly necessary.
The feud of the Capulets and Montagues was as nothing

compared with the obstacles of every sort which must have been surmounted, the special eliminations which nature has had to submit to the hazards, already far from common, which result in love, before a retired tailor, who was intending to set off soberly for his office, can stand quivering in ecstasy before a stoutish man of fifty; this Romeo and this Juliet may believe with good reason that their love is not the caprice of a moment but a true predestination, prepared by the harmonies of their temperaments, and not only by their own personal temperaments but by those of their ancestors, by their most distant strains of heredity, so much so that the fellow creature who is conjoined with them has belonged to them from before their birth, has attracted them by a force comparable to that which governs the worlds on which we passed our former lives. M. de Charlus had distracted me from looking to see whether the bee was bringing to the orchid the pollen it had so long been waiting to receive, and had no chance of receiving save by an accident so unlikely that one might call it a sort of miracle. But this was a miracle also that I had just witnessed, almost of the same order and no less marvellous. As soon as I had considered their meeting from this point of view, everything about it seemed to me instinct with beauty. The most extraordinary devices that nature has invented to compel insects to ensure the fertilisation of flowers which without their intervention could not be fertilised because the male flower is too far away from the female—or when, if it is the wind that must provide for the transportation of the pollen, she makes that pollen so much more simply detachable from the male, so much more easily arrested in its flight by the female flower, by eliminating the secretion of nectar which is no longer of any use since there is no insect to be attracted, and, that the flower may be kept free for the pollen which it needs, which can fructify only in itself, makes it secrete a liquid which renders it immune to all other pollens—seemed to me no more marvellous than the existence of the sub-variety of inverts destined to guarantee the pleasures of love to the invert who is growing old: men who are attracted not by all other men, but—by a phenomenon of correspondence and harmony similar to those that precede the fertilisation of heterostyle trimorphous flowers like the *lythrum salicoria*—only by men considerably older than themselves. Of this subvariety Jupien had just furnished me with an example less striking however than certain others, which every collector of a human herbary, every moral botanist can observe in spite of their rarity, and which will present to the eye a delicate youth who is waiting for the advances of a robust and paunchy quinquagenarian, remaining as indifferent to those of other young men as the hermaphrodite flowers of the short-styled *primula veris* so long as they are fertilised only by other *primulae veris* of short style also, whereas they welcome with joy the pollen of the *primula veris* with the long styles. As for M. de Charlus's part in the transaction, I noticed afterwards that there were for him various kinds of conjunction, some of which, by their multiplicity, their almost invisible speed and above all the absence of contact between the two actors, recalled still more forcibly those flowers that in a garden are fertilised by the pollen of a neighbouring flower which they may never touch. There were in fact certain persons whom it was sufficient for him to make come to his house, hold for an hour or two under the domination of his talk, for his desire, quickened by some earlier encounter, to be assuaged. By a simple use of words the conjunction was effected, as simply as it can be among the infusoria. Sometimes, as had doubtless been the case with me on the evening on which I had been summoned by him after the Guermantes dinner-party, the relief was effected by a violent ejaculation which the Baron made in his visitor's face, just as certain flowers, furnished with a hidden spring, sprinkle from within the unconsciously collaborating and disconcerted insect. M. de Charlus, from vanquished turning victor, feeling himself purged of his uneasiness and calmed, would send away the visitor who had at once ceased to appear to him desirable. Finally, inasmuch as inversion itself springs from the fact that the invert is too closely akin to woman to be capable of having any effective relations with her, it comes under a higher law which ordains that so many hermaphrodite flowers shall remain unfertile, that is to say the law of the sterility of autofecundation. It is true that inverts, in their search for a male person, will often be found to put up with other inverts as effeminate as themselves. But it is enough that they do not belong to the female sex, of which they have in them an embryo which they can put to no useful purpose, such as we find in so many hermaphrodite flowers, and even in certain hermaphrodite animals, such as the snail, which cannot be fertilised by themselves, but can by other hermaphrodites. In this respect the race of inverts, who eagerly connect themselves with Oriental antiquity or the Golden Age in Greece, might be traced back farther still, to those experimental epochs in which there existed neither dioecious plants nor monosexual animals, to that initial hermaphroditism of which certain rudiments of male organs in the anatomy of the woman and of female organs in that of the man seem still to preserve the trace. I found the pantomine, incomprehensible to me at first, of Jupien and M. de Charlus as curious as those seductive gestures addressed, Darwin tells us, to insects not only by the flowers called composite which erect the florets of their capitals so as to be seen from a greater distance, such as a certain heterostyle which turns back its stamens and bends them to open the way for the insect, or offers him an ablution, or, to take an immediate instance, the nectar-fragrance and vivid hue of the corollae that were at that moment attracting insects to our courtyard. From this day onwards M. de Charlus was to alter the time of his visits to Mme. de Villeparisis, not that he could not see Jupien elsewhere and with greater convenience, but because to him just as much as to me the afternoon sunshine and the blossoming plant were, no doubt, linked together in memory. Apart from this, he did not confine himself to recommending the Jupiens to Mme. de Villeparisis, to the Duchesse de Guermantes, to a whole brilliant list of patrons, who were all the more assiduous in their attentions to the young seamstress when they saw that the few ladies who had held out, or had merely delayed their submission, were subjected to the direst reprisals by the Baron, whether in order that they might serve as an example, or because they had aroused his wrath and had stood out against his attempted domination; he made Jupien's position more and more lucrative, until he definitely engaged him as his secretary and established him in the state in which we

42

shall see him later on. "Ah, now! There is a happy man, if you like, that Julien," said Françoise, who had a tendency to minimise or exaggerate people's generosity according as it was bestowed on herself or on others. Not that, in this instance, she had any need to exaggerate, nor for that matter did she feel any jealousy, being genuinely fond of Jupien. "Oh, he's such a good man, the Baron," she went on, "such a well-behaved, religious, proper sort of man. If I had a daughter to marry and was one of the rich myself, I would give her to the Baron with my eyes shut." "But, Françoise," my mother observed gently, "she'ld be well supplied with husbands, that daughter of yours. Don't forget you've already promised her to Jupien." "Ah! Lordy, now," replied Françoise, "there's another of them that would make a woman happy. It doesn't matter whether you're rich or poor, it makes no difference to your nature. The Baron and Julien, they're just the same sort of person."

However, I greatly exaggerated at the time, on the strength of this first revelation, the elective character of so carefully selected a combination. Admittedly, every man of the kind of M. de Charlus is an extraordinary creature since, if he does not make concessions to the possibilities of life, he seeks out essentially the love of a man of the other race, that is to say a man who is a lover of women (and incapable consequently of loving him); in contradiction of what I had imagined in the courtyard, where I had seen Jupien turning towards M. de Charlus like the orchid making overtures to the bee, these exceptional creatures whom we commiserate are a vast crowd, as we shall see in the course of this work, for a reason which will be disclosed only at the end of it, and commiserate themselves for being too many rather than too few. For the two angels who were posted at the gates of Sodom to learn whether its inhabitants (according to Genesis) had indeed done all the things the report of which had ascended to the Eternal Throne must have been, and of this one can only be glad, exceedingly ill chosen by the Lord, Who ought not to have entrusted the task to any but a Sodomite. Such an one the excuses: " Father of six children—I keep two mistresses," and so forth could never have persuaded benevolently to lower his flaming sword and to mitigate the punishment; he would have answered: " Yes, and your wife lives in a torment of jealousy. But even when these women have not been chosen by you from Gomorrah, you spend your nights with a watcher of flocks upon Hebron." And he would at once have made him retrace his steps to the city which the rain of fire and brimstone was to destroy. On the contrary, they allowed to escape all the shame-faced Sodomites, even if these, on catching sight of a boy, turned their heads, like Lot's wife, though without being on that account changed like her into pillars of salt. With the result that they engendered a numerous posterity with whom this gesture has continued to be habitual, like that of the dissolute women who, while apparently studying a row of shoes displayed in a shop window, turn their heads to keep track of a passing student. These descendants of the Sodomites, so numerous that we may apply to them that other verse of Genesis: " If a man can number the dust of the earth, then shall thy seed also be numbered," have established themselves throughout the entire world; they have had access to every profession and pass so easily into the most ex-

44

clusive clubs that, whenever a Sodomite fails to secure election, the black balls are, for the most part, cast by other Sodomites, who are anxious to penalise sodomy, having inherited the falsehood that enabled their ancestors to escape from the accursed city. It is possible that they may return there one day. Certainly they form in every land an Oriental colony, cultured, musical, malicious, which has certain charming qualities and intolerable defects. We shall study them with greater thoroughness in the course of the following pages; but I have thought it as well to utter here a provisional warning against the lamentable error of proposing (just as people have encouraged a Zionist movement) to create a Sodomist movement and to rebuild Sodom. For, no sooner had they arrived there than the Sodomites would leave the town so as not to have the appearance of belonging to it, would take wives, keep mistresses in other cities where they would find, incidentally, every diversion that appealed to them. They would repair to Sodom only on days of supreme necessity, when their own town was empty, at those seasons when hunger drives the wolf from the woods; in other words, everything would go on very much as it does to-day in London, Berlin, Rome, Petrograd or Paris.

Anyhow, on the day in question, before paying my call on the Duchess, I did not look so far ahead, and I was distressed to find that I had, by my engrossment in the Jupien-Charlus conjunction, missed perhaps an opportunity of witnessing the fertilisation of the blossom by the bee.

PART II

CHAPTER I

M. de Charlus in Society.—A physician.—Typical physiognomy of
Mme. de Vaugoubert.—Mme. d'Arpajon, the Hubert Robert
fountain and the merriment of the Grand Duke Vladimir.—Mmes.
d'Amoncourt, de Citri, de Saint-Euverte, etc.—Curious conversation
between Swann and the Prince de Guermantes.—Albertine on the
telephone.—My social life in the interval before my second and
final visit to Balbec. Arrival at Balbec.—The heart's intermissions.

AS I was in no haste to arrive at this party at the
Guermantes', to which I was not certain that I
had been invited, I remained sauntering out of
doors; but the summer day seemed to be in no greater
haste than myself to stir. Albeit it was after nine o'clock,
it was still the light of day that on the Place de la Con-
corde was giving the Luxor obelisk the appearance of
being made of pink nougat. Then it diluted the tint and
changed the surface to a metallic substance, so that the
obelisk not only became more precious but seemed to
have grown more slender and almost flexible. You imagined that you might have twisted it in your fingers, had
perhaps already slightly distorted its outline. The moon
was now in the sky like a section of orange delicately
peeled although slightly bruised. But presently she was
to be fashioned of the most enduring gold. Sheltering
alone behind her, a poor little star was to serve as sole
companion to the lonely moon, while she, keeping her
friend protected, but bolder and striding ahead, would
brandish like an irresistible weapon, like an Oriental
symbol, her broad and marvellous crescent of gold.

Outside the mansion of the Princesse de Guermantes,

I met the Duc de Châtellerault; I no longer remembered
that half an hour earlier I had still been persecuted by
the fear—which, for that matter, was speedily to grip
me again—that I might be entering the house uninvited.
We grow uneasy, and it is sometimes long after the hour
of danger, which a subsequent distraction has made us
forget, that we remember our uneasiness. I greeted the
young Duke and made my way into the house. But here
I must first of all record a trifling incident, which will
enable us to understand something that was presently to
occur.

There was one person who, on that evening as on the
previous evenings, had been thinking a great deal about
the Duc de Châtellerault, without however suspecting
who he was: this was the usher (styled at that time the
aboyeur) of Mme. de Guermantes. M. de Châtellerault,
so far from being one of the Princess's intimate friends,
albeit he was one of her cousins, had been invited to her
house for the first time. His parents, who had not been
on speaking terms with her for the last ten years, had
been reconciled to her within the last fortnight, and,
obliged to be out of Paris that evening, had requested
their son to fill their place. Now, a few days earlier, the
Princess's usher had met in the Champs-Elysées a young
man whom he had found charming but whose identity
he had been unable to establish. Not that the young
man had not shewn himself as obliging as he had been
generous. All the favours that the usher had supposed
that he would have to bestow upon so young a gentleman,
he had on the contrary received. But M. de Châtellerault was as reticent as he was rash; he was all the more
determined not to disclose his incognito since he did not

48

know with what sort of person he was dealing; his fear
would have been far greater, although quite unfounded,
if he had known. He had confined himself to posing as
an Englishman, and to all the passionate questions with
which he was plied by the usher, desirous to meet again
a person to whom he was indebted for so much pleasure
and so ample a gratuity, the Duke had merely replied,
from one end of the Avenue Gabriel to the other: "I do
not speak French."

Albeit, in spite of everything—remembering his cousin
Gilbert's maternal ancestry—the Duc de Guermantes pretended to find a touch of Courvoisier in the drawing-room
of the Princesse de Guermantes-Bavière, the general estimate of that lady's initiative spirit and intellectual superiority was based upon an innovation that was to be
found nowhere else in her set. After dinner, however
important the party that was to follow, the chairs, at the
Princesse de Guermantes's, were arranged in such a way
as to form little groups, in which people might have to
turn their backs upon one another. The Princess then
displayed her social sense by going to sit down, as though
by preference, in one of these. Not that she was afraid
to pick out and attract to herself a member of another
group. If, for instance, she had remarked to M. Detaille,
who naturally agreed with her, on the beauty of Mme. de
Villemur's neck, of which that lady's position in another
group made her present a back view, the Princess did not
hesitate to raise her voice: "Madame de Villemur, M.
Detaille, with his wonderful painter's eye, has just been
admiring your neck." Mme. de Villemur interpreted this
as a direct invitation to join in the conversation; with the
agility of a practised horsewoman, she made her chair

rotate slowly through three quadrants of a circle, and, without in the least disturbing her neighbours, came to rest almost facing the Princess. "You don't know M. Detaille?" exclaimed their hostess, for whom her guest's nimble and modest tergiversation was not sufficient. "I do not know him, but I know his work," replied Mme. de Villemur, with a respectful, engaging air, and a promptitude which many of the onlookers envied her, addressing the while to the celebrated painter whom this invocation had not been sufficient to introduce to her in a formal manner, an imperceptible bow. "Come, Monsieur Detaille," said the Princess, "let me introduce you to Mme. de Villemur." That lady thereupon shewed as great ingenuity in making room for the creator of the *Dream* as she had shewn a moment earlier in wheeling round to face him. And the Princess drew forward a chair for herself; she had indeed invoked Mme. de Villemur only to have an excuse for quitting the first group, in which she had spent the statutory ten minutes, and bestowing a similar allowance of her time upon the second. In three quarters of an hour, all the groups had received a visit from her, which seemed to have been determined in each instance by impulse and predilection, but had the paramount object of making it apparent how naturally "a great lady knows how to entertain." But now the guests for the party were beginning to arrive, and the lady of the house was seated not far from the door—erect and proud in her semi-regal majesty, her eyes ablaze with their own incandescence—between two unattractive Royalties and the Spanish Ambassadress.

I stood waiting behind a number of guests who had arrived before me. Facing me was the Princess, whose

beauty is probably not the only thing, where there were
so many beauties, that reminds me of this party. But
the face of my hostess was so perfect; stamped like so
beautiful a medal, that it has retained a commemorative
force in my mind. The Princess was in the habit of
saying to her guests when she met them a day or two
before one of her parties: " You will come, won't you? "
as though she felt a great desire to talk to them. But as,
on the contrary, she had nothing to talk to them about,
when they entered her presence she contented herself,
without rising, with breaking off for an instant her vapid
conversation with the two Royalties and the Ambassadress and thanking them with: " How good of you to
have come," not that she thought that the guest had
shewn his goodness by coming, but to enhance her own;
then, at once dropping him back into the stream, she
would add: " You will find M. de Guermantes by the
garden door," so that the guest proceeded on his way and
ceased to bother her. To some indeed she said nothing,
contenting herself with shewing them her admirable onyx
eyes, as though they had come merely to visit an exhibition of precious stones.

The person immediately in front of me was the Duc
de Châtellerault.

Having to respond to all the smiles, all the greetings
waved to him from inside the drawing-room, he had not
noticed the usher. But from the first moment the usher
had recognised him. The identity of this stranger, which
he had so ardently desired to learn, in another minute he
would know. When he asked his " Englishman " of the
other evening what name he was to announce, the usher
was not merely stirred, he considered that he was being

indiscreet, indelicate. He felt that he was about to reveal to the whole world (which would, however, suspect nothing) a secret which it was criminal of him to force like this and to proclaim in public. Upon hearing the guest's reply: "Le duc de Châtellerault," he felt such a burst of pride that he remained for a moment speechless. The Duke looked at him, recognised him, saw himself ruined, while the servant, who had recovered his composure and was sufficiently versed in heraldry to complete for himself an appellation that was too modest, shouted with a professional vehemence softened by an emotional tenderness: "Son Altesse Monseigneur le duc de Châtellerault!" But it was now my turn to be announced. Absorbed in contemplation of my hostess, who had not yet seen me, I had not thought of the function—terrible to me, although not in the same sense as to M. de Châtellerault—of this usher garbed in black like a headsman, surrounded by a group of lackeys in the most cheerful livery, lusty fellows ready to seize hold of an intruder and cast him out of doors. The usher asked me my name, I told him it as mechanically as the condemned man allows himself to be strapped to the block. At once he lifted his head majestically and, before I could beg him to announce me in a lowered tone so as to spare my own feelings if I were not invited and those of the Princesse de Guermantes if I were, shouted the disturbing syllables with a force capable of bringing down the roof.

The famous Huxley (whose grandson occupies an unassailable position in the English literary world of to-day) relates that one of his patients dared not continue to go into society because often, on the actual chair that was pointed out to her with a courteous gesture, she saw an old gentleman already seated. She could be quite certain that either the gesture of invitation or the old gentleman's presence was a hallucination, for her hostess would not have offered her a chair that was already occupied. And when Huxley, to cure her, forced her to reappear in society, she felt a moment of painful hesitation when she asked herself whether the friendly sign that was being made to her was the real thing, or, in obedience to a non-existent vision, she was about to sit down in public upon the knees of a gentleman in flesh and blood. Her brief uncertainty was agonising. Less so perhaps than mine. From the moment at which I had taken in the sound of my name, like the rumble that warns us of a possible cataclysm, I was bound, to plead my own good faith in either event, and as though I were not tormented by any doubt, to advance towards the Princess with a resolute air.

She caught sight of me when I was still a few feet away and (to leave me in no doubt that I was the victim of a conspiracy), instead of remaining seated, as she had done for her other guests, rose and came towards me. A moment later, I was able to heave the sigh of relief of Huxley's patient, when, having made up her mind to sit down on the chair, she found it vacant and realised that it was the old gentleman that was a hallucination. The Princess had just held out her hand to me with a smile. She remained standing for some moments with the kind of charm enshrined in the verse of Malherbe which ends:

"To do them honour all the angels rise."

She apologised because the Duchess had not yet come, as though I must be bored there without her. In order

53

to give me this greeting, she wheeled round me, holding me by the hand, in a graceful revolution by the whirl of which I felt myself carried off my feet. I almost expected that she would next offer me, like the leader of a cotillon, an ivory-headed cane or a watch-bracelet. She did not, however, give me anything of the sort, and as though, instead of dancing the Boston, she had been listening to a sacred quartet by Beethoven the sublime strains of which she was afraid of interrupting, she cut short the conversation there and then, or rather did not begin it, and, still radiant at having seen me come in, merely informed me where the Prince was to be found.

I moved away from her and did not venture to approach her again, feeling that she had absolutely nothing to say to me and that, in her vast kindness, this woman marvellously tall and handsome, noble as were so many great ladies who stepped so proudly upon the scaffold, could only, short of offering me a draught of honeydew, repeat what she had already said to me twice: " You will find the Prince in the garden." Now, to go in search of the Prince was to feel my doubts revive in a fresh form.

In any case I should have to find somebody to introduce me. One could hear, above all the din of conversation, the interminable chatter of M. de Charlus, talking to H. E. the Duke of Sidonia, whose acquaintance he had just made. Members of the same profession find one another out, and so it is with a common vice. M. de Charlus and M. de Sidonia had each of them immediately detected the other's vice, which was in both cases that of soliloquising in society, to the extent of not being able to stand any interruption. Having decided at once that, in the words of a famous sonnet, there was " no help," they had made up their minds not to be silent but each to go on talking without any regard to what the other might say. This had resulted in the confused babble produced in Molière's comedies by a number of people saying different things simultaneously. The Baron, with his deafening voice, was moreover certain of keeping the upper hand, of drowning the feeble voice of M. de Sidonia; without however discouraging him, for, whenever M. de Charlus paused for a moment to breathe, the interval was filled by the murmurs of the Grandee of Spain who had imperturbably continued his discourse. I could easily have asked M. de Charlus to introduce me to the Prince de Guermantes, but I feared (and with good reason) that he might be cross with me. I had treated him in the most ungrateful fashion by letting his offer pass unheeded for the second time and by never giving him a sign of my existence since the evening when he had so affectionately escorted me home. And yet I could not plead the excuse of having anticipated the scene which I had just witnessed, that very afternoon, enacted by himself and Jupien. I suspected nothing of the sort. It is true that shortly before this, when my parents reproached me with my laziness and with not having taken the trouble to write a line to M. de Charlus, I had violently reproached them with wishing me to accept a degrading proposal. But anger alone, and the desire to hit upon the expression that would be most offensive to them had dictated this mendacious retort. In reality, I had imagined nothing sensual, nothing sentimental even, underlying the Baron's offers. I had said this to my parents with entire irresponsibility. But sometimes the future is latent in us without our knowledge, and our words which we suppose to be false forecast an imminent reality.

M. de Charlus would doubtless have forgiven me my want of gratitude. But what made him furious was that my presence this evening at the Princesse de Guermantes's, as for some time past at her cousin's, seemed to be a defiance of his solemn declaration: "There is no admission to those houses save through me." A grave fault, a crime that was perhaps inexpiable, I had not followed the conventional path. M. de Charlus knew well that the thunderbolts which he hurled at those who did not comply with his orders, or to whom he had taken a dislike, were beginning to be regarded by many people, however furiously he might brandish them, as mere pasteboard, and had no longer the force to banish anybody from anywhere. But he believed perhaps that his diminished power, still considerable, remained intact in the eyes of novices like myself. And so I did not consider it well advised to ask a favour of him at a party at which the mere fact of my presence seemed an ironical denial of his pretensions.

I was buttonholed at that moment by a man of a distinctly common type, Professor E——. He had been surprised to see me at the Guermantes'. I was no less surprised to see him there, for nobody had ever seen before or was ever to see again a person of his sort at one of the Princess's parties. He had just succeeded in curing the Prince, after the last rites had been administered, of a septic pneumonia, and the special gratitude that Mme. de Guermantes felt towards him was the reason for her thus departing from custom and inviting him to her house. As he knew absolutely nobody in the rooms, and could not wander about there indefinitely by himself, like a minister of death, having recognised me, he had discovered, for the first time in his life, that he had an infinite number of things to say to me, which enabled him to assume an air of composure, and this was one of the reasons for his advancing upon me. There was also another. He attached great importance to his never being mistaken in his diagnoses. Now his correspondence was so numerous that he could not always bear in mind, when he had seen a patient once only, whether the disease had really followed the course that he had traced for it. The reader may perhaps remember that, immediately after my grandmother's stroke, I had taken her to see him, on the afternoon when he was having all his decorations stitched to his coat. After so long an interval, he no longer remembered the formal announcement which had been sent to him at the time. "Your grandmother *is* dead, isn't she?" he said to me in a voice in which a semi-certainty calmed a slight apprehension. "Ah! Indeed! Well, from the moment I saw her my prognosis was extremely grave, I remember it quite well."

It was thus that Professor E—— learned or recalled the death of my grandmother, and (I must say this to his credit, which is that of the medical profession as a whole), without displaying, without perhaps feeling any satisfaction. The mistakes made by doctors are innumerable. They err habitually on the side of optimism as to treatment, of pessimism as to the outcome. "Wine? In moderation, it can do you no harm, it is always a tonic. . . . Sexual enjoyment? After all it is a natural function. I allow you to use, but not to abuse it, you understand. Excess in anything is wrong." At once, what a temptation to the patient to renounce those two life-givers, water and chastity. If, on the other hand, he has any trouble with his heart, albumen, and so forth, it never lasts for long. Disorders that are grave but purely functional are at once ascribed to an imaginary cancer. It is useless to continue visits which are powerless to eradicate an incurable malady. Let the patient, left to his own devices, thereupon subject himself to an implacable regime, and in time recover, or merely survive, and the doctor, to whom he touches his hat in the Avenue de l'Opéra, when he supposed him to have long been lying in Père Lachaise, will interpret the gesture as an act of insolent defiance. An innocent stroll, taken beneath his nose and venerable beard, would arouse no greater wrath in the Assize Judge who, two years earlier, had sentenced the rascal, now passing him with apparent impunity, to death. Doctors (we do not here include them all, of course, and make a mental reservation of certain admirable exceptions), are in general more displeased, more irritated by the quashing of their sentence than pleased by its execution. This explains why Professor E——, despite the intellectual satisfaction that he doubtless felt at finding that he had not been mistaken, was able to speak to me only with regret of the blow that had fallen upon us. He was in no hurry to cut short the conversation, which kept him in countenance and gave him a reason for remaining. He spoke to me of the great heat through which we were passing, but, albeit he was a well-read man and capable of expressing himself in good French, said to me: "You are none the worse for this hyperthermia?" The fact is that medicine has made some slight advance in knowledge since Molière's days,

58

but none in its vocabulary. My companion went on: "The great thing is to avoid the sudations that are caused by weather like this, especially in superheated rooms. You can remedy them, when you go home and feel thirsty, by the application of heat" (by which he apparently meant hot drinks).

Owing to the circumstances of my grandmother's death, the subject interested me, and I had recently read in a book by a great specialist that perspiration was injurious to the kidneys, by making moisture pass through the skin when its proper outlet was elsewhere. I thought with regret of those dog-days at the time of my grandmother's death, and was inclined to blame them for it. I did not mention this to Dr. E——, but of his own accord he said to me: "The advantage of this very hot weather in which perspiration is abundant is that the kidney is correspondingly relieved." Medicine is not an exact science.

Keeping me engaged in talk, Professor E—— asked only not to be forced to leave me. But I had just seen, making a series of sweeping bows to right and left of the Princesse de Guermantes, stepping back a pace first, the Marquis de Vaugoubert. M. de Norpois had recently introduced me to him and I hoped that I might find in him a person capable of presenting me to our host. The proportions of this work do not permit me to explain here in consequence of what incidents in his youth M. de Vaugoubert was one of the few men (possibly the only man) in society who happened to be in what is called at Sodom the "confidence" of M. de Charlus. But, if our Minister to the Court of King Theodosius had certain defects in common with the Baron, they were only a very pale reflexion. It was merely in an infinitely softened, sentimental and simple form that he displayed those alternations of affection and hatred through which the desire to attract, and then the fear—equally imaginary—of being, if not scorned, at any rate unmasked, made the Baron pass. Made ridiculous by a chastity, a "platonicism" (to which as a man of keen ambition he had, from the moment of passing his examination, sacrificed all pleasure), above all by his intellectual nullity, these alternations M. de Vaugoubert did, nevertheless, display. But whereas in M. de Charlus the immoderate praises were proclaimed with a positive burst of eloquence, and seasoned with the subtlest, the most mordant banter which marked a man for ever, by M. de Vaugoubert, on the other hand, the affection was expressed with the banality of a man of the lowest intelligence, and of a public official, the grievances (worked up generally into a complete indictment, as with the Baron) by a malevolence which, though relentless, was at the same time spiritless, and was all the more startling inasmuch as it was invariably a direct contradiction of what the Minister had said six months earlier and might soon perhaps be saying again: a regularity of change which gave an almost astronomic poetry to the various phases of M. de Vaugoubert's life, albeit apart from this nobody was ever less suggestive of a star.

The greeting that he gave me had nothing in common with that which I should have received from M. de Charlus. To this greeting M. de Vaugoubert, apart from the thousand mannerisms which he supposed to be indicative of good breeding and diplomacy, imparted a cavalier, brisk, smiling air, which should make him seem on the one hand to be rejoicing at being alive—at a time when he was inwardly chewing the mortification of a career with no prospect of advancement and with the threat of enforced retirement—and on the other hand young, virile and charming, when he could see and no longer ventured to go and examine in the glass the lines gathering upon a face which he would have wished to keep full of seduction. Not that he would have hoped for effective conquests, the mere thought of which filled him with terror on account of what people would say, scandals, blackmail. Having passed from an almost infantile corruption to an absolute continence dating from the day on which his thoughts had turned to the Quai d'Orsay and he had begun to plan a great career for himself, he had the air of a caged animal, casting in every direction glances expressive of fear, appetite and stupidity. This last was so dense that he did not reflect that the street-arabs of his adolescence were boys no longer, and when a newsvendor bawled in his face: "*La Presse!*" even more than with longing he shuddered with terror, imagining himself recognised and denounced.

But in default of the pleasures sacrificed to the ingratitude of the Quai d'Orsay, M. de Vaugoubert—and it was for this that he was anxious still to attract—was liable to sudden stirrings of the heart. Heaven knows with how many letters he would overwhelm the Ministry (what personal ruses he would employ, the drafts that he made upon the credit of Mme. de Vaugoubert, who, on account of her corpulence, her exalted birth, her masculine air, and above all the mediocrity of her husband, was reputed to be endowed with eminent capacities and to be herself for all practical purposes the Minister), to introduce without any valid reason a young man destitute of all merit into the staff of the Legation. It is true that a few months, a few years later, the insignificant attaché had only to appear, without the least trace of any hostile intention, to have shewn signs of coldness towards his chief for the latter, supposing himself scorned or betrayed, to devote the same hysterical ardour to punishing him with which he had showered favours upon him in the past. He would move heaven and earth to have him recalled and the Director of Political Affairs would receive a letter daily: "Why don't you hurry up and rid me of that lascar. Give him a dressing down in his own interest. What he needs is a slice of humble pie." The post of attaché at the court of King Theodosius was on this account far from enjoyable. But in all other respects, thanks to his perfect common sense as a man of the world, M. de Vaugoubert was one of the best representatives of the French Government abroad. When a man who was reckoned a superior person, a Jacobin, with an expert knowledge of all subjects, replaced him later on, it was not long before war broke out between France and the country over which that monarch reigned.

M. de Vaugoubert, like M. de Charlus, did not care to be the first to give a greeting. Each of them preferred to "respond," being constantly afraid of the gossip which the person to whom otherwise they might have offered their hand might have heard about them since their last meeting. In my case, M. de Vaugoubert had no need to ask himself this question, I had as a matter of fact gone up of my own accord to greet him, if only because of the difference in our ages. He replied with an air of wonder and delight, his eyes continuing to stray as though

there had been a patch of clover on either side of me
upon which he was forbidden to graze. I felt that it
would be more becoming to ask him to introduce me to
Mme. de Vaugoubert, before effecting that introduction
to the Prince which I decided not to mention to him until
afterwards. The idea of making me acquainted with his
wife seemed to fill him with joy, for his own sake as well
as for hers, and he led me at a solemn pace towards the
Marquise. Arriving in front of her, and indicating me
with his hand and eyes, with every conceivable mark of
consideration, he nevertheless remained silent and withdrew after a few moments, in a sidelong fashion, leaving
me alone with his wife. She had at once given me her
hand, but without knowing to whom this token of friendship was addressed, for I realised that M. de Vaugoubert
had forgotten my name, perhaps even had failed to
recognise me, and being unwilling, from politeness, to
confess his ignorance had made the introduction consist
in a mere dumb show. And so I was no farther advanced; how was I to get myself introduced to my host
by a woman who did not know my name? Worse still,
I found myself obliged to remain for some moments talking to Mme. de Vaugoubert. And this annoyed me for
two reasons. I had no wish to remain all night at this
party, for I had arranged with Albertine (I had given her
a box for *Phèdre*) that she was to pay me a visit shortly
before midnight. Certainly I was not in the least in love
with her; I was yielding, in making her come this evening,
to a wholly sensual desire, albeit we were at that torrid
period of the year when sensuality, evaporating, visits
more readily the organ of taste, seeks above all things
coolness. More than for the kiss of a girl, it thirsts for

orangeade, for a cold bath, or even to gaze at that peeled and juicy moon which was quenching the thirst of heaven. I counted however upon ridding myself, in Albertine's company—which, moreover, reminded me of the coolness of the sea—of the regret that I should not fail to feel for many charming faces (for it was a party quite as much for girls as for married women that the Princess was giving. On the other hand, the face of the imposing Mme. de Vaugoubert, Bourbonian and morose, was in no way attractive).

People said at the Ministry, without any suggestion of malice, that in their household it was the husband who wore the petticoats and the wife the trousers. Now there was more truth in this saying than was supposed. Mme. de Vaugoubert was really a man. Whether she had always been one, or had grown to be as I saw her, matters little, for in either case we have to deal with one of the most touching miracles of nature which, in the latter alternative especially, makes the human kingdom resemble the kingdom of flowers. On the former hypothesis— if the future Mme. de Vaugoubert had always been so clumsily manlike—nature, by a fiendish and beneficent ruse, bestows on the girl the deceiving aspect of a man. And the youth who has no love for women and is seeking to be cured greets with joy this subterfuge of discovering a bride who figures in his eyes as a market porter. In the alternative case, if the woman has not originally these masculine characteristics, she adopts them by degrees, to please her husband, and even unconsciously, by that sort of mimicry which makes certain flowers assume the appearance of the insects which they seek to attract. Her regret that she is not loved, that she is not a man,

64

virilises her. Indeed, quite apart from the case that we are now considering, who has not remarked how often the most normal couples end by resembling each other, at times even by an exchange of qualities? A former German Chancellor, Prince von Bülow, married an Italian. In the course of time, on the Pincio, it was remarked how much the Teutonic husband had absorbed of Italian delicacy, and the Italian Princess of German coarseness. To turn aside to a point without the province of the laws which we are now tracing, everyone knows an eminent French diplomat, whose origin was at first suggested only by his name, one of the most illustrious in the East. As he matured, as he grew old, there was revealed in him the Oriental whom no one had ever suspected, and now when we see him we regret the absence of the fez that would complete the picture.

To revert to habits completely unknown to the ambassador whose profile, coarsened by heredity, we have just recalled, Mme. de Vaugoubert realised the acquired or predestined type, the immortal example of which is the Princess Palatine, never out of a riding habit, who, having borrowed from her husband more than his virility, championing the defects of the men who do not care for women, reports in her familiar correspondence the mutual relations of all the great noblemen of the court of Louis XIV. One of the reasons which enhance still farther the masculine air of women like Mme. de Vaugoubert is that the neglect which they receive from their husbands, the shame that they feel at such neglect, destroy in them by degrees everything that is womanly. They end by acquiring both the good and the bad qualities which their husbands lack. The more frivolous, effeminate, indiscreet their husbands are, the more they grow into the effigy, devoid of charm, of the virtues which their husbands ought to practise.

Traces of abasement, boredom, indignation, marred the regular features of Mme. de Vaugoubert. Alas, I felt that she was regarding me with interest and curiosity as one of those young men who appealed to M. de Vaugoubert, and one of whom she herself would so much have liked to be, now that her husband, growing old, shewed a preference for youth. She was gazing at me with the close attention shewn by provincial ladies who from an illustrated catalogue copy the tailor-made dress so becoming to the charming person in the picture (actually, the same person on every page, but deceptively multiplied into different creatures, thanks to the differences of pose and the variety of attire). The instinctive attraction which urged Mme. de Vaugoubert towards me was so strong that she went the length of seizing my arm, so that I might take her to get a glass of orangeade. But I released myself, alleging that I must presently be going, and had not yet been introduced to our host.

This distance between me and the garden door where he stood talking to a group of people was not very great. But it alarmed me more than if, in order to cross it, I should have to expose myself to a continuous hail of fire.

A number of women from whom I felt that I might be able to secure an introduction were in the garden, where, while feigning an ecstatic admiration, they were at a loss for an occupation. Parties of this sort are as a rule premature. They have little reality until the following day, when they occupy the attention of the people who were not invited. A real author, devoid of the foolish self-esteem of so many literary people, if, when he reads an article by a critic who has always expressed the greatest admiration for his works, he sees the names of various inferior writers mentioned, but not his own, has no time to stop and consider what might be to him a matter for astonishment: his books are calling him. But a society woman has nothing to do and, on seeing in the *Figaro:* "Last night the Prince and Princesse de Guermantes gave a large party," etc., exclaims: "What! Only three days ago I talked to Marie-Gilbert for an hour, and she never said a word about it!" and racks her brains to discover how she can have offended the Guermantes. It must be said that, so far as the Princess's parties were concerned, the astonishment was sometimes as great among those who were invited as among those who were not. For they would burst forth at the moment when one least expected them, and summoned in people whose existence Mme. de Guermantes had forgotten for years. And almost all the people in society are so insignificant that others of their sort adopt, in judging them, only the measure of their social success, cherish them if they are invited, if they are omitted detest them. As to the latter, if it was the fact that the Princess often, even when they were her friends, did not invite them, that was often due to her fear of annoying "Palamède," who had excommunicated them. And so I might be certain that she had not spoken of me to M. de Charlus, for otherwise I should not have found myself there. He meanwhile was posted between the house and the garden, by the side of the German Ambassador, leaning upon the balustrade of the great staircase which led from the garden to the house, so that the other guests, in spite of the three or four feminine admirers who were grouped round the Baron and almost concealed him, were obliged to greet him as they passed. He responded by naming each of them in turn. And one heard an incessant: " Good evening, Monsieur du Hazay, good evening, Madame de la Tour du Pin-Verclause, good evening, Madame de la Tour du Pin-Gouvernet, good evening, Philibert, good evening, my dear Ambassadress," and so on. This created a continuous barking sound, interspersed with benevolent suggestions or inquiries (to the answers to which he paid no attention), which M. de Charlus addressed to them in a tone softened, artificial to shew his indifference, and benign: " Take care the child doesn't catch cold, it is always rather damp in the gardens. Good evening, Madame de Brantes. Good evening, Madame de Mecklembourg. Have you brought your daughter? Is she wearing that delicious pink frock? Good evening, Saint-Géran." Certainly there was an element of pride in this attitude, for M. de Charlus was aware that he was a Guermantes, and that he occupied a supreme place at this party. But there was more in it than pride, and the very word *fête* suggested, to the man with aesthetic gifts, the luxurious, curious sense that it might bear if this party were being given not by people in contemporary society but in a painting by Carpaccio or Veronese. It is indeed highly probable that the German Prince that M. de Charlus was must rather have been picturing to himself the reception that occurs in *Tannhäuser,* and himself as the Margrave, standing at the entrance to the Warburg with a kind word of condescension for each of his guests, while their procession into the castle or the park is greeted by the long phrase, a hundred times renewed, of the famous March.

I must, however, make up my mind. I could distinguish beneath the trees various women with whom I was more or less closely acquainted, but they seemed transformed because they were at the Princess's and not at her cousin's, and because I saw them seated not in front of Dresden china plates but beneath the boughs of a chestnut. The refinement of their setting mattered nothing. Had it been infinitely less refined than at Oriane's, I should have felt the same uneasiness. When the electric light in our drawing-room fails, and we are obliged to replace it with oil lamps, everything seems altered. I was recalled from my uncertainty by Mme. de Souvré. "Good evening," she said as she approached me. "Have you seen the Duchesse de Guermantes lately?" She excelled in giving to speeches of this sort an intonation which proved that she was not uttering them from sheer silliness, like people who, not knowing what to talk about, come up to you a thousand times over to mention some bond of common acquaintance, often extremely slight. She had on the contrary a fine conducting wire in her glance which signified:" Don't suppose for a moment that I haven't recognised you. You are the young man I met at the Duchesse de Guermantes. I remember quite well." Unfortunately, this protection, extended over me by this phrase, stupid in appearance but delicate in intention, was extremely fragile, and vanished as soon as I tried to make use of it. Madame de Souvré had the art, if called upon to convey a request to some influential person, of appearing at the same time, in the petitioner's eyes, to be recommending him, and in those of the influential person not to be recommending the petitioner, so that her ambiguous gesture opened a credit balance of gratitude to her with the latter without placing her in any way in debt to the former. Encouraged by this lady's civilities to ask her to introduce me to M. de Guermantes, I found that she took advantage of a moment when our host was not looking in our direction, laid a motherly hand on my shoulder, and, smiling at the averted face of the Prince who was unable to see her, thrust me towards him with a gesture of feigned protection, but deliberately ineffective, which left me stranded almost at my starting point. Such is the cowardice of people in society.

That of a lady who came to greet me, addressing me by my name, was greater still. I tried to recall her own name as I talked to her; I remembered quite well having met her at dinner, I could remember things that she had said. But my attention, concentrated upon the inward region in which these memories of her lingered, was unable to discover her name there. It was there, nevertheless. My thoughts began playing a sort of game with it to grasp its outlines, its initial letter, and so finally to bring the whole name to light. It was labour in vain, I could more or less estimate its mass, its weight, but as for its forms, confronting them with the shadowy captive lurking in the inward night, I said to myself: "It is not that." Certainly my mind would have been capable of creating the most difficult names. Unfortunately, it had not to create but to reproduce. All action by the mind is easy, if it is not subjected to the test of reality. Here, I was forced to own myself beaten. Finally, in a flash, the name came back to me as a whole: "Madame d'Arpajon." I am wrong in saying that it came, for it did not, I think, appear to me by a spontaneous propulsion. I do not think either that the many slight memories which associated me with the lady, and to which I did not cease to appeal for help (by such exhortations as: " Come now, it is the lady who is a friend of Mme. de Souvré, who feels for Victor Hugo so artless an admiration, mingled with so much alarm and horror,")—I do not believe that all these memories, hovering between me and her name, served in any way to bring it to light. In that great game of hide and seek which is played in our memory when we seek to recapture a name, there is not any series of gradual approximations. We see nothing, then suddenly the name appears in its exact form and very different from what we thought we could make out. It is not the name that has come to us. No, I believe rather that, as we go on living, we pass our time in keeping away from the zone in which a name is distinct, and it was by an exercise of my will and attention which increased the acuteness of my inward vision that all of a sudden I had pierced the semi-darkness and seen daylight. In any case, if there are transitions between oblivion and memory, then, these transitions are unconscious. For the intermediate names through which we pass, before finding the real name, are themselves false, and bring us nowhere nearer to it. They are not even, properly speaking, names at all, but often mere consonants which are not to be found in the recaptured name. And yet, this operation of the mind passing from a blank to reality is so mysterious, that it is possible after all that these false consonants are really handles, awkwardly held out to enable us to seize hold of the correct name. " All this," the reader will remark, " tells us nothing as to the lady's failure to oblige; but since you have made so long a digression, allow me, gentle author, to waste another moment of your time in telling you that it is a pity that, young as you were (or as your hero was, if he be not yourself), you had already so feeble a memory that you could not recall the name of a lady whom you knew quite well." It is indeed a pity, gentle reader. And sadder than you think when one feels the time approaching when names and words will vanish from the clear zone of consciousness, and when one must for ever cease to name to oneself the people whom one has known most intimately. It is indeed a pity that one should require this effort, when one is still young, to recapture names which one knows quite well. But if this infirmity occurred only in the case of names barely known, quite naturally forgotten, names which one would not take the trouble to remember, the infirmity would not be without its advantages. "And what are they, may I ask?" Well, Sir, that the malady alone makes us remark and apprehend, and allows us to dissect the mechanism of which otherwise we should know nothing. A man who, night after night, falls like a lump of lead upon his bed, and ceases to live until the moment when he wakes and rises, will such a man ever dream of making, I do not say great discoveries, but even minute observations upon sleep? He barely knows that he does sleep. A little insomnia is not without its value in making us appreciate sleep, in throwing a ray of light upon that darkness. A memory without fault is not a very powerful incentive to studying the phenomena of memory. "In a word, did Mme. d'Arpajon introduce you to the Prince?" No, but be quiet and let me go on with my story.

- Mme. d'Arpajon was even more cowardly than Mme.

de Souvré, but there was more excuse for her cowardice. She knew that she had always had very little influence in society. This influence, such as it was, had been reduced still farther by her connexion with the Duc de Guermantes; his desertion of her dealt it the final blow. The resentment which she felt at my request that she should introduce me to the Prince produced a silence which, she was artless enough to suppose, conveyed the impression that she had not heard what I said. She was not even aware that she was knitting her brows with anger. Perhaps, on the other hand, she was aware of it, did not bother about the inconsistency, and made use of it for the lesson which she was thus able to teach me without undue rudeness; I mean a silent lesson, but none the less eloquent for that.

Apart from this, Mme. d'Arpajon was extremely annoyed; many eyes were raised in the direction of a renaissance balcony at the corner of which, instead of one of those monumental statues which were so often used as ornaments at that period, there leaned, no less sculptural than they, the magnificent Marquise de Surgis-le-Duc, who had recently succeeded Mme. d'Arpajon in the heart of Basin de Guermantes. Beneath the flimsy white tulle which protected her from the cool night air, one saw the supple form of a winged victory. I had no recourse left save to M. de Charlus, who had withdrawn to a room downstairs which opened on the garden. I had plenty of time (as he was pretending to be absorbed in a fictitious game of whist which enabled him to appear not to notice people) to admire the deliberate, artistic simplicity of his evening coat which, by the merest trifles which only a tailor's eye could have picked out, had the air of a " Harmony in Black and White" by Whistler; black, white and red, rather, for M. de Charlus was wearing, hanging from a broad ribbon pinned to the lapel of his coat, the Cross, in white, black and red enamel, of a Knight of the religious Order of Malta. At that moment the Baron's game was interrupted by Mme. de Gallardon, leading her nephew, the Vicomte de Courvoisier, a young man with an attractive face and an impertinent air. "Cousin," said Mme. de Gallardon, "allow me to introduce my nephew Adalbert. Adalbert, you remember the famous Uncle Palamède of whom you have heard so much." "Good evening, Madame de Gallardon," M. de Charlus replied. And he added, without so much as a glance at the young man: "Good evening, Sir," with a truculent air and in a tone so violently discourteous that everyone in the room was stupefied. Perhaps M. de Charlus, knowing that Mme. de Gallardon had her doubts as to his morals and guessing that she had not been able to resist, for once in a way, the temptation to allude to them, was determined to nip in the bud any scandal that she might have embroidered upon a friendly reception of her nephew, making at the same time a resounding profession of indifference with regard to young men in general; perhaps he had not considered that the said Adalbert had responded to his aunt's speech with a sufficiently respectful air; perhaps, desirous of making headway in time to come with so attractive a cousin, he chose to give himself the advantage of a preliminary assault, like those sovereigns who, before engaging upon diplomatic action, strengthen it by an act of war.

It was not so difficult as I supposed to secure M. de Charlus's consent to my request that he should introduce

74

me to the Prince de Guermantes. For one thing, in the course of the last twenty years, this Don Quixote had tilted against so many windmills (often relatives who, he imagined, had behaved badly to him), he had so frequently banned people as being "impossible to have in the house" from being invited by various male or female Guermantes, that these were beginning to be afraid of quarrelling with all the people they knew and liked, of condemning themselves to a lifelong deprivation of the society of certain newcomers whom they were curious to meet, by espousing the thunderous but unexplained rancours of a brother-in-law or cousin who expected them to abandon for his sake, wife, brother, children. More intelligent than the other Guermantes, M. de Charlus realised that people were ceasing to pay any attention, save once in a while, to his veto, and, looking to the future, fearing lest one day it might be with his society that they would dispense, he had begun to make allowances, to reduce, as the saying is, his terms. Furthermore, if he had the faculty of ascribing for months, for years on end, an identical life to a detested person—to such an one he would not have tolerated their sending an invitation, and would have fought, rather, like a trooper, against a queen, the status of the person who stood in his way ceasing to count for anything in his eyes; on the other hand, his explosions of wrath were too frequent not to be somewhat fragmentary. "The imbecile, the rascal! We shall have to put him in his place, sweep him into the gutter, where unfortunately he will not be innocuous to the health of the town," he would scream, even when he was alone in his own room, while reading a letter that he considered irreverent, or upon recalling some remark that had been repeated to him. But a fresh outburst against a second imbecile cancelled the first, and the former victim had only to shew due deference for the crisis that he had occasioned to be forgotten, it not having lasted long enough to establish a foundation of hatred upon which to build. And so, I might perhaps—despite his ill-humour towards me—have been successful when I asked him to introduce me to the Prince, had I not been so ill-inspired as to add, from a scruple of conscience, and so that he might not suppose me guilty of the indelicacy of entering the house at a venture, counting upon him to enable me to remain there: "You are aware that I know them quite well, the Princess has been very kind to me." "Very well, if you know them, why do you need me to introduce you?" he replied in a sharp tone, and, turning his back, resumed his make-believe game with the Nuncio, the German Ambassador and another personage whom I did not know by sight.

Then, from the depths of those gardens where in days past the Duc d'Aiguillon used to breed rare animals, there came to my ears, through the great, open doors, the sound of a sniffing nose that was savouring all those refinements and determined to miss none of them. The sound approached, I moved at a venture in its direction, with the result that the words *good evening* were murmured in my ear by M. de Bréauté, not like the rusty metallic sound of a knife being sharpened on a grindstone, even less like the cry of the wild boar, devastator of tilled fields, but like the voice of a possible saviour.

Less influential than Mme. de Souvré, but less deeply ingrained than she with the incapacity to oblige, far more at his ease with the Prince than was Mme. d'Arpajon, entertaining some illusion perhaps as to my position in the Guermantes set, or perhaps knowing more about it than myself, I had nevertheless for the first few moments some difficulty in arresting his attention, for, with fluttering, distended nostrils, he was turning in every direction, inquisitively protruding his monocle, as though he found himself face to face with five hundred matchless works of art. But, having heard my request, he received it with satisfaction, led me towards the Prince and presented me to him with a relishing, ceremonious, vulgar air, as though he had been handing him, with a word of commendation, a plate of cakes. Just as the greeting of the Duc de Guermantes was, when he chose, friendly, instinct with good fellowship, cordial and familiar, so I found that of the Prince stiff, solemn, haughty. He barely smiled at me, addressed me gravely as " Sir." I had often heard the Duke make fun of his cousin's stiffness. But from the first words that he addressed to me, which by their cold and serious tone formed the most entire contrast with the language of Basin, I realised at once that the fundamentally disdainful man was the Duke, who spoke to you at your first meeting with him as " man to man," and that, of the two cousins, the one who was really simple was the Prince. I found in his reserve a stronger feeling, I do not say of equality, for that would have been inconceivable to him, but at least of the consideration which one may shew for an inferior, such as may be found in all strongly hierarchical societies, in the Law Courts, for instance; in a Faculty, where a public prosecutor or dean, conscious of their high charge, conceal perhaps more genuine simplicity, and, when you come to know them better, more kindness, true simplicity, cordiality,

beneath their traditional aloofness than the more modern
brethren beneath their jocular affectation of comradeship.
" Do you intend to follow the career of Monsieur, your
father? " he said to me with a distant but interested air.
I answered his question briefly, realising that he had
asked it only out of politeness, and moved away to allow
him to greet the fresh arrivals.

I caught sight of Swann, and meant to speak to him,
but at that moment I saw that the Prince de Guermantes,
instead of waiting where he was to receive the greeting
of Odette's husband, had immediately, with the force of
a suction pump, carried him off to the farther end of the
garden, in order, as some said, " to shew him the door."

So entirely absorbed in the company that I did not learn
until two days later, from the newspapers, that a Czech
orchestra had been playing throughout the evening, and
that Bengal lights had been burning in constant succession,
I recovered some power of attention with the idea of going to look at the celebrated fountain of Hubert Robert.

In a clearing surrounded by fine trees several of which
were as old as itself, set in a place apart, one could see it
in the distance, slender, immobile, stiffened, allowing the
breeze to stir only the lighter fall of its pale and quivering plume. The eighteenth century had refined the elegance of its lines, but, by fixing the style of the jet, seemed
to have arrested its life; at this distance one had the
impression of a work of art rather than the sensation of
water. The moist cloud itself that was perpetually gathering at its crest preserved the character of the period
like those that in the sky assemble round the palaces of
Versailles. But from a closer view one realised that,
while it respected, like the stones of an ancient palace, the

THE EVENING PARTY AT
THE PRINCESSE DE GUERMANTES

THE EVENING PARTY AT
THE PRINCESSE DE GUERMANTES

design traced for it beforehand, it was a constantly changing stream of water that, springing upwards and seeking to obey the architect's traditional orders, performed them to the letter only by seeming to infringe them, its thousand separate bursts succeeding only at a distance in giving the impression of a single flow. This was in reality as often interrupted as the scattering of the fall, whereas from a distance it had appeared to me unyielding, solid, unbroken in its continuity. From a little nearer, one saw that this continuity, apparently complete, was assured, at every point in the ascent of the jet, wherever it must otherwise have been broken, by the entering into line, by the lateral incorporation of a parallel jet which mounted higher than the first and was itself, at an altitude greater but already a strain upon its endurance, relieved by a third. Seen close at hand, drops without strength fell back from the column of water crossing on their way their climbing sisters and, at times, torn, caught in an eddy of the night air, disturbed by this ceaseless flow, floated awhile before being drowned in the basin. They teased with their hesitations, with their passage in the opposite direction, and blurred with their soft vapour the vertical tension of that stem, bearing aloft an oblong cloud composed of a thousand tiny drops, but apparently painted in an unchanging, golden brown which rose, unbreakable, constant, urgent, swift, to mingle with the clouds in the sky. Unfortunately, a gust of wind was enough to scatter it obliquely on the ground; at times indeed a single jet, disobeying its orders, swerved and, had they not kept a respectful distance, would have drenched to their skins the incautious crowd of gazers.

One of these little accidents, which could scarcely occur

save when the breeze freshened for a moment, was distinctly unpleasant. Somebody had told Mme. d'Arpajon that the Duc de Guermantes, who as a matter of fact had not yet arrived, was with Mme. de Surgis in one of the galleries of pink marble to which one ascended by the double colonnade, hollowed out of the wall, which rose from the brink of the fountain. Now, just as Mme. d'Arpajon was making for one of these staircases, a strong gust of warm air made the jet of water swerve and inundated the fair lady so completely that, the water streaming down from her open bosom inside her dress, she was soaked as if she had been plunged into a bath. Whereupon, a few feet away, a rhythmical roar resounded, loud enough to be heard by a whole army, and at the same time protracted in periods as though it were being addressed not to the army as a whole but to each unit in turn; it was the Grand Duke Vladimir, who was laughing whole-heartedly upon seeing the immersion of Mme. d'Arpajon, one of the funniest sights, as he was never tired of repeating afterwards, that he had ever seen in his life. Some charitable persons having suggested to the Muscovite that a word of sympathy from himself was perhaps deserved and would give pleasure to the lady who, notwithstanding her tale of forty winters fully told, wiping herself with her scarf, without appealing to anyone for help, was stepping clear in spite of the water that was maliciously spilling over the edge of the basin, the Grand Duke, who had a kind heart, felt that he must say a word in season, and, before the last military tattoo of his laughter had altogether subsided, one heard a fresh roar, more vociferous even than the last. "Bravo, old girl!" he cried, clapping his hands as though at the theatre.

Mme. d'Arpajon was not at all pleased that her dexterity should be commended at the expense of her youth. And when some one remarked to her, in a voice drowned by the roar of the water, over which nevertheless rose the princely thunder: "I think His Imperial Highness said something to you." "No! It was to Mme. de Souvré," was her reply.

I passed through the gardens and returned by the stair, upon which the absence of the Prince, who had vanished with Swann, enlarged the crowd of guests round M. de Charlus, just as, when Louis XIV was not at Versailles, there was a more numerous attendance upon Monsieur, his brother. I was stopped on my way by the Baron, while behind me two ladies and a young man came up to greet him.

"It is nice to see you here," he said to me, as he held out his hand. "Good evening, Madame de la Trémoïlle, good evening, my dear Herminie." But doubtless the memory of what he had said to me as to his own supreme position in the Hôtel Guermantes made him wish to appear to be feeling, with regard to a matter which annoyed him but which he had been unable to prevent, a satisfaction which his high-and-mighty impertinence and his hysterical excitement immediately invested in a cloak of exaggerated irony. "It is nice," he repeated, "but it is, really, very odd." And he broke into peals of laughter which appeared to be indicative at once of his joy and of the inadequacy of human speech to express it. Certain persons, meanwhile, who knew both how difficult he was of access and how prone to insolent retorts, had been drawn towards us by curiosity, and, with an almost indecent haste, broke into a run. "Come, now, don't be cross,"

I   G

he said to me, patting me gently on the shoulder, "you know that I am your friend. Good evening, Antioche, good evening, Louis-René. Have you been to look at the fountain?" he asked me in a tone that was affirmative rather than questioning. "It is quite pretty, ain't it? It is marvellous. It might be made better still, naturally, if certain things were removed, and then there would be nothing like it in France. But even as it stands, it is quite one of the best things. Bréauté will tell you that it was a mistake to put lamps round it, to try and make people forget that it was he who was responsible for that absurd idea. But after all he has only managed to spoil it a very little. It is far more difficult to deface a great work of art than to create one. Not that we had not a vague suspicion all the time that Bréauté was not quite a match for Hubert Robert."

I drifted back into the stream of guests who were entering the house. "Have you seen my delicious cousin Oriane lately?" I was asked by the Princess who had now deserted her post by the door and with whom I was making my way back to the rooms. "She's sure to be here to-night, I saw her this afternoon," my hostess added. "She promised me to come. I believe too that you will be dining with us both to meet the Queen of Italy, at the Embassy, on Thursday. There are to be all the Royalties imaginable, it will be most alarming." They could not in any way alarm the Princesse de Guermantes, whose rooms swarmed with them, and who would say: "My little Coburgs" as she might have said "my little dogs." And so Mme. de Guermantes said: "It will be most alarming," out of sheer silliness, which, among people in society, overrides even their vanity. With regard to her own pedigree, she knew less than a passman in history. As for the people of her circle, she liked to shew that she knew the nicknames with which they had been labelled. Having asked me whether I was dining, the week after, with the Marquise de la Pommelière, who was often called "la Pomme," the Princess, having elicited a reply in the negative, remained silent for some moments. Then, without any other motive than a deliberate display of instinctive erudition, banality, and conformity to the prevailing spirit, she added: "She's not a bad sort, the Pomme!"

While the Princess was talking to me, it so happened that the Duc and Duchesse de Guermantes made their entrance. But I could not go at once to greet them, for I was waylaid by the Turkish Ambassadress, who, pointing to our hostess whom I had just left, exclaimed as she seized me by the arm: "Ah! What a delicious woman the Princess is! What a superior being! I feel sure that, if I were a man," she went on, with a trace of Oriental servility and sensuality, "I would give my life for that heavenly creature." I replied that I did indeed find her charming, but that I knew her cousin, the Duchess, better. "But there is no comparison," said the Ambassadress. "Oriane is a charming society woman who gets her wit from Mémé and Babal, whereas Marie-Gilbert is *somebody*."

I never much like to be told like this, without a chance to reply, what I ought to think about people whom I know. And there was no reason why the Turkish Ambassadress should be in any way better qualified than myself to judge of the worth of the Duchesse de Guermantes.

On the other hand (and this explained also my annoy-

ance with the Ambassadress), the defects of a mere acquaintance, and even of a friend, are to us real poisons,
against which we are fortunately " mithridated."

But, without applying any standard of scientific comparison and talking of anaphylaxis, let us say that, at the
heart of our friendly or purely social relations, there lurks
a hostility momentarily cured but recurring by fits and
starts. As a rule, we suffer little from these poisons, so
long as people are " natural." By saying " Babal " and
" Mémé " to indicate people with whom she was not acquainted, the Turkish Ambassadress suspended the effects of the " mithridatism " which, as a rule, made me
find her tolerable. She annoyed me, which was all the
more unfair, inasmuch as she did not speak like this to
make me think that she was an intimate friend of
" Mémé," but owing to a too rapid education which made
her name these noble lords according to what she believed to be the custom of the country. She had crowded
her course into a few months, and had not picked up the
rules. But, on thinking it over, I found another reason
for my disinclination to remain in the Ambassadress's
company. It was not so very long since, at Oriane's,
this same diplomatic personage had said to me, with a
purposeful and serious air, that she found the Princesse
de Guermantes frankly antipathetic. I felt that I need
not stop to consider this change of front: the invitation
to the party this evening had brought it about. The
Ambassadress was perfectly sincere when she told me
that the Princesse de Guermantes was a sublime creature.
She had always thought so. But, having never before
been invited to the Princess's house, she had felt herself
bound to give this non-invitation the appearance of a

deliberate abstention on principle. Now that she had been asked, and would presumably continue to be asked in the future, she could give free expression to her feelings. There is no need, in accounting for three out of four of the opinions that we hold about other people, to go so far as crossed love or exclusion from public office. Our judgment remains uncertain: the withholding or bestowal of an invitation determines it. Anyhow, the Turkish Ambassadress, as the Baronne de Guermantes remarked while making a tour of inspection through the rooms with me, " was all right." She was, above all, extremely useful. The real stars of society are tired of appearing there. He who is curious to gaze at them must often migrate to another hemisphere, where they are more or less alone. But women like the Ottoman Ambassadress, of quite recent admission to society, are never weary of shining there, and, so to speak, everywhere at once. They are of value at entertainments of the sort known as *soirée* or *rout,* to which they would let themselves be dragged from their deathbeds rather than miss one. They are the supers upon whom a hostess can always count, determined never to miss a party. And so, the foolish young men, unaware that they are false stars, take them for the queens of fashion, whereas it would require a formal lecture to explain to them by virtue of what reasons Mme. Standish, who, her existence unknown to them, lives remote from the world, painting cushions, is at least as great a lady as the Duchesse de Doudeauville.

In the ordinary course of life, the eyes of the Duchesse de Guermantes were absent and slightly melancholy, she made them sparkle with a flame of wit only when she had to say how-d'ye-do to a friend; precisely as though the said friend had been some witty remark, some charming touch, some titbit for delicate palates, the savour of which has set on the face of the connoisseur an expression of refined joy. But upon big evenings, as she had too many greetings to bestow, she decided that it would be tiring to have to switch off the light after each. Just as an ardent reader, when he goes to the theatre to see a new piece by one of the masters of the stage, testifies to his certainty that he is not going to spend a dull evening by having, while he hands his hat and coat to the attendant, his lip adjusted in readiness for a sapient smile, his eye kindled for a sardonic approval; similarly it was at the moment of her arrival that the Duchess lighted up for the whole evening. And while she was handing over her evening cloak, of a magnificent Tiepolo red, exposing a huge collar of rubies round her neck, having cast over her gown that final rapid, minute and exhaustive dress-maker's glance which is also that of a woman of the world, Oriane made sure that her eyes, just as much as her other jewels, were sparkling. In vain might sundry "kind friends" such as M. de Janville fling themselves upon the Duke to keep him from entering: "But don't you know that poor Mama is at his last gasp? He has had the Sacraments." "I know, I know," answered M. de Guermantes, thrusting the tiresome fellow aside in order to enter the room. "The viaticum has acted splendidly," he added, with a smile of pleasure at the thought of the ball which he was determined not to miss after the Prince's party. "We did not want people to know that we had come back," the Duchess said to me. She never suspected that the Princess had already disproved this

statement by telling me that she had seen her cousin for
a moment, who had promised to come. The Duke, after
a protracted stare with which he proceeded to crush his
wife for the space of five minutes, observed: " I told Oriane about your misgivings." Now that she saw that they
were unfounded, and that she herself need take no action
in the attempt to dispel them, she pronounced them absurd, and continued to chaff me about them. "The idea
of supposing that you were not invited! Besides, wasn't
I there? Do you suppose that I should be unable to get
you an invitation to my cousin's house?" I must admit
that frequently, after this, she did things for me that were
far more difficult; nevertheless, I took care not to interpret her words in the sense that I had been too modest.
I was beginning to learn the exact value of the language,
spoken or mute, of aristocratic affability, an affability that
is happy to shed balm upon the sense of inferiority in
those persons towards whom it is directed, though not to
the point of dispelling that sense, for in that case it would
no longer have any reason to exist. "But you are our
equal, if not our superior," the Guermantes seemed, in all
their actions, to be saying; and they said it in the most
courteous fashion imaginable, to be loved, admired, but
not to be believed; that one should discern the fictitious
character of this affability was what they called being
well-bred; to suppose it to be genuine, a sign of ill-
breeding. I was to receive, as it happened, shortly after
this, a lesson which gave me a full and perfect understanding of the extent and limitations of certain forms of
aristocratic affability. It was at an afternoon party given
by the Duchesse de Montmorency to meet the Queen of
England; there was a sort of royal procession to the

buffet, at the head of which walked Her Majesty on the arm of the Duc de Guermantes. I happened to arrive at that moment. With his disengaged hand the Duke conveyed to me, from a distance of nearly fifty yards, a thousand signs of friendly invitation, which appeared to mean that I need not be afraid to approach, that I should not be devoured alive instead of the sandwiches. But I, who was becoming word-perfect in the language of the court, instead of going even one step nearer, keeping my fifty yards' interval, made a deep bow, but without smiling, the sort of bow that I should have made to some one whom I scarcely knew, then proceeded in the opposite direction. Had I written a masterpiece, the Guermantes would have given me less credit for it than I earned by that bow. Not only did it not pass unperceived by the Duke, albeit he had that day to acknowledge the greetings of more than five hundred people, it caught the eye of the Duchess, who, happening to meet my mother, told her of it, and, so far from suggesting that I had done wrong, that I ought to have gone up to him, said that her husband had been lost in admiration of my bow, that it would have been impossible for anyone to put more into it. They never ceased to find in that bow every possible merit, without however mentioning that which had seemed the most priceless of all, to wit that it had been discreet, nor did they cease either to pay me compliments which I understood to be even less a reward for the past than a hint for the future, after the fashion of the hint delicately conveyed to his pupils by the headmaster of a school: "Do not forget, my boys, that these prizes are intended not so much for you as for your parents, so that they may send you back next term." So it was that

Mme. de Marsantes, when some one from a different world entered her circle, would praise in his hearing the discreet people whom "you find at home when you go to see them, and who at other times let you forget their existence," as one warns by an indirect allusion a servant who has an unpleasant smell, that the practice of taking a bath is beneficial to the health.

While, before she had even left the entrance hall, I was talking to Mme. de Guermantes, I could hear a voice of a sort which, for the future, I was to be able to classify without the possibility of error. It was, in this particular instance, the voice of M. de Vaugoubert talking to M. de Charlus. A skilled physician need not even make his patient unbutton his shirt, nor listen to his breathing, the sound of his voice is enough. How often, in time to come, was my ear to be caught in a drawing-room by the intonation or laughter of some man, who, for all that, was copying exactly the language of his profession or the manners of his class, affecting a stern aloofness or a coarse familiarity, but whose artificial voice was enough to indicate: "He is a Charlus" to my trained ear, like the note of a tuning fork. At that moment the entire staff of one of the Embassies went past, pausing to greet M. de Charlus. For all that my discovery of the sort of malady in question dated only from that afternoon (when I had surprised M. de Charlus with Jupien) I should have had no need, before giving a diagnosis, to put questions, to auscultate. But M. de Vaugoubert, when talking to M. de Charlus, appeared uncertain. And yet he must have known what was in the air after the doubts of his adolescence. The invert believes himself to be the only one of his kind in the universe; it is only in later years that

he imagines—another exaggeration—that the unique exception is the normal man. But, ambitious and timorous,
M. de Vaugoubert had not for many years past surrendered himself to what would to him have meant
pleasure. The career of diplomacy had had the same
effect upon his life as a monastic profession. Combined
with his assiduous frequentation of the School of Political
Sciences, it had vowed him from his twentieth year to the
chastity of a professing Christian. And so, as each of our
senses loses its strength and vivacity, becomes atrophied
when it is no longer exercised, M. de Vaugoubert, just as
the civilised man is no longer capable of the feats of
strength, of the acuteness of hearing of the cave-dweller,
had lost that special perspicacity which was rarely at
fault in M. de Charlus; and at official banquets, whether
in Paris or abroad, the Minister Plenipotentiary was no
longer capable of identifying those who, beneath the disguise of their uniform, were at heart his congeners. Certain names mentioned by M. de Charlus, indignant if he
himself was cited for his peculiarities, but always delighted to give away those of other people, caused M. de
Vaugoubert an exquisite surprise. Not that, after all
these years, he dreamed of profiting by any windfall.
But these rapid revelations, similar to those which in
Racine's tragedies inform Athalie and Abner that Joas is
of the House of David, that Esther, enthroned in the
purple, comes of a Yiddish stock, changing the aspect of
the X—— Legation, or of one or another department of
the Ministry of Foreign Affairs, rendered those palaces
as mysterious, in retrospect, as the Temple of Jerusalem
or the Throne-room at Susa. At the sight of the youthful staff of this Embassy advancing in a body to shake

hands with M. de Charlus, M. de Vaugoubert assumed the astonished air of Elise exclaiming, in *Esther:* "Great heavens! What a swarm of innocent beauties issuing from all sides presents itself to my gaze! How charming a modesty is depicted on their faces!" Then, athirst for more definite information, he cast at M. de Charlus a smiling glance fatuously interrogative and concupiscent: "Why, of course they are," said M. de Charlus with the knowing air of a learned man speaking to an ignoramus. From that instant M. de Vaugoubert (greatly to the annoyance of M. de Charlus) could not tear his eyes from these young secretaries whom the X—— Ambassador to France, an old stager, had not chosen blindfold. M. de Vaugoubert remained silent, I could only watch his eyes. But, being accustomed from my childhood to apply, even to what is voiceless, the language of the classics, I made M. de Vaugoubert's eyes repeat the lines in which Esther explains to Elise that Mardochée, in his zeal for his religion, has made it a rule that only those maidens who profess it shall be employed about the Queen's person. "And now his love for our nation has peopled this palace with daughters of Sion, young and tender flowers wafted by fate, transplanted like myself beneath a foreign sky. In a place set apart from profane eyes, he" (the worthy Ambassador) "devotes his skill and labour to shaping them."

At length M. de Vaugoubert spoke, otherwise than with his eyes. "Who knows," he said sadly, "that in the country where I live the same thing does not exist also?" "It is probable," replied M. de Charlus, "starting with King Theodosius, not that I know anything definite about him." "Oh, dear, no! Nothing of that sort!" "Then he has no right to look it so completely. Besides, he has all the little tricks. He had that 'my dear' manner, which I detest more than anything in the world. I should never dare to be seen walking in the street with him. Anyhow, you must know what he is, they all call him the White Wolf." "You are entirely mistaken about him. He is quite charming, all the same. The day on which the agreement with France was signed, the King kissed me. I have never been so moved." "That was the moment to tell him what you wanted." "Oh, good heavens! What an idea! If he were even to suspect such a thing! But I have no fear in that direction." A conversation which I could hear, for I was standing close by, and which made me repeat to myself: "The King unto this day knows not who I am, and this secret keeps my tongue still enchained."

This dialogue, half mute, half spoken, had lasted but a few moments, and I had barely entered the first of the drawing-rooms with the Duchesse de Guermantes when a little dark lady, extremely pretty, stopped her:

"I've been looking for you everywhere. D'Annunzio saw you from a box in the theatre, he has written the Princesse de T—— a letter in which he says that he never saw anything so lovely. He would give his life for ten minutes' conversation with you. In any case, even if you can't or won't, the letter is in my possession. You must fix a day to come and see me. There are some secrets which I cannot tell you here. I see you don't remember me," she added, turning to myself; "I met you at the Princesse de Parme's" (where I had never been). "The Emperor of Russia is anxious for your father to be sent to Petersburg. If you could come in on Monday,

Isvolski himself will be there, he will talk to you about it. I have a present for you, my dear," she went on, returning to the Duchess, "which I should not dream of giving to anyone but you. The manuscripts of three of Ibsen's plays, which he sent to me by his old attendant. I shall keep one and give you the other two."

The Duc de Guermantes was not overpleased by these offers. Uncertain whether Ibsen and D'Annunzio were dead or alive, he could see in his mind's eye a tribe of authors, playwrights, coming to call upon his wife and putting her in their works. People in society are too apt to think of a book as a sort of cube one side of which has been removed, so that the author can at once " put in " the people he meets. This is obviously disloyal, and authors are a pretty low class. Certainly, it would not be a bad thing to meet them once in a way, for thanks to them, when one reads a book or an article, one can " read between the lines," " unmask " the characters. After all, though, the wisest thing is to stick to dead authors. M. de Guermantes considered " quite all right " only the gentleman who did the funeral notices in the *Gaulois*. He, at any rate, confined himself to including M. de Guermantes among the people " conspicuous by their presence " at funerals at which the Duke had given his name. When he preferred that his name should not appear, instead of giving it, he sent a letter of condolence to the relatives of the deceased, assuring them of his deep and heartfelt sympathy. If, then, the family sent to the paper " among the letters received, we may mention one from the Duc de Guermantes," etc., this was the fault not of the ink-slinger but of the son, brother, father of the deceased whom the Duke thereupon described as upstarts, and with whom he decided for the future to have no further dealings (what he called, not being very well up in the meaning of such expressions, "having a crow to pick"). In any event, the names of Ibsen and D'Annunzio, and his uncertainty as to their survival, brought a frown to the brows of the Duke, who was not far enough away from us to escape hearing the various blandishments of Mme. Timoléon d'Amoncourt. This was a charming woman, her wit, like her beauty, so entrancing that either of them by itself would have made her shine. But, born outside the world in which she now lived, having aspired at first merely to a literary salon, the friend successively—and nothing more than a friend, for her morals were above reproach—and exclusively of every great writer, who gave her all his manuscripts, wrote books for her, chance having once introduced her into the Faubourg Saint-Germain, these literary privileges were of service to her there. She had now an established position, and no longer needed to dispense other graces than those that were shed by her presence. But, accustomed in times past to act as go-between, to render services, she persevered in them even when they were no longer necessary. She had always a state secret to reveal to you, a potentate whom you must meet, a watercolour by a master to present to you. There was indeed in all these superfluous attractions a trace of falsehood, but they made her life a comedy that scintillated with complications, and it was no exaggeration to say that she appointed prefects and generals.

As she strolled by my side, the Duchesse de Guermantes allowed the azure light of her eyes to float in front of her, but vaguely, so as to avoid the people with whom she did not wish to enter into relations, whose presence she discerned at times, like a menacing reef in the distance. We advanced between a double hedge of guests, who, conscious that they would never come to know "Oriane," were anxious at least to point her out, as a curiosity, to their wives: "Quick, Ursule, come and look at Madame de Guermantes talking to that young man." And one felt that in another moment they would be clambering upon the chairs, for a better view, as at the Military Review on the 14th of July, or the Grand Prix. Not that the Duchesse de Guermantes had a more aristocratic salon than her cousin. The former's was frequented by people whom the latter would never have been willing to invite, principally on account of her husband. She would never have been at home to Mme. Alphonse de Rothschild, who, an intimate friend of Mme. de la Trémoïlle and of Mme. de Sagan, as was Oriane herself, was constantly to be seen in the house of the last-named. It was the same with Baron Hirsch, whom the Prince of Wales had brought to see her, but not to the Princess, who would not have approved of him, and also with certain outstandingly notorious Bonapartists or even Republicans, whom the Duchess found interesting but whom the Prince, a convinced Royalist, would not have allowed inside his house. His antisemitism also being founded on principle did not yield before any social distinction, however strongly accredited, and if he was at home to Swann, whose friend he had been since their boyhood, being, however, the only one of the Guermantes who addressed him as Swann and not as Charles, this was because, knowing that Swann's grandmother, a Protestant married to a Jew, had been the Duc de Berri's mistress,

95

he endeavoured, from time to time, to believe in the legend which made out Swann's father to be a natural son of that Prince. By this hypothesis, which incidentally was false, Swann, the son of a Catholic father, himself the son of a Bourbon by a Catholic mother, was a Christian to his finger-tips.

"What, you don't know these glories?" said the Duchess, referring to the rooms through which we were moving. But, having given its due meed of praise to her cousin's "palace," she hastened to add that she a thousand times preferred her own "humble den." "This is an admirable house to *visit*. But I should die of misery if I had to stay behind and sleep in rooms that have witnessed so many historic events. It would give me the feeling of having been left after closing-time, forgotten, in the Chateau of Blois, or Fontainebleau, or even the Louvre, with no antidote to my depression except to tell myself that I was in the room in which Monaldeschi was murdered. As a sedative, that is not good enough. Why, here comes Mme. de Saint-Euverte. We've just been dining with her. As she is giving her great annual beanfeast to-morrow, I supposed she would be going straight to bed. But she can never miss a party. If this one had been in the country, she would have jumped on a lorry rather than not go to it."

As a matter of fact, Mme. de Saint-Euverte had come this evening, less for the pleasure of not missing another person's party than in order to ensure the success of her own, recruit the latest additions to her list, and, so to speak, hold an eleventh hour review of the troops who were on the morrow to perform such brilliant evolutions at her garden party. For, in the long course of years, the guests at the Saint-Euverte parties had almost entirely changed. The female celebrities of the Guermantes world, formerly so sparsely scattered, had—loaded with attentions by their hostess—begun gradually to bring their friends. At the same time, by an enterprise equally progressive, but in the opposite direction, Mme. de Saint-Euverte had, year by year, reduced the number of persons unknown to the world of fashion. You had ceased to see first one of them, then another. For some time the "batch" system was in operation, which enabled her, thanks to parties over which a veil of silence was drawn, to summon the ineligibles separately to entertain one another, which dispensed her from having to invite them with the nice people. What cause had they for complaint? Were they not given (*panem et circenses*) light refreshments and a select musical programme? And so, in a kind of symmetry with the two exiled duchesses whom, in years past, when the Saint-Euverte salon was only starting, one used to see holding up, like a pair of Caryatides, its unstable crest, in these later years one could distinguish, mingling with the fashionable throng, only two heterogeneous persons, old Mme. de Cambremer and the architect's wife with a fine voice who was always having to be asked to sing. But, no longer knowing anybody at Mme. de Saint-Euverte's, bewailing their lost comrades, feeling that they were in the way, they stood about with a frozen-to-death air, like two swallows that have not migrated in time. And so, the following year, they were not invited; Mme. de Franquetot made an attempt on behalf of her cousin, who was so fond of music. But as she could obtain for her no more explicit reply than the words: "Why, people can always come in and listen to music, if they like; there is nothing criminal about that!" Mme. de Cambremer did not find the invitation sufficiently pressing, and abstained.

Such a transformation having been effected by Mme. de Saint-Euverte, from a leper hospice to a gathering of great ladies (the latest form, apparently in the height of fashion, that it had assumed), it might seem odd that the person who on the following day was to give the most brilliant party of the season should need to appear over-night to address a last word of command to her troops. But the fact was that the pre-eminence of Mme. de Saint-Euverte's drawing-room existed only for those whose social life consists entirely in reading the accounts of afternoon and evening parties in the *Gaulois* or *Figaro*, without ever having been present at one. To these worldlings who see the world only as reflected in the newspapers, the enumeration of the British, Austrian, etc., Ambassadresses, of the Duchesses d'Uzès, de la Trémoïlle, etc., etc., was sufficient to make them instinc-tively imagine the Saint-Euverte drawing-room to be the first in Paris, whereas it was among the last. Not that the reports were mendacious. The majority of the per-sons mentioned had indeed been present. But each of them had come in response to entreaties, civilities, serv-ices, and with the sense of doing infinite honour to Mme. de Saint-Euverte. Such drawing-rooms, shunned rather than sought after, to which people are so to speak roped in, deceive no one but the fair readers of the " Society " column. They pass over a really fashionable party, the sort at which the hostess, who could have had all the duchesses in existence, they being athirst to be " num-bered among the elect," invites only two or three and does not send any list of her guests to the papers. And so these hostesses, ignorant or contemptuous of the power that publicity has acquired to-day, are considered fashionable by the Queen of Spain but are overlooked by the crowd, because the former knows and the latter does not know who they are.

Mme. de Saint-Euverte was not one of these women, and, with an eye to the main chance, had come to gather up for the morrow everyone who had been invited. M. de Charlus was not among these, he had always refused to go to her house. But he had quarrelled with so many people that Mme. de Saint-Euverte might put this down to his peculiar nature.

Assuredly, if it had been only Oriane, Mme. de Saint-Euverte need not have put herself to the trouble, for the invitation had been given by word of mouth, and, what was more, accepted with that charming, deceiving grace in the exercise of which those Academicians are unsurpassed from whose door the candidate emerges with a melting heart, never doubting that he can count upon their support. But there were others as well. The Prince d'Agrigente, would he come? And Mme. de Durfort? And so, with an eye to business, Mme. de Saint-Euverte had thought it expedient to appear on the scene in person. Insinuating with some, imperative with others, to all alike she hinted in veiled words at inconceivable attractions which could never be seen anywhere again, and promised each that he should find at her party the person he most wished, or the personage he most wanted to meet. And this sort of function with which she was invested on one day in the year—like certain public offices in the ancient world—of the person who is to give on the morrow the biggest garden-party of the season conferred upon her a momentary authority. Her lists were made up and closed, so that while she wandered slowly through the Princess's rooms to drop into one ear after another: "You won't forget about me to-morrow," she had the ephemeral glory of turning away her eyes, while continuing to smile, if she caught sight of some horrid creature who was to be avoided or some country squire for whom the bond of a schoolboy friendship had secured admission to Gilbert's, and whose presence at her garden-party would be no gain. She preferred not to speak to him, so as to be able to say later on: "I issued my invitations verbally, and unfortunately I didn't see you anywhere." And so she, a mere Saint-Euverte, set to work with her gimlet eyes to pick and choose among the guests at the Princess's party. And she imagined herself, in so doing, to be every inch a Duchesse de Guermantes.

It must be admitted that the latter lady had not, either, whatever one might suppose, the unrestricted use of her greetings and smiles. To some extent, no doubt, when she withheld them, it was deliberately: "But the woman bores me to tears," she would say, "am I expected to talk to her about her party for the next hour?"

A duchess of swarthy complexion went past, whom her ugliness and stupidity, and certain irregularities of behaviour had exiled not from society as a whole but from certain small and fashionable circles. "Ah!" murmured Mme. de Guermantes, with the sharp, unerring glance of the connoisseur who is shewn a false jewel, "So they have that sort here?" By the mere sight of this semi-tarnished lady, whose face was burdened with a surfeit of moles from which black hairs sprouted, Mme. de Guermantes gauged the mediocre importance of this party. They had been brought up together, but she had severed all relations with the lady; and responded to her greeting only with the curtest little nod. "I cannot understand," she said to me, "how Marie-Gilbert can invite us with all that scum. You might say there was a deputation of paupers from every parish. Mélanie Pourtalès arranged things far better. She could have the Holy Synod and the Oratoire Chapel in her house if she liked, but at least she didn't invite us on the same day." But, in many cases, it was from timidity, fear of a scene with her husband, who did not like her to entertain artists and such like (Marie-Gilbert took a kindly interest in dozens of them, you had to take care not to be accosted by some illustrious German diva), from some misgivings, too, with regard to Nationalist feeling, which, inasmuch as she was endowed, like M. de Charlus, with the wit of the Guermantes, she despised from the social point of view (people were now, for the greater glory of the General Staff, sending a plebeian general in to dinner before certain dukes), but to which, nevertheless, as she knew that she was considered unsound in her views, she made liberal concessions, even dreading the prospect of having to offer her hand to Swann in these anti-semitic surroundings. With regard to this, her mind was soon set at rest, for she learned that the Prince had refused to have Swann in the house, and had had "a sort of an altercation" with him. There was no risk of her having to converse in public with "poor Charles," whom she preferred to cherish in private.

"And who in the world is that?" Mme. de Guermantes

exclaimed, upon seeing a little lady with a slightly lost air, in a black gown so simple that you would have taken her for a pauper, greet her, as did also the lady's husband, with a sweeping bow. She did not recognise the lady and, in her insolent way, drew herself up as though offended and stared at her without responding. "Who is that person, Basin?" she asked with an air of astonishment, while M. de Guermantes, to atone for Oriane's impoliteness, was bowing to the lady and shaking hands with her husband. "Why, it is Mme. de Chaussepierre, you were most impolite." "I have never heard of anybody called Chaussepierre." "Old mother Chanlivault's nephew." "I haven't the faintest idea what you're talking about. Who is the woman, and why does she bow to me?" "But you know her perfectly, she's Mme. de Charleval's daughter, Henriette Montmorency." "Oh, but I knew her mother quite well, she was charming, extremely intelligent. What made her go and marry all these people I never heard of? You say that she calls herself Mme. de Chaussepierre?" she said, isolating each syllable of the name with a questioning air, and as though she were afraid of making a mistake. "It is not so ridiculous as you appear to think, to call oneself Chaussepierre! Old Chaussepierre was the brother of the aforesaid Chanlivault, of Mme. de Sennecour and of the Vicomtesse de Merlerault. They're a good family." "Oh, do stop," cried the Duchess, who, like a lion-tamer, never cared to appear to be allowing herself to be intimidated by the devouring glare of the animal. "Basin, you are the joy of my life. I can't imagine where you picked up those names, but I congratulate you on them. If I did not know Chaussepierre, I have at least read

Balzac, you are not the only one, and I have even read Labiche. I can appreciate Chanlivault, I do not object to Charleval, but I must confess that Merlerault is a masterpiece. However, let us admit that Chaussepierre is not bad either. You must have gone about collecting them, it's not possible. You mean to write a book," she turned to myself, "you ought to make a note of Charleval and Merlerault. You will find nothing better." "He will find himself in the dock, and will go to prison; you are giving him very bad advice, Oriane." "I hope, for his own sake, that he has younger people than me at his disposal if he wishes to ask for bad advice; especially if he means to follow it. But if he means to do nothing worse than write a book!" At some distance from us, a wonderful, proud young woman stood out delicately from the throng in a white dress, all diamonds and tulle. Madame de Guermantes watched her talking to a whole group of people fascinated by her grace. "Your sister is the belle of the ball, as usual; she is charming to-night," she said, as she took a chair, to the Prince de Chimay who went past. Colonel de Froberville (the General of that name was his uncle) came and sat down beside us, as did M. de Bréauté, while M. de Vaugoubert, after hovering about us (by an excess of politeness which he maintained even when playing tennis when, by dint of asking leave of the eminent personages present before hitting the ball, he invariably lost the game for his partner) returned to M. de Charlus (until that moment almost concealed by the huge skirt of the Comtesse Molé, whom he professed to admire above all other women), and, as it happened, at the moment when several members of the latest diplomatic mission to Paris were greeting the Baron. At the sight of a young secretary with a particularly intelligent air, M. de Vaugoubert fastened on M. de Charlus a smile upon which there bloomed visibly one question only. M. de Charlus would, no doubt, readily have compromised some one else, but to feel himself compromised by this smile formed on another person's lips, which, moreover, could have but one meaning, exasperated him. " I know absolutely nothing about the matter, I beg you to keep your curiosity to yourself. It leaves me more than cold. Besides, in this instance, you are making a mistake of the first order. I believe this young man to be absolutely the opposite." Here M. de Charlus, irritated at being thus given away by a fool, was not speaking the truth. The secretary would, had the Baron been correct, have formed an exception to the rule of his Embassy. It was, as a matter of fact, composed of widely different personalities, many of them extremely second-rate, so that, if one sought to discover what could have been the motive of the selection that had brought them together, the only one possible seemed to be inversion. By setting at the head of this little diplomatic Sodom an Ambassador who on the contrary ran after women with the comic exaggeration of an old buffer in a revue, who made his battalion of male impersonators toe the line, the authorities seemed to have been obeying the law of contrasts. In spite of what he had beneath his nose, he did not believe in inversion. He gave an immediate proof of this by marrying his sister to a Chargé d'Affaires whom he believed, quite mistakenly, to be a womaniser. After this he became rather a nuisance and was soon replaced by a fresh Excellency who ensured the homogeneity of the party. Other Embassies sought to rival this one, but could never dispute the prize (as in the matriculation examinations, where a certain school always heads the list), and more than ten years had to pass before, heterogeneous attachés having been introduced into this too perfect whole, another might at last wrest the grim trophy from it and march at the head.

Reassured as to her fear of having to talk to Swann, Mme. de Guermantes felt now merely curious as to the subject of the conversation he had had with their host. "Do you know what it was about?" the Duke asked M. de Bréauté. "I did hear," the other replied, "that it was about a little play which the writer Bergotte produced at their house. It was a delightful show, as it happens. But it seems the actor made up as Gilbert, whom, as it happens, Master Bergotte had intended to take off." "Oh, I should have loved to see Gilbert taken off," said the Duchess, with a dreamy smile. "It was about this little performance," M. de Bréauté went on, thrusting forward his rodent jaw, "that Gilbert demanded an explanation from Swann, who merely replied what everyone thought very witty: 'Why, not at all, it wasn't the least bit like you, you are far funnier!' It appears, though," M. de Bréauté continued, "that the little play was quite delightful. Mme. Molé was there, she was immensely amused." "What, does Mme. Molé go there?" said the Duchess in astonishment. "Ah! That must be Mémé's doing. That is what always happens, in the end, to that sort of house. One fine day everybody begins to flock to it, and I, who have deliberately remained aloof, upon principle, find myself left to mope alone in my corner." Already, since M. de Bréauté's speech, the Duchesse de Guermantes (with regard if not to Swann's house, at least to the hypothesis of encountering him at any moment) had, as we see, adopted a fresh point of view. "The explanation that you have given us," said Colonel de Froberville to M. de Bréauté, "is entirely unfounded. I have good reason to know. The Prince purely and simply gave Swann a dressing down and would have him to know, as our forebears used to say, that he was not to shew his face in the house again, seeing the opinions he flaunts. And, to my mind, my uncle Gilbert was right a thousand times over, not only in giving Swann a piece of his mind, he ought to have finished six months ago with an out and out Drey-fusard."

Poor M. de Vaugoubert, changed now from a too cautious tennis-player to a mere inert tennis ball which is driven to and fro without compunction, found himself projected towards the Duchesse de Guermantes to whom he made obeisance. He was none too well received, Oriane living in the belief that all the diplomats—or politicians—of her world were nincompoops.

M. de Froberville had greatly benefited by the social privileges that had of late been accorded to military men. Unfortunately, if the wife of his bosom was a quite authentic relative of the Guermantes, she was also an extremely poor one, and, as he himself had lost his fortune, they went scarcely anywhere, and were the sort of people who were apt to be overlooked except on great occasions, when they had the good fortune to bury or marry a relative. Then, they did really enter into communion with the world of fashion, like those nominal Catholics who approach the holy table but once in the year. Their material situation would indeed have been deplorable had not Mme. de Saint-Euverte, faithful to her affection for the late General de Froberville, done everything to help the household, providing frocks and entertainments for the two girls. But the Colonel, though generally considered a good fellow, had not the spirit of gratitude. He was envious of the splendours of a benefactress who extolled them herself without pause or measure. The annual garden party was for him, his wife and children, a marvellous pleasure which they would not have missed for all the gold in the world, but a pleasure poisoned by the thought of the joys of satisfied pride that Mme. de Saint-Euverte derived from it. The accounts of this garden party in the newspapers, which, after giving detailed reports, would add with Machiavellian guile: "We shall refer again to this brilliant gathering," the complementary details of the women's costume, appearing for several days in succession, all this was so obnoxious to the Frobervilles, that they, cut off from most pleasures and knowing that they could count upon the pleasure of this one afternoon, were moved every year to hope that bad weather would spoil the success of the party, to consult the barometer and to anticipate with ecstasy the threatenings of a storm that might ruin everything.

"I shall not discuss politics with you, Froberville," said M. de Guermantes, "but, so far as Swann is concerned, I can tell you frankly that his conduct towards ourselves has been beyond words. Introduced into society, in the past, by ourselves, by the Duc de Chartres, they tell me now that he is openly a Dreyfusard. I should never have believed it of him, an epicure, a man of practical judgment, a collector, who goes in for old books, a member of the Jockey, a man who enjoys the respect of all that know him, who knows all the good addresses, and used to send us the best port wine you could wish to drink, a dilettante, the father of a family. Oh! I have been greatly deceived. I do not complain for myself, it is understood that I am only an old fool, whose opinion counts for nothing, mere rag tag and bobtail, but if only for Oriane's sake, he ought to have openly disavowed the Jews and the partisans of the man Dreyfus.

"Yes, after the friendship my wife has always shewn him," went on the Duke, who evidently considered that to denounce Dreyfus as guilty of high treason, whatever opinion one might hold in one's own conscience as to his guilt, constituted a sort of thank-offering for the manner in which one had been received in the Faubourg Saint-Germain, "he ought to have disassociated himself. For, you can ask Oriane, she had a real friendship for him." The Duchess, thinking that an ingenuous, calm tone would give a more dramatic and sincere value to her words, said in a schoolgirl voice, as though she were simply letting the truth fall from her lips, merely giving a slightly melancholy expression to her eyes: "It is quite true, I have no reason to conceal the fact that I did feel a sincere affection for Charles!" "There, you see, I don't have to make her say it. And after that, he carries his ingratitude to the point of being a Dreyfusard!"

"Talking of Dreyfusards," I said, "it appears, Prince Von is one." "Ah, I am glad you reminded me of him," exclaimed M. de Guermantes, "I was forgetting that he had asked me to dine with him on Monday. But whether he is a Dreyfusard or not is entirely immaterial, since he is a foreigner. I don't give two straws for his opinion. With a Frenchman, it is another matter. It is true that Swann is a Jew. But, until to-day—forgive me, Froberville—I have always been foolish enough to believe that a Jew can be a Frenchman, that is to say, an honourable Jew, a man of the world. Now, Swann was that in every sense of the word. Ah, well! He forces me to admit that I have been mistaken, since he has taken the side of this Dreyfus (who, guilty or not, never moved in his world, he cannot ever have met him) against a society that had adopted him, had treated him as one of ourselves. It goes without saying, we were all of us prepared to vouch for Swann, I would have answered for his patriotism as for my own. Ah! He is rewarding us very badly:I must confess that I should never have expected such a thing from him. I thought better of him. He was a man of intelligence (in his own line, of course). I know that he had already made that insane, disgraceful marriage. By which token, shall I tell you some one who was really hurt by Swann's marriage: my wife. Oriane often has what I might call an affectation of insensibility. But at heart she feels things with extraordinary keenness." Mme. de Guermantes, delighted by this analysis of her character, listened to it with a modest air but did not utter a word, from a scrupulous reluctance to acquiesce in it, but principally from fear of cutting it short. M. de Guermantes might have gone on talking for an hour on this subject, she would have sat as still, or even stiller than if she had been listening to music. "Very well! I remember, when she heard of Swann's marriage, she felt hurt; she considered that it was wrong in a person to whom we had given so much friendship. She was very fond of Swann; she was deeply grieved. Am I not right, Oriane?" Mme. de Guermantes felt that she ought to reply to so direct a challenge, upon a point of fact, which would allow her, unobtrusively, to confirm the tribute which, she felt, had come to an end. In a shy and simple tone, and with an air all the more studied in that it sought to shew genuine " feeling," she said with a meek reserve, " It is true, Basin is quite right." " Still, that was not quite the same. After all, love is love, although, in my opinion, it ought to confine itself within certain limits. I might excuse a young fellow, a mere boy, for letting himself be caught by an infatuation. But Swann, a man of intelligence, of proved refinement, a good judge of pictures, an intimate friend of the Duc de Chartres, of Gilbert himself!" The tone in which M. de Guermantes said this was, for that matter, quite inoffensive, without a trace of the vulgarity which he too often shewed. He spoke with a slightly indignant melancholy, but everything about him was steeped in that gentle gravity which constitutes the broad and unctuous charm of certain portraits by Rembrandt, that of the Burgomaster Six, for example. One felt that the question of the immorality of Swann's conduct with regard to " the Case " never even presented itself to the Duke, so confident was he of the answer; it caused him the grief of a father who sees one of his sons, for whose education he has made the utmost sacrifices, deliberately ruin the magnificent position he has created for him and dishonour, by pranks which the principles or prejudices of his family cannot allow, a respected name. It is true that M. de Guermantes had not displayed so profound and pained an astonishment when he learned that Saint-Loup was a Dreyfusard. But, for one thing, he regarded his nephew as a young man gone astray, as to whom nothing, until he began to mend his ways, could be surprising, whereas Swann was what M. de Guermantes called "a man of weight, a man occupying a position in the front rank." Moreover and above all, a considerable interval of time had elapsed during which, if, from the historical point of view, events had, to some extent, seemed to justify the Dreyfusard argument, the anti-Dreyfusard opposition had doubled its violence, and, from being purely political, had become social. It was now a question of militarism, of patriotism, and the waves of anger that had been stirred up in society had had time to gather the force which they never have at the beginning of a storm. "Don't you see," M. de Guermantes went on, "even from the point of view of his beloved Jews, since he is absolutely determined to stand by them, Swann has made a blunder of an incalculable magnitude. He has shewn that they are to some extent forced to give their support to anyone of their own race, even if they do not know him personally. It is a public danger. We have evidently been too easy going, and the mistake Swann is making will create all the more stir since he was respected, not to say received, and was almost the only Jew that anyone knew. People will say: *Ab uno disce omnes.*" (His satisfaction at having hit, at the right moment, in his memory, upon so apt a quotation, alone brightened with a proud smile the melancholy of the great nobleman conscious of betrayal.)

I was longing to know what exactly had happened between the Prince and Swann, and to catch the latter, if he had not already gone home. "I don't mind telling you," the Duchess answered me when I spoke to her of this desire, "that I for my part am not over anxious to see him, because it appears, by what I was told just now at Mme. de Saint-Euverte's, that he would like me before he dies to make the acquaintance of his wife and daughter. Good heavens, it distresses me terribly that he should be ill, but, I must say, I hope it is not so serious as all that. And besides, it is not really a reason at all, because if it were it would be so childishly simple. A writer with no talent would have only to say: 'Vote for me at the Academy because my wife is dying and I wish to give her this last happiness.' There would be no more entertaining if one was obliged to make friends with all the dying people. My coachman might come to me with: 'My daughter is seriously ill, get me an invitation to the Princesse de Parme's.' I adore Charles, and I should hate having to refuse him, and so that is why I prefer to avoid the risk of his asking me. I hope with all my heart that he is not dying, as he says, but really, if it has to happen, it would not be the moment for me to make the acquaintance of those two creatures who have deprived me of the most amusing of my friends for the last fifteen years, with the additional disadvantage that I should not even be able to make use of their society to see him, since he would be dead!"

Meanwhile M. de Bréauté had not ceased to ruminate the contradiction of his story by Colonel de Froberville. "I do not question the accuracy of your version, my dear fellow," he said, "but I had mine from a good source. It was the Prince de la Tour d'Auvergne who told me."

"I am surprised that an educated man like yourself should still say 'Prince de la Tour d'Auvergne,'" the Duc de Guermantes broke in, "you know that he is nothing of

the kind. There is only one member of that family left.
Oriane's uncle, the Duc de Bouillon."

"The brother of Mme. de Villeparisis?" I asked, remembering that she had been Mlle. de Bouillon. "Precisely. Oriane, Mme. de Lambresac is bowing to you."
And indeed, one saw at certain moments form and fade
like a shooting star a faint smile directed by the Duchesse
de Lambresac at somebody whom she had recognised.
But this smile, instead of taking definite shape in an
active affirmation, in a language mute but clear, was
drowned almost immediately in a sort of ideal ecstasy
which expressed nothing, while her head drooped in a
gesture of blissful benediction, recalling the inclination
towards the crowd of communicants of the head of a
somewhat senile prelate. There was not the least trace of
senility about Mme. de Lambresac. But I was acquainted already with this special type of old-fashioned
distinction. At Combray and in Paris, all my grandmother's friends were in the habit of greeting one another
at a social gathering with as seraphic an air as if they
had caught sight of some one of their acquaintance in
church, at the moment of the Elevation or during a
funeral, and were casting him a gentle "Good morning"
which ended in prayer. At this point a remark made by
M. de Guermantes was to complete the likeness that I
was tracing. "But you have seen the Duc de Bouillon,"
he said to me. "He was just going out of my library this
afternoon as you came in, a short person with white hair."
It was the person whom I had taken for a man of business from Combray, and yet, now that I came to think
it over, I could see the resemblance to Mme. de Villeparisis. The similarity between the evanescent greetings

of the Duchesse de Lambresac and those of my grand-mother's friends had first aroused my interest, by shew-ing me how in all narrow and exclusive societies, be they those of the minor gentry or of the great nobility, the old manners persist, allowing us to recapture, like an archae-ologist, what might have been the standard of upbringing, and the side of life which it reflects, in the days of the Vicomte d'Arlincourt and Loïsa Puget. Better still now, the perfect conformity in appearance between a man of business from Combray of his generation and the Duc de Bouillon reminded me of what had already struck me so forcibly when I had seen Saint-Loup's maternal grand-father, the Duc de La Rochefoucauld, in a daguerreotype in which he was exactly similar, in dress, air and manner, to my great-uncle, that social, and even individual differ-ences are merged when seen from a distance in the uni-formity of an epoch. The truth is that the similarity of dress, and also the reflexion, from a person's face, of the spirit of his age occupy so much more space than his caste, which bulks largely only in his own self-esteem and the imagination of other people, that in order to discover that a great nobleman of the time of Louis Philippe differs less from a citizen of the time of Louis Philippe than from a great nobleman of the time of Louis XV, it is not neces-sary to visit the galleries of the Louvre.

At that moment, a Bavarian musician with long hair, whom the Princesse de Guermantes had taken under her wing, bowed to Oriane. She responded with an inclina-tion of her head, but the Duke, furious at seeing his wife bow to a person whom he did not know, who had a curi-ous style, and, so far as M. de Guermantes understood, an extremely bad reputation, turned upon his wife with a terrible inquisitorial air, as much as to say: "Who in the world is that Ostrogoth?" Poor Mme. de Guermantes's position was already distinctly complicated, and if the musician had felt a little pity for this martyred wife, he would have made off as quickly as possible. But, whether from a desire not to remain under the humiliation that had just been inflicted on him in public, before the eyes of the Duke's oldest and most intimate friends, whose presence there had perhaps been responsible to some extent for his silent bow, and to shew that it was on the best of grounds and not without knowing her already that he had greeted the Duchesse de Guermantes, or else in obedience to the obscure but irresistible impulse to commit a blunder which drove him—at a moment when he ought to have trusted to the spirit—to apply the whole letter of the law, the musician came closer to Mme. de Guermantes and said to her: "Madame la Duchesse, I should like to request the honour of being presented to the Duke." Mme. de Guermantes was indeed in a quandary. But after all, she might well be a forsaken wife, she was still Duchesse de Guermantes and could not let herself appear to have forfeited the right to introduce to her husband the people whom she knew. "Basin," she said, "allow me to present to you M. d'Herweck."

"I need not ask whether you are going to Madame de Saint-Euverte's to-morrow," Colonel de Froberville said to Mme. de Guermantes, to dispel the painful impression produced by M. d'Herweck's ill-timed request. "The whole of Paris will be there." Meanwhile, turning with a single movement and as though he were carved out of a solid block towards the indiscreet musician, the Duc de Guermantes, fronting his suppliant, monumental, mute, wroth, like Jupiter Tonans, remained motionless like this for some seconds, his eyes ablaze with anger and astonishment, his waving locks seeming to issue from a crater. Then, as though carried away by an impulse which alone enabled him to perform the act of politeness that was demanded of him, and after appearing by his attitude of defiance to be calling the entire company to witness that he did not know the Bavarian musician, clasping his white-gloved hands behind his back, he jerked his body forward and bestowed upon the musician a bow so profound, instinct with such stupefaction and rage, so abrupt, so violent, that the trembling artist recoiled, stooping as he went, so as not to receive a formidable butt in the stomach. "Well, the fact is, I shall not be in Paris," the Duchess answered Colonel de Froberville. "I may as well tell you (though I ought to be ashamed to confess such a thing) that I have lived all these years without seeing the windows at Montfort-l'Amaury. It is shocking, but there it is. And so, to make amends for my shameful ignorance, I decided that I would go and see them to-morrow." M. de Bréauté smiled a subtle smile. He quite understood that, if the Duchess had been able to live all these years without seeing the windows at Montfort-l'Amaury, this artistic excursion did not all of a sudden take on the urgent character of an expedition "hot-foot" and might without danger, after having been put off for more than twenty-five years, be retarded for twenty-four hours. The plan that the Duchess had formed was simply the Guermantes way of issuing the decree that the Saint-Euverte establishment was definitely not a "really nice" house, but a house to which you were invited that you might be

utilised afterwards in the account in the *Gaulois*, a house
that would set the seal of supreme smartness upon those,
or at any rate upon her (should there be but one) who
did not go to it. The delicate amusement of M. de
Bréauté, enhanced by that poetical pleasure which people
in society felt when they saw Mme. de Guermantes do
things which their own inferior position did not allow
them to imitate, but the mere sight of which brought to
their lips the smile of the peasant thirled to the soil when
he sees freer and more fortunate men pass by above his
head, this delicate pleasure could in no way be compared
with the concealed but frantic ecstasy that was at once
felt by M. de Froberville.

The efforts that this gentleman was making so that
people should not hear his laughter had made him turn
as red as a turkey-cock, in spite of which it was only
with a running interruption of hiccoughs of joy that he
exclaimed in a pitying tone: "Oh! Poor Aunt Saint-
Euverte, she will take to her bed! No! The unhappy
woman is not to have her Duchess, what a blow, why, it
is enough to kill her!" he went on, convulsed with laughter. And in his exhilaration he could not help stamping
his feet and rubbing his hands. Smiling out of one eye
and with the corner of her lips at M. de Froberville,
whose amiable intention she appreciated, but found the
deadly boredom of his society quite intolerable, Mme. de
Guermantes decided finally to leave him.

"Listen, I shall be obliged to bid you good night," she
said to him as she rose with an air of melancholy resignation, and as though it had been a bitter grief to her.
Beneath the magic spell of her blue eyes her gently musical voice made one think of the poetical lament of a

fairy. "Basin wants me to go and talk to Marie for a little." In reality, she was tired of listening to Froberville, who did not cease to envy her her going to Montfort-l'Amaury, when she knew quite well that he had never heard of the windows before in his life, nor for that matter would he for anything in the world have missed going to the Saint-Euverte party. "Good-bye, I've barely said a word to you, it is always like that at parties, we never see the people, we never say the things we should like to say, but it is the same everywhere in this life. Let us hope that when we are dead things will be better arranged. At any rate we shall not always be having to put on low dresses. And yet, one never knows. We may perhaps have to display our bones and worms on great occasions. Why not? Look, there goes old Rampillon, do you see any great difference between her and a skeleton in an open dress? It is true that she has every right to look like that, for she must be at least a hundred. She was already one of those sacred monsters before whom I refused to bow the knee when I made my first appearance in society. I thought she had been dead for years; which for that matter would be the only possible explanation of the spectacle she presents. It is impressive and liturgical; quite *Camposanto!*" The Duchess had moved away from Froberville; he came after her: "Just one word in your ear." Slightly annoyed: "Well, what is it now?" she said to him stiffly. And he, having been afraid lest, at the last moment, she might change her mind about Montfort-l'Amaury: "I did not like to mention it for Mme. de Saint-Euverte's sake, so as not to get her into trouble, but since you don't intend to be there, I may tell you that I am glad for your sake, for she has measles in the house!" "Oh, good gracious!" said Oriane, who had a horror of illnesses. "But that wouldn't matter to me, I've had them already. You can't get them twice." "So the doctors say; I know people who've had them four times. Anyhow, you are warned." As for himself, these fictitious measles would have needed to attack him in reality and to chain him to his bed before he would have resigned himself to missing the Saint-Euverte party to which he had looked forward for so many months. He would have the pleasure of seeing so many smart people there! The still greater pleasure of remarking that certain things had gone wrong, and the supreme pleasures of being able for long afterwards to boast that he had mingled with the former and, while exaggerating or inventing them, of deploring the latter.

I took advantage of the Duchess's moving to rise also in order to make my way to the smoking-room and find out the truth about Swann. "Do not believe a word of what Babal told us," she said to me. "Little Molé would never poke her nose into a place like that. They tell us that to draw us. Nobody ever goes to them and they are never asked anywhere either. He admits it himself: 'We spend the evenings alone by our own fire-side.' As he always says *we*, not like royalty, but to include his wife, I do not press him. But I know all about it," the Duchess added. We passed two young men whose great and dissimilar beauty took its origin from one and the same woman. They were the two sons of Mme. de Surgis, the latest mistress of the Duc de Guermantes. Both were resplendent with their mother's perfections, but each in his own way. To one had passed, rippling through a virile body, the royal presence of Mme. de Surgis and the same pallor, ardent, flushed and sacred, flooded the marble cheeks of mother and son; but his brother had received the Grecian brow, the perfect nose, the statuesque throat, the eyes of infinite depth; composed thus of separate gifts, which the goddess had shared between them, their twofold beauty offered one the abstract pleasure of thinking that the cause of that beauty was something outside themselves; one would have said that the principal attributes of their mother were incarnate in two different bodies; that one of the young men was his mother's stature and her complexion, the other her gaze, like those divine beings who were no more than the strength and beauty of Jupiter or Minerva. Full of respect for M. de Guermantes, of whom they said: "He is a great friend of our parents," the elder nevertheless thought that it would be wiser not to come up and greet the Duchess, of whose hostility towards his mother he was aware, though without perhaps understanding the reason for it, and at the sight of us he slightly averted his head. The younger, who copied his brother in everything, because, being stupid and short-sighted to boot, he did not venture to own a personal opinion, inclined his head at the same angle, and the pair slipped past us towards the card-room, one behind the other, like a pair of allegorical figures.

Just as I reached this room, I was stopped by the Marquise de Citri, still beautiful but almost foaming at the mouth. Of decently noble birth, she had sought and made a brilliant match in marrying M. de Citri, whose great-grandmother had been an Aumale-Lorraine. But no sooner had she tasted this satisfaction than her natural cantankerousness gave her a horror of people in society which did not cut her off absolutely from social life. Not only, at a party, did she deride everyone present, her derision of them was so violent that mere laughter was not sufficiently bitter, and changed into a guttural hiss. " Ah!" she said to me, pointing to the Duchesse de Guermantes who had now left my side and was already some way off, " what defeats me is that she can lead this sort of existence." Was this the speech of a righteously indignant Saint, astonished that the Gentiles did not come of their own accord to perceive the Truth, or that of an anarchist athirst for carnage? In any case there could be no possible justification for this apostrophe. In the first place, the " existence led " by Mme. de Guermantes differed hardly perceptibly (except in indignation) from that led by Mme. de Citri. Mme. de Citri was stupefied when she saw the Duchess capable of that mortal sacrifice: attendance at one of Marie-Gilbert's parties. It must be said in this particular instance that Mme. de Citri was genuinely fond of the Princess, who was indeed the kindest of women, and knew that, by attending her party, she was giving her great pleasure. And so she had put off, in order to come to the party, a dancer whom she regarded as a genius, and who was to have initiated her into the mysteries of Russian choreography. Another reason which to some extent stultified the concentrated rage which Mme. de Citri felt on seeing Oriane greet one or other of the guests was that Mme. de Guermantes, albeit at a far less advanced stage, shewed the symptoms of the malady that was devouring Mme. de Citri. We have seen, moreover, that she had carried the germs of it from her birth. In fact, being more intelligent than Mme. de Citri, Mme. de Guermantes would have had better right than she to this nihilism (which was more than merely social), but it is true that certain good qualities help us rather to endure the defects of our neighbour than they make us suffer from them; and a man of great talent will normally pay less attention to other people's folly than would a fool. We have already described at sufficient length the nature of the Duchess's wit to convince the reader that, if it had nothing in common with great intellect, it was at least wit, a wit adroit in making use (like a translator) of different grammatical forms. Now nothing of this sort seemed to entitle Mme. de Citri to look down upon qualities so closely akin to her own. She found everyone idiotic, but in her conversation, in her letters, shewed herself distinctly inferior to the people whom she treated with such disdain. She had moreover such a thirst for destruction that, when she had almost given up society, the pleasures that she then sought were subjected, each in turn, to her terrible disintegrating force. After she had given up parties for musical evenings, she used to say: " You like listening to that sort of thing, to music? Good gracious, it all depends on what it is. It can be simply deadly! Oh! Beethoven! What a bore!" With Wagner, then with Franck, Debussy, she did not even take the trouble to say the word *barbe,* but merely passed her hand over her face with a tonsorial gesture.

Presently, everything became boring. " Beautiful things are such a bore. Oh! Pictures! They're enough to drive one mad. How right you are, it is such a bore having to write letters!" Finally it was life itself that she declared to be *rasante,* leaving her hearers to wonder where she applied the term.

I do not know whether it was the effect of what the
Duchesse de Guermantes, on the evening when I first
dined at her house, had said of this interior, but the card,
or smoking-room, with its pictorial floor, its tripods, its
figures of gods and animals that gazed at you, the
sphinxes stretched out along the arms of the chairs, and
most of all the huge table, of marble or enamelled mosaic,
covered with symbolical signs more or less imitated from
Etruscan and Egyptian art, gave me the impression of a
magician's cell. And, on a chair drawn up to the glittering, augural table, M. de Charlus, in person, never touching a card, unconscious of what was going on round about
him, incapable of observing that I had entered the room,
seemed precisely a magician applying all the force of his
will and reason to drawing a horoscope. Not only that,
but, like the eyes of a Pythian on her tripod, his eyes were
starting from his head, and that nothing might distract
him from labours which required the cessation of the most
simple movements, he had (like a calculator who will do
nothing else until he has solved his problem) laid down
beside him the cigar which he had previously been holding between his lips, but had no longer the necessary
detachment of mind to think of smoking. Seeing the
two crouching deities borne upon the arms of the chair
that stood facing him, one might have thought that the
Baron was endeavouring the solve the enigma of the
Sphinx, had it not been that, rather, of a young and living
Oedipus, seated in that very armchair, where he had
come to join in the game. Now, the figure to which M.
de Charlus was applying with such concentration all his
mental powers, and which was not, to tell the truth, one
of the sort that are commonly studied *more geometrico,*

was that of the proposition set him by the lineaments of the young Comte de Surgis; it appeared, so profound was M. de Charlus's absorption in front of it, to be some rebus, some riddle, some algebraical problem, of which he must try to penetrate the mystery or to work out the formula. In front of him the sibylline signs and the figures inscribed upon that Table of the Law seemed the gramarye which would enable the old sorcerer to tell in what direction the young man's destiny was shaping. Suddenly he became aware that I was watching him, raised his head as though he were waking from a dream, smiled at me and blushed. At that moment Mme. de Surgis's other son came up behind the one who was playing, to look at his cards. When M. de Charlus had learned from me that they were brothers, his features could not conceal the admiration that he felt for a family which could create masterpieces so splendid and so diverse. And what added to the Baron's enthusiasm was the discovery that the two sons of Mme. de Surgis-le-Duc were sons not only of the same mother but of the same father. The children of Jupiter are dissimilar, but that is because he married first Metis, whose destiny it was to bring into the world wise children, then Themis, and after her Eurynome, and Mnemosyne, and Leto, and only as a last resort Juno. But to a single father Mme. de Surgis had borne these two sons who had each received beauty from her, but a different beauty.

I had at length the pleasure of seeing Swann come into this room, which was very big, so big that he did not at first catch sight of me. A pleasure mingled with sorrow, with a sorrow which the other guests did not, perhaps, feel, their feeling consisting rather in that sort of fascination which is exercised by the strange and unexpected forms of an approaching death, a death that a man already has, in the popular saying, written on his face. And it was with a stupefaction that was almost offensive, into which entered indiscreet curiosity, cruelty, a scrutiny at once quiet and anxious (a blend of *suave mari magno* and *memento quia pulvis,* Robert would have said), that all eyes were fastened upon that face the cheeks of which had been so eaten away by disease, like a waning moon, that, except at a certain angle, the angle doubtless at which Swann looked at himself, they stopped short like a flimsy piece of scenery to which only an optical illusion can add the appearance of solidity. Whether because of the absence of those cheeks, no longer there to modify it, or because arterio-sclerosis, which also is a form of intoxication, had reddened it, as would drunkenness, or deformed it, as would morphine, Swann's punchinello nose, absorbed for long years in an attractive face, seemed now enormous, tumid, crimson, the nose of an old Hebrew rather than of a dilettante Valois. Perhaps too in him, in these last days, the race was making appear more pronounced the physical type that characterises it, at the same time as the sentiment of a moral solidarity with the rest of the Jews, a solidarity which Swann seemed to have forgotten throughout his life, and which, one after another, his mortal illness, the Dreyfus case and the anti-semitic propaganda had revived. There are certain Israelites, superior people for all that and refined men of the world, in whom there remain in reserve and in the wings, ready to enter at a given moment in their lives, as in a play, a bounder and a prophet. Swann had arrived at the age of the prophet. Certainly, with his face from which, by the action of his disease, whole segments had vanished, as when a block of ice melts and slabs of it fall off bodily, he had greatly altered. But I could not help being struck by the discovery how far more he had altered in relation to myself. This man, excellent, cultivated, whom I was far from annoyed at meeting, I could not bring myself to understand how I had been able to invest him long ago in a mystery so great that his appearance in the Champs-Elysées used to make my heart beat so violently that I was too bashful to approach his silk-lined cape, that at the door of the flat in which such a being dwelt I could not ring the bell without being overcome by boundless emotion and dismay; all this had vanished not only from his home, but from his person, and the idea of talking to him might or might not be agreeable to me, but had no effect whatever upon my nervous system.

And besides, how he had altered since that very afternoon, when I had met him—after all, only a few hours earlier—in the Duc de Guermantes's study. Had he really had a scene with the Prince, and had it left him crushed? The supposition was not necessary. The slightest efforts that are demanded of a person who is very ill quickly become for him an excessive strain. He has only to be exposed, when already tired, to the heat of a crowded drawing-room, for his countenance to decompose and turn blue, as happens in a few hours with an overripe pear or milk that is ready to turn. Besides, Swann's hair was worn thin in patches, and, as Mme. de Guermantes remarked, needed attention from the furrier, looked as if it had been camphored, and camphored badly. I was just crossing the room to speak to Swann when unfortunately a hand fell upon my shoulder:

"Hallo, old boy, I am in Paris for forty-eight hours. I called at your house, they told me you were here, so that it is to you that my aunt is indebted for the honour of my company at her party." It was Saint-Loup. I told him how greatly I admired the house. "Yes, it makes quite a historic edifice. Personally, I think it appalling. We mustn't go near my uncle Palamède, or we shall be caught. Now that Mme. Molé has gone (for it is she that is ruling the roast just now), he is quite at a loose end. It seems it was as good as a play, he never let her out of his sight for a moment, and only left her when he had put her safely into her carriage. I bear my uncle no ill will, only I do think it odd that my family council, which has always been so hard on me, should be composed of the very ones who have led giddy lives themselves, beginning with the giddiest of the lot, my uncle Charlus, who is my official guardian, has had more women than Don Juan, and is still carrying on in spite of his age. There was a talk at one time of having me made a ward of court. I bet, when all those gay old dogs met to consider the question, and had me up to preach to me and tell me that I was breaking my mother's heart, they dared not look one another in the face for fear of laughing. Just think of the fellows who formed the council, you would think they had deliberately chosen the biggest womanisers." Leaving out of account M. de Charlus, with regard to whom my friend's astonishment no longer seemed to me to be justified, but for different reasons, and reasons which, moreover, were afterwards to undergo modification in my mind, Robert was quite wrong in finding it extraordinary that lessons in worldly wisdom should be given to a young man by people who had done foolish things, or were still doing them.

Even if we take into account only atavism, family like-nesses, it is inevitable that the uncle who delivers the lecture should have more or less the same faults as the nephew whom he has been deputed to scold. Nor is the uncle in the least hypocritical in so doing, taken in as he is by the faculty that people have of believing, in every fresh experience, that "this is quite different," a faculty which allows them to adopt artistic, political and other errors without perceiving that they are the same errors which they exposed, ten years ago, in another school of painters, whom they condemned, another political affair which, they considered, merited a loathing that they no longer feel, and espouse those errors without recognising them in a fresh disguise. Besides, even if the faults of the uncle are different from those of the nephew, heredity may none the less be responsible, for the effect does not always resemble the cause, as a copy resembles its orig-inal, and even if the uncle's faults are worse, he may easily believe them to be less serious.

When M. de Charlus made indignant remonstrances to Robert, who moreover was unaware of his uncle's true inclinations, at that time, and indeed if it had still been the time when the Baron used to scarify his own inclina-tions, he might perfectly well have been sincere in con-sidering, from the point of view of a man of the world, that Robert was infinitely more to blame than himself. Had not Robert, at the very moment when his uncle had been deputed to make him listen to reason, come within an inch of getting himself ostracised by society, had he not very nearly been blackballed at the Jockey, had he not made himself a public laughing stock by the vast sums that he threw away upon a woman of the lowest order, by his friendships with people—authors, actors, Jews—not one of whom moved in society, by his opinions, which were indistinguishable from those held by traitors, by the grief he was causing to all his relatives? In what respect could it be compared, this scandalous existence, with that of M. de Charlus who had managed, so far, not only to retain but to enhance still further his position as a Guermantes, being in society an absolutely privileged person, sought after, adulated in the most exclusive circles, and a man who, married to a Bourbon Princess, a woman of eminence, had been able to ensure her happiness, had shewn a devotion to her memory more fervent, more scrupulous than is customary in society, and had thus been as good a husband as a son!

"But are you sure that M. de Charlus has had all those mistresses?" I asked, not, of course, with any diabolical intent of revealing to Robert the secret that I had surprised, but irritated, nevertheless, at hearing him maintain an erroneous theory with so much certainty and assurance. He merely shrugged his shoulders in response to what he took for ingenuousness on my part. "Not that I blame him in the least, I consider that he is perfectly right." And he began to sketch in outline a theory of conduct that would have horrified him at Balbec (where he was not content with denouncing seducers, death seeming to him then the only punishment adequate to their crime). Then, however, he had still been in love and jealous. He went so far as to sing me the praises of houses of assignation. "They're the only places where you can find a shoe to fit you, sheath your weapon, as we say in the regiment." He no longer felt for places of that sort the disgust that had inflamed him at Balbec when I made an allusion to them, and, hearing what he now said, I told him that Bloch had introduced me to one, but Robert replied that the one which Bloch frequented must be "extremely mixed, the poor man's paradise!—It all depends, though: where is it?" I remained vague, for I had just remembered that it was the same house at which one used to have for a louis that Rachel whom Robert had so passionately loved. "Anyhow, I can take you to some far better ones, full of stunning women." Hearing me express the desire that he would take me as soon as possible to the ones he knew, which must indeed be far superior to the house to which Bloch had taken me, he expressed a sincere regret that he could not, on this occasion, as he would have to leave Paris next day. "It will have to be my next leave," he said. "You'll see, there are young girls there, even," he added with an air of mystery. "There is a little Mademoiselle de . . . I think it's d'Orgeville, I can let you have the exact name, who is the daughter of quite tip-top people; her mother was by way of being a La Croix-l'Evêque, and they're a really decent family, in fact they're more or less related, if I'm not mistaken, to my aunt Oriane. Anyhow, you have only to see the child, you can tell at once that she comes of decent people" (I could detect, hovering for a moment over Robert's voice, the shadow of the genius of the Guermantes, which passed like a cloud, but at a great height and without stopping). "It seems to me to promise marvellous developments. The parents are always ill and can't look after her. Gad, the child must have some amusement, and I count upon you to provide it!" "Oh! When are you coming back?" "I don't know, if you don't absolutely insist upon Duchesses" (Duchess being in aristocracy the only title that denotes a particularly brilliant rank, as the lower orders talk of "Princesses"), "in a different class of goods, there is Mme. Putbus's maid."

At this moment, Mme. de Surgis entered the room in search of her sons. As soon as he saw her M. de Charlus went up to her with a friendliness by which the Marquise was all the more agreeably surprised, in that an icy frigidity was what she had expected from the Baron, who had always posed as Oriane's protector and alone of the family—the rest being too often inclined to forgive the Duke his irregularities by the glamour of his position and their own jealousy of the Duchess—kept his brother's mistresses pitilessly at a distance. And so Mme. de Surgis had fully understood the motives of the attitude that she dreaded to find in the Baron, but never for a moment suspected those of the wholly different welcome that she did receive from him. He spoke to her with admiration of the portrait that Jacquet had painted of her years before. This admiration waxed indeed to an enthusiasm which, if it was partly deliberate, with the object of preventing the Marquise from going away, of "hooking" her, as Robert used to say of enemy armies when you seek to keep their effective strength engaged at one point, might also be sincere. For, if everyone was delighted to admire in her sons the regal bearing and eyes of Mme. de Surgis, the Baron could taste an inverse but no less keen pleasure in finding those charms combined in the mother, as in a portrait which does not by itself excite desire, but feeds with the aesthetic admiration that it does excite the desires that it revives. These came now to give, in retrospect, a voluptuous charm to Jacquet's portrait itself, and at that moment the Baron would gladly have purchased it to study upon its surface the physiognomic pedigree of the two young Surgis.

"You see, I wasn't exaggerating," Robert said in my ear. "Just look at the way my uncle is running after Mme. de Surgis. Though I must say, that does surprise me. If Oriane knew, she would be furious. Really, there are enough women in the world without his having to go and sprawl over that one," he went on; like everybody who is not in love, he imagined that one chose the person whom one loved after endless deliberations and on the strength of various qualities and advantages. Besides, while completely mistaken about his uncle, whom he supposed to be devoted to women, Robert, in his rancour, spoke too lightly of M. de Charlus. We are not always somebody's nephew with impunity. It is often through him that a hereditary habit is transmitted to us sooner or later. We might indeed arrange a whole gallery of portraits, named like the German comedy: *Uncle and Nephew,* in which we should see the uncle watching jealously, albeit unconsciously, for his nephew to end by becoming like himself.

I go so far as to say that this gallery would be incomplete were we not to include in it the uncles who are not really related by blood, being the uncles only of their nephews' wives. The Messieurs de Charlus are indeed so convinced that they themselves are the only good husbands, what is more the only husbands of whom their wives are not jealous, that generally, out of affection for their niece, they make her marry another Charlus. Which tangles the skein of family likenesses. And, to affection for the niece, is added at times affection for her betrothed as well. Such marriages are not uncommon, and are often what are called happy.

"What were we talking about? Oh yes, that big, fair girl, Mme. Putbus's maid. She goes with women too, but I don't suppose you mind that, I can tell you frankly, I have never seen such a gorgeous creature." "I imagine her rather Giorgione?" "Wildly Giorgione! Oh, if I only had a little time in Paris, what wonderful things there are to be done! And then, one goes on to the next. For love is all rot, mind you, I've finished with all that." I soon discovered, to my surprise, that he had equally finished with literature, whereas it was merely with regard to literary men that he had struck me as being disillusioned at our last meeting. ("They're practically all a pack of scoundrels," he had said to me, a saying that might be explained by his justified resentment towards certain of Rachel's friends. They had indeed persuaded her that she would never have any talent if she allowed "Robert, scion of an alien race" to acquire an influence over her, and with her used to make fun of him, to his face, at the dinners to which he entertained them.) But in reality Robert's love of Letters was in no sense profound, did not spring from his true nature, was only a by-product of his love of Rachel, and he had got rid of it, at the same time as of his horror of voluptuaries and his religious respect for the virtue of women.

"There is something very strange about those two young men. Look at that curious passion for gambling, Marquise," said M. de Charlus, drawing Mme. de Surgis's attention to her own sons, as though he were completely unaware of their identity. "They must be a pair of Orientals, they have certain characteristic features, they are perhaps Turks," he went on, so as both to give further support to his feint of innocence and to exhibit a vague antipathy, which, when in due course it gave place to affability, would prove that the latter was addressed to the young men solely in their capacity as sons of Mme. de Surgis, having begun only when the Baron discovered who they were. Perhaps too M. de Charlus, whose insolence was a natural gift which he delighted in exercising, took advantage of the few moments in which he was supposed not to know the name of these two young men to have a little fun at Mme. de Surgis's expense, and to indulge in his habitual sarcasm, as Scapin takes advantage of his master's disguise to give him a sound drubbing.

"They are my sons," said Mme. de Surgis, with a blush which would not have coloured her cheeks had she been more discerning, without necessarily being more virtuous. She would then have understood that the air of absolute indifference or of sarcasm which M. de Charlus displayed towards a young man was no more sincere than the wholly superficial admiration which he shewed for a woman, did not express his true nature. The woman to whom he could go on indefinitely paying the prettiest compliments might well be jealous of the look which, while talking to her, he shot at a man whom he would pretend afterwards not to have noticed. For that look was not of the sort which M. de Charlus kept for women; a special look, springing from the depths, which even at a party could not help straying innocently in the direction of the young men, like the look in a tailor's eye which betrays his profession by immediately fastening upon your attire.

"Oh, how very strange!" replied M. de Charlus, not without insolence, as though his mind had to make a long journey to arrive at a reality so different from what he had pretended to suppose. "But I don't know them!" he added, fearing lest he might have gone a little too far in the expression of his antipathy, and have thus paralysed the Marquise's intention to let him make their acquaintance. "Would you allow me to introduce them to you?" Mme. de Surgis inquired timidly. "Why, good gracious, just as you please, I shall be delighted, I am perhaps not very entertaining company for such young people," M. de Charlus intoned with the air of hesitation and coldness of a person who is letting himself be forced into an act of politeness.

"Arnulphe, Victurnien, come here at once," said Mme. de Surgis. Victurnien rose with decision. Arnulphe, though he could not see where his brother was going, followed him meekly.

"It's the sons' turn, now," muttered Saint-Loup. "It's enough to make one die with laughing. He tries to curry favour with every one, down to the dog in the yard. It is all the funnier, as my uncle detests pretty boys. And just look how seriously he is listening to them. If it had been I who tried to introduce them to him, he would have given me what for. Listen, I shall have to go and say how d'ye do to Oriane. I have so little time in Paris that I want to try and see all the people here that I ought to leave cards on."

"What a well-bred air they have, what charming manners," M. de Charlus was saying. "You think so?" Mme. de Surgis replied, highly delighted.

Swann having caught sight of me came over to Saint-Loup and myself. His Jewish gaiety was less refined than his witticisms as a man of the world. "Good evening," he said to us. "Heavens! All three of us together, people will think it is a meeting of the Syndicate. In another minute they'll be looking for the safe!" He had not observed that M. de Monserfeuil was just behind his back and could hear what he said. The General could not help wincing. We heard the voice of M. de Charlus close beside us: "What, you are called Victurnien, after the *Cabinet des Antiques*," the Baron was saying, to prolong his conversation with the two young men. "By Balzac, yes," replied the elder Surgis, who had never read a line of that novelist's work, but to whom his tutor had remarked, a few days earlier, upon the similarity of his Christian name and d'Esgrignon's. Mme. de Surgis was delighted to see her son shine, and at M. de Charlus's ecstasy before such a display of learning.

"It appears that Loubet is entirely on our side, I have it from an absolutely trustworthy source," Swann informed Saint-Loup, but this time in a lower tone so as not to be overheard by the General. Swann had begun to find his wife's Republican connexions more interesting now that the Dreyfus case had become his chief preoccupation. "I tell you this because I know that your heart is with us."

"Not quite to that extent; you are entirely mistaken," was Robert's answer. "It's a bad business, and I'm sorry I ever had a finger in it. It was no affair of mine.

If it were to begin over again, I should keep well clear of it. I am a soldier, and my first duty is to support the Army. If you will stay with M. Swann for a moment, I shall be back presently, I must go and talk to my aunt." But I saw that it was with Mlle. d'Ambresac that he went to talk, and was distressed by the thought that he had lied to me about the possibility of their engagement. My mind was set at rest when I learned that he had been introduced to her half an hour earlier by Mme. de Marsantes, who was anxious for the marriage, the Ambresacs being extremely rich.

"At last," said M. de Charlus to Mme. de Surgis, " I find a young man with some education, who has read, who knows what is meant by Balzac. And it gives me all the more pleasure to meet him where that sort of thing has become most rare, in the house of one of my peers, one of ourselves," he added, laying stress upon the words. It was all very well for the Guermantes to profess to regard all men as equal; on the great occasions when they found themselves among people who were "born," especially if they were not quite so well born as themselves, whom they were anxious and able to flatter, they did not hesitate to trot out old family memories. "At one time," the Baron went on, "the word aristocrat meant the best people, in intellect, in heart. Now, here is the first person I find among ourselves who has ever heard of Victurnien d'Esgrignon. I am wrong in saying the first. There are also a Polignac and a Montesquiou," added M. de Charlus, who knew that this twofold association must inevitably thrill the Marquise. "However, your sons have every reason to be learned, their maternal grandfather had a famous collection of eighteenth century stuff. I will shew you mine if you will do me the pleasure of coming to luncheon with me one day," he said to the young Victurnien. "I can shew you an interesting edition of the *Cabinet des Antiques* with corrections in Balzac's own hand. I shall be charmed to bring the two Victurniens face to face."

I could not bring myself to leave Swann. He had arrived at that stage of exhaustion in which a sick man's body becomes a mere retort in which we study chemical reactions. His face was mottled with tiny spots of Prussian blue, which seemed not to belong to the world of living things, and emitted the sort of odour which, at school, after the " experiments," makes it so unpleasant to have to remain in a " science " classroom. I asked him whether he had not had a long conversation with the Prince de Guermantes and if he would tell me what it had been about. " Yes," he said, " but go for a moment first with M. de Charlus and Mme. de Surgis, I shall wait for you here."

Indeed, M. de Charlus, having suggested to Mme. de Surgis that they should leave this room which was too hot, and go and sit for a little in another, had invited not the two sons to accompany their mother, but myself. In this way he made himself appear, after he had successfully hooked them, to have lost all interest in the two young men. He was moreover paying me an inexpensive compliment, Mme. de Surgis being in distinctly bad odour.

Unfortunately, no sooner had we sat down in an alcove from which there was no way of escape than Mme. de Saint-Euverte, a butt for the Baron's jibes, came past. She, perhaps to mask or else openly to shew her contempt for the ill will which she inspired in M. de Charlus, and

above all to shew that she was on intimate terms with a
woman who was talking so familiarly to him, gave a dis-
dainfully friendly greeting to the famous beauty, who
acknowledged it, peeping out of the corner of her eye at
M. de Charlus with a mocking smile. But the alcove was
so narrow that Mme. de Saint-Euverte, when she tried
to continue, behind our backs, her canvass of her guests
for the morrow, found herself a prisoner, and had some
difficulty in escaping, a precious moment which M. de
Charlus, anxious that his insolent wit should shine before
the mother of the two young men, took good care not to
let slip. A silly question which I had put to him, without
malice aforethought, gave him the opportunity for a
hymn of triumph of which the poor Saint-Euverte, almost
immobilised behind us, could not have lost a word.
"Would you believe it, this impertinent young man," he
said, indicating me to Mme. de Surgis, "asked me just
now, without any sign of that modesty which makes us
keep such expeditions private, if I was going to Mme. de
Saint-Euverte's, which is to say, I suppose, if I was
suffering from the colic. I should endeavour, in any
case, to relieve myself in some more comfortable place
than the house of a person who, if my memory serves
me, was celebrating her centenary when I first began
to go about town, though not, of course, to her house.
And yet who could be more interesting to listen to?
What a host of historic memories, seen and lived through
in the days of the First Empire and the Restoration, and
secret history too, which could certainly have nothing of
the "saint" about it, but must be decidedly "verdant"
if we are to judge by the amount of kick still left in the
old trot's shanks. What would prevent me from ques-

tioning her about those passionate times is the acuteness of my olfactory organ. The proximity of the lady is enough. I say to myself all at once: oh, good lord, some one has broken the lid of my cesspool, when it is simply the Marquise opening her mouth to emit some invitation. And you can understand that if I had the misfortune to go to her house, the cesspool would be magnified into a formidable sewage-cart. She bears a mystic name, though, which has always made me think with jubilation, although she has long since passed the date of her jubilee, of that stupid line of poetry called deliquescent: 'Ah, green, how green my soul was on that day. . . .' But I require a cleaner sort of verdure. They tell me that the indefatigable old street-walker gives 'garden-parties,' I should describe them as 'invitations to explore the sewers.' Are you going to wallow there?" he asked Mme. de Surgis, who this time was annoyed. Wishing to pretend for the Baron's benefit that she was not going, and knowing that she would give days of her life rather than miss the Saint-Euverte party, she got out of it by taking a middle course, that is to say uncertainty. This uncertainty took so clumsily amateurish, so sordidly material a form, that M. de Charlus, with no fear of offending Mme. de Surgis, whom nevertheless he was anxious to please, began to laugh to shew her that "it cut no ice with him."

"I always admire people who make plans," she said; "I often change mine at the last moment. There is a question of a summer frock which may alter everything. I shall act upon the inspiration of the moment."

For my part, I was furious at the abominable little speech that M. de Charlus had just made. I would have liked to shower blessings upon the giver of garden-parties. Unfortunately, in the social as in the political world, the victims are such cowards that one cannot for long remain indignant with their tormentors. Mme. de Saint-Euverte, who had succeeded in escaping from the alcove to which we were barring the entry, brushed against the Baron inadvertently as she passed him, and, by a reflex action of snobbishness which wiped out all her anger, perhaps even in the hope of securing an opening, at which this could not be the first attempt, exclaimed: "Oh! I beg your pardon, Monsieur de Charlus, I hope I did not hurt you," as though she were kneeling before her lord and master. The latter did not deign to reply save by a broad ironical smile, and conceded only a "Good evening," which, uttered as though he were only now made aware of the Marquise's presence after she had greeted him, was an insult the more. Lastly, with a supreme want of spirit which pained me for her sake, Mme. de Saint-Euverte came up to me and, drawing me aside, said in my ear: "Tell me, what have I done to offend M. de Charlus? They say that he doesn't consider me smart enough for him," she said, laughing from ear to ear. I remained serious. For one thing, I thought it stupid of her to appear to believe or to wish other people to believe that nobody, really, was as smart as herself. For another thing, people who laugh so heartily at what they themselves have said, when it is not funny, dispense us accordingly, by taking upon themselves the responsibility for the mirth, from joining in it.

"Other people assure me that he is cross because I do not invite him. But he does not give me much encouragement. He seems to avoid me." (This expression

struck me as inadequate.) "Try to find out, and come
and tell me to-morrow. And if he feels remorseful and
wishes to come too, bring him. I shall forgive and forget. Indeed, I shall be quite glad to see him, because it
will annoy Mme. de Surgis. I give you a free hand.
You have the most perfect judgment in these matters and
I do not wish to appear to be begging my guests to come.
In any case, I count upon you absolutely."

It occurred to me that Swann must be getting tired of
waiting for me. I did not wish, moreover, to be too late
in returning home, because of Albertine, and, taking
leave of Mme. de Surgis and M. de Charlus, I went in
search of my sick man in the card-room. I asked him
whether what he had said to the Prince in their conversation in the garden was really what M. de Bréauté (whom
I did not name) had reported to us, about a little play
by Bergotte. He burst out laughing: "There is not a
word of truth in it, not one, it is entirely made up and
would have been an utterly stupid thing to say. Really,
it is unheard of, this spontaneous generation of falsehood.
I do not ask who it was that told you, but it would be
really interesting, in a field as limited as this, to work
back from one person to another and find out how the
story arose. Anyhow, what concern can it be of other
people, what the Prince said to me? People are very inquisitive. I have never been inquisitive, except when I
was in love, and when I was jealous. And a lot I ever
learned! Are you jealous?" I told Swann that I had
never experienced jealousy, that I did not even know
what it was. "Indeed! I congratulate you. A little
jealousy is not at all a bad thing, from two points of view.
For one thing, because it enables people who are not

inquisitive to take an interest in the lives of others, or of one other at any rate. And besides, it makes one feel the pleasure of possession, of getting into a carriage with a woman, of not allowing her to go about by herself. But that occurs only in the very first stages of the disease, or when the cure is almost complete. In the interval, it is the most agonising torment. However, even the two pleasures I have mentioned, I must own to you that I have tasted very little of them: the first, by the fault of my own nature, which is incapable of sustained reflexion; the second, by force of circumstances, by the fault of the woman, I should say the women, of whom I have been jealous. But that makes no difference. Even when one is no longer interested in things, it is still something to have been interested in them; because it was always for reasons which other people did not grasp. The memory of those sentiments is, we feel, to be found only in ourselves; we must go back into ourselves to study it. You mustn't laugh at this idealistic jargon, what I mean to say is that I have been very fond of life and very fond of art. Very well! Now that I am a little too weary to live with other people, those old sentiments, so personal and individual, that I felt in the past, seem to me—it is the mania of all collectors—very precious. I open my heart to myself like a sort of showcase, and examine one by one ever so many love affairs of which the rest of the world can have known nothing. And of this collection, to which I am now even more attached than to my others, I say to myself, rather as Mazarin said of his library, but still without any keen regret, that it will be very tiresome to have to leave it all. But, to come back to my conversation with the Prince, I shall repeat it to one person only, and that person is going to be yourself." My attention was distracted by the conversation that M. de Charlus, who had returned to the card-room, was prolonging indefinitely close beside us. "And are you a reader too? What do you do?" he asked Comte Arnulphe, who had never heard even the name of Balzac. But his short-sightedness, as he saw everything very small, gave him the appearance of seeing to great distances, so that, rare poetry in a sculptural Greek god, there seemed to be engraved upon his pupils remote, mysterious stars.

"Suppose we took a turn in the garden, Sir," I said to Swann, while Comte Arnulphe, in a lisping voice which seemed to indicate that mentally at least his development was incomplete, replied to M. de Charlus with an artlessly obliging precision: "I, oh, golf chiefly, tennis, football, running, polo I'm really keen on." So Minerva, being subdivided, ceased in certain cities to be the goddess of wisdom, and incarnated part of herself in a purely sporting, horse-loving deity, Athene Hippia. And he went to Saint Moritz also to ski, for Pallas Trilogeneia frequents the high peaks and outruns swift horsemen. "Ah!" replied M. de Charlus with the transcendent smile of the intellectual who does not even take the trouble to conceal his derision, but, on the other hand, feels himself so superior to other people and so far despises the intelligence of those who are the least stupid, that he barely differentiates between them and the most stupid, the moment they can be attractive to him in some other way. While talking to Arnulphe, M. de Charlus felt that by the mere act of addressing him he was conferring upon him a superiority which everyone else must recognise and envy. "No," Swann replied, "I am too tired to walk about, let us sit down somewhere in a corner, I cannot remain on my feet any longer." This was true, and yet the act of beginning to talk had already given him back a certain vivacity. This was because, in the most genuine exhaustion, there is, especially in neurotic people, an element that depends upon attracting their attention and is kept going only by an act of memory. We at once feel tired as soon as we are afraid of feeling tired, and, to throw off our fatigue, it suffices us to forget about it. To be sure, Swann was far from being one of those indefatigable invalids who, entering a room worn out and ready to drop, revive in conversation like a flower in water and are able for hours on end to draw from their own words a reserve of strength which they do not, alas, communicate to their hearers, who appear more and more exhausted the more the talker comes back to life. But Swann belonged to that stout Jewish race, in whose vital energy, its resistance to death, its individual members seem to share. Stricken severally by their own diseases, as it is stricken itself by persecution, they continue indefinitely to struggle against terrible suffering which may be prolonged beyond every apparently possible limit, when already one sees nothing more than a prophet's beard surmounted by a huge nose which dilates to inhale its last breath, before the hour strikes for the ritual prayers and the punctual procession begins of distant relatives advancing with mechanical movements, as upon an Assyrian frieze.

We went to sit down, but, before moving away from the group formed by M. de Charlus with the two young Surgis and their mother, Swann could not resist fastening upon the lady's bosom the slow expansive concupiscent gaze of a connoisseur. He put up his monocle, for a better view, and, while he talked to me, kept glancing in the direction of the lady. "This is, word for word," he said to me when we were seated, "my conversation with the Prince, and if you remember what I said to you just now, you will see why I choose you as my confidant. There is another reason as well, which you shall one day learn.—'My dear Swann,' the Prince de Guermantes said to me, 'you must forgive me if I have appeared to be avoiding you for some time past.' (I had never even noticed it, having been ill and avoiding society myself.) 'In the first place, I had heard it said that, as I fully expected, in the unhappy affair which is splitting the country in two your views were diametrically opposed to mine. Now, it would have been extremely painful to me to have to hear you express them. So sensitive were my nerves that when the Princess, two years ago, heard her brother-in-law, the Grand Duke of Hesse, say that Dreyfus was innocent, she was not content with promptly denying the assertion but refrained from repeating it to me in order not to upset me. About the same time, the Crown Prince of Sweden came to Paris and, having probably heard some one say that the Empress Eugénie was a Dreyfusist, confused her with the Princess (a strange confusion, you will admit, between a woman of the rank of my wife and a Spaniard, a great deal less well born than people make out, and married to a mere Bonaparte), and said to her: Princess, I am doubly glad to meet you, for I know that you hold the same view as myself of the Dreyfus case, which does not surprise me since Your Highness is Bavarian. Which drew down upon the Prince the answer: Sir, I am nothing now but a French Princess, and I share the views of all my fellow-countrymen. Now, my dear Swann, about eighteen months ago, a conversation I had with General de Beaucerfeuil made me suspect that not an error, but grave illegalities had been committed in the procedure of the trial.'"

We were interrupted (Swann did not wish people to overhear his story) by the voice of M. de Charlus who (without, as it happened, paying us the slightest attention) came past escorting Mme. de Surgis, and stopped in the hope of detaining her for a moment longer, whether on account of her sons or from that reluctance common to all the Guermantes to bring anything to an end, which kept them plunged in a sort of anxious inertia. Swann informed me, in this connexion, a little later, of something that stripped the name Surgis-le-Duc, for me, of all the poetry that I had found in it. The Marquise de Surgis-le-Duc boasted a far higher social position, far finer connexions by marriage than her cousin the Comte de Surgis, who had no money and lived on his estate in the country. But the words that ended her title "le Duc" had not at all the origin which I ascribed to them, and which had made me associate it in my imagination with Bourg-l'Abbé, Bois-le-Roi, etc. All that had happened was that a Comte de Surgis had married, during the Restoration, the daughter of an immensely rich industrial magnate, M. Leduc, or Le Duc, himself the son of a chemical manufacturer, the richest man of his day, and a Peer of France. King Charles X had created for the son born of this marriage the Marquisate of Surgis-le-Duc, a Marquisate of Surgis existing already in the family.

The addition of the plebeian surname had not prevented this branch from allying itself, on the strength of its enormous fortune, with the first families of the realm. And the present Marquise de Surgis-le-Duc, herself of exalted birth, might have moved in the very highest circles. A demon of perversity had driven her, scorning the position ready made for her, to flee from the conjugal roof, to live a life of open scandal. Whereupon the world which she had scorned at twenty, when it was at her feet, had cruelly failed her at thirty, when, after ten years, everybody, except a few faithful friends, had ceased to bow to her, and she set to work to reconquer laboriously, inch by inch, what she had possessed as a birthright. (An outward and return journey which are not uncommon.)

As for the great nobles, her kinsmen, whom she had disowned in the past, and who in their turn had now disowned her, she found an excuse for the joy that she would feel in gathering them again to her bosom in the memories of childhood that they would be able to recall. And in so saying, to cloak her snobbishness, she was perhaps less untruthful than she supposed. "Basin is all my girlhood!" she said on the day on which he came back to her. And as a matter of fact there was a grain of truth in the statement. But she had miscalculated when she chose him for her lover. For all the women friends of the Duchesse de Guermantes were to rally round her, and so Mme. de Surgis must descend for the second time that slope up which she had so laboriously toiled. "Well!" M. de Charlus was saying to her, in his attempt to prolong the conversation. "You will lay my tribute at the feet of the beautiful portrait. How is it? What has become of it?" "Why," replied Mme. de Surgis, "you know I haven't got it now; my husband wasn't pleased with it." "Not pleased! With one of the greatest works of art of our time, equal to Nattier's Duchesse de Châteauroux, and, moreover, perpetuating no less majestic and heart-shattering a goddess. Oh! That little blue collar! I swear, Vermeer himself never painted a fabric more consummately, but we must not say it too loud or Swann will fall upon us to avenge his favourite painter, the Master of Delft." The Marquise, turning round, addressed a smile and held out her hand to Swann, who had risen to greet her. But almost without concealment, whether in his declining days he had lost all wish for concealment, by indifference to opinion, or the physical power, by the excitement of his desire and the weakening of the control that helps us to conceal it, as soon as Swann, on taking the Marquise's hand, saw her bosom at close range and from above, he plunged an attentive, serious, absorbed, almost anxious gaze into the cavity of her bodice, and his nostrils, drugged by the lady's perfume, quivered like the wings of a butterfly about to alight upon a half-hidden flower. He checked himself abruptly on the edge of the precipice, and Mme. de Surgis herself, albeit annoyed, stifled a deep sigh, so contagious can desire prove at times. "The painter was cross," she said to M. de Charlus, "and took it back. I have heard that it is now at Diane de Saint-Euverte's." "I decline to believe," said the Baron, "that a great picture can have such bad taste."

"He is talking to her about her portrait. I could talk to her about that portrait just as well as Charlus," said Swann, affecting a drawling, slangy tone as he followed

the retreating couple with his gaze. "And I should certainly enjoy talking about it more than Charlus," he
added. I asked him whether the things that were said
about M. de Charlus were true, in doing which I was
lying twice over, for, if I had no proof that anybody ever
had said anything, I had on the other hand been perfectly aware for some hours past that what I was hinting
at was true. Swann shrugged his shoulders, as though I
had suggested something quite absurd. "It's quite true
that he's a charming friend. But, need I add, his friendship is purely platonic. He is more sentimental than
other men, that is all; on the other hand, as he never goes
very far with women, that has given a sort of plausibility
to the idiotic rumours to which you refer. Charlus is
perhaps greatly attached to his men friends, but you may
be quite certain that the attachment is only in his head
and in his heart. At last, we may perhaps be left in
peace for a moment. Well, the Prince de Guermantes
went on to say: 'I don't mind telling you that this idea
of a possible illegality in the procedure of the trial was
extremely painful to me, because I have always, as you
know, worshipped the army; I discussed the matter again
with the General, and, alas, there could be no two ways of
looking at it. I don't mind telling you frankly that, all
this time, the idea that an innocent man might be under-
going the most degrading punishment had never even
entered my mind. But, starting from this idea of illegality, I began to study what I had always declined to
read, and then the possibility not, this time, of illegal
procedure but of the prisoner's innocence began to haunt
me. I did not feel that I could talk about it to the Princess. Heaven knows that she has become just as French

as myself. You may say what you like, from the day of our marriage, I took such pride in shewing her our country in all its beauty, and what to me is the most splendid thing in it, our Army, that it would have been too painful to me to tell her of my suspicions, which involved, it is true, a few officers only. But I come of a family of soldiers, I did not like to think that officers could be mistaken. I discussed the case again with Beaucerfeuil, he admitted that there had been culpable intrigues, that the *bordereau* was possibly not in Dreyfus's writing, but that an overwhelming proof of his guilt did exist. This was the Henry document. And, a few days later, we learned that it was a forgery. After that, without letting the Princess see me, I began to read the *Siècle* and the *Aurore* every day; soon I had no doubt left, it kept me awake all night. I confided my distress to our friend, the abbé Poiré, who, I was astonished to find, held the same conviction, and I got him to say masses for the intention of Dreyfus, his unfortunate wife and their children. Meanwhile, one morning as I was going to the Princess's room, I saw her maid trying to hide something from me that she had in her hand. I asked her, chaffingly, what it was, she blushed and refused to tell me. I had the fullest confidence in my wife, but this incident disturbed me considerably (and the Princess too, no doubt, who must have heard of it from her woman), for my dear Marie barely uttered a word to me that day at luncheon. I asked the abbé Poiré whether he could say my mass for Dreyfus on the following morning. . . .' And so much for that!" exclaimed Swann, breaking off his narrative. I looked up, and saw the Duc de Guermantes bearing down upon us. "Forgive me for interrupting you, boys. My lad," he went on, addressing myself, "I am instructed to give you a message from Oriane. Marie and Gilbert have asked her to stay and have supper at their table with only five or six other people: the Princess of Hesse, Mme. de Ligné, Mme. de Tarente, Mme. de Chevreuse, the Duchesse d'Arenberg. Unfortunately, we can't wait, we are going on to a little ball of sorts." I was listening, but whenever we have something definite to do at a given moment, we depute a certain person who is accustomed to that sort of duty to keep an eye on the clock and warn us in time. This indwelling servant reminded me, as I had asked him to remind me a few hours before, that Albertine, who at the moment was far from my thoughts, was to come and see me immediately after the theatre. And so I declined the invitation to supper. This does not mean that I was not enjoying myself at the Princesse de Guermantes's. The truth is that men can have several sorts of pleasure. The true pleasure is that for which they abandon the other. But the latter, if it is apparent, or rather if it alone is apparent, may put people off the scent of the other, reassure or mislead the jealous, create a false impression. And yet, all that is needed to make us sacrifice it to the other is a little happiness or a little suffering. Sometimes a third order of pleasures, more serious but more essential, does not yet exist for us, in whom its potential existence is indicated only by its arousing regrets, discouragement. And yet it is to these pleasures that we shall devote ourselves in time to come. To give an example of quite secondary importance, a soldier in time of peace will sacrifice a social existence to love, but, once war is declared (and without there being any need to introduce the idea of a patriotic duty), will sacrifice love to the passion, stronger than love, for fighting. It was all very well Swann's saying that he enjoyed telling me his story, I could feel that his conversation with me, because of the lateness of the hour, and because he himself was so ill, was one of those fatigues at which those who know that they are killing themselves by sitting up late, by overexerting themselves, feel when they return home an angry regret, similar to that felt at the wild extravagance of which they have again been guilty by the spendthrifts who will not, for all that, be able to restrain themselves to-morrow from throwing money out of the windows. After we have passed a certain degree of enfeeblement, whether it be caused by age or by ill health, all pleasure taken at the expense of sleep, in departure from our habits, every breach of the rules becomes a nuisance. The talker continues to talk, out of politeness, from excitement, but he knows that the hour at which he might still have been able to go to sleep has already passed, and he knows also the reproaches that he will heap upon himself during the insomnia and fatigue that must ensue. Already, moreover, even the momentary pleasure has come to an end, body and brain are too far drained of their strength to welcome with any readiness what seems to the other person entertaining. They are like a house on the morning before a journey or removal, where visitors become a perfect plague, to be received sitting upon locked trunks, with our eyes on the clock. "At last we are alone," he said; "I quite forget where I was. Oh yes, I had just told you, hadn't I, that the Prince asked the abbé Poiré if he could say his mass next day for Dreyfus. 'No, the abbé informed me' (I say *me* to you," Swann explained to me, "because it is the Prince who is speaking, you understand?), 'for I have another mass that I have been asked to say for him to-morrow as well.—What, I said to him, is there another Catholic as well as myself who is convinced of his innocence?—It appears so.—But this other supporter's conviction must be of more recent growth than mine.—Maybe, but this other was making me say masses when you still believed Dreyfus guilty.—Ah, I can see that it is not anyone in our world.—On the contrary!—Indeed! There are Dreyfusists among us, are there? You intrigue me; I should like to unbosom myself to this rare bird, if I know him.—You do know him. —His name?—The Princesse de Guermantes. While I was afraid of shocking the Nationalist opinions, the French faith of my dear wife, she had been afraid of alarming my religious opinions, my patriotic sentiments. But privately she had been thinking as I did, though for longer than I had. And what her maid had been hiding as she went into her room, what she went out to buy for her every morning, was the *Aurore*. My dear Swann, from that moment I thought of the pleasure that I should give you when I told you how closely akin my views upon this matter were to yours; forgive me for not having done so sooner. If you bear in mind that I had never said a word to the Princess, it will not surprise you to be told that thinking the same as yourself must at that time have kept me farther apart from you than thinking differently. For it was an extremely painful topic for me to approach. The more I believe that an error, that crimes even have been committed, the more my heart bleeds for the Army. It had never occurred to me that opinions like mine could possibly cause you similar pain, until I was told the other day that you were emphatically protesting against the insults to the Army and against the Dreyfusists for consenting to ally themselves with those who insulted it. That settled it, I admit that it has been most painful for me to confess to you what I think of certain officers, few in number fortunately, but it is a relief to me not to have to keep at armslength from you any longer, and especially that you should quite understand that if I was able to entertain other sentiments, it was because I had not a shadow of doubt as to the soundness of the verdict. As soon as my doubts began, I could wish for only one thing, that the mistake should be rectified.' I must tell you that this speech of the Prince de Guermantes moved me profoundly. If you knew him as I do, if you could realise the distance he has had to traverse in order to reach his present position, you would admire him as he deserves. Not that his opinion surprises me, his is such a straightforward nature!" Swann was forgetting that in the afternoon he had on the contrary told me that people's opinions as to the Dreyfus case were dictated by atavism. At the most he had made an exception in favour of intelligence, because in Saint-Loup it had managed to overcome atavism and had made a Dreyfusard of him. Now he had just seen that this victory had been of short duration and that Saint-Loup had passed into the opposite camp. And so it was to straightforwardness now that he assigned the part which had previously devolved upon intelligence. In reality we always discover afterwards that our adversaries had a reason for being on the side they espoused, which has nothing to do with any element of right that there may be on that side, and that those who think as we do do so because their intelligence, if their moral nature is too base to be invoked, or their straightforwardness, if their penetration is feeble, has compelled them.

Swann now found equally intelligent anybody who was of his opinion, his old friend the Prince de Guermantes and my schoolfellow Bloch, whom previously he had avoided and whom he now invited to luncheon. Swann interested Bloch greatly by telling him that the Prince de Guermantes was a Dreyfusard. "We must ask him to sign our appeal for Picquart; a name like his would have a tremendous effect." But Swann, blending with his ardent conviction as an Israelite the diplomatic moderation of a man of the world, whose habits he had too thoroughly acquired to be able to shed them at this late hour, refused to allow Bloch to send the Prince a circular to sign, even on his own initiative. "He cannot do such a thing, we must not expect the impossible," Swann repeated. "There you have a charming man who has travelled thousands of miles to come over to our side. He can be very useful to us. If he were to sign your list, he would simply be compromising himself with his own people, would be made to suffer on our account, might even repent of his confidences and not confide in us again." Nor was this all, Swann refused his own signature. He felt that his name was too Hebraic not to create a bad effect. Besides, even if he approved of all the attempts to secure a fresh trial, he did not wish to be mixed up in any way in the antimilitarist campaign. He wore, a thing he had never done previously, the decoration he had won as a young militiaman, in '70, and added a codicil to his will asking that, contrary to his previous

156

dispositions, he might be buried with the military honours due to his rank as Chevalier of the Legion of Honour. A request which assembled round the church of Combray a whole squadron of those troopers over whose fate Françoise used to weep in days gone by, when she envisaged the prospect of a war. In short, Swann refused to sign Bloch's circular, with the result that, if he passed in the eyes of many people as a fanatical Dreyfusard, my friend found him lukewarm, infected with Nationalism, and a militarist.

Swann left me without shaking hands so as not to be forced into a general leave-taking in this room which swarmed with his friends, but said to me: "You ought to come and see your friend Gilberte. She has really grown up now and altered, you would not know her. She would be so pleased!" I was no longer in love with Gilberte. She was for me like a dead person for whom one has long mourned, then forgetfulness has come, and if she were to be resuscitated, she could no longer find any place in a life which has ceased to be fashioned for her. I had no desire now to see her, not even that desire to shew her that I did not wish to see her which, every day, when I was in love with her, I vowed to myself that I would flaunt before her, when I should be in love with her no longer.

And so, seeking now only to give myself, in Gilberte's eyes, the air of having longed with all my heart to meet her again and of having been prevented by circumstances of the kind called "beyond our control" albeit they only occur, with any certainty at least, when we have done nothing to prevent them, so far from accepting Swann's invitation with reserve, I would not let him go until he had promised to explain in detail to his daughter the mischances that had prevented and would continue to prevent me from going to see her. "Anyhow, I am going to write to her as soon as I go home," I added. "But be sure you tell her it will be a threatening letter, for in a month or two I shall be quite free, and then let her tremble, for I shall be coming to your house as regularly as in the old days."

Before parting from Swann, I said a word to him about his health. "No, it is not as bad as all that," he told me. "Still, as I was saying, I am quite worn out, and I accept with resignation whatever may be in store for me. Only, I must say that it would be most annoying to die before the end of the Dreyfus case. Those scoundrels have more than one card up their sleeves. I have no doubt of their being defeated in the end, but still they are very powerful, they have supporters everywhere. Just as everything is going on splendidly, it all collapses. I should like to live long enough to see Dreyfus rehabilitated and Picquart a colonel."

When Swann had left, I returned to the great drawing-room in which was to be found that Princesse de Guermantes with whom I did not then know that I was one day to be so intimate. Her passion for M. de Charlus did not reveal itself to me at first. I noticed only that the Baron, after a certain date, and without having taken one of those sudden dislikes, which were not surprising in him, to the Princesse de Guermantes, while continuing to feel for her just as strong an affection, a stronger affection perhaps than ever, appeared worried and annoyed whenever anyone mentioned her name to him. He never included it now in his list of the people whom he wished to meet at dinner.

It is true that before this time I had heard an extremely malicious man about town say that the Princess had completely changed, that she was in love with M. de Charlus, but this slander had appeared to me absurd and had made me angry. I had indeed remarked with astonishment that, when I was telling her something that concerned myself, if M. de Charlus's name cropped up in the middle, the Princess immediately screwed up her attention to the narrower focus of a sick man who, hearing us talk about ourselves, and listening, in consequence, in a careless and distracted fashion, suddenly realises that a name we have mentioned is that of the disease from which he is suffering, which at once interests and delights him. So, if I said to her: "Why, M. de Charlus told me . . ." the Princess at once gathered up the slackened reins of her attention. And having on one occasion said in her hearing that M. de Charlus had at that moment a warm regard for a certain person, I was astonished to see appear in the Princess's eyes that momentary change of colour, like the line of a fissure in the pupil, which is due to a thought that our words have unconsciously aroused in the mind of the person to whom we are talking, a secret thought that will not find expression in words, but will rise from the depths which we have stirred to the surface—altered for an instant—of his gaze. But if my remark had moved the Princess, I did not then suspect in what fashion.

Anyhow, shortly after this, she began to talk to me about M. de Charlus, and almost without ambiguity. If she made any allusion to the rumours which a few people here and there were spreading about the Baron, it was merely as though to absurd and scandalous inventions. But, on the other hand, she said: " I feel that any woman who fell in love with a man of such priceless worth as Palamède ought to have sufficient breadth of mind, enough devotion, to accept him and understand him as a whole, for what he is, to respect his freedom, humour his fancies, seek only to smooth out his difficulties and console him in his griefs." Now, by such a speech, vague as it was, the Princesse de Guermantes revealed the weakness of the character she was seeking to extol, just as M. de Charlus himself did at times. Have I not heard him, over and again, say to people who until then had been uncertain whether or not he was being slandered: " I, who have climbed many hills and crossed many valleys in my life, who have known all manner of people, burglars as well as kings, and indeed, I must confess, with a slight preference for the burglars, who have pursued beauty in all its forms," and so forth; and by these words which he thought adroit, and in contradicting rumours the currency of which no one suspected (or to introduce, from inclination, moderation, love of accuracy, an element of truth which he was alone in regarding as insignificant), he removed the last doubts of some of his hearers, inspired others, who had not yet begun to doubt him, with their first. For the most dangerous of all forms of concealment is that of the crime itself in the mind of the guilty party. His permanent consciousness of it prevents him from imagining how generally it is unknown, how readily a complete lie would be accepted, and on the other hand from realising at what degree of truth other people will detect, in words which he believes to be innocent, a confession. Not that he would not be entirely wrong in seeking to hush it up, for there is no vice that does not find ready support in the best society, and one has seen a country house turned upside down in order that two sisters might sleep in adjoining rooms as soon as their hostess learned that theirs was a more than sisterly affection. But what revealed to me all of a sudden the Princess's love was a trifling incident upon which I shall not dwell here, for it forms part of quite another story, in which M. de Charlus allowed a Queen to die rather than miss an appointment with the hairdresser who was to singe his hair for the benefit of an omnibus conductor who filled him with alarm. However, to be done with the Princess's love, let us say what the trifle was that opened my eyes. I was, on the day in question, alone with her in her carriage. As we were passing a post office she stopped the coachman. She had come out without a footman. She half drew a letter from her muff and was preparing to step down from the carriage to put it into the box. I tried to stop her, she made a show of resistance, and we both realised that our instinctive movements had been, hers compromising, in appearing to be guarding a secret, mine indiscreet, in attempting to pass that guard. She was the first to recover. Suddenly turning very red, she gave me the letter. I no longer dared not to take it, but, as I slipped it into the box, I could not help seeing that it was addressed to M. de Charlus.

To return to this first evening at the Princesse de Guermantes's, I went to bid her good-night, for her cousins, who had promised to take me home, were in a hurry to be gone. M. de Guermantes wished, however, to say good-bye to his brother, Mme. de Surgis having found time to mention to the Duke as she left that M. de Charlus had been charming to her and to her sons. This great courtesy on his brother's part, the first moreover that he had ever shewn in that line, touched Basin deeply and aroused in him old family sentiments which were never asleep for long. At the moment when we were saying good-bye to the Princess he was attempting, without actually thanking M. de Charlus, to give expression to his fondness for him, whether because he really found a difficulty in controlling it or in order that the Baron might remember that actions of the sort that he had performed this evening did not escape the eyes of a brother, just as, with the object of creating a chain of pleasant associations in the future, we give sugar to a dog that has done its trick. "Well, little brother!" said the Duke, stopping M. de Charlus and taking him lovingly by the arm, "so this is how one walks past one's elders and betters without so much as a word. I never see you now, Mémé, and you can't think how I miss you. I was turning over some old letters just now and came upon some from poor Mamma, which are all so full of love for you." "Thank you, Basin," replied M. de Charlus in a broken voice, for he could never speak without emotion of their mother. "You must make up your mind to let me fix up bachelor quarters for you at Guermantes," the Duke went on. "It is nice to see the two brothers so affectionate towards each other," the Princess said to Oriane. "Yes, indeed! I don't suppose you could find many brothers like that. I shall invite you to meet him," she promised me. "You've not quarrelled with him? . . . But what can they be talking about?" she added in an

anxious tone, for she could catch only an occasional word
of what they were saying. She had always felt a certain
jealousy of the pleasure that M. de Guermantes found in
talking to his brother of a past from which he was inclined to keep his wife shut out. She felt that, when they
were happy at being together like this, and she, unable
to restrain her impatient curiosity, came and joined them,
her coming did not add to their pleasure. But this
evening, this habitual jealousy was reinforced by another.
For if Mme. de Surgis had told M. de Guermantes how
kind his brother had been to her so that the Duke might
thank his brother, at the same time certain devoted female friends of the Guermantes couple had felt it their
duty to warn the Duchess that her husband's mistress
had been seen in close conversation with his brother.
And this information was torture to Mme. de Guermantes. "Think of the fun we used to have at Guermantes long ago," the Duke went on. "If you came
down sometimes in summer we could take up our old
life again. Do you remember old Father Courveau:
'Why is Pascal vexing? Because he is vec . . .
vec . . .?'" "*Said!*" put in M. de Charlus as though
he were still answering his tutor's question. "And why
is Pascal vexèd; because he is vec . . . because he is
vec . . . *Sing!* Very good, you will pass, you are certain to be mentioned, and Madame la Duchesse will give
you a Chinese dictionary." "How it all comes back to
me, young Mémé, and the old china vase Hervey brought
you from Saint-Denis, I can see it now. You used to
threaten us that you would go and spend your life in
China, you were so fond of the country; even then you
used to love wandering about all night. Ah! You were

a peculiar type, for I can honestly say that never in anything did you have the same tastes as other people. . . ." But no sooner had he uttered these words than the Duke flamed up, as the saying is, for he was aware of his brother's reputation, if not of his actual habits. As he never made any allusion to them before his brother, he was all the more annoyed at having said something which might be taken to refer to them, and more still at having shewn his annoyance. After a moment's silence: "Who knows," he said, to cancel the effect of his previous speech, "you were perhaps in love with a Chinese girl, before loving so many white ones and finding favour with them, if I am to judge by a certain lady to whom you have given great pleasure this evening by talking to her. She was delighted with you." The Duke had vowed that he would not mention Mme. de Surgis, but, in the confusion that the blunder he had just made had wrought in his ideas, he had fallen upon the first that occurred to him, which happened to be precisely the one that ought not to have appeared in the conversation, although it had started it. But M. de Charlus had observed his brother's blush. And, like guilty persons who do not wish to appear embarrassed that you should talk in their presence of the crime which they are supposed not to have committed, and feel that they ought to prolong a dangerous conversation: "I am charmed to hear it," he replied, "but I should like to go back to what you were saying before, which struck me as being profoundly true. You were saying that I never had the same ideas as other people, how right you are, you said that I had peculiar tastes." "No," protested M. de Guermantes who, as a matter of fact, had not used those words, and may not have believed that their meaning was applicable to his brother. Besides, what right had he to bully him about eccentricities which in any case were vague enough or secret enough to have in no way impaired the Baron's tremendous position in society? What was more, feeling that the resources of his brother's position were about to be placed at the service of his mistresses, the Duke told himself that this was well worth a little tolerance in exchange; had he at that moment known of some "peculiar" intimacy of his brother, M. de Guermantes would, in the hope of the support that the other was going to give him, have passed it over, shutting his eyes to it, and if need be lending a hand. "Come along, Basin; good night, Palamède," said the Duchess, who, devoured by rage and curiosity, could endure no more, "if you have made up your minds to spend the night here, we might just as well have stayed to supper. You have been keeping Marie and me standing for the last half-hour." The Duke parted from his brother after a significant pressure of his hand, and the three of us began to descend the immense staircase of the Princess's house.

On either side of us, on the topmost steps, were scattered couples who were waiting for their carriages to come to the door. Erect, isolated, flanked by her husband and myself, the Duchess kept to the left of the staircase, already wrapped in her Tiepolo cloak, her throat clasped in its band of rubies, devoured by the eyes of women and men alike, who sought to divine the secret of her beauty and distinction. Waiting for her carriage upon the same step of the stair as Mme. de Guermantes, but at the opposite side of it, Mme. de Gallardon, who had long abandoned all hope of ever receiving a visit from her cousin, turned her back so as not to appear to have seen her, and, what was more important, so as not furnish a proof of the fact that the other did not greet her. Mme. de Gallardon was in an extremely bad temper because some gentlemen in her company had taken it upon themselves to speak to her of Oriane: "I have not the slightest desire to see her," she had replied to them, "I did see her, as a matter of fact, just now, she is beginning to shew her age; it seems she can't get over it. Basin says so himself. And, good lord, I can understand that, for, as she has no brains, is as michievous as a weevil, and has shocking manners, she must know very well that, once her looks go, she will have nothing left to fall back upon."

I had put on my greatcoat, for which M. de Guermantes, who dreaded chills, reproached me, as we went down together, because of the heated atmosphere indoors. And the generation of noblemen which more or less passed through the hands of Mgr. Dupanloup speaks such bad French (except the Castellane brothers) that the Duke expressed what was in his mind thus: "It is better not to put on your coat before going out of doors, at least *as a general rule*." I can see all that departing crowd now, I can see, if I be not mistaken in placing him upon that staircase, a portrait detached from its frame, the Prince de Sagan, whose last appearance in society this must have been, baring his head to offer his homage to the Duchess, with so sweeping a revolution of his tall hat in his white-gloved hand (harmonising with the gardenia in his buttonhole), that one felt surprised that it was not a plumed felt hat of the old regime, several ancestral faces from which were exactly reproduced in the face of this great gentleman. He stopped for but a short time in front of her, but even his momentary attitudes were sufficient to compose a complete tableau vivant, and, as it were, an historical scene. Moreover, as he has since then died, and as I never had more than a glimpse of him in his lifetime, he has so far become for me a character in history, social history at least, that I am quite astonished when I think that a woman and a man whom I know are his sister and nephew.

While we were going downstairs, there came up, with an air of weariness that suited her, a woman who appeared to be about forty, but was really older. This was the Princesse d'Orvillers, a natural daughter, it was said, of the Duke of Parma, whose pleasant voice rang with a vaguely Austrian accent. She advanced, tall, stooping, in a gown of white flowered silk, her exquisite, throbbing, cankered bosom heaving beneath a harness of diamonds and sapphires. Tossing her head like a royal palfrey embarrassed by its halter of pearls, of an incalculable value but an inconvenient weight, she let fall here and there a gentle, charming gaze, of an azure which, as time began to fade it, became more caressing than ever, and greeted most of the departing guests with a friendly nod. "You choose a nice time to arrive, Paulette!" said the Duchess. "Yes, I am so sorry! But really it was a physical impossibility," replied the Princesse d'Orvillers, who had acquired this sort of expression from the Duchesse de Guermantes, but added to it her own natural sweetness and the air of sincerity conveyed by the force of a remotely Teutonic accent in so tender a voice. She appeared to be alluding to complications of life too elaborate to be related, and not merely to evening parties, although she had just come on from a succession of these. But it was not they that obliged her to come so late. As the Prince de Guermantes had for many years forbidden his wife to receive Mme. d'Orvillers, that lady, when the ban was withdrawn, contented herself with replying to the other's invitations, so as not to appear to be thirsting after them, by simply leaving cards. After two or three years of this method, she came in person, but very late, as though after the theatre. In this way she gave herself the appearance of attaching no importance to the party, nor to being seen at it, but simply of having come to pay the Prince and Princess a visit, for their own sakes, because she liked them, at an hour when, the great majority of their guests having already gone, she would " have them more to herself."

" Oriane has really sunk very low," muttered Mme. de Gallardon. " I cannot understand Basin's allowing her to speak to Mme. d'Orvillers. I am sure M. de Gallardon would never have allowed me." For my part, I had recognised in Mme. d'Orvillers the woman who, outside the Hôtel Guermantes, used to cast languishing glances at me, turn round, stop and gaze into shop windows. Mme. de Guermantes introduced me, Mme. d'Orvillers was charming, neither too friendly nor annoyed. She gazed at me as at everyone else out of her gentle eyes. . . . But I was never again, when I met her, to receive from her one of those overtures with which she had seemed to be offering herself. There is a special kind of glance, apparently of recognition, which a young man never receives from certain women—nor from certain men—after the day on which they have made his

acquaintance and have learned that he is the friend of
people with whom they too are intimate.

We were told that the carriage was at the door. Mme.
de Guermantes gathered up her red skirt as though to
go downstairs and get into the carriage, but, seized perhaps by remorse, or by the desire to give pleasure, and
above all to profit by the brevity which the material
obstacle to prolonging it imposed upon so boring an
action, looked at Mme. de Gallardon; then, as though
she had only just caught sight of her, acting upon a
sudden inspiration, before going down tripped across the
whole width of the step and, upon reaching her delighted
cousin, held out her hand. "Such a long time," said the
Duchess who then, so as not to have to develop all the
regrets and legitimate excuses that this formula might be
supposed to contain, turned with a look of alarm towards
the Duke, who as a matter of fact, having gone down
with me to the carriage, was storming with rage when he
saw that his wife had gone over to Mme. de Gallardon
and was holding up the stream of carriages behind.
"Oriane is still very good looking, after all!" said Mme.
de Gallardon. "People amuse me when they say that
we have quarrelled; we may (for reasons which we have
no need to tell other people) go for years without seeing
one another, we have too many memories in common
ever to be separated, and in her heart she must know that
she cares far more for me than for all sorts of people
whom she sees every day and who are not of her rank."
Mme. de Gallardon was in fact like those scorned lovers
who try desperately to make people believe that they are
better loved than those whom their fair one cherishes.
And (by the praises which, without heeding their contra-

diction of what she had been saying a moment earlier, she now lavished in speaking of the Duchesse de Guermantes) she proved indirectly that the other was thoroughly conversant with the maxims that ought to guide in her career a great lady of fashion who, at the selfsame moment when her most marvellous gown is exciting an admiration not unmixed with envy, must be able to cross the whole width of a staircase to disarm it. "Do at least take care not to wet your shoes" (a brief but heavy shower of rain had fallen), said the Duke, who was still furious at having been kept waiting.

On our homeward drive, in the confined space of the coupé, the red shoes were of necessity very close to mine, and Mme. de Guermantes, fearing that she might actually have touched me, said to the Duke: "This young man will have to say to me, like the person in the caricature: 'Madame, tell me at once that you love me, but don't tread on my feet like that.'" My thoughts, however, were far from Mme. de Guermantes. Ever since Saint-Loup had spoken to me of a young girl of good family who frequented a house of ill-fame, and of the Baroness Putbus's maid, it was in these two persons that were coalesced and embodied the desires inspired in me day by day by countless beauties of two classes, on the one hand the plebeian and magnificent, the majestic lady's maids of great houses, swollen with pride and saying "we" when they spoke of Duchesses, on the other hand those girls of whom it was enough for me sometimes, without even having seen them go past in carriages or on foot, to have read the names in the account of a ball for me to fall in love with them and, having conscientiously searched the year-book for the country houses in which they spent the summer (as often as not letting myself be led astray by a similarity of names), to dream alternately of going to live amid the plains of the West, the sandhills of the North, the pine-forests of the South. But in vain might I fuse together all the most exquisite fleshly matter to compose, after the ideal outline traced for me by Saint-Loup, the young girl of easy virtue and Mme. Putbus's maid, my two possessible beauties still lacked what I should never know until I had seen them: individual character. I was to wear myself out in seeking to form a mental picture, during the months in which I would have preferred a lady's maid, of the maid of Mme. Putbus. But what peace of mind after having been perpetually troubled by my restless desires, for so many fugitive creatures whose very names I often did not know, who were in any case so hard to find again, harder still to become acquainted with, impossible perhaps to captivate, to have subtracted from all that scattered, fugitive, anonymous beauty, two choice specimens duly labelled, whom I was at least certain of being able to procure when I chose. I kept putting off the hour for devoting myself to this twofold pleasure, as I put off that for beginning to work, but the certainty of having it whenever I chose dispensed me almost from the necessity of taking it, like those soporific tablets which one has only to have within reach of one's hand not to need them and to fall asleep. In the whole universe I desired only two women, of whose faces I could not, it is true, form any picture, but whose names Saint-Loup had told me and had guaranteed their consent. So that, if he had, by what he had said this evening, set my imagination a heavy task, he had at the same time procured an appreciable relaxation, a prolonged rest for my will.

"Well!" said the Duchess to me, "apart from your balls, can't I be of any use to you? Have you found a house where you would like me to introduce you?" I replied that I was afraid the only one that tempted me was hardly fashionable enough for her. "Whose is that?" she asked in a hoarse and menacing voice, scarcely opening her lips. "Baroness Putbus." This time she pretended to be really angry. "No, not that! I believe you're trying to make a fool of me. I don't even know how I come to have heard the creature's name. But she is the dregs of society. It's just as though you were to ask me for an introduction to my milliner. And worse than that, for my milliner is charming. You are a little bit cracked, my poor boy. In any case, I beg that you will be polite to the people to whom I have introduced you, leave cards on them, and go and see them, and not talk to them about Baroness Putbus of whom they have never heard." I asked whether Mme. d'Orvillers was not inclined to be flighty. "Oh, not in the least, you are thinking of some one else, why, she's rather a prude, if anything. Ain't she, Basin?" "Yes, in any case I don't thing there has ever been anything to be said about her," said the Duke.

"You won't come with us to the ball?" he asked me. "I can lend you a Venetian cloak and I know some one who will be damned glad to see you there—Oriane for one, that I needn't say—but the Princesse de Parme. She's never tired of singing your praises, and swears by you alone. It's fortunate for you—since she is a trifle mature—that she is the model of virtue. Otherwise she

would certainly have chosen you as a sigisbee, as it was
called in my young days, a sort of cavaliere servente.

I was interested not in the ball but in my appointment
with Albertine. And so I refused. The carriage had
stopped, the footman was shouting for the gate to be
opened, the horses pawing the ground until it was flung
apart and the carriage passed into the courtyard. "Till
we meet again," said the Duke. "I have sometimes regretted living so close to Marie," the Duchess said to me,
"because I may be very fond of her, but I am not quite
so fond of her company. But I have never regretted it so
much as to-night, since it has allowed me so little of
yours." "Come, Oriane, no speechmaking." The
Duchess would have liked me to come inside for a minute.
She laughed heartily, as did the Duke, when I said that
I could not because I was expecting a girl to call at any
moment. "You choose a funny time to receive visitors,"
she said to me.

"Come along, my child, there is no time to waste,"
said M. de Guermantes to his wife. "It is a quarter to
twelve, and time we were dressed. . . ." He came in
collision, outside his front door which they were grimly
guarding, with the two ladies of the walking-sticks, who
had not been afraid to descend at dead of night from their
mountain-top to prevent a scandal. "Basin, we felt we
must warn you, in case you were seen at that ball: poor
Amanien has just passed away, an hour ago." The Duke
felt a momentary alarm. He saw the delights of the
famous ball snatched from him as soon as these accursed
mountaineers had informed him of the death of M. d'Os-
mond. But he quickly recovered himself and flung at his

cousins a retort into which he introduced, with his deter-
mination not to forego a pleasure, his incapacity to
assimilate exactly the niceties of the French language:
"He is dead! No, no, they exaggerate, they exaggerate!" And without giving a further thought to his two
relatives who, armed with their alpenstocks, were preparing to make their nocturnal ascent, he fired off a string of
questions at his valet:

"Are you sure my helmet has come?" "Yes, Monsieur le Duc." "You're sure there's a hole in it I can
breathe through? I don't want to be suffocated, damn
it!" "Yes, Monsieur le Duc." "Oh, thunder of
heaven, this is an unlucky evening. Oriane, I forgot to
ask Babal whether the shoes with pointed toes were
for you!" "But, my dear, the dresser from the Opéra-
Comique is here, he will tell us. I don't see how they
could go with your spurs." "Let us go and find the
dresser," said the Duke. "Good-bye, my boy, I should
ask you to come in while we are trying on, it would
amuse you. But we should only waste time talking, it
is nearly midnight and we must not be late in getting
there or we shall spoil the set."

I too was in a hurry to get away from M. and Mme. de
Guermantes as quickly as possible. *Phèdre* finished at
about half past eleven. Albertine must have arrived by
now. I went straight to Françoise: "Is Mlle. Albertine
in the house?" "No one has called."

Good God, that meant that no one would call! I was
in torment, Albertine's visit seeming to me now all the
more desirable, the less certain it had become.

Françoise was cross too, but for quite a different reason. She had just installed her daughter at the table for a succulent repast. But, on hearing me come in, and seeing that there was not time to whip away the dishes and put out needles and thread as though it were a work party and not a supper party: " She has just been taking a spoonful of soup," Françoise explained to me, " I forced her to gnaw a bit of bone," to reduce thus to nothing her daughter's supper, as though the crime lay in its abundance. Even at luncheon or dinner, if I committed the error of entering the kitchen, Françoise would pretend that they had finished, and would even excuse herself with: " I just felt I could eat a *scrap*," or " a *mouthful*." But I was speedily reassured on seeing the multitude of the plates that covered the table, which Françoise, surprised by my sudden entry, like a thief in the night which she was not, had not had time to conjure out of sight. Then she added: " Go along to your bed now, you have done enough work to-day " (for she wished to make it appear that her daughter not only cost us nothing, lived by privations, but was actually working herself to death in our service). " You are only crowding up the kitchen, and disturbing Monsieur, who is expecting a visitor. Go on, upstairs," she repeated, as though she were obliged to use her authority to send her daughter to bed, who, the moment supper was out of the question, remained in the kitchen only for appearance's sake, and if I had stayed five minutes longer would have withdrawn of her own accord. And turning to me, in that charming popular and yet, somehow, personal French which was her spoken language : " Monsieur doesn't see that her face is just cut in two with want of sleep." I remained, delighted at not having to talk to Françoise's daughter.

I have said that she came from a small village which was quite close to her mother's, and yet differed from it in the nature of the soil, its cultivation, in dialect; above all in certain characteristics of the inhabitants. Thus the "butcheress" and Françoise's niece did not get on at all well together, but had this point in common, that, when they went out on an errand, they would linger for hours at "the sister's" or "the cousin's," being themselves incapable of finishing a conversation, in the course of which the purpose with which they had set out faded so completely from their minds that, if we said to them on their return:

"Well! Will M. le Marquis de Norpois be at home at a quarter past six?" they did not even beat their brows and say: "Oh, I forgot all about it," but "Oh! I didn't understand that Monsieur wanted to know that, I thought I had just to go and bid him good day." If they "lost their heads" in this manner about a thing that had been said to them an hour earlier, it was on the other hand impossible to get out of their heads what they had once heard said, by "the" sister or cousin. Thus, if the butcheress had heard it said that the English made war upon us in '70 at the same time as the Prussians, and I had explained to her until I was tired that this was not the case, every three weeks the butcheress would repeat to me in the course of conversation: "It's all because of that war the English made on us in '70, with the Prussians." "But I've told you a hundred times that you are wrong."—She would then answer, implying that her conviction was in no way shaken: "In any case, that's no reason for wishing them any harm. Plenty of water has run under the bridges since '70," and so forth. On another occasion, advocating a war with England which I opposed, she said: "To be sure, it's always better not to go to war; but when you must, it's best to do it at once. As the sister was explaining just now, ever since that war the English made on us in '70, the commercial treaties have ruined us. After we've beaten them, we won't allow one Englishman into France, unless he pays three hundred francs to come in, as we have to pay now to land in England."

Such was, in addition to great honesty and, when they were speaking, an obstinate refusal to allow any interruption, going back twenty times over to the point at which they had been interrupted, which ended by giving to their talk the unshakable solidity of a Bach fugue, the character of the inhabitants of this tiny village which did not boast five hundred, set among its chestnuts, its willows, and its fields of potatoes and beetroot.

Françoise's daughter, on the other hand, spoke (regarding herself as an up-to-date woman who had got out of the old ruts) Parisian slang and was well versed in all the jokes of the day. Françoise having told her that I had come from the house of a Princess: "Oh, indeed! The Princess of Brazil, I suppose, where the nuts come from." Seeing that I was expecting a visitor, she pretended to suppose that my name was Charles. I replied innocently that it was not, which enabled her to get in: "Oh, I thought it was! And I was just saying to myself, *Charles attend* (charlatan)." This was not in the best of taste. But I was less unmoved when, to console me for Albertine's delay, she said to me: "I expect you'll go on waiting till doomsday. She's never coming. Oh! These modern flappers!"

And so her speech differed from her mother's; but, what is more curious, her mother's speech was not the same as that of her grandmother, a native of Bailleau-le-Pin, which was so close to Françoise's village. And yet the dialects differed slightly, like the scenery. Françoise's mother's village, scrambling down a steep bank into a ravine, was overgrown with willows. And, miles away from either of them, there was, on the contrary, a small district of France where the people spoke almost precisely the same dialect as at Méséglise. I made this discovery only to feel its drawbacks. In fact, I once came upon Françoise eagerly conversing with a neighbour's housemaid, who came from this village and spoke its dialect. They could more or less understand one another, I did not understand a word, they knew this but did not however cease (excused, they felt, by the joy of being fellow-countrywomen although born so far apart) to converse in this strange tongue in front of me, like people who do not wish to be understood. These picturesque studies in linguistic geography and comradeship belowstairs were continued weekly in the kitchen, without my deriving any pleasure from them.

Since, whenever the outer gate opened, the doorkeeper pressed an electric button which lighted the stairs, and since all the occupants of the building had already come in, I left the kitchen immediately and went to sit down in the hall, keeping watch, at a point where the curtains did not quite meet over the glass panel of the outer door, leaving visible a vertical strip of semi-darkness on the stair. If, all of a sudden, this strip turned to a golden yellow, that would mean that Albertine had just entered the building and would be with me in a minute; nobody else could be coming at that time of night. And I sat there, unable to take my eyes from the strip which persisted in remaining dark; I bent my whole body forward to make certain of noticing any change; but, gaze as I might, the vertical black band, despite my impassioned longing, did not give me the intoxicating delight that I should have felt had I seen it changed by a sudden and significant magic to a luminous bar of gold. This was a great to do to make about that Albertine to whom I had not given three minutes' thought during the Guermantes party! But, reviving my feelings when in the past I had been kept waiting by other girls, Gilberte especially, when she delayed her coming, the prospect of having to forego a simple bodily pleasure caused me an intense mental suffering.

I was obliged to retire to my room. Françoise followed me. She felt that, as I had come away from my party, there was no point in my keeping the rose that I had in my buttonhole, and approached to take it from me. Her action, by reminding me that Albertine was perhaps not coming, and by obliging me also to confess that I wished to look smart for her benefit, caused an irritation that was increased by the fact that, in tugging myself free, I crushed the flower and Françoise said to me: "It would have been better to let me take it than to go and spoil it like that." But anything that she might say exasperated me. When we are kept waiting, we suffer so keenly from the absence of the person for whom we are longing that we cannot endure the presence of anyone else.

When Françoise had left my room, it occurred to me that, if it only meant that now I wanted to look my best before Albertine, it was a pity that I had so many times let her see me unshaved, with several days' growth of beard, on the evenings when I let her come in to renew our caresses. I felt that she took no interest in me and was giving me the cold shoulder. To make my room look a little brighter, in case Albertine should still come, and because it was one of the prettiest things that I possessed, I set out, for the first time for years, on the table by my bed, the turquoise-studded cover which Gilberte had had made for me to hold Bergotte's pamphlet, and which, for so long a time, I had insisted on keeping by me while I slept, with the agate marble. Besides, as much perhaps as Albertine herself, who still did not come, her presence at that moment in an " alibi " which she had evidently found more attractive, and of which I knew nothing, gave me a painful feeling which, in spite of what I had said, barely an hour before, to Swann, as to my incapacity for being jealous, might, if I had seen my friend at less protracted intervals, have changed into an anxious need to know where, with whom, she was spending her time. I dared not send round to Albertine's house, it was too late, but in the hope that, having supper perhaps with some other girls, in a café, she might take it into her head to telephone to me, I turned the switch and, restoring the connexion to my own room, cut it off between the post office and the porter's lodge to which it was generally switched at that hour. A receiver in the little passage on which Françoise's room opened would have been simpler, less inconvenient, but useless. The advance of civilisation enables each of us to display unsuspected merits or fresh defects which make him dearer or more insupportable to his friends. Thus Dr. Bell's invention had enabled Françoise to acquire an additional defect, which was that of refusing, however important, however urgent the occasion might be, to make use of the telephone. She would manage to disappear whenever anybody was going to teach her how to use it, as people disappear when it is time for them to be vaccinated. And so the telephone was installed in my bedroom, and, that it might not disturb my parents, a rattle had been substituted for the bell. I did not move, for fear of not hearing it sound. So motionless did I remain that, for the first time for months, I noticed the tick of the clock. Françoise came in to make the room tidy. She began talking to me, but I hated her conversation, beneath the uniformly trivial continuity of which my feelings were changing from one minute to another, passing from fear to anxiety; from anxiety to complete disappointment. Belying the words of vague satisfaction which I thought myself obliged to address to her, I could feel that my face was so wretched that I pretended to be suffering from rheumatism, to account for the discrepancy between my feigned indifference and my woebegone expression; besides, I was afraid that her talk, which, for that matter, Françoise carried on in an undertone (not on account of Albertine, for she considered that all possibility of her coming was long past), might prevent me from hearing the saving call which now would not sound. At length Françoise went off to bed; I dismissed her with an abrupt civility, so that the noise she made in leaving the room should not drown that of the telephone. And I settled down again to listen, to suffer; when we are kept waiting, from the ear which takes in sounds to the mind which dissects and analyses them, and from the mind to the heart, to which it transmits its results, the double journey is so rapid that we cannot even detect its course, and imagine that we have been listening directly with our heart.

I was tortured by the incessant recurrence of my longing, ever more anxious and never to be gratified, for the sound of a call; arrived at the culminating point of a tortuous ascent through the coils of my lonely anguish, from the heart of the populous, nocturnal Paris that had suddenly come close to me, there beside my bookcase, I heard all at once, mechanical and sublime, like, in *Tristan*, the fluttering veil or the shepherd's pipe, the purr of the telephone. I sprang to the instrument, it was Albertine. " I'm not disturbing you, ringing you up at this hour? " " Not at all . . ." I said, restraining my joy, for her remark about the lateness of the hour was doubtless meant as an apology for coming, in a moment, so late, and did not mean that she was not coming. " Are you coming round? " I asked in a tone of indifference. " Why . . . no, unless you absolutely must see me."

Part of me which the other part sought to join was in Albertine. It was essential that she came, but I did not tell her so at first; now that we were in communication, I said to myself that I could always oblige her at the last moment either to come to me or to let me hasten to her. " Yes, I am near home," she said, " and miles away from you; I hadn't read your note properly. I have just found it again and was afraid you might be waiting up for me." I felt sure that she was lying, and it was now, in my fury, from a desire not so much to see her as to upset her plans that I determined to make her come. But I felt it better to refuse at first what in a few moments I should try to obtain from her. But where was she? With the sound of her voice were blended other sounds: the braying of a bicyclist's horn, a woman's voice singing, a brass band in the distance rang out as distinctly as the beloved voice, as though to shew me that it was indeed Albertine in her actual surroundings who was beside me at that moment, like a clod of earth with which we have carried away all the grass that was growing from it. The same sounds that I heard were striking her ear also, and were distracting her attention: details of truth, extraneous to the subject under discussion, valueless in themselves, all the more necessary to our perception of the miracle for what it was; elements sober and charming, descriptive of some street in Paris, elements heart-rending also and cruel of some unknown festivity which, after she came away from *Phèdre*, had prevented Albertine from coming to me. " I must warn you first of all that I don't in the least want you to come, because, at this time of night, it will be a frightful nuisance . . ." I said to her, " I'm dropping with sleep. Besides, oh, well, there are endless complications. I am bound to say that there was no possibility of your misunderstanding my letter. You answered that it was all right. Very well, if you hadn't understood, what did you mean by that? " " I said it was all right, only I couldn't quite remember what we had arranged. But I see you're cross with me, I'm sorry. I wish now I'd never gone to *Phèdre*. If I'd known there was going to be all this fuss about it . . ." she went on, as people invariably do when, being in the wrong over one thing, they pretend to suppose that they are being blamed for another. " I am not in the least annoyed about *Phèdre*, seeing it was I that asked you to go to it." " Then you are angry with me;

it's a nuisance it's so late now, otherwise I should have come to you, but I shall call to-morrow or the day after and make it up." "Oh, please, Albertine, I beg of you not to, after making me waste an entire evening, the least you can do is to leave me in peace for the next few days. I shan't be free for a fortnight or three weeks. Listen, if it worries you to think that we seem to be parting in anger, and perhaps you are right, after all, then I greatly prefer, all things considered, since I have been waiting for you all this time and you have not gone home yet, that you should come at once. I shall take a cup of coffee to keep myself awake." "Couldn't you possibly put it off till to-morrow? Because the trouble is. . . ." As I listened to these words of deprecation, uttered as though she did not intend to come, I felt that, with the longing to see again the velvet-blooming face which in the past, at Balbec, used to point all my days to the moment when, by the mauve September sea, I should be walking by the side of that roseate flower, a very different element was painfully endeavouring to combine. This terrible need of a person, at Combray I had learned to know it in the case of my mother, and to the pitch of wanting to die if she sent word to me by Françoise that she could not come upstairs. This effort on the part of the old sentiment, to combine and form but a single element with the other, more recent, which had for its voluptuous object only the coloured surface, the rosy complexion of a flower of the beach, this effort results often only in creating (in the chemical sense) a new body, which can last for but a few moments. This evening, at any rate, and for long afterwards, the two elements remained apart. But already, from the last words that had reached me over the telephone, I was beginning to understand that Albertine's life was situated (not in a material sense, of course) at so great a distance from mine that I should always have to make a strenuous exploration before I could lay my hand on her, and, what was more, organised like a system of earthworks, and, for greater security, after the fashion which, at a later period, we learned to call camouflaged. Albertine, in fact, belonged, although at a slightly higher social level, to that type of person to whom her door-keeper promises your messenger that she will deliver your letter when she comes in (until the day when you realise that it is precisely she, the person whom you met out of doors, and to whom you have allowed yourself to write, who is the door-keeper. So that she does indeed live (but in the lodge, only) at the address she has given you, which for that matter is that of a private brothel, in which the door-keeper acts as pander), or who gives as her address a house where she is known to accomplices who will not betray her secret to you, from which your letters will be forwarded to her, but in which she does not live, keeps at the most a few articles of toilet. Lives entrenched behind five or six lines of defence, so that when you try to see the woman, or to find out about her, you invariably arrive too far to the right, or to the left, or too early, or too late, and may remain for months on end, for years even, knowing nothing. About Albertine, I felt that I should never find out anything, that, out of that tangled mass of details of fact and falsehood, I should never unravel the truth: and that it would always be so, unless I were to shut her up in prison (but prisoners escape) until the end. This evening, this conviction gave me only a vague uneasiness, in which however I could detect a shuddering anticipation of long periods of suffering to come.

"No," I replied, "I told you a moment ago that I should not be free for the next three weeks—no more tomorrow than any other day." "Very well, in that case . . . I shall come this very instant . . . it's a nuisance, because I am at a friend's house, and she. . . ." I saw that she had not believed that I would accept her offer to come, which therefore was not sincere, and I decided to force her hand. "What do you suppose I care about your friend, either come or don't, it's for you to decide, it wasn't I that asked you to come, it was you who suggested it to me." "Don't be angry with me, I am going to jump into a cab now and shall be with you in ten minutes." And so from that Paris out of whose murky depths there had already emanated as far as my room, delimiting the sphere of action of an absent person, a voice which was now about to emerge and appear, after this preliminary announcement, it was that Albertine whom I had known long ago beneath the sky of Balbec, when the waiters of the Grand Hotel, as they laid the tables, were blinded by the glow of the setting sun, when, the glass having been removed from all the windows, every faintest murmur of the evening passed freely from the beach where the last strolling couples still lingered, into the vast dining-room in which the first diners had not yet taken their places, and, across the mirror placed behind the cashier's desk, there passed the red reflexion of the hull, and lingered long after it the grey reflexion of the smoke of the last steamer for Rivebelle. I no longer asked myself what could have made Albertine late, and, when Françoise came into my room to inform me: "Mademoiselle Albertine is here," if I answered without even turning my head, that was only to conceal my emotion: "What in the world makes Mademoiselle Albertine come at this time of night!" But then, raising my eyes to look at Françoise, as though curious to hear her answer which must corroborate the apparent sincerity of my question, I perceived, with admiration and wrath, that, capable of rivalling Berma herself in the art of endowing with speech inanimate garments and the lines of her face, Françoise had taught their part to her bodice, her hair—the whitest threads of which had been brought to the surface, were displayed there like a birth-certificate—her neck bowed by weariness and obedience. They commiserated her for having been dragged from her sleep and from her warm bed, in the middle of the night, at her age, obliged to bundle into her clothes in haste, at the risk of catching pneumonia. And so, afraid that I might have seemed to be apologising for Albertine's late arrival: "Anyhow, I'm very glad she has come, it's just what I wanted," and I gave free vent to my profound joy. It did not long remain unclouded, when I had heard Françoise's reply. Without uttering a word of complaint, seeming indeed to be doing her best to stifle an irrepressible cough, and simply folding her shawl over her bosom as though she were feeling cold, she began by telling me everything that she had said to Albertine, whom she had not forgotten to ask after her aunt's health. "I was just saying, Monsieur must have been afraid that Mademoiselle was not coming, because this is no time to pay visits, it's nearly morning. But she must have been in some place where she was enjoying herself, because she never even said as much as that she was sorry she had kept Monsieur waiting, she answered me with a devil-may-care look, 'Better late than never!'" And Françoise added, in words that pierced my heart: "When she spoke like that she gave herself away. She would have liked to hide what she was thinking, perhaps, but. . . ."

I had no cause for astonishment. I said, a few pages back, that Françoise rarely paid attention, when she was sent with a message, if not to what she herself had said, which she would willingly relate in detail, at any rate to the answer that we were awaiting. But if, making an exception, she repeated to us the things that our friends had said, however short they might be, she generally arranged, appealing if need be to the expression, the tone that, she assured us, had accompanied them, to make them in some way or other wounding. At a pinch, she would bow her head beneath an insult (probably quite imaginary) which she had received from a tradesman to whom we had sent her, provided that, being addressed to her as our representative, who was speaking in our name, the insult might indirectly injure us. The only thing would have been to tell her that she had misunderstood the man, that she was suffering from persecution mania and that the shopkeepers were not at all in league against her. However, their sentiments affected me little. It was a very different matter, what Albertine's sentiments were. And, as she repeated the ironical words: "Better late than never!" Françoise at once made me see the friends in whose company Albertine had finished the evening, preferring their company, therefore, to mine. "She's a comical sight, she has a little flat hat on, with those big eyes of hers, it does make her look funny, especially with her cloak which she did ought to have sent to the amender's, for it's all in holes. She amuses me," added, as though laughing at Albertine, Françoise who rarely shared my impressions, but felt a need to communicate her own. I refused even to appear to understand that this laugh was indicative of scorn, but, to give tit for tat, replied, although I had never seen the little hat to which she referred: "What you call a 'little flat hat' is a simply charming. . . ." "That is to say, it's just nothing at all," said Françoise, giving expression, frankly this time, to her genuine contempt. Then (in a mild and leisurely tone so that my mendacious answer might appear to be the expression not of my anger but of the truth), wasting no time, however, so as not to keep Albertine waiting, I heaped upon Françoise these cruel words: "You are excellent," I said to her in a honeyed voice, "you are kind, you have a thousand merits, but you have never learned a single thing since the day when you first came to Paris, either about ladies' clothes or about how to pronounce words without making silly blunders." And this reproach was particularly stupid, for those French words which we are so proud of pronouncing accurately are themselves only blunders made by the Gallic lips which mispronounced Latin or Saxon, our language being merely a defective pronunciation of several others.

The genius of language in a living state, the future and past of French, that is what ought to have interested me in Françoise's mistakes. Her "amender" for "mender" was not so curious as those animals that survive from remote ages, such as the whale or the giraffe, and shew us the states through which animal life has passed. "And," I went on, "since you haven't managed to learn in all these years, you never will. But don't let that distress you, it doesn't prevent you from being a very good soul, and making spiced beef with jelly to perfection, and lots of other things as well. The hat that you think so simple is copied from a hat belonging to the Princesse de Guermantes which cost five hundred francs. However, I mean to give Mlle. Albertine an even finer one very soon." I knew that what would annoy Françoise more than anything was the thought of my spending money upon people whom she disliked. She answered me in a few words which were made almost unintelligible by a sudden attack of breathlessness. When I discovered afterwards that she had a weak heart, how remorseful I felt that I had never denied myself the fierce and sterile pleasure of making these retorts to her speeches. Françoise detested Albertine, moreover, because, being poor, Albertine could not enhance what Françoise regarded as my superior position. She smiled benevolently whenever I was invited by Mme. de Villeparisis. On the other hand, she was indignant that Albertine did not practise reciprocity. It came to my being obliged to invent fictitious presents which she was supposed to have given me, in the existence of which Françoise never for an instant believed. This want of reciprocity shocked her most of all in the matter of food. That Albertine should accept dinners from Mamma, when we were not invited to Mme. Bontemps's (who for that matter spent half her time out of Paris, her husband accepting " posts " as in the old days when he had had enough of the Ministry), seemed to her an indelicacy on the part of my friend which she rebuked indirectly by repeating a saying current at Combray:

"Let's eat my bread."

"Ay, that's the stuff."

"Let's eat thy bread."

"I've had enough."

I pretended that I was obliged to write a letter. "To whom were you writing?" Albertine asked me as she entered the room. "To a pretty little friend of mine, Gilberte Swann. Don't you know her?" "No." I decided not to question Albertine as to how she had spent the evening, I felt that I should only find fault with her and that we should not have any time left, seeing how late it was already, to be reconciled sufficiently to pass to kisses and caresses. And so it was with these that I chose to begin from the first moment. Besides, if I was a little calmer, I was not feeling happy. The loss of all orientation, of all sense of direction that we feel when we are kept waiting, still continues, after the coming of the person awaited, and, taking the place, inside us, of the calm spirit in which we were picturing her coming as so great a pleasure, prevents us from deriving any from it. Albertine was in the room: my unstrung nerves, continuing to flutter, were still expecting her. "I want a nice kiss, Albertine." "As many as you like," she said to me in her kindest manner. I had never seen her looking so pretty. "Another?" "Why, you know it's a great, great pleasure to me." "And a thousand times greater to me," she replied. "Oh! What a pretty book-cover you have there!" "Take it, I give it to you as a keepsake." "You are too kind. . . ." People would be cured for ever of romanticism if they could make up their minds, in thinking of the girl they love, to try to be the man they will be when they are no longer in love with

191

her. Gilberte's book-cover, her agate marble, must have derived their importance in the past from some purely inward distinction, since now they were to me a book-cover, a marble like any others.

I asked Albertine if she would like something to drink. "I seem to see oranges over there and water," she said. "That will be perfect." I was thus able to taste with her kisses that refreshing coolness which had seemed to me to be better than they, at the Princesse de Guermantes's. And the orange squeezed into the water seemed to yield to me, as I drank, the secret life of its ripening growth, its beneficent action upon certain states of that human body which belongs to so different a kingdom, its powerlessness to make that body live, but on the other hand the process of irrigation by which it was able to benefit it, a hundred mysteries concealed by the fruit from my senses, but not from my intellect.

When Albertine had gone, I remembered that I had promised Swann that I would write to Gilberte, and courtesy, I felt, demanded that I should do so at once. It was without emotion and as though drawing a line at the foot of a boring school essay, that I traced upon the envelope the name *Gilberte Swann,* with which at one time I used to cover my exercise-books to give myself the illusion that I was corresponding with her. For if, in the past, it had been I who wrote that name, now the task had been deputed by Habit to one of the many secretaries whom she employs. He could write down Gilberte's name with all the more calm, in that, placed with me only recently by Habit, having but recently entered my service, he had never known Gilberte, and knew only, without attaching any reality to the words, because he had heard me speak of her, that she was a girl with whom I had once been in love.

I could not accuse her of hardness. The person that I now was in relation to her was the clearest possible proof of what she herself had been: the book-cover, the agate marble had simply become for me in relation to Albertine what they had been for Gilberte, what they would have been to anybody who had not suffused them with the glow of an internal flame. But now I felt a fresh disturbance which in its turn distorted the real force of things and words. And when Albertine said to me, in a further outburst of gratitude: " I do love turquoises! " I answered her: " Do not let these die," entrusting to them as to some precious jewel the future of our friendship, which however was no more capable of inspiring a sentiment in Albertine than it had been of preserving the sentiment that had bound me in the past to Gilberte.

There appeared about this time a phenomenon which deserves mention only because it recurs in every important period of history. At the same moment when I was writing to Gilberte, M. de Guermantes, just home from his ball, still wearing his helmet, was thinking that next day he would be compelled to go into formal mourning, and decided to proceed a week earlier to the cure that he had been ordered to take. When he returned from it three weeks later (to anticipate for a moment, since I am still finishing my letter to Gilberte), those friends of the Duke who had seen him, so indifferent at the start, turn into a raving anti-Dreyfusard, were left speechless with amazement when they heard him (as though the action of the cure had not been confined to his bladder) answer:

" Oh, well, there'll be a fresh trial and he'll be acquitted; you can't sentence a fellow without any evidence against him. Did you ever see anyone so gaga as Froberville? An officer, leading the French people to the shambles, heading straight for war. Strange times we live in." The fact was that, in the interval, the Duke had met, at the spa, three charming ladies (an Italian princess and her two sisters-in-law). After hearing them make a few remarks about the books they were reading, a play that was being given at the Casino, the Duke had at once understood that he was dealing with women of superior intellect, by whom, as he expressed it, he would be knocked out in the first round. He was all the more delighted to be asked to play bridge by the Princess. But, the moment he entered her sitting room, as he began, in the fervour of his double-dyed anti-Dreyfusism: "Well, we don't hear very much more of the famous Dreyfus and his appeal," his stupefaction had been great when he heard the Princess and her sisters-in-law say: "It's becoming more certain every day. They can't keep a man in prison who has done nothing." "Eh? Eh?" the Duke had gasped at first, as at the discovery of a fantastic nickname employed in this household to turn to ridicule a person whom he had always regarded as intelligent. But, after a few days, as, from cowardice and the spirit of imitation, we shout "Hallo, Jojotte," without knowing why at a great artist whom we hear so addressed by the rest of the household, the Duke, still greatly embarrassed by the novelty of this attitude, began nevertheless to say: "After all, if there is no evidence against him." The three charming ladies decided that he was not progressing rapidly enough and began to bully him: "But really, nobody with a grain of intelligence can ever have believed for a moment that there was anything." Whenever any revelation came out that was "damning" to Dreyfus, and the Duke, supposing that now he was going to convert the three charming ladies, came to inform them of it, they burst out laughing and had no difficulty in proving to him, with great dialectic subtlety, that his argument was worthless and quite absurd. The Duke had returned to Paris a frantic Dreyfusard. And certainly we do not suggest that the three charming ladies were not, in this instance, messengers of truth. But it is to be observed that, every ten years or so, when we have left a man filled with a genuine conviction, it so happens that an intelligent couple, or simply a charming lady, comes in touch with him and after a few months he is won over to the opposite camp. And in this respect there are plenty of countries that behave like the sincere man, plenty of countries which we have left full of hatred for another race, and which, six months later, have changed their attitude and broken off all their alliances.

I ceased for some time to see Albertine, but continued, failing Mme. de Guermantes who no longer spoke to my imagination, to visit other fairies and their dwellings, as inseparable from themselves as is from the mollusc that fashioned it and takes shelter within it the pearly or enamelled valve or crenellated turret of its shell. I should not have been able to classify these ladies, the difficulty being that the problem was so vague in its terms and impossible not merely to solve but to set. Before coming to the lady, one had first to approach the faery mansion. Now as one of them was always at home after luncheon in the summer months, before I reached her house I was obliged to close the hood of my cab, so scorching were the sun's rays, the memory of which was, without my realising it, to enter into my general impression. I supposed that I was merely being driven to the Cours-la-Reine; in reality, before arriving at the gathering which a man of wider experience would perhaps have despised, I received, as though on a journey through Italy, a delicious, dazzled sensation from which the house was never afterwards to be separated in my memory. What was more, in view of the heat of the season and the hour, the lady had hermetically closed the shutters of the vast rectangular saloons on the ground floor in which she entertained her friends. I had difficulty at first in recognising my hostess and her guests, even the Duchesse de Guermantes, who in her hoarse voice bade me come and sit down next to her, in a Beauvais armchair illustrating the Rape of Europa. Then I began to make out on the walls the huge eighteenth century tapestries representing vessels whose masts were hollyhocks in blossom, beneath which I sat as though in the palace not of the Seine but of Neptune, by the brink of the river Oceanus, where the Duchesse de Guermantes became a sort of goddess of the waters. I should never stop if I began to describe all the different types of drawing-room. This example is sufficient to shew that I introduced into my social judgments poetical impressions which I never included among the items when I came to add up the sum, so that, when I was calculating the importance of a drawing-room, my total was never correct.

Certainly, these were by no means the only sources of error, but I have no time left now, before my departure for Balbec (where to my sorrow I am going to make a second stay which will also be my last), to start upon a series of pictures of society which will find their place in due course. I need here say only that to this first errone-ous reason (my relatively frivolous existence which made people suppose that I was fond of society) for my letter to Gilberte, and for that reconciliation with the Swann family to which it seemed to point, Odette might very well, and with equal inaccuracy, have added a second. I have suggested hitherto the different aspects that the social world assumes in the eyes of a single person only by supposing that, if a woman who, the other day, knew nobody now goes everywhere, and another who occupied a commanding position is ostracised, one is inclined to regard these changes merely as those purely personal ups and downs of fortune which from time to time bring about in a given section of society, in consequence of specula-tions on the stock exchange, a crashing downfall or en-richment beyond the dreams of avarice. But there is more in it than that. To a certain extent social mani-festations (vastly less important than artistic movements, political crises, the evolution that sweeps the public taste in the direction of the theatre of ideas, then of impres-sionist painting, then of music that is German and compli-cated, then of music that is Russian and simple, or of ideas of social service, justice, religious reaction, patriotic outbursts) are nevertheless an echo of them, remote, broken, uncertain, disturbed, changing. So that even drawing-rooms cannot be portrayed in a static immobil-ity which has been conventionally employed up to this point for the study of characters, though these too must be carried along in an almost historical flow. The thirst for novelty that leads men of the world who are more or less sincere in their eagerness for information as to intellectual evolution to frequent the circles in which they can trace its development makes them prefer as a rule some hostess as yet undiscovered, who represents still in their first freshness the hopes of a superior culture so faded and tarnished in the women who for long years have wielded the social sceptre and who, having no secrets from these men, no longer appeal to their imagination. And every age finds itself personified thus in fresh women, in a fresh group of women, who, closely adhering to whatever may at that moment be the latest object of interest, seem, in their attire, to be at that moment making their first public appearance, like an unknown species, born of the last deluge, irresistible beauties of each new Consulate, each new Directory. But very often the new hostess is simply like certain statesmen who may be in office for the first time but have for the last forty years been knocking at every door without seeing any open, women who were not known in society but who nevertheless had been receiving, for years past, and failing anything better, a few " chosen friends " from its ranks. To be sure, this is not always the case, and when, with the prodigious flowering of the Russian Ballet, revealing one after another Bakst, Nijinski, Benoist, the genius of Stravinski, Princess Yourbeletieff, the youthful sponsor of all these new great men, appeared bearing on her head an immense, quivering egret, unknown to the women of Paris, which they all sought to copy, one might have supposed that this marvellous creature had been imported in their innumerable baggage, and as their most priceless treasure, by the Russian dancers; but when presently, by her side, in her stage box, we see, at every performance of

the "Russians," seated like a true fairy godmother, unknown until that moment to the aristocracy, Mme. Verdurin, we shall be able to tell the society people who naturally supposed that Mme. Verdurin had recently entered
the country with Diaghileff's troop, that this lady had
already existed in different periods, and had passed
through various avatars of which this is remarkable only
in being the first that is bringing to pass at last, assured
henceforth, and at an increasingly rapid pace, the success
so long awaited by the Mistress. In Mme. Swann's case,
it is true, the novelty she represented had not the same
collective character. Her drawing-room was crystallised
round a man, a dying man, who had almost in an instant
passed, at the moment when his talent was exhausted,
from obscurity to a blaze of glory. The passion for
Bergotte's works was unbounded. He spent the whole
day, on show, at Mme. Swann's, who would whisper to
some influential man: "I shall say a word to him, he will
write an article for you." He was, for that matter, quite
capable of doing so and even of writing a little play for
Mme. Swann. A stage nearer to death, he was not quite
so feeble as at the time when he used to come and inquire
after my grandmother. This was because intense physical suffering had enforced a regime on him. Illness is
the doctor to whom we pay most heed: to kindness, to
knowledge we make promises only; pain we obey.

It is true that the Verdurins and their little clan had at
this time a far more vital interest than the drawing-room
faintly nationalist, more markedly literary, and pre-
eminently Bergottic of Mme. Swann. The little clan was
in fact the active centre of a long political crisis which
had reached its maximum of intensity: Dreyfusism. But

society people were for the most part so violently opposed to the appeal that a Dreyfusian house seemed to them as inconceivable a thing as, at an earlier period, a Communard house. The Principessa di Caprarola, who had made Mme. Verdurin's acquaintance over a big exhibition which she had organised, had indeed been to pay her a long call, in the hope of seducing a few interesting specimens of the little clan and incorporating them in her own drawing-room, a call in the course of which the Princess (playing the Duchesse de Guermantes in miniature) had made a stand against current ideas, declared that the people in her world were idiots, all of which, thought Mme. Verdurin, shewed great courage. But this courage was not, in the sequel, to go the length of venturing, under fire of the gaze of nationalist ladies, to bow to Mme. Verdurin at the Balbec races. With Mme. Swann, on the contrary, the anti-Dreyfusards gave her credit for being " sound," which, in a woman married to a Jew, was doubly meritorious. Nevertheless, the people who had never been to her house imagined her as visited only by a few obscure Israelites and disciples of Bergotte. In this way we place women far more outstanding than Mme. Swann on the lowest rung of the social ladder, whether on account of their origin, or because they do not care about dinner parties and receptions at which we never see them, and suppose this, erroneously, to be due to their not having been invited, or because they never speak of their social connexions, but only of literature and art, or because people conceal the fact that they go to their houses, or they, to avoid impoliteness to yet other people, conceal the fact that they open their doors to these, in short for a thousand reasons which, added together, make of one or other of them in certain people's eyes, the sort of woman whom one does not know. So it was with Odette. Mme. d'Epinoy, when busy collecting some subscription for the "Patrie Française," having been obliged to go and see her, as she would have gone to her dressmaker, convinced moreover that she would find only a lot of faces that were not so much impossible as completely unknown, stood rooted to the ground when the door opened not upon the drawing-room she imagined but upon a magic hall in which, as in the transformation scene of a pantomime, she recognised in the dazzling chorus, half reclining upon divans, seated in armchairs, addressing their hostess by her Christian name, the royalties, the duchesses, whom she, the Princesse d'Epinoy, had the greatest difficulty in enticing into her own drawing-room, and to whom at that moment, beneath the benevolent eyes of Odette, the Marquis du Lau, Comte Louis de Turenne, Prince Borghese, the Duc d'Estrées, carrying orangeade and cakes, were acting as cupbearers and henchmen. The Princesse d'Epinoy, as she instinctively made people's social value inherent in themselves, was obliged to disincarnate Mme. Swann and reincarnate her in a fashionable woman. Our ignorance of the real existence led by the women who do not advertise it in the newspapers draws thus over certain situations (thereby helping to differentiate one house from another) a veil of mystery. In Odette's case, at the start, a few men of the highest society, anxious to meet Bergotte, had gone to dine, quite quietly, at her house. She had had the tact, recently acquired, not to advertise their presence, they found when they went there, a memory perhaps of the little nucleus, whose traditions Odette had preserved in spite of the schism, a place laid for them at table, and so forth. Odette took them with Bergotte (whom these excursions, incidentally, finished off) to interesting first nights. They spoke of her to various women of their own world who were capable of taking an interest in such a novelty. These women were convinced that Odette, an intimate friend of Bergotte, had more or less collaborated in his works, and believed her to be a thousand times more intelligent than the most outstanding women of the Faubourg, for the same reason that made them pin all their political faith to certain Republicans of the right shade such as M. Doumer and M. Deschanel, whereas they saw France doomed to destruction were her destinies entrusted to the Monarchy men who were in the habit of dining with them, men like Charette or Doudeauville. This change in Odette's status was carried out, so far as she was concerned, with a discretion that made it more secure and more rapid but allowed no suspicion to filter through to the public that is prone to refer to the social columns of the *Gaulois* for evidence as to the advance or decline of a house, with the result that one day, at the dress rehearsal of a play by Bergotte, given in one of the most fashionable theatres in aid of a charity, the really dramatic moment was when people saw enter the box opposite, which was that reserved for the author, and sit down by the side of Mme. Swann, Mme. de Marsantes and her who, by the gradual self-effacement of the Duchesse de Guermantes (glutted with fame, and retiring to save the trouble of going on), was on the way to becoming the lion, the queen of the age, Comtesse Molé. "We never even supposed that she had begun to climb," people

said of Odette as they saw Comtesse Molé enter her box,
" and look, she has reached the top of the ladder."

So that Mme. Swann might suppose that it was from
snobbishness that I was taking up again with her daughter.

Odette, notwithstanding her brilliant escort, listened
with close attention to the play, as though she had come
there solely to see it performed, just as in the past she
used to walk across the Bois for her health, as a form of
exercise. Men who in the past had shewn less interest
in her came to the edge of the box, disturbing the whole
audience, to reach up to her hand and so approach the
imposing circle that surrounded her. She, with a smile
that was still more friendly than ironical, replied patiently
to their questions, affecting greater calm than might have
been expected, a calm which was, perhaps, sincere, this
exhibition being only the belated revelation of a habitual
and discreetly hidden intimacy. Behind these three
ladies to whom every eye was drawn was Bergotte flanked
by the Prince d'Agrigente, Comte Louis de Turenne, and
the Marquis de Bréauté. And it is easy to understand
that, to men who were received everywhere and could not
expect any further advancement save as a reward for
original research, this demonstration of their merit which
they considered that they were making in letting themselves succumb to a hostess with a reputation for profound intellectuality, in whose house they expected to
meet all the dramatists and novelists of the day, was
more exciting, more lively than those evenings at the
Princesse de Guermantes's, which, without any change of
programme or fresh attraction, had been going on year
after year, all more or less like the one we have described

in such detail. In that exalted sphere, the sphere of the Guermantes, in which people were beginning to lose interest, the latest intellectual fashions were not incarnate in entertainments fashioned in their image, as in those sketches that Bergotte used to write for Mme. Swann, or those positive committees of public safety (had society been capable of taking an interest in the Dreyfus case) at which, in Mme. Verdurin's drawing-room, used to assemble Picquart, Clémenceau, Zola, Reinach and Labori.

Gilberte, too, helped to strengthen her mother's position, for an uncle of Swann had just left nearly twenty-four million francs to the girl, which meant that the Faubourg Saint-Germain was beginning to take notice of her. The reverse of the medal was that Swann (who, however, was dying) held Dreyfusard opinions, though this as a matter of fact did not injure his wife, but was actually of service to her. It did not injure her because people said: "He is dotty, his mind has quite gone, nobody pays any attention to him, his wife is the only person who counts and she is charming." But even Swann's Dreyfusism was useful to Odette. Left to herself, she would quite possibly have allowed herself to make advances to fashionable women which would have been her undoing. Whereas on the evenings when she dragged her husband out to dine in the Faubourg Saint-Germain, Swann, sitting sullenly in his corner, would not hesitate, if he saw Odette seeking an introduction to some Nationalist lady, to exclaim aloud: "Really, Odette, you are mad. Why can't you keep yourself to yourself. It is idiotic of you to get yourself introduced to anti-semites. I forbid you." People in society whom everyone else runs after are not accustomed either to such pride or to such ill-breeding. For the first time they beheld some one who thought himself " superior " to them. The fame of Swann's mutterings was spread abroad, and cards with turned-down corners rained upon Odette. When she came to call upon Mme. d'Arpajon there was a brisk movement of friendly curiosity. " You didn't mind my introducing her to you," said Mme. d'Arpajon. " She is so nice. It was Marie de Marsantes that told me about her." " No, not at all, I hear she's so wonderfully clever, and she is charming. I had been longing to meet her; do tell me where she lives." Mme. d'Arpajon told Mme. Swann that she had enjoyed herself hugely at the latter's house the other evening, and had joyfully forsaken Mme. de Saint-Euverte for her. And it was true, for to prefer Mme. Swann was to shew that one was intelligent, like going to concerts instead of to tea-parties. But when Mme. de Saint-Euverte called on Mme. d'Arpajon at the same time as Odette, as Mme. de Saint-Euverte was a great snob and Mme. d'Arpajon, albeit she treated her without ceremony, valued her invitations, she did not introduce Odette, so that Mme. de Saint-Euverte should not know who it was. The Marquise imagined that it must be some Princess who never went anywhere, since she had never seen her before, prolonged her call, replied indirectly to what Odette was saying, but Mme. d'Arpajon remained adamant. And when Mme. de Saint-Euverte owned herself defeated and took her leave: " I did not introduce you," her hostess told Odette, " because people don't much care about going to her parties and she is always inviting one; you would never hear the last of her." " Oh, that is all right," said Odette with a pang of regret. But she retained the idea that people did not care about going to Mme. de Saint-Euverte's, which was to a certain extent true, and concluded that she herself held a position in society vastly superior to Mme. de Saint-Euverte's, albeit that lady held a very high position, and Odette, so far, had none at all.

That made no difference to her, and, albeit all Mme. de Guermantes's friends were friends also of Mme. d'Arpajon, whenever the latter invited Mme. Swann, Odette would say with an air of compunction: "I am going to Mme. d'Arpajon's; you will think me dreadfully old-fashioned, I know, but I hate going, for Mme. de Guermantes's sake" (whom, as it happened, she had never met). The distinguished men thought that the fact that Mme. Swann knew hardly anyone in good society meant that she must be a superior woman, probably a great musician, and that it would be a sort of extra distinction, as for a Duke to be a Doctor of Science, to go to her house. The completely unintelligent women were attracted by Odette for a diametrically opposite reason; hearing that she attended the Colonne concerts and professed herself a Wagnerian, they concluded from this that she must be "rather a lark," and were greatly excited by the idea of getting to know her. But, being themselves none too firmly established, they were afraid of compromising themselves in public if they appeared to be on friendly terms with Odette, and if, at a charity concert, they caught sight of Mme. Swann, would turn away their heads, deeming it impossible to bow, beneath the very nose of Mme. de Rochechouart, to a woman who was perfectly capable of having been to Bayreuth, which was as good as saying that she would stick at nothing.

Everybody becomes different upon entering another person's house. Not to speak of the marvellous metamorphoses that were accomplished thus in the faery palaces, in Mme. Swann's drawing-room, M. de Bréauté, acquiring a sudden importance from the absence of the people by whom he was normally surrounded, by his air of satisfaction at finding himself there, just as if instead of going out to a party he had slipped on his spectacles to shut himself up in his study and read the *Revue des Deux Mondes,* the mystic rite that he appeared to be performing in coming to see Odette, M. de Bréauté himself seemed another man. I would have given anything to see what alterations the Duchesse de Montmorency-Luxembourg would undergo in this new environment. But she was one of the people who could never be induced to meet Odette. Mme. de Montmorency, a great deal kinder to Oriane than Oriane was to her, surprised me greatly by saying, with regard to Mme. de Guermantes: "She knows some quite clever people, everybody likes her, I believe that if she had just had a slightly more coherent mind, she would have succeeded in forming a salon. The fact is, she never bothered about it, she is quite right, she is very well off as she is, with everybody running after her." If Mme. de Guermantes had not a "salon," what in the world could a "salon" be? The stupefaction in which this speech plunged me was no greater than that which I caused Mme. de Guermantes when I told her that I should like to be invited to Mme. de Montmorency's. Oriane thought her an old idiot. "I go there," she said, "because I'm forced to, she's my aunt, but you! She don't even know how to get nice people to come to her house." Mme. de Guermantes did not realise that nice people left me cold, that when she spoke to me of the Arpajon drawing-room I saw a yellow butterfly, and the Swann drawing-room (Mme. Swann was at home in the winter months between 6 and 7) a black butterfly, its wings powdered with snow. Even this last drawing-room, which was not a " salon " at all, she considered, albeit out of bounds for herself, permissible to me, on account of the " clever people " to be found there. But Mme. de Luxembourg! Had I already produced something that had attracted attention, she would have concluded that an element of snobbishness may be combined with talent. But I put the finishing touch to her disillusionment; I confessed to her that I did not go to Mme. de Montmorency's (as she supposed) to " take notes " and " make a study." Mme. de Guermantes was in this respect no more in error than the social novelists who analyse mercilessly from outside the actions of a snob or supposed snob, but never place themselves in his position, at the moment when a whole social springtime is bursting into blossom in his imagination. I myself, when I sought to discover what was the great pleasure that I found in going to Mme. de Montmorency's, was somewhat taken aback. She occupied, in the Faubourg Saint-Germain, an old mansion ramifying into pavilions which were separated by small gardens. In the outer hall a statuette, said to be by Falconnet, represented a spring which did, as it happened, exude a perpetual moisture. A little farther on the doorkeeper, her eyes always red, whether from grief or neurasthenia, a headache or a cold in the head, never answered your inquiry, waved her arm vaguely to indicate that the Duchess was at home, and let a drop or two trickle from her eyelids into a bowl filled with forget-me-nots. The pleasure that I felt on seeing the statuette, because it reminded me of a " little gardener " in plaster that stood in one of the Combray gardens, was nothing to that which was given me by the great staircase, damp and resonant, full of echoes, like the stairs in certain old-fashioned bathing establishments, with the vases filled with cinerarias—blue against blue— in the entrance hall and most of all the tinkle of the bell, which was exactly that of the bell in Eulalie's room. This tinkle raised my enthusiasm to a climax, but seemed to me too humble a matter for me to be able to explain it to Mme. de Montmorency, with the result that she in-variably saw me in a state of rapture of which she might never guess the cause.

THE HEART'S INTERMISSIONS

MY second arrival at Balbec was very different from the other. The manager had come in person to meet me at Pont-à-Couleuvre, reiterating how greatly he valued his titled patrons, which made me afraid that he had ennobled me, until I realised that, in the obscurity of his grammatical memory, *titré* meant simply *attitré*, or accredited. In fact, the more new languages he learned the worse he spoke the others. He informed he that he had placed me at the very top of the hotel. "I hope," he said, "that you will not interpolate this as a want of discourtesy, I was sorry to give you a room of which you are unworthy, but I did it in connexion with the noise, because in that room you will not have anyone above your head to disturb your trepanum" (tympanum). "Don't be alarmed, I shall have the windows closed, so that they shan't bang. Upon that point, I am intolerable" (the last word expressing not his own thought, which was that he would always be found inexorable in that respect, but, quite possibly, the thoughts of his underlings). The rooms were, as it proved, those we had had before. They were no humbler, but I had risen in the manager's esteem. I could light a fire if I liked (for, by the doctors' orders, I had left Paris at Easter), but he was afraid there might be "fixtures" in the ceiling. "See that you always wait before alighting a fire until the preceding one is extenuated" (extinct). "The important thing is to take care not to avoid setting fire to the chimney, especially as, to cheer things up a bit, I have put an old china pottage on the mantelpiece which might become insured."

He informed me with great sorrow of the death of the leader of the Cherbourg bar: "He was an old retainer," he said (meaning probably "campaigner") and gave me to understand that his end had been hastened by the quickness, otherwise the fastness, of his life. "For some time past I noticed that after dinner he would take a doss in the reading-room" (take a doze, presumably). "The last times, he was so changed that if you hadn't known who it was, to look at him, he was barely recognisant" (presumably, recognisable).

A happy compensation: the chief magistrate of Caen had just received his "bags" (badge) as Commander of the Legion of Honour. "Surely to goodness, he has capacities, but seems they gave him it principally because of his general 'impotence.'" There was a mention of this decoration, as it happened, in the previous day's *Echo de Paris*, of which the manager had as yet read only "the first paradox" (meaning paragraph). The paper dealt admirably with M. Caillaux's policy. "I consider, they're quite right," he said. "He is putting us too much under the thimble of Germany" (under the thumb). As the discussion of a subject of this sort with a hotel-keeper seemed to me boring, I ceased to listen. I thought of the visual images that had made me decide to return to Balbec. They were very different from those of the earlier time, the vision in quest of which I came was as dazzlingly clear as the former had been clouded; they were to prove deceitful nevertheless. The images selected by memory are as arbitrary, as narrow, as intangible as those which imagination had formed and reality has destroyed. There is no reason why, existing outside ourself, a real place should conform to the pictures in our memory rather than to those in our dreams. And besides, a fresh reality will perhaps make us forget, detest even, the desires that led us forth upon our journey.

Those that had led me forth to Balbec sprang to some extent from my discovery that the Verdurins (whose invitations I had invariably declined, and who would certainly be delighted to see me, if I went to call upon them in the country with apologies for never having been able to call upon them in Paris), knowing that several of the faithful would be spending the holidays upon that part of the coast, and having, for that reason, taken for the whole season one of M. de Cambremer's houses (La Raspelière), had invited Mme. Putbus to stay with them. The evening on which I learned this (in Paris) I lost my head completely and sent our young footman to find out whether the lady would be taking her Abigail to Balbec with her. It was eleven o'clock. Her porter was a long time in opening the front door, and, for a wonder, did not send my messenger packing, did not call the police, merely gave him a dressing down, but with it the information that I desired. He said that the head lady's maid would indeed be accompanying her mistress, first of all to the waters in Germany, then to Biarritz, and at the end of the season to Mme. Verdurin's. From that moment my mind had been at rest, and glad to have this iron in the fire. I had been able to dispense with those pursuits in the streets, in which I had not that letter of introduction to the beauties I encountered which I should have to the "Giorgione" in the fact of my having dined that very evening, at the Verdurins', with her mistress. Besides, she might form a still better opinion of me perhaps when she learned that I knew not merely the

213

middle class tenants of La Raspelière but its owners, and above all Saint-Loup who, prevented from commending me personally to the maid (who did not know him by name), had written an enthusiastic letter about me to the Cambremers. He believed that, quite apart from any service that they might be able to render me, Mme. de Cambremer, the Legrandin daughter-in-law, would interest me by her conversation. "She is an intelligent woman," he had assured me. "She won't say anything final" (*final* having taken the place of *sublime* things with Robert, who, every five or six years, would modify a few of his favourite expressions, while preserving the more important intact), "but it is an interesting nature, she has a personality, intuition; she has the right word for everything. Every now and then she is maddening, she says stupid things on purpose, to seem smart, which is all the more ridiculous as nobody could be less smart than the Cambremers, she is not always in the picture, but, taking her all round, she is one of the people it is more or less possible to talk to."

No sooner had Robert's letter of introduction reached them than the Cambremers, whether from a snobbishness that made them anxious to oblige Saint-Loup, even indirectly, or from gratitude for what he had done for one of their nephews at Doncières, or (what was most likely) from kindness of heart and traditions of hospitality, had written long letters insisting that I should stay with them, or, if I preferred to be more independent, offering to find me lodgings. When Saint-Loup had pointed out that I should be staying at the Grand Hotel, Balbec, they replied that at least they would expect a call from me as soon as I arrived and, if I did not appear, would come without fail to hunt me out and invite me to their garden parties.

No doubt there was no essential connexion between Mme. Putbus's maid and the country round Balbec; she would not be for me like the peasant girl whom, as I strayed alone along the Méséglise way, I had so often sought in vain to evoke, with all the force of my desire. But I had long since given up trying to extract from a woman as it might be the square root of her unknown quantity, the mystery of which a mere introduction was generally enough to dispel. Anyhow at Balbec, where I had not been for so long, I should have this advantage, failing the necessary connexion which did not exist between the place and this particular woman, that my sense of reality would not be destroyed by familiarity, as in Paris, where, whether in my own home or in a bedroom that I already knew, pleasure indulged in with a woman could not give me for one instant, amid everyday surroundings, the illusion that it was opening the door for me to a new life. (For if habit is a second nature, it prevents us from knowing our original nature, whose cruelties it lacks and also its enchantments.) Now this illusion I might perhaps feel in a strange place, where one's sensibility is revived by a ray of sunshine, and where my ardour would be raised to a climax by the lady's maid whom I desired: we shall see, in the course of events, not only that this woman did not come to Balbec, but that I dreaded nothing so much as the possibility of her coming, so that the principal object of my expedition was neither attained, nor indeed pursued. It was true that Mme. Putbus was not to be at the Verdurins' so early in the season; but these pleasures which we have chosen beforehand may be remote, if their coming is assured, and if, in the interval of waiting, we can devote ourselves to the pastime of seeking to attract, while powerless to love. Moreover, I was not going to Balbec in the same practical frame of mind as before; there is always less egoism in pure imagination than in recollection; and I knew that I was going to find myself in one of those very places where fair strangers most abound; a beach presents them as numerously as a ball-room, and I looked forward to strolling up and down outside the hotel, on the front, with the same sort of pleasure that Mme. de Guermantes would have procured me if, instead of making other hostesses invite me to brilliant dinner-parties, she had given my name more frequently for their lists of partners to those of them who gave dances. To make female acquaintances at Balbec would be as easy for me now as it had been difficult before, for I was now as well supplied with friends and resources there as I had been destitute of them on my former visit.

I was roused from my meditations by the voice of the manager, to whose political dissertations I had not been listening. Changing the subject, he told me of the chief magistrate's joy on hearing of my arrival, and that he was coming to pay me a visit in my room, that very evening. The thought of this visit so alarmed me (for I was beginning to feel tired) that I begged him to prevent it (which he promised to do, and, as a further precaution, to post members of his staff on guard, for the first night, on my landing). He did not seem overfond of his staff. " I am obliged to keep running after them all the time because they are lacking in inertia. If I was not there they would never stir. I shall post the lift-boy on sentry outside your door." I asked him if the boy had yet become "head page." "He is not old enough yet in the house," was the answer. "He has comrades more aged than he is. It would cause an outcry. We must act with granulation in everything. I quite admit that he strikes a good aptitude" (meaning attitude) "at the door of his lift. But he is still a trifle young for such positions. With others in the place of longer standing, it would make a contrast. He is a little wanting in seriousness, which is the primitive quality" (doubtless, the primordial, the most important quality). "He needs his leg screwed on a bit tighter" (my informant meant to say his head). "Anyhow, he can leave it all to me. I know what I'm about. Before I won my stripes as manager of the Grand Hotel, I smelt powder under M. Paillard." I was impressed by this simile, and thanked the manager for having come in person as far as Pont-à-Couleuvre. "Oh, that's nothing! The loss of time has been quite infinite" (for infinitesimal). Meanwhile, we had arrived.

Complete physical collapse. On the first night, as I was suffering from cardiac exhaustion, trying to master my pain, I bent down slowly and cautiously to take off my boots. But no sooner had I touched the topmost button than my bosom swelled, filled with an unknown, a divine presence, I shook with sobs, tears streamed from my eyes. The person who came to my rescue, who saved me from barrenness of spirit, was the same who, years before, in a moment of identical distress and loneliness, in a moment when I was no longer in any way myself, had come in, and had restored me to myself, for that person was myself and more than myself (the container that is greater than the contents, which it was bringing to me). I had just perceived, in my memory, bending over my weariness, the tender, preoccupied, dejected face of my grandmother, as she had been on that first evening of our arrival, the face not of that grandmother whom I was astonished—and reproached myself —to find that I regretted so little and who was no more of her than just her name, but of my own true grandmother, of whom, for the first time since that afternoon in the Champs-Elysées on which she had had her stroke, I now recaptured, by an instinctive and complete act of recollection, the living reality. That reality has no existence for us, so long as it has not been created anew by our mind (otherwise the men who have been engaged in a Titanic conflict would all of them be great epic poets); and so, in my insane desire to fling myself into her arms, it was not until this moment, more than a year after her burial, because of that anachronism which so often prevents the calendar of facts from corresponding to that of our feelings, that I became conscious that she was dead. I had often spoken about her in the interval, and thought of her also, but behind my words and thoughts, those of an ungrateful, selfish, cruel youngster, there had never been anything that resembled my grandmother, because, in my frivolity, my love of pleasure, my familiarity with the spectacle of her ill health, I retained only in a potential state the memory of what she had been. At whatever moment we estimate it, the total value of our spiritual nature is more or less fictitious, notwithstanding the long inventory of its treasures, for now one, now another of these is unrealisable, whether we are considering actual treasures or those of the imagination, and, in my own case, fully as much as the ancient name of Guermantes, this other, how far more important item, my real memory of my grandmother. For with the troubles of memory are closely linked the heart's intermissions. It is, no doubt, the existence of our body, which we may compare to a jar containing our spiritual nature, that leads us to suppose that all our inward wealth, our past joys, all our sorrows, are perpetually in our possession. Perhaps it is equally inexact to suppose that they escape or return. In any case, if they remain within us, it is, for most of the time, in an unknown region where they are of no service to us, and where even the most ordinary are crowded out by memories of a different kind, which preclude any simultaneous occurrence of them in our consciousness. But if the setting of sensations in which they are preserved be recaptured, they acquire in turn the same power of expelling everything that is incompatible with them, of installing alone in us the self that originally lived them. Now, inasmuch as the self that I had just suddenly become once again had not existed since that evening long ago when my grandmother undressed me after my arrival at Balbec, it was quite naturally, not at the end of the day that had just passed, of which that self knew nothing, but—as though there were in time different and parallel series—without loss of continuity, immediately after the first evening at Balbec long ago, that I clung to the minute in which my grandmother had leaned over me. The self that I then was, that had so long disappeared, was once again so close to me that I seemed still to hear the words that had just been spoken, albeit they were nothing more now than illusion, as a man who is half awake thinks he can still make out close at hand the sounds of his receding dream. I was nothing now but the person who sought a refuge in his grandmother's arms, sought to wipe away the traces of his suffering by giving her kisses, that person whom I should have had as great difficulty in imagining when I was one or other of those persons which, for some time past, I had successively been, as the efforts, doomed in any event to sterility, that I should now have had to make to feel the desires and joys of any of those which, for a time at least, I no longer was. I reminded myself how, an hour before the moment at which my grandmother had stooped down like that, in her dressing gown, to unfasten my boots, as I wandered along the stiflingly hot street, past the pastry-cook's, I had felt that I could never, in my need to feel her arms round me, live through the hour that I had still to spend without her. And now that this same need was reviving in me, I knew that I might wait hour after hour, that she would never again be by my side, I had only just discovered this because I had only just, on feeling her for the first time, alive, authentic, making my heart swell to breaking-point, on finding her at last, learned that I had lost her for ever. Lost for ever; I could not understand and was struggling to bear the anguish of this contradiction: on the one hand an existence, an affection, surviving in me as I had known them, that is to say created for me, a love in whose eyes everything found in me so entirely its complement, its goal, its constant lodestar, that the genius of great men, all the genius that might have existed from the beginning of the world would have been less precious to my grandmother than a single one of my defects; and on the other hand, as soon as I had lived over again that bliss, as though it were present, feeling it shot through by the certainty, throbbing like a physical anguish, of an annihilation that had effaced my image of that affection, had destroyed that existence, abolished in retrospect our interwoven destiny, made of my grandmother at the moment when I found her again as in a mirror, a mere stranger whom chance had allowed to spend a few years in my company, as it might have been in anyone's else, but to whom, before and after those years, I was, I could be nothing.

Instead of the pleasures that I had been experiencing of late, the only pleasure that it would have been possible for me to enjoy at that moment would have been, by modifying the past, to diminish the sorrows and sufferings of my grandmother's life. Now, I did not recall her only in that dressing-gown, a garment so appropriate as to have become almost their symbol to the labours, foolish no doubt but so lovable also, that she performed for me, gradually I began to remember all the opportunities that I had seized, by letting her perceive, by exaggerating if necessary my sufferings, to cause her a grief which I imagined as being obliterated immediately by my kisses, as though my affection had been as capable as my happiness of creating hers; and, what was worse, I, who could conceive no other happiness now than in finding happiness shed in my memory over the contours of that face, moulded and bowed by love, had set to work with frantic efforts, in the past, to destroy even its most modest pleasures, as on the day when Saint-Loup had taken my grandmother's photograph and I, unable to conceal from her what I thought of the ridiculous childishness of the coquetry with which she posed for him, with her wide-brimmed hat, in a flattering half light, had allowed myself to mutter a few impatient, wounding words, which, I had perceived from a contraction of her features, had carried, had pierced her; it was I whose heart they were rending now that there was no longer possible, ever again, the consolation of a thousand kisses.

But never should I be able to wipe out of my memory that contraction of her face, that anguish of her heart, or rather of my own: for as the dead exist only in us, it is ourselves that we strike without ceasing when we persist in recalling the blows that we have dealt them. To these griefs, cruel as they were, I clung with all my might and main, for I realised that they were the effect of my memory of my grandmother, the proof that this memory which I had of her was really present within me. I felt that I did not really recall her save by grief and should have liked to feel driven yet deeper into me these nails which fastened the memory of her to my consciousness. I did not seek to mitigate my suffering, to set it off, to pretend that my grandmother was only somewhere else and momentarily invisible, by addressing to her photograph (the one taken by Saint-Loup, which I had beside me) words and prayers as to a person who is separated from us but, retaining his personality, knows us and remains bound to us by an indissoluble harmony. Never did I do this, for I was determined not merely to suffer, but to respect the original form of my suffering, as it had suddenly come upon me unawares, and I wished to continue to feel it, according to its own laws, whenever those strange contradictory impressions of survival and obliteration crossed one another again in my mind. This painful and, at the moment, incomprehensible impression,

I knew—not, forsooth, whether I should one day distil a grain of truth from it—but that if I ever should succeed in extracting that grain of truth, it could only be from it, from so singular, so spontaneous an impression, which had been neither traced by my intellect nor attenuated by my pusillanimity, but which death itself, the sudden revelation of death, had, like a stroke of lightning, carved upon me, along a supernatural, inhuman channel, a two-fold and mysterious furrow. (As for the state of forget-fulness of my grandmother in which I had been living until that moment, I could not even think of turning to it to extract truth from it; since in itself it was nothing but a negation, a weakening of the mind incapable of recre-ating a real moment of life and obliged to substitute for it conventional and neutral images.) Perhaps, however, as the instinct of preservation, the ingenuity of the mind in safeguarding us from grief, had begun already to build upon still smouldering ruins, to lay the first courses of its serviceable and ill-omened structure, I relished too keenly the delight of recalling this or that opinion held by my dear one, recalling them as though she had been able to hold them still, as though she existed, as though I con-tinued to exist for her. But as soon as I had succeeded in falling asleep, at that more truthful hour when my eyes closed to the things of the outer world, the world of sleep (on whose frontier intellect and will, momentarily paralysed, could no longer strive to rescue me from the cruelty of my real impressions) reflected, refracted the agonising synthesis of survival and annihilation, in the mysteriously lightened darkness of my organs. World of sleep in which our inner consciousness, placed in bond-age to the disturbances of our organs, quickens the rhythm of heart or breath because a similar dose of terror, sorrow, remorse acts with a strength magnified an hundredfold if it is thus injected into our veins; as soon as, to traverse the arteries of the subterranean city, we have embarked upon the dark current of our own blood as upon an inward Lethe meandering sixfold, huge solemn forms appear to us, approach and glide away, leaving us in tears. I sought in vain for my grandmother's form when I had stepped ashore beneath the sombre portals; I knew, indeed, that she did still exist, but with a diminished vitality, as pale as that of memory; the darkness was increasing, and the wind; my father, who was to take me where she was, did not appear. Suddenly my breath failed me, I felt my heart turn to stone; I had just remembered that for week after week I had forgotten to write to my grandmother. What must she be thinking of me? "Great God!" I said to myself, "how wretched she must be in that little room which they have taken for her, no bigger than what one would take for an old servant, where she is all alone with the nurse they have put there to look after her, from which she cannot stir, for she is still slightly paralysed and has always refused to rise from her bed. She must be thinking that I have forgotten her now that she is dead; how lonely she must be feeling, how deserted! Oh, I must run to see her, I mustn't lose a minute, I mustn't wait for my father to come, even—but where is it, how can I have forgotten the address, will she know me again, I wonder? How can I have forgotten her all these months?" It is so dark, I shall not find her; the wind is keeping me back; but look! there is my father walking ahead of me; I call out to him: "Where is grandmother? Tell me her address. Is she all right? Are you quite sure she has everything she wants?" "Why," says my father, "you need not alarm yourself. Her nurse is well trained. We send her a trifle, from time to time, so that she can get your grandmother anything she may need. She asks, sometimes, how you are getting on. She was told that you were going to write a book. She seemed pleased. She wiped away a tear." And then I fancied I could remember that, a little time after her death, my grandmother had said to me, crying, with a humble expression, like an old servant who has been given notice to leave, like a stranger, in fact: "You will let me see something of you occasionally, won't you; don't let too many years go by without visiting me. Remember that you were my grandson, once, and that grandmothers never forget." And seeing again that face, so submissive, so sad, so tender, which was hers, I wanted to run to her at once and say to her, as I ought to have said to her then: "Why, grandmother, you can see me as often as you like, I have only you in the world, I shall never leave you any more." What tears my silence must have made her shed through all those months in which I have never been to the place where she lies, what can she have been saying to herself about me? And it is in a voice choked with tears that I too shout to my father: "Quick, quick, her address, take me to her." But he says: "Well . . . I don't know whether you will be able to see her. Besides, you know, she is very frail now, very frail, she is not at all herself, I am afraid you would find it rather painful. And I can't be quite certain of the number of the avenue." "But tell me, you who know, it is not true that the dead have ceased to exist. It can't possibly be true, in spite

I   225   Q

of what they say, because grandmother does exist still."
My father smiled a mournful smile: "Oh, hardly at all,
you know, hardly at all. I think that it would be better
if you did not go. She has everything that she wants.
They come and keep the place tidy for her." "But she
is often left alone?" "Yes, but that is better for her. It
is better for her not to think, which could only be bad for
her. It often hurts her, when she tries to think. Besides, you know, she is quite lifeless now. I shall leave a
note of the exact address, so that you can go to her; but
I don't see what good you can do there, and I don't suppose the nurse will allow you to see her." "You know
quite well I shall always stay beside her, dear, deer, deer,
Francis Jammes, fork." But already I had retraced the
dark meanderings of the stream, had ascended to the
surface where the world of living people opens, so that if
I still repeated: "Francis Jammes, deer, deer," the se-
quence of these words no longer offered me the limpid
meaning and logic which they had expressed to me so
naturally an instant earlier and which I could not now
recall. I could not even understand why the word
"Aias" which my father had just said to me, had immediately signified: "Take care you don't catch cold,"
without any possible doubt. I had forgotten to close the
shutters, and so probably the daylight had awakened
me. But I could not bear to have before my eyes those
waves of the sea which my grandmother could formerly
contemplate for hours on end; the fresh image of their
heedless beauty was at once supplemented by the thought
that she did not see them; I should have liked to stop my
ears against their sound, for now the luminous plenitude
of the beach carved out an emptiness in my heart; every-

thing seemed to be saying to me, like those paths and lawns of a public garden in which I had once lost her, long ago, when I was still a child: "We have not seen her," and beneath the hemisphere of the pale vault of heaven I felt myself crushed as though beneath a huge bell of bluish glass, enclosing an horizon within which my grandmother was not. To escape from the sight of it, I turned to the wall, but alas what was now facing me was that partition which used to serve us as a morning messenger, that partition which, as responsive as a violin in rendering every fine shade of sentiment, reported so exactly to my grandmother my fear at once of waking her and, if she were already awake, of not being heard by her and so of her not coming, then immediately, like a second instrument taking up the melody, informed me that she was coming and bade me be calm. I dared not put out my hand to that wall, any more than to a piano on which my grandmother had played and which still throbbed from her touch. I knew that I might knock now, even louder, that I should hear no response, that my grandmother would never come again. And I asked nothing better of God, if a Paradise exists, than to be able, there, to knock upon that wall the three little raps which my grandmother would know among a thousand, and to which she would reply with those other raps which said: "Don't be alarmed, little mouse, I know you are impatient, but I am just coming," and that He would let me remain with her throughout eternity which would not be too long for us.

The manager came in to ask whether I would not like to come down. He had most carefully supervised my "placement" in the dining-room. As he had seen no sign of me, he had been afraid that I might have had another of my choking fits. He hoped that it might be only a little " sore throats " and assured me that he had heard it said that they could be soothed with what he called " calyptus."

He brought me a message from Albertine. She was not supposed to be coming to Balbec that year but, having changed her plans, had been for the last three days not in Balbec itself but ten minutes away by the tram at a neighbouring watering-place. Fearing that I might be tired after the journey, she had stayed away the first evening, but sent word now to ask when I could see her. I inquired whether she had called in person, not that I wished to see her, but so that I might arrange not to see her. " Yes," replied the manager. " But she would like it to be as soon as possible, unless you have not some quite necessitous reasons. You see," he concluded, " that everybody here desires you, definitively." But for my part, I wished to see nobody.

And yet the day before, on my arrival, I had felt myself recaptured by the indolent charm of a seaside existence. The same taciturn lift-boy, silent this time from respect and not from scorn, and glowing with pleasure, had set the lift in motion. As I rose upon the ascending column, I had passed once again through what had formerly been for me the mystery of a strange hotel, in which when you arrive, a tourist without protection or position, each old resident returning to his room, each chambermaid passing along the eery perspective of a corridor, not to mention the young lady from America with her companion, on their way down to dinner, give you a look in which you can read nothing that you would have liked to see. This time on the contrary I had felt the entirely soothing pleasure of passing up through an hotel that I knew, where I felt myself at home, where I had performed once again that operation which we must always start afresh, longer, more difficult than the turning outside in of an eyelid, which consists in investing things with the spirit that is familiar to us instead of their own which we found alarming. Must I always, I had asked myself, little thinking of the sudden change of mood that was in store for me, be going to strange hotels where I should be dining for the first time, where Habit would not yet have killed upon each landing, outside every door, the terrible dragon that seemed to be watching over an enchanted life, where I should have to approach those strange women whom fashionable hotels, casinos, watering-places, seem to draw together and endow with a common existence.

I had found pleasure even in the thought that the boring chief magistrate was so eager to see me, I could see, on that first evening, the waves, the azure mountain ranges of the sea, its glaciers and its cataracts, its elevation and its careless majesty—merely upon smelling for the first time after so long an interval, as I washed my hands, that peculiar odour of the over-scented soaps of the Grand Hotel—which, seeming to belong at once to the present moment and to my past visit, floated between them like the real charm of a particular form of existence to which one returns only to change one's necktie. The sheets on my bed, too fine, too light, too large, impossible to tuck in, to keep in position, which billowed out from beneath the blankets in moving whorls had distressed me before. Now they merely cradled upon the awkward,

swelling fulness of their sails the glorious sunrise, big
with hopes, of my first morning. But that sun had not
time to appear. In the dead of night, the awful, godlike
presence had returned to life. I asked the manager to
leave me, and to give orders that no one was to enter my
room. I told him that I should remain in bed and rejected his offer to send to the chemist's for the excellent
drug. He was delighted by my refusal for he was afraid
that other visitors might be annoyed by the smell of the
" calyptus." It earned me the compliment: " You are in
the movement " (he meant: " in the right "), and the
warning: " take care you don't defile yourself at the
door, I've had the lock ' elucidated ' with oil; if any of
the servants dares to knock at your door, he'll be beaten
' black and white.' And they can mark my words, for
I'm not a repeater " (this evidently meant that he did not
say a thing twice). " But wouldn't you care for a drop
of old wine, just to set you up; I have a pig's head of it
downstairs " (presumably hogshead). " I shan't bring
it to you on a silver dish like the head of Jonathan, and
I warn you that it is not Château-Lafite, but it is virtu-
ously equivocal " (virtually equivalent). " And as it's
quite light, they might fry you a little sol." I declined
everything, but was surprised to hear the name of the fish
(sole) pronounced like that of the King of Israel, Saul,
by a man who must have ordered so many in his life.

Despite the manager's promises, they brought me in a
little later the turned down card of the Marquise de Cambremer. Having come over to see me, the old lady had
sent to inquire whether I was there and when she heard
that I had arrived only the day before, and was unwell,
had not insisted, but (not without stopping, doubtless, at

the chemist's or the haberdasher's, while the footman jumped down from the box and went in to pay a bill or to give an order) had driven back to Féterne, in her old barouche upon eight springs, drawn by a pair of horses. Not infrequently did one hear the rumble and admire the pomp of this carriage in the streets of Balbec and of various other little places along the coast, between Balbec and Féterne. Not that these halts outside shops were the object of these excursions. It was on the contrary some tea-party or garden-party at the house of some squire or functionary, socially quite unworthy of the Marquise. But she, although completely overshadowing, by her birth and wealth, the petty nobility of the district, was in her perfect goodness and simplicity of heart so afraid of disappointing anyone who had sent her an invitation that she would attend all the most insignificant social gatherings in the neighbourhood. Certainly, rather than travel such a distance to listen, in the stifling heat of a tiny drawing-room, to a singer who generally had no voice and whom in her capacity as the lady bountiful of the countryside and as a famous musician she would afterwards be compelled to congratulate with exaggerated warmth, Mme. de Cambremer would have preferred to go for a drive or to remain in her marvellous gardens at Féterne, at the foot of which the drowsy waters of a little bay float in to die amid the flowers. But she knew that the probability of her coming had been announced by the host, whether he was a noble or a free burgess of Maineville-la Teinturière or of Chattoncourt-l'Orgueilleux. And if Mme. de Cambremer had driven out that afternoon without making a formal appearance at the party, any of the guests who had come from one or other of the little places that lined the coast might have seen and heard the Marquise's barouche, which would deprive her of the excuse that she had not been able to get away from Féterne. On the other hand, these hosts might have seen Mme. de Cambremer, time and again, appear at concerts given in houses which, they considered, were no place for her; the slight depreciation caused thereby, in their eyes, to the position of the too obliging Marquise vanished as soon as it was they who were entertaining her, and it was with feverish anxiety that they kept asking themselves whether or not they were going to have her at their " small party." What an allaying of the doubts and fears of days if, after the first song had been sung by the daughter of the house or by some amateur on holiday in the neighbourhood, one of the guests announced (an infallible sign that the Marquise was coming to the party) that he had seen the famous barouche and pair drawn up outside the watchmaker's or the chemist's! Thereupon Mme. de Cambremer (who indeed was to enter before long followed by her daughter-in-law, the guests who were staying with her at the moment and whom she had asked permission, granted with such joy, to bring) shone once more with undiminished lustre in the eyes of her host and hostess, to whom the hoped-for reward of her coming had perhaps been the determining if unavowed cause of the decision they had made a month earlier: to burden themselves with the trouble and expense of an afternoon party. Seeing the Marquise present at their gathering, they remembered no longer her readiness to attend those given by their less deserving neighbours, but the antiquity of her family, the splendour of her house, the rudeness of her daughter-in-law, born Legrandin, who by her arrogance emphasised the slightly insipid good-nature of the dowager. Already they could see in their mind's eye, in the social column of the *Gaulois*, the paragraph which they would draft themselves in the family circle, with all the doors shut and barred, upon "the little corner of Brittany which is at present a whirl of gaiety, the select party from which the guests could hardly tear themselves away, promising their charming host and hostess that they would soon pay them another visit." Day after day they watched for the newspaper to arrive, worried that they had not yet seen any notice in it of their party, and afraid lest they should have had Mme. de Cambremer for their other guests alone and not for the whole reading public. At length the blessed day arrived: "The season is exceptionally brilliant this year at Balbec. Small afternoon concerts are the fashion. . . ." Heaven be praised, Mme. de Cambremer's name was spelt correctly, and included "among others we may mention" but at the head of the list. All that remained was to appear annoyed at this journalistic indiscretion which might get them into difficulties with people whom they had not been able to invite, and to ask hypocritically in Mme. de Cambremer's hearing who could have been so treacherous as to send the notice, upon which the Marquise, every inch the lady bountiful, said: "I can understand your being annoyed, but I must say I am only too delighted that people should know I was at your party."

On the card that was brought me, Mme. de Cambremer had scribbled the message that she was giving an afternoon party "the day after to-morrow." To be sure, as recently as the day before yesterday, tired as I was of the social round, it would have been a real pleasure to me to taste it, transplanted amid those gardens in which there grew in the open air, thanks to the exposure of Féterne, fig trees, palms, rose bushes extending down to a sea as blue and calm often as the Mediterranean, upon which the host's little yacht sped across, before the party began, to fetch from the places on the other side of the bay the most important guests, served, with its awnings spread to shut out the sun, after the party had assembled, as an open air refreshment room, and set sail again in the evening to take back those whom it had brought. A charming luxury, but so costly that it was partly to meet the expenditure that it entailed that Mme. de Cambremer had sought to increase her income in various ways, and notably by letting, for the first time, one of her properties, very different from Féterne: la Raspelière. Yes, two days earlier, how welcome such a party, peopled with minor nobles all unknown to me, would have been to me as a change from the " high life " of Paris. But now pleasures had no longer any meaning for me. And so I wrote to Mme. de Cambremer to decline, just as, an hour ago, I had put off Albertine: grief had destroyed in me the possibility of desire as completely as a high fever takes away one's appetite. . . . My mother was to arrive on the morrow. I felt that I was less unworthy to live in her company, that I should understand her better, now that an alien and degrading existence had wholly given place to the resurging, heartrending memories that wreathed and ennobled my soul, like her own, with their crown of thorns. I thought so: in reality there is a world of difference between real griefs, like my mother's, which literally crush out our life for years if not for ever, when we have lost the person we love—and those other griefs, transitory when all is said, as mine was to be, which pass as quickly as they have been slow in coming, which we do not realise until long after the event, because, in order to feel them, we need first to understand them; griefs such as so many people feel, from which the grief that was torturing me at this moment differed only in assuming the form of unconscious memory.

That I was one day to experience a grief as profound as that of my mother, we shall find in the course of this narrative, but it was neither then nor thus that I imagined it. Nevertheless, like a principal actor who ought to have learned his part and to have been in his place long beforehand but has arrived only at the last moment and, having read over once only what he has to say, manages to "gag" so skilfully when his cue comes that nobody notices his unpunctuality, my new found grief enabled me, when my mother came, to talk to her as though it had existed always. She supposed merely that the sight of these places which I had visited with my grandmother (which was not at all the case) had revived it. For the first time then, and because I felt a sorrow which was nothing compared with hers, but which opened my eyes, I realised and was appalled to think what she must be suffering. For the first time I understood that the fixed and tearless gaze (which made Françoise withhold her sympathy) that she had worn since my grandmother's death had been arrested by that incomprehensible contradiction of memory and nonexistence. Besides, since she was, although still in deep mourning, more fashionably dressed in this strange place, I was more struck by the transformation that had occurred in her. It is not enough to say that she had lost all her gaiety; melted, congealed into a sort of imploring image, she seemed to be afraid of shocking by too sudden a movement, by too loud a tone, the sorrowful presence that never parted from her. But, what struck me most of all, when I saw her cloak of crape, was—what had never occurred to me in Paris—that it was no longer my mother that I saw before me, but my grandmother. As, in royal and princely families, upon the death of the head of the house his son takes his title and, from being Duc d'Orléans, Prince de Tarente or Prince des Laumes, becomes King of France, Duc de la Trémoïlle, Duc de Guermantes, so by an accession of a different order and more remote origin, the dead man takes possession of the living who becomes his image and successor, carries on his interrupted life. Perhaps the great sorrow that follows, in a daughter such as Mamma, the death of her mother only makes the chrysalis break open a little sooner, hastens the metamorphosis and the appearance of a person whom we carry within us and who, but for this crisis which annihilates time and space, would have come more gradually to the surface. Perhaps, in our regret for her who is no more, there is a sort of auto-suggestion which ends by bringing out on our features resemblances which potentially we already bore, and above all a cessation of our most characteristically personal activity (in my mother, her common sense, the sarcastic gaiety that she inherited from her father) which we did not shrink, so long as the beloved was alive, from exercising, even at her expense, and which counterbalanced the traits that we derived exclusively from her. Once she is dead, we should hesitate to be different, we begin to admire only what she was, what we ourselves already were only blended with something else,

236

and what in future we are to be exclusively. It is in this sense (and not in that other, so vague, so false, in which the phrase is generally used) that we may say that death is not in vain, that the dead man continues to react upon us. He reacts even more than a living man because, true reality being discoverable only by the mind, being the object of a spiritual operation, we acquire a true knowledge only of things that we are obliged to create anew by thought, things that are hidden from us in everyday life. . . . Lastly, in our mourning for our dead we pay an idolatrous worship to the things that they liked. Not only could not my mother bear to be parted from my grandmother's bag, become more precious than if it had been studded with sapphires and diamonds, from her muff, from all those garments which served to enhance their personal resemblance, but even from the volumes of Mme. de Sévigné which my grandmother took with her everywhere, copies which my mother would not have exchanged for the original manuscript of the letters. She had often teased my grandmother who could never write to her without quoting some phrase of Mme. de Sévigné or Mme. de Beausergent. In each of the three letters that I received from Mamma before her arrival at Balbec, she quoted Mme. de Sévigné to me, as though those three letters had been written not by her to me but by my grandmother and to her. She must at once go out upon the front to see that beach of which my grandmother had spoken to her every day in her letters. Carrying her mother's sunshade, I saw her from my window advance, a sable figure, with timid, pious steps, over the sands that beloved feet had trodden before her, and she looked as though she were going down to find a corpse which the waves would cast up at her feet. So that she should not have to dine by herself, I was to join her downstairs. The chief magistrate and the barrister's widow asked to be introduced to her. And everything that was in any way connected with my grandmother was so precious to her that she was deeply touched, remembered ever afterwards with gratitude what the chief magistrate had said to her, just as she was hurt and indignant that the barrister's wife had not a word to say in memory of the dead. In reality, the chief magistrate was no more concerned about my grandmother than the barrister's wife. The heartfelt words of the one and the other's silence, for all that my mother imagined so vast a difference between them, were but alternative ways of expressing that indifference which we feel towards the dead. But I think that my mother found most comfort in the words in which, quite involuntarily, I conveyed to her a little of my own anguish. It could not but make Mamma happy (notwithstanding all her affection for myself), like everything else that guaranteed my grandmother survival in our hearts. Daily after this my mother went down and sat upon the beach, so as to do exactly what her mother had done, and read her mother's two favourite books, the *Memoirs* of Madame de Beausergent and the *Letters* of Madame de Sévigné. She, like all the rest of us, could not bear to hear the latter lady called the " spirituelle Marquise " any more than to hear La Fontaine called " le Bonhomme." But when, in reading the *Letters,* she came upon the words: " My daughter," she seemed to be listening to her mother's voice.

She had the misfortune, upon one of these pilgrimages during which she did not like to be disturbed, to meet upon the beach a lady from Combray, accompanied by her daughters. Her name was, I think, Madame Poussin. But among ourselves we always referred to her as the " Pretty Kettle of Fish," for it was by the perpetual repetition of this phrase that she warned her daughters of the evils that they were laying up for themselves, saying for instance if one of them was rubbing her eyes: " When you go and get ophthalmia, that will be a pretty kettle of fish." She greeted my mother from afar with slow and melancholy bows, a sign not of condolence but of the nature of her social training. We might never have lost my grandmother, or had any reason to be anything but happy. Living in comparative retirement at Combray within the walls of her large garden, she could never find anything soft enough to her liking, and subjected to a softening process the words and even the proper names of the French language. She felt " spoon " to be too hard a word to apply to the piece of silver which measured out her syrups, and said, in consequence, " spune "; she would have been afraid of hurting the feelings of the sweet singer of Télémaque by calling him bluntly Fénelon—as I myself said with a clear conscience, having had as a friend the dearest and cleverest of men, good and gallant, never to be forgotten by any that knew him, Bertrand de Fénelon—and never said anything but " Fénélon," feeling that the acute accent added a certain softness. The far from soft son-in-law of this Madame Poussin, whose name I have forgotten, having been a lawyer at Combray, ran off with the contents of the safe, and relieved my uncle among others of a considerable sum of money. But most of the people of Combray were on such friendly terms with the rest of the family that no coolness ensued and her neighbours said merely that they were sorry for Madame Poussin. She never entertained, but whenever people passed by her railings they would stop to admire the delicious shade of her trees, which was the only thing that could be made out. She gave us no trouble at Balbec, where I encountered her only once, at a moment when she was saying to a daughter who was biting her nails: "When they begin to fester, that will be a pretty kettle of fish."

While Mamma sat reading on the beach I remained in my room by myself. I recalled the last weeks of my grandmother's life, and everything connected with them, the outer door of the flat which had been propped open when I went out with her for the last time. In contrast to all this the rest of the world seemed scarcely real and my anguish poisoned everything in it. Finally my mother insisted upon my going out. But at every step, some forgotten view of the casino, of the street along which, as I waited until she was ready, that first evening, I had walked as far as the monument to Duguay-Trouin, prevented me, like a wind against which it is hopeless to struggle, from going farther; I lowered my eyes in order not to see. And after I had recovered my strength a little I turned back towards the hotel, the hotel in which I knew that it was henceforth impossible that, however long I might wait, I should find my grandmother, whom I had found there before, on the evening of our arrival. As it was the first time that I had gone out of doors, a number of servants whom I had not yet seen were gazing at me curiously. Upon the very threshold of the hotel a young page took off his cap to greet me and at once put it on again. I supposed that Aimé had, to borrow his own expression, " given him the office " to treat me with respect. But I saw a moment later that, as some one else entered the hotel, he doffed it again. The fact of the matter was that this young man had no other occupation in life than to take off and put on his cap, and did it to perfection. Having realised that he was incapable of doing anything else and that in this art he excelled, he practised it as often as was possible daily, which won him a discreet but widespread regard from the visitors, coupled with great regard from the hall porter upon whom devolved the duty of engaging the boys and who, until this rare bird alighted, had never succeeded in finding one who did not receive notice within a week, greatly to the astonishment of Aimé who used to say: " After all, in that job they've only got to be polite, which can't be so very difficult." The manager required in addition that they should have what he called a good " presence," meaning thereby that they should not be absent from their posts, or perhaps having heard the word " presence " used of personal appearance. The appearance of the lawn behind the hotel had been altered by the creation of several flower-beds and by the removal not only of an exotic shrub but of the page who, at the time of my former visit, used to provide an external decoration with the supple stem of his figure crowned by the curious colouring of his hair. He had gone with a Polish countess who had taken him as her secretary, following the example of his two elder brothers and their typist sister, torn from the hotel by persons of different race and sex who had been attracted by their charm. The only one remaining was the youngest, whom nobody wanted, because he squinted. He was highly delighted when the Polish countess or the protectors of the other two brothers came on a visit to the hotel at Balbec. For, albeit he was jealous of his brothers, he was fond of them and could in this way cultivate his family affections for a few weeks in the year. Was not the Abbess of Fontevrault accustomed, deserting her nuns for the occasion, to come and partake of the hospitality which Louis XIV offered to that other Mortemart, his mistress, Madame de Montespan? The boy was still in his first year at Balbec; he did not as yet know me, but having heard his comrades of longer standing supplement the word "Monsieur," when they addressed me, with my surname, he copied them from the first with an air of satisfaction, whether at shewing his familiarity with a person whom he supposed to be well-known, or at conforming with a custom of which five minutes earlier he had never heard but which he felt it to be indispensable that he should not fail to observe. I could quite well appreciate the charm that this great "Palace" might have for certain persons. It was arranged like a theatre, and a numerous cast filled it to the doors with animation. For all that the visitor was only a sort of spectator, he was perpetually taking part in the performance, and that not as in one of those theatres where the actors perform a play among the audience, but as though the life of the spectator were going on amid the sumptuous fittings of the stage. The lawn-tennis player might come in wearing a white flannel blazer, the porter would have put on a blue frock coat with silver braid before handing him his letters. If this lawn-tennis player did not choose to walk upstairs, he was equally involved with the actors in having by his side, to propel the lift, its attendant no less richly attired. The corridors on each landing engulfed a flying band of nymphlike chambermaids, fair visions against the sea, at whose modest chambers the admirers of feminine beauty arrived by cunning detours. Downstairs, it was the masculine element that predominated and made this hotel, in view of the extreme and effortless youth of the servants, a sort of Judaeo-Christian tragedy given bodily form and perpetually in performance. And so I could not help repeating to myself, when I saw them, not indeed the lines of Racine that had come into my head at the Princesse de Guermantes's while M. de Vaugoubert stood watching young secretaries of embassy greet M. de Charlus, but other lines of Racine, taken this time not from *Esther* but from *Athalie:* for in the doorway of the hall, what in the seventeenth century was called the portico, "a flourishing race" of young pages clustered, especially at tea-time, like the young Israelites of Racine's choruses. But I do not believe that one of them could have given even the vague answer that Joas finds to satisfy Athalie when she inquires of the infant Prince: "What is your office, then?" for they had none. At the most, if one had asked of any of them, like the new Queen: "But all this race, what do they then, imprisoned in this place?" he might have said: "I watch the solemn pomp and bear my part." Now and then one of the young supers would approach some more important personage, then this young beauty would rejoin the chorus, and, unless it were the moment for a spell of contemplative relaxation, they would proceed with their useless, reverent, decorative, daily evolutions. For, except on their "day off," "reared in seclusion from the world" and never crossing the threshold, they led the same ecclesiastical existence as the Levites in *Athalie,* and as I gazed at that "young and faithful troop" playing at the foot of the steps draped with sumptuous carpets, I felt inclined to ask myself whether I were entering the Grand Hotel at Balbec or the Temple of Solomon.

I went straight up to my room. My thoughts kept constantly turning to the last days of my grandmother's illness, to her sufferings which I lived over again, intensifying them with that element which is even harder to endure than the sufferings of other people, and is added to them by our merciless pity; when we think that we are merely reviving the pains of a beloved friend, our pity exaggerates them; but perhaps it is our pity that is in the right, more than the sufferers' own consciousness of their pains, they being blind to that tragedy of their own existence which pity sees and deplores. Certainly my pity would have taken fresh strength and far exceeded my grandmother's sufferings had I known then what I did not know until long afterwards, that my grandmother, on the eve of her death, in a moment of consciousness and after making sure that I was not in the room, had taken Mamma's hand, and, after pressing her fevered lips to it, had said: "Farewell, my child, farewell for ever." And this may perhaps have been the memory upon which my mother never ceased to gaze so fixedly. Then more pleasant memories returned to me. She was my grandmother and I was her grandson. Her facial expressions seemed written in a language intended for me alone; she was everything in my life, other people existed merely in relation to her, to the judgment that she would pass upon them; but no, our relations were too fleeting to have been anything but accidental. She no longer knew me, I should never see her again. We had not been created solely for one another, she was a stranger to me. This stranger was before my eyes at the moment in the photograph taken of her by Saint-Loup. Mamma, who had met Albertine, insisted upon my seeing her, because of the nice things that she had said about my grandmother and myself. I had accordingly made an appointment with her. I told the manager that she was coming, and asked him to let her wait for me in the drawing-room. He informed me that he had known her for years, her and her friends, long before they had attained "the age of purity" but that he was annoyed with them because of certain things that they had said about the hotel. "They can't be very 'gentlemanly' if they talk like that. Unless people have been slandering them." I had no difficulty in guessing that "purity" here meant "puberty." As I waited until it should be time to go down and meet Albertine, I was keeping my eyes fixed, as upon a picture which one ceases to see by dint of staring at it, upon the photograph that Saint-Loup had taken, when all of a sudden I thought once again: "It's grandmother, I am her grandson" as a man who has lost his memory remembers his name, as a sick man changes his personality. Françoise came in to tell me that Albertine was there, and, catching sight of the photograph: "Poor Madame, it's the very image of her, even the beauty spot on her cheek; that day the Marquis took her picture, she was very poorly, she had been taken bad twice. 'Whatever happens, Françoise,' she said, 'you must never let my grandson know.' And she kept it to herself, she was always bright with other people. When she was by herself, though, I used to find that she seemed to be in rather monotonous spirits now and then. But that soon passed away. And then she said to me, she said: 'If anything were to happen to me, he ought to have a picture of me to keep. And I have never had one done in my life.' So then she sent me along with a message to the Marquis, and he was never to let you know that it was she who had asked him, but could he take her photograph. But when I came back and told her that he would, she had changed her mind again, because she was looking so poorly. 'It would be even worse,' she said to me, 'than no picture at all.' But she was a clever one, she was, and in the end she got herself up so well in that big shady hat that it didn't shew at all when she was out of the sun. She was very glad to have that photograph, because at that time she didn't think she would ever leave Balbec alive.' It was no use my saying to her: 'Madame, it's wrong to talk like that, I don't like to hear Madame talk like that,' she had got it into her head. And, lord, there were plenty days when she couldn't eat a thing. That was why she used to make Monsieur go and dine away out in the country with M. le Marquis. Then, instead of going in to dinner, she would pretend to be reading a book, and as soon as the Marquis's carriage had started, up she would go to bed. Some days she wanted to send word to Madame, to come down and see her in time. And then she was afraid of alarming her, as she had said nothing to her about it. 'It will be better for her to stay with her husband, don't you see, Françoise.'" Looking me in the face, Françoise asked me all of a sudden if I was "feeling indisposed." I said that I was not; whereupon she: "And you make me waste my time talking to you. Your visitor has been here all this time. I must go down and tell her. She is not the sort of person to have here. Why, a fast one like that, she may be gone again by now. She doesn't like to be kept waiting. Oh, nowadays, Mademoiselle Albertine, she's somebody!" "You are quite wrong, she is a very respectable person, too respectable for this place. But go and tell her that I shan't be able to see her to-day."

What compassionate declamations I should have provoked from Françoise if she had seen me cry. I carefully hid myself from her. Otherwise I should have had her sympathy. But I gave her mine. We do not put ourselves sufficiently in the place of these poor maidservants who cannot bear to see us cry, as though crying were bad for us; or bad, perhaps, for them, for Françoise used to say to me when I was a child: "Don't cry like that, I don't like to see you crying like that." We dislike highfalutin language, asseverations, we are wrong, we close our hearts to the pathos of the countryside, to the legend which the poor servant girl, dismissed, unjustly perhaps, for theft, pale as death, grown suddenly more humble than if it were a crime merely to be accused, unfolds, invoking her father's honesty, her mother's principles, her grandam's counsels. It is true that those same servants who cannot bear our tears will have no hesitation in letting us catch pneumonia, because the maid downstairs likes draughts and it would not be polite to her to shut the windows. For it is necessary that even those who are right, like Françoise, should be wrong also, so that Justice may be made an impossible thing. Even the humble pleasures of servants provoke either the refusal or the ridicule of their masters. For it is always a mere nothing, but foolishly sentimental, unhygienic. And so, they are in a position to say: "How is it that I ask for only this one thing in the whole year, and am not allowed it." And yet the masters will allow them something far more difficult, which was not stupid and dangerous for the servants—or for themselves. To be sure, the humility of the wretched maid, trembling, ready to confess the crime that she has not committed, saying "I shall leave to-night if you wish it," is a thing that nobody can resist. But we must learn also not to remain unmoved, despite the solemn, menacing fatuity of the things that she says, her maternal heritage and the dignity of the family "kailyard," before an old cook draped in the honour of her life and of her ancestry, wielding her broom like a sceptre, donning the tragic buskin, stifling her speech with sobs, drawing herself up with majesty. That afternoon, I remembered or imagined scenes of this sort which I associated with our old servant, and from then onwards, in spite of all the harm that she might do to Albertine, I loved Françoise with an affection, intermittent it is true, but of the strongest kind, the kind that is founded upon pity.

To be sure, I suffered agonies all that day, as I sat gazing at my grandmother's photograph. It tortured me. Not so acutely, though, as the visit I received that evening from the manager. After I had spoken to him about my grandmother, and he had reiterated his condolences, I heard him say (for he enjoyed using the words that he pronounced wrongly): "Like the day when Madame your grandmother had that sincup, I wanted to tell you about it, because of the other visitors, don't you know, it might have given the place a bad name. She ought really to have left that evening. But she begged me to say nothing about it and promised me that she wouldn't have another sincup, or the first time she had one, she would go. The floor waiter reported to me that she had had another. But, lord, you were old friends that we try to please, and so long as nobody made any complaint." And so my grandmother had had syncopes which she had never mentioned to me. Perhaps at the very moment when I was being most beastly to her, when she was obliged, amid her pain, to see that she kept her temper, so as not to anger me, and her looks, so as not to be turned out of the hotel. " Sincup " was a word which, so pronounced, I should never have imagined, which might perhaps, applied to other people, have struck me as ridiculous, but which in its strange sonorous novelty, like that of an original discord, long retained the faculty of arousing in me the most painful sensations.

Next day I went, at Mamma's request, to lie down for a little on the sands, or rather among the dunes, where one is hidden by their folds, and I knew that Albertine and her friends would not be able to find me. My drooping eyelids allowed but one kind of light to pass, all rosy, the light of the inner walls of the eyes. Then they shut altogether. Whereupon my grandmother appeared to me, seated in an armchair. So feeble she was, she seemed to be less alive than other people. And yet I could hear her breathe; now and again she made a sign to shew that she had understood what we were saying, my father and I. But in vain might I take her in my arms, I failed utterly to kindle a spark of affection in her eyes, a flush of colour in her cheeks. Absent from herself, she appeared somehow not to love me, not to know me, perhaps not to see me. I could not interpret the secret of her indifference, of her dejection, of her silent resentment. I drew my father aside. "You can see, all the same," I said to him, "there's no doubt about it, she understands everything perfectly. It is a perfect imitation of life. If we could have your cousin here, who maintains that the dead don't live. Why, she's been dead for more than a year now, and she's still alive. But why won't she give me a kiss?" "Look, her poor head is drooping again." "But she wants to go, now, to the Champs-Elysées." "It's madness!" "You really think it can do her any harm, that she can die any further? It isn't possible that she no longer loves me. I keep on hugging her, won't she ever smile at me again?" "What can you expect, when people are dead they are dead."

A few days later I was able to look with pleasure at the photograph that Saint-Loup had taken of her; it did not revive the memory of what Françoise had told me, because that memory had never left me and I was growing used to it. But with regard to the idea that I had received of the state of her health—so grave, so painful—on that day, the photograph, still profiting by the ruses that my grandmother had adopted, which succeeded in taking me in even after they had been disclosed to me, shewed me her so smart, so care-free, beneath the hat which partly hid her face, that I saw her looking less unhappy and in better health than I had imagined. And yet, her cheeks having unconsciously assumed an expression of their own, livid, haggard, like the expression of an animal that feels that it has been marked down for slaughter, my grandmother had an air of being under sentence of death, an air involuntarily sombre, unconsciously tragic, which passed unperceived by me but prevented Mamma from ever looking at that photograph, that photograph which seemed to her a photograph not so much of her mother as of her mother's disease, of an insult that the disease was offering to the brutally buffeted face of my grandmother.

Then one day I decided to send word to Albertine that I would see her presently. This was because, on a morning of intense and premature heat, the myriad cries of children at play, of bathers disporting themselves, of newsvendors, had traced for me in lines of fire, in wheeling, interlacing flashes, the scorching beach which the little waves came up one after another to sprinkle with their coolness; then had begun the symphonic concert mingled with the splashing of the water, through which the violins hummed like a swarm of bees that had strayed out over the sea. At once I had longed to hear again Albertine's laughter, to see her friends, those girls outlined against the waves who had remained in my memory the inseparable charm, the typical flora of Balbec; and I had determined to send a line by Françoise to Albertine, making an appointment for the following week, while, gently rising, the sea as each wave uncurled completely buried in layers of crystal the melody whose phrases appeared to be separated from one another like those angel lutanists which on the roof of the Italian cathedral rise between the peaks of blue porphyry and foaming jasper. But on the day on which Albertine came, the weather had turned dull and cold again, and moreover I had no opportunity of hearing her laugh; she was in a very bad temper. "Balbec is deadly dull this year," she said to me. "I don't mean to stay any longer than I can help. You know I've been here since Easter, that's more than a month. There's not a soul here. You can imagine what fun it is." Notwithstanding the recent rain and a sky that changed every moment, after escorting Albertine as far as Epreville, for she was, to borrow her expression, "on the run" between that little watering-place, where Mme. Bontemps had her villa, and Parville, where she had been taken "en pension" by Rosemonde's family, I went off by myself in the direction of the highroad that Mme. de Villeparisis's carriage had taken when we went for a drive with my grandmother; pools of water which the sun, now bright again, had not dried made a regular quagmire of the ground, and I thought of my grandmother who, in the old days, could not walk a yard without covering herself in mud. But on reaching the road I found a dazzling spectacle. Where I had seen with my grandmother in the month of August only the green leaves and, so to speak, the disposition of the apple-trees, as far as the eye could reach they were in full bloom, marvellous in their splendour, their feet in the mire beneath their ball-dresses, taking no precaution not to spoil the most marvellous pink satin that was ever seen, which glittered in the sunlight; the distant horizon of the sea gave the trees the background of a Japanese print; if I raised my head to gaze at the sky through the blossom, which made its serene blue appear almost violent, the trees seemed to be drawing apart to reveal the immensity of their paradise. Beneath that azure a faint but cold breeze set the blushing bouquets gently trembling. Blue tits came and perched upon the branches and fluttered among the flowers, indulgent, as though it had been an amateur of exotic art and colours who had artificially created this living beauty. But it moved one to tears because, to whatever lengths the artist went in the refinement of his creation, one felt that it was natural, that these apple-trees were there in the heart of the country, like peasants, upon one of the highroads of France. Then the rays of the sun gave place suddenly to those of the rain; they streaked the whole horizon, caught the line of apple-trees in their grey net. But these continued to hold aloft their beauty, pink and blooming, in the wind that had turned icy beneath the drenching rain: it was a day in spring.

CHAPTER II

IN my fear lest the pleasure I found in this solitary excursion might weaken my memory of my grandmother, I sought to revive this by thinking of some great mental suffering that she had undergone; in response to my appeal that suffering tried to build itself in my heart, threw up vast pillars there; but my heart was doubtless too small for it, I had not the strength to bear so great a grief, my attention was distracted at the moment when it was approaching completion, and its arches collapsed before joining as, before they have perfected their curve, the waves of the sea totter and break.

And yet, if only from my dreams when I was asleep, I might have learned that my grief for my grandmother's death was diminishing, for she appeared in them less crushed by the idea that I had formed of her non-existence. I saw her an invalid still, but on the road to recovery, I found her in better health. And if she made any allusion to what she had suffered, I stopped her mouth with my kisses and assured her that she was now permanently cured. I should have liked to call the sceptics to witness that death is indeed a malady from which one recovers. Only, I no longer found in my grandmother the rich spontaneity of old times. Her words were no more than a feeble, docile response, almost a mere echo of mine; she was nothing more than the reflexion of my own thoughts.

Incapable as I still was of feeling any fresh physical desire, Albertine was beginning nevertheless to inspire in me a desire for happiness. Certain dreams of shared affection, always floating on the surface of our minds, ally themselves readily by a sort of affinity with the memory (provided that this has already become slightly vague) of a woman with whom we have taken our pleasure. This sentiment recalled to me aspects of Albertine's face, more gentle, less gay, quite different from those that would have been evoked by physical desire; and as it was also less pressing than that desire I would gladly have postponed its realisation until the following winter, without seeking to see Albertine again at Balbec, before her departure. But even in the midst of a grief that is still keen physical desire will revive. From my bed, where I was made to spend hours every day resting, I longed for Albertine to come and resume our former amusements. Do we not see, in the very room in which they have lost a child, its parents soon come together again to give the little angel a baby brother? I tried to distract my mind from this desire by going to the window to look at that day's sea. As in the former year, the seas, from one day to another, were rarely the same. Nor, however, did they at all resemble those of that first year, whether because we were now in spring with its storms, or because even if I had come down at the same time as before, the different, more changeable weather might have discouraged from visiting this coast certain seas, indolent, vaporous and fragile, which I had seen throughout long, scorching days, asleep upon the beach, their bluish bosoms, only, faintly stirring, with a soft palpitation, or, as was most probable, because my eyes, taught by Elstir to retain precisely those elements that before I had deliberately rejected, would now gaze for hours at what in the former year they had been incapable of seeing. The contrast that used then to strike me so forcibly between the country drives that I took with Mme. de Villeparisis and this proximity, fluid, inaccessible, mythological, of the eternal Ocean, no longer existed for me. And there were days now when, on the contrary, the sea itself seemed almost rural. On the days, few and far between, of really fine weather, the heat had traced upon the waters, as it might be across country, a dusty white track, at the end of which the pointed mast of a fishing-boat stood up like a village steeple. A tug, of which one could see only the funnel, was smoking in the distance like a factory amid the fields, while alone against the horizon a convex patch of white, sketched there doubt-less by a sail but apparently a solid plastered surface, made one think of the sunlit wall of some isolated build-ing, an hospital or a school. And the clouds and the wind, on days when these were added to the sun, com-pleted if not the error of judgment, at any rate the illu-sion of the first glance, the suggestion that it aroused in the imagination. For the alternation of sharply defined patches of colour like those produced in the country by the proximity of different crops, the rough, yellow, almost muddy irregularities of the marine surface, the banks, the slopes that hid from sight a vessel upon which a crew of nimble sailors seemed to be reaping a harvest, all this upon stormy days made the ocean a thing as varied, as solid, as broken, as populous, as civilised as the earth with its carriage roads over which I used to travel, and was soon to be travelling again. And once, unable any longer to hold out against my desire, instead of going back to bed I put on my clothes and started off to Incarville, to find Albertine. I would ask her to come with me to Douville, where I would pay calls at Féterne upon Mme. de Cambremer and at la Raspelière upon Mme. Verdurin. Albertine would wait for me meanwhile upon the beach and we would return together after dark. I went to take the train on the local light railway, of which I had picked up, the time before, from Albertine and her friends all the nicknames current in the district, where it was known as the *Twister* because of its numberless windings, the *Crawler* because the train never seemed to move, the *Transatlantic* because of a horrible siren which it sounded to clear people off the line, the *Decauville* and the *Funi*, albeit there was nothing funicular about it but because it climbed the cliff, and, although not, strictly speaking, a Decauville, had a 60 centimetre gauge, the *B. A. G.* because it ran between Balbec and Grattevast *via* Angerville, the *Tram* and the *T. S. N.* because it was a branch of the Tramways of Southern Normandy. I took my seat in a compartment in which I was alone; it was a day of glorious sunshine, and stiflingly hot; I drew down the blue blind which shut off all but a single ray of sunlight. But immediately I beheld my grandmother, as she had appeared sitting in the train, on our leaving Paris for Balbec, when, in her sorrow at seeing me drink beer, she had preferred not to look, to shut her eyes and pretend to be asleep. I, who in my childhood had been unable to endure her anguish when my grandfather tasted brandy, I had inflicted this anguish upon her, not merely of seeing me accept, at the invitation of another, a drink which she regarded as bad for me, I had forced her to leave me free to swill it down to my heart's content, worse still, by my bursts of passion, my choking fits, I had forced her to help, to advise me to do so, with a supreme resignation of which I saw now in my memory the mute, despairing image, her eyes closed to shut out the sight. So vivid a memory had, like the stroke of a magic wand, restored the mood that I had been gradually outgrowing for some time past; what had I to do with Rosemonde when my lips were wholly possessed by the desperate longing to kiss a dead woman, what had I to say to the Cambremers and Verdurins when my heart was beating so violently because at every moment there was being renewed in it the pain that my grandmother had suffered. I could not remain in the compartment. As soon as the train stopped at Maineville-la-Teinturière, abandoning all my plans, I alighted. Maineville had of late acquired considerable importance and a reputation all its own, because a director of various casinos, a caterer in pleasure, had set up, just outside it, with a luxurious display of bad taste that could vie with that of any smart hotel, an establishment to which we shall return anon, and which was, to put it briefly, the first brothel for "exclusive" people that it had occurred to anyone to build upon the coast of France. It was the only one. True, every port has its own, but intended for sailors only, and for lovers of the picturesque whom it amuses to see, next door to the primeval parish church, the bawd, hardly less ancient, venerable and moss-grown, standing outside her ill-famed door, waiting for the return of the fishing fleet.

Hurrying past the glittering house of "pleasure," insolently erected there despite the protests which the heads of families had addressed in vain to the mayor, I reached the cliff and followed its winding paths in the direction of

Balbec. I heard, without responding to it, the appeal of the hawthorns. Neighbours, in humbler circumstances, of the blossoming apple trees, they found them very coarse, without denying the fresh complexion of the rosy-petalled daughters of those wealthy brewers of cider. They knew that, with a lesser dowry, they were more sought after, and were attractive enough by themselves in their tattered whiteness.

On my return, the hotel porter handed me a black-bordered letter in which the Marquis and the Marquise de Gonneville, the Vicomte and the Vicomtesse d'Amfreville, the Comte and the Comtesse de Berneville, the Marquis and the Marquise de Graincourt, the Comte d'Amenoncourt, the Comtesse de Maineville, the Comte and the Comtesse de Franquetot, the Comtesse de Chaverny *née* d'Aigleville, begged to announce, and from which I understood at length why it had been sent to me when I caught sight of the names of the Marquise de Cambremer *née* du Mesnil la Guichard, the Marquis and the Marquise de Cambremer, and saw that the deceased, a cousin of the Cambremers, was named Éléonore-Euphrasie-Humbertine de Cambremer, Comtesse de Criquetot. In the whole extent of this provincial family, the enumeration of which filled the closely printed lines, not a single commoner, and on the other hand not a single title that one knew, but the entire muster-roll of the nobles of the region who made their names—those of all the interesting spots in the neighbourhood—ring out their joyous endings in *ville*, in *court*, sometimes on a duller note (in *tot*). Garbed in the roof-tiles of their castle or in the roughcast of their parish church, their nodding heads barely reaching above the vault of the nave or banqueting hall, and then only to cap themselves with the Norman lantern or the dovecot of the pepperpot turret, they gave the impression of having sounded the rallying call to all the charming villages straggling or scattered over a radius of fifty leagues, and to have paraded them in massed formation, without one absentee, one intruder, on the compact, rectangular chess-board of the aristocratic letter edged with black.

My mother had gone upstairs to her room, meditating the phrase of Madame de Sévigné: "I see nothing of the people who seek to distract me from you; the truth of the matter is that they are seeking to prevent me from thinking of you, and that annoys me."—because the chief magistrate had told her that she ought to find some distraction. To me he whispered: "That's the Princesse de Parme!" My fears were dispelled when I saw that the woman whom the magistrate pointed out to me bore not the slightest resemblance to Her Royal Highness. But as she had engaged a room in which to spend the night after paying a visit to Mme. de Luxembourg, the report of her coming had the effect upon many people of making them take each newcomer for the Princesse de Parme—and upon me of making me go and shut myself up in my attic.

I had no wish to remain there by myself. It was barely four o'clock. I asked Françoise to go and find Albertine, so that she might spend the rest of the afternoon with me.

It would be untrue, I think, to say that there were already symptoms of that painful and perpetual mistrust which Albertine was to inspire in me, not to mention the special character, emphatically Gomorrhan, which that mistrust was to assume. Certainly, even that afternoon

—but this was not the first time—I grew anxious as I was kept waiting. Françoise, once she had started, stayed away so long that I began to despair. I had not lighted the lamp. The daylight had almost gone. The wind was making the flag over the Casino flap. And, fainter still in the silence of the beach over which the tide was rising, and like a voice rendering and enhancing the troubling emptiness of this restless, unnatural hour, a little barrel organ that had stopped outside the hotel was playing Viennese waltzes. At length Françoise arrived, but unaccompanied. "I have been as quick as I could but she wouldn't come because she didn't think she was looking smart enough. If she was five minutes painting herself and powdering herself, she was an hour by the clock. You'll be having a regular scentshop in here. She's coming, she stayed behind to tidy herself at the glass. I thought I should find her here." There was still a long time to wait before Albertine appeared. But the gaiety, the charm that she shewed on this occasion dispelled my sorrow. She informed me (in contradiction of what she had said the other day) that she would be staying for the whole season and asked me whether we could not arrange, as in the former year, to meet daily. I told her that at the moment I was too melancholy and that I would rather send for her from time to time at the last moment, as I did in Paris. "If ever you're feeling worried, or feel that you want me, do not hesitate," she told me, "to send for me, I shall come immediately, and if you are not afraid of its creating a scandal in the hotel, I shall stay as long as you like." Françoise, in bringing her to me, had assumed the joyous air she wore whenever she had gone out of her way to please me and had been successful. But Albertine herself contributed nothing to her joy, and the very next day Françoise was to greet me with the profound observation: "Monsieur ought not to see that young lady. I know quite well the sort she is, she'll land you in trouble." As I escorted Albertine to the door I saw in the lighted dining-room the Princesse de Parme. I merely gave her a glance, taking care not to be seen. But I must say that I found a certain grandeur in the royal politeness which had made me smile at the Guermantes'. It is a fundamental rule that sovereign princes are at home wherever they are, and this rule is conventionally expressed in obsolete and useless customs such as that which requires the host to carry his hat in his hand, in his own house, to shew that he is not in his own home but in the Prince's. Now the Princesse de Parme may not have formulated this idea to herself, but she was so imbued with it that all her actions, spontaneously invented to suit the circumstances, pointed to it. When she rose from table she handed a lavish tip to Aimé, as though he had been there solely for her and she were rewarding, before leaving a country house, a footman who had been detailed to wait upon her. Nor did she stop at the tip, but with a gracious smile bestowed on him a few friendly, flattering words, with a store of which her mother had provided her. Another moment, and she would have told him that, just as the hotel was perfectly managed, so Normandy was a garden of roses and that she preferred France to any other country in the world. Another coin slipped from the Princess's fingers, for the wine waiter, for whom she had sent and to whom she made a point of expressing her satisfaction like a general after an inspection. The lift-boy had come up at that moment with a message for her; he too received a little speech, a smile and a tip, all this interspersed with encouraging and humble words intended to prove to them that she was only one of themselves. As Aimé, the wine waiter, the lift-boy and the rest felt that it would be impolite not to grin from ear to ear at a person who smiled at them, she was presently surrounded by a cluster of servants with whom she chatted kindly; such ways being unfamiliar in smart hotels, the people who passed by, not knowing who she was, thought they beheld a permanent resident at Balbec, who, because of her humble origin, or for professional reasons (she was perhaps the wife of an agent for champagne) was less different from the domestics than the really smart visitors. As for me, I thought of the palace at Parma, of the counsels, partly religious, partly political, given to this Princess, who behaved towards the lower orders as though she had been obliged to conciliate them in order to reign over them one day. Or indeed, as though she were already reigning.

I went upstairs again to my room, but I was not alone there. I could hear some one softly playing Schumann. No doubt it happens at times that people, even those whom we love best, become saturated with the melancholy or irritation that emanates from us. There is nevertheless an inanimate object which is capable of a power of exasperation to which no human being will ever attain: to wit, a piano.

Albertine had made me take a note of the dates on which she would be going away for a few days to visit various girl friends, and had made me write down their addresses as well, in case I should want her on one of those evenings, for none of them lived very far away.

This meant that when I tried to find her, going from one girl to another, she became more and more entwined in ropes of flowers. I must confess that many of her friends —I was not yet in love with her—gave me, at one watering-place or another, moments of pleasure. These obliging young comrades did not seem to me to be very many. But recently I have thought it over, their names have recurred to me. I counted that, in that one season, a dozen conferred on me their ephemeral favours. A name came back to me later, which made thirteen. I then, with almost a child's delight in cruelty, dwelt upon that number. Alas, I realised that I had forgotten the first of them all, Albertine who no longer existed and who made the fourteenth.

I had, to resume the thread of my narrative, written down the names and addresses of the girls with whom I should find her upon the days when she was not to be at Incarville, but privately had decided that I would devote those days rather to calling upon Mme. Verdurin. In any case, our desire for different women varies in intensity. One evening we cannot bear to let one out of our sight who, after that, for the next month or two, will never enter our mind. Then there is the law of change, for a study of which this is not the place, under which, after an over-exertion of the flesh, the woman whose image haunts our momentary senility is one to whom we would barely give more than a kiss on the brow. As for Albertine, I saw her seldom, and only upon the very infrequent evenings when I felt that I could not live without her. If this desire seized me when she was too far from Balbec for Françoise to be able to go and fetch her, I used to send the lift-boy to Epreville, to La Sogne, to

Saint-Frichoux, asking him to finish his work a little earlier than usual. He would come into my room, but would leave the door open for, albeit he was conscientious at his " job " which was pretty hard, consisting in endless cleanings from five o'clock in the morning, he could never bring himself to make the effort to shut a door, and, if one were to remark to him that it was open, would turn back and, summoning up all his strength, give it a gentle push. With the democratic pride that marked him, a pride to which, in more liberal careers, the members of a profession that is at all numerous never attain, barristers, doctors and men of letters speaking simply of a " brother " barrister, doctor or man of letters, he, employing, and rightly, a term that is confined to close corporations like the Academy, would say to me in speaking of a page who was in charge of the lift upon alternate days: " I shall get my *colleague* to take my place." This pride did not prevent him from accepting, with a view to increasing what he called his " salary," remuneration for his errands, a fact which had made Françoise take a dislike to him: " Yes, the first time you see him you would give him the sacrament without confession, but there are days when his tongue is as smooth as a prison door. It's your money he's after." This was the category in which she had so often included Eulalie, and in which, alas (when I think of all the trouble that was one day to come of it), she already placed Albertine, because she saw me often asking Mamma, on behalf of my impecunious friend, for trinkets and other little presents, which Françoise held to be inexcusable because Mme. Bontemps had only a general servant. A moment later the lift-boy, having removed what I should have called his livery and he called

266

his tunic, appeared wearing a straw hat, carrying a cane, holding himself stiffly erect, for his mother had warned him never to adopt the "working-class" or "pageboy" style. Just as, thanks to books, all knowledge is open to a working man, who ceases to be such when he has finished his work, so, thanks to a "boater" hat and a pair of gloves, elegance became accessible to the lift-boy who, having ceased for the evening to take the visitors upstairs, imagined himself, like a young surgeon who has taken off his overall, or Serjeant Saint-Loup out of uniform, a typical young man about town. He was not for that matter lacking in ambition, or in talent either in manipulating his machine and not bringing you to a standstill between two floors. But his vocabulary was defective. I credited him with ambition because he said in speaking of the porter, under whom he served: "My porter," in the same tone in which a man who owned what the page would have called a "private mansion" in Paris would have referred to his footman. As for the lift-boy's vocabulary. it is curious that anybody who heard people, fifty times a day, calling for the "lift," should never himself call it anything but a "left." There were certain things about this boy that were extremely annoying: whatever I might be saying to him he would interrupt with a phrase: "I should say so!" or "I say!" which seemed either to imply that my remark was so obvious that anybody would have thought of it, or else to take all the credit for it to himself, as though it were he that was drawing my attention to the subject. "I should say so!" or "I say!" exclaimed with the utmost emphasis, issued from his lips every other minute, over matters to which he had never given a thought, a trick which irritated me so much that I immediately began to say the opposite to shew him that he knew nothing about it. But to my second assertion, albeit it was incompatible with the first, he replied none the less stoutly: "I should say so!" "I say!" as though these words were inevitable. I found it difficult, also, to forgive him the trick of employing certain terms proper to his calling, which would therefore have sounded perfectly correct in their literal sense, in a figurative sense only, which gave them an air of feeble witticism, for instance the verb to pedal. He never used it when he had gone anywhere on his bicycle. But if, on foot, he had hurried to arrive somewhere in time, then, to indicate that he had walked fast, he would exclaim: "I should say I didn't half pedal!" The lift-boy was on the small side, clumsily built and by no means good looking. This did not prevent him, whenever one spoke to him of some tall, slim, handsome young man, from saying: "Oh, yes, I know, a fellow who is just my height." And one day when I was expecting him to bring me the answer to a message, hearing somebody come upstairs, I had in my impatience opened the door of my room and caught sight of a page as beautiful as Endymion, with incredibly perfect features, who was bringing a message to a lady whom I did not know. When the lift-boy returned, in telling him how impatiently I had waited for the answer, I mentioned to him that I had thought I heard him come upstairs but that it had turned out to be a page from the Hôtel de Normandie. "Oh, yes, I know," he said, "they have only the one, a boy about my build. He's so like me in face, too, that we're always being mistaken; anybody would think he was my brother." Lastly, he always wanted to appear to have understood you perfectly from the first second, which meant that as soon as you asked him to do anything he would say: " Yes, yes, yes, yes, I understand all that," with a precision and a tone of intelligence which for some time deceived me; but other people, as we get to know them, are like a metal dipped in an acid bath, and we see them gradually lose their good qualities (and their bad qualities too, at times). Before giving him my instructions, I saw that he had left the door open; I pointed this out to him, I was afraid that people might hear us; he acceded to my request and returned, having reduced the gap. " Anything to oblige. But there's nobody on this floor except us two." Immediately I heard one, then a second, then a third person go by. This annoyed me partly because of the risk of my being overheard, but more still because I could see that it did not in the least surprise him and was a perfectly normal occurrence. " Yes, that'll be the maid next door going for her things. Oh, that's of no importance, it's the bottler putting away his keys. No, no, it's nothing, you can say what you want, it's my colleague just going on duty." Then, as the reasons that all these people had for passing did not diminish my dislike of the thought that they might overhear me, at a formal order from me he went, not to shut the door, which was beyond the strength of this bicyclist who longed for a " motor," but to push it a little closer to. " Now we shall be quite quiet." So quiet were we that an American lady burst in and withdrew with apologies for having mistaken the number of her room. " You are going to bring this young lady back with you," I told him, after first going and banging the door with all my might (which brought in another page to see whether a window had been left

open). "You remember the name: Mlle. Albertine Si-
monet. Anyhow, it's on the envelope. You need only
say to her that it's from me. She will be delighted to
come," I added, to encourage him and preserve a scrap
of my own self-esteem. "I should say so!" "Not at
all, there is not the slightest reason to suppose that she
will be glad to come. It's a great nuisance getting here
from Berneville." "I understand!" "You will tell her
to come with you." "Yes, yes, yes, yes, I understand
perfectly," he replied, in that sharp, precise tone which
had long ceased to make a "good impression" upon me
because I knew that it was almost mechanical and covered with its apparent clearness plenty of uncertainty and
stupidity. "When will you be back?" "Haven't any
too much time," said the lift-boy, who, carrying to ex-
tremes the grammatical rule that forbids the repetition of
personal pronouns before coordinate verbs, omitted the
pronoun altogether. "Can go there all right. Leave
was stopped this afternoon, because there was a dinner
for twenty at luncheon. And it was my turn off duty
to-day. So it's all right if I go out a bit this evening.
Take my bike with me. Get there in no time." And an
hour later he reappeared and said: "Monsieur's had to
wait, but the young lady's come with me. She's down
below." "Oh, thanks very much; the porter won't be
cross with me?" "Monsieur Paul? Doesn't even know
where I've been. The head of the door himself can't say
a word." But once, after I had told him: "You absolutely must bring her back with you," he reported to me
with a smile: "You know, I couldn't find her. She's not
there. Couldn't wait any longer; was afraid of getting
it like my colleague who was 'missed from the hotel'"

(for the lift-boy, who used the word "rejoin" of a profession which one joined for the first time, "I should like to rejoin the post-office," to make up for this, or to mitigate the calamity, were his own career at stake, or to insinuate it more delicately and treacherously were the victim some one else, elided the prefix and said: "I know he's been 'missed"). It was not with any evil intent that he smiled, but from sheer timidity. He thought that he was diminishing the magnitude of his crime by making a joke of it. In the same way, if he had said to me: "*You know*, I couldn't find her," this did not mean that he really thought that I knew it already. On the contrary, he was all too certain that I did not know it, and, what was more, was afraid to tell me. And so he said "you know" to ward off the terror which menaced him as he uttered the words that were to bring me the knowledge. We ought never to lose our tempers with people who, when we find fault with them, begin to titter. They do so not because they are laughing at us, but because they are trembling lest we should be angry. Let us shew all pity and tenderness to those who laugh. For all the world like a stroke, the lift-boy's anxiety had wrought in him not merely an apoplectic flush but an alteration in his speech which had suddenly become familiar. He wound up by telling me that Albertine was not at Epreville, that she would not be coming back there before nine o'clock, and that if betimes (which meant, by chance) she came back earlier, my message would be given her, and in any case she would be with me before one o'clock in the morning.[1]

[1] In the French text of *Sodome et Gomorrhe,* Volume I ends at this point.

It was not this evening, however, that my cruel mistrust began to take solid form. No, to make no mystery about it, although the incident did not occur until some weeks later, it arose out of a remark made by Cottard. Albertine and her friends had insisted that day upon dragging me to the casino at Incarville where, as luck would have it, I should not have joined them (having intended to go and see Mme. Verdurin who had invited me again and again), had I not been held up at Incarville itself by a breakdown of the tram which it would take a considerable time to repair. As I strolled up and down waiting for the men to finish working at it, I found myself all of a sudden face to face with Doctor Cottard, who had come to Incarville to see a patient. I almost hesitated to greet him as he had not answered any of my letters. But friendship does not express itself in the same way in different people. Not having been brought up to observe the same fixed rules of behaviour as well-bred people, Cottard was full of good intentions of which one knew nothing, even denying their existence, until the day when he had an opportunity of displaying them. He apologised, had indeed received my letters, had reported my whereabouts to the Verdurins who were most anxious to see me and whom he urged me to go and see. He even proposed to take me to them there and then, for he was waiting for the little local train to take him back there for dinner. As I hesitated and as he had still some time before his train (for there was bound to be still a considerable delay), I made him come with me to the little casino, one of those that had struck me as being so gloomy on the evening of my first arrival, now filled with the tumult of the girls, who, in the absence

ANDRÉE DANCING WITH ALBERTINE

ANDRÉE DANCING WITH ALBERTINE

of male partners, were dancing together. Andrée came sliding along the floor towards me; I was meaning to go off with Cottard in a moment to the Verdurins', when I definitely declined his offer, seized by an irresistable desire to stay with Albertine. The fact was, I had just heard her laugh. And her laugh at once suggested the rosy flesh, the fragrant portals between which it had just made its way, seeming also, as strong, sensual and revealing as the scent of geraniums, to carry with it some microscopic particles of their substance, irritant and secret.

One of the girls, a stranger to me, sat down at the piano, and Andrée invited Albertine to waltz with her. Happy in the thought that I was going to remain in this little casino with these girls, I remarked to Cottard how well they danced together. But he, taking the professional point of view of a doctor and with an ill-breeding which overlooked the fact that they were my friends, although he must have seen me shaking hands with them, replied: "Yes, but parents are very rash to allow their daughters to form such habits. I should certainly never let mine come here. Are they nice-looking, though? I can't see their faces. There now, look," he went on, pointing to Albertine and Andrée who were waltzing slowly, tightly clasped together, "I have left my glasses behind and I don't see very well, but they are certainly keenly roused. It is not sufficiently known that women derive most excitement from their breasts. And theirs' as you see, are completely touching." And indeed the contact had been unbroken between the breasts of Andrée and of Albertine. I do not know whether they heard or guessed Cottard's observation, but they gently broke the contact while continuing to waltz. At that moment Andrée said something to Albertine, who laughed, the same deep and penetrating laugh that I had heard before. But all that it wafted to me this time was a feeling of pain; Albertine appeared to be revealing by it, to be making Andrée share some exquisite, secret thrill. It rang out like the first or the last strains of a ball to which one has not been invited. I left the place with Cottard, distracted by his conversation, thinking only at odd moments of the scene I had just witnessed. This does not mean that Cottard's conversation was interesting. It had indeed, at that moment, become bitter, for we had just seen Doctor du Boulbon go past without noticing us. He had come down to spend some time on the other side of Balbec bay, where he was greatly in demand. Now, albeit Cottard was in the habit of declaring that he did no professional work during the holidays, he had hoped to build up a select practice along the coast, a hope which du Boulbon's presence there doomed to disappointment. Certainly, the Balbec doctor could not stand in Cottard's way. He was merely a thoroughly conscientious doctor who knew everything, and to whom you could not mention the slightest irritation of the skin without his immediately prescribing, in a complicated formula, the ointment, lotion or liniment that would put you right. As Marie Gineste used to say, in her charming speech, he knew how to " charm " cuts and sores. But he was in no way eminent. He had indeed caused Cottard some slight annoyance. The latter, now that he was anxious to exchange his Chair for that of Therapeutics, had begun to specialise in toxic actions. These, a perilous innovation in medicine, give an excuse for changing the labels in the chemists' shops, where every preparation is declared to be in no way toxic, unlike its substitutes, and indeed to be disintoxicant. It is the fashionable cry; at the most there may survive below in illegible lettering, like the faint trace of an older fashion, the assurance that the preparation has been carefully disinfected. Toxic actions serve also to reassure the patient, who learns with joy that his paralysis is merely a toxic disturbance. Now, a Grand Duke who had come for a few days to Balbec and whose eye was extremely swollen had sent for Cottard who, in return for a wad of hundred-franc notes (the Professor refused to see anyone for less), had put down the inflammation to a toxic condition and prescribed a disintoxicant treatment. As the swelling did not go down, the Grand Duke fell back upon the general practitioner of Balbec, who in five minutes had removed a speck of dust. The following day, the swelling had gone. A celebrated specialist in nervous diseases was, however, a more dangerous rival. He was a rubicund, jovial person, since, for one thing, the constant society of nervous wrecks did not prevent him from enjoying excellent health, but also so as to reassure his patients by the hearty merriment of his " Good morning " and " Good-bye," while quite ready to lend the strength of his muscular arms to fastening them in strait-waistcoats later on. Nevertheless, whenever you spoke to him at a party, whether of politics or of literature, he would listen to you with a kindly attention, as though he were saying: "What is it all about? " without at once giving an opinion, as though it were a matter for consultation. But anyhow he, whatever his talent might be, was a specialist. And so the whole of Cottard's rage was heaped upon du Boulbon. But I soon bade good-bye to the Verdurins' professional friend, and returned to Balbec, after promising him that I would pay them a visit before long.

The mischief that his remarks about Albertine and Andrée had done me was extreme, but its worst effects were not immediately felt by me, as happens with those forms of poisoning which begin to act only after a certain time.

Albertine, on the night after the lift-boy had gone in search of her, did not appear, notwithstanding his assurances. Certainly, personal charm is a less frequent cause of love than a speech such as: "No, this evening I shall not be free." We barely notice this speech if we are with friends; we are gay all the evening, a certain image never enters our mind; during those hours it remains dipped in the necessary solution; when we return home we find the plate developed and perfectly clear. We become aware that life is no longer the life which we would have surrendered for a trifle the day before, because, even if we continue not to fear death, we no longer dare think of a parting.

From, however, not one o'clock in the morning (the limit fixed by the lift-boy), but three o'clock, I no longer felt as in former times the anguish of seeing the chance of her coming diminish. The certainty that she would not now come brought me a complete, refreshing calm; this night was simply a night like all the rest during which I did not see her, such was the idea from which I started. After which, the thought that I should see her in the morning, or some other day, outlining itself upon the blank which I submissively accepted, became pleasant. Sometimes, during these nights of waiting, our anguish is due to a drug which we have taken. The sufferer, misinterpreting his own symptoms, thinks that he is anxious about the woman who fails to appear. Love is engendered in these cases, as are certain nervous maladies, by the inaccurate explanation of a state of discomfort. An explanation which it is useless to correct, at any rate so far as love is concerned, a sentiment which (whatever its cause) is invariably in error.

Next day, when Albertine wrote to me that she had only just got back to Epreville, and so had not received my note in time, and was coming, if she might, to see me that evening, behind the words of her letter, as behind those that she had said to me once over the telephone, I thought I could detect the presence of pleasures, of people whom she had preferred to me. Once again, I was stirred from head to foot by the painful longing to know what she could have been doing, by the latent love which we always carry within us; I almost thought for a moment that it was going to attach me to Albertine, but it confined itself to a stationary throbbing, the last echo of which died away without the machine's having been set in motion.

I had failed during my first visit to Balbec—and perhaps, for that matter, Andrée had failed equally—to understand Albertine's character. I had put it down as frivolous, but had not known whether our combined supplications might not succeed in keeping her with us and making her forego a garden-party, a donkey ride, a picnic. During my second visit to Balbec, I began to suspect that this frivolity was only for show, the garden-party a mere screen, if not an invention. She shewed herself in various

colours in the following incident (by which I mean the
incident as seen by me, from my side of the glass which
was by no means transparent, and without my having
any means of determining what reality there was on the
other side). Albertine was making me the most passionate protestations of affection. She looked at the time
because she had to go and call upon a lady who was at
home, it appeared, every afternoon at five o'clock, at
Infreville. Tormented by suspicion, and feeling at the
same time far from well, I asked Albertine, I implored
her to remain with me. It was impossible (and indeed
she could wait only five minutes longer) because it would
annoy the lady who was far from hospitable, highly sus-
ceptible and, said Albertine, a perfect nuisance. "But
one can easily cut a call." "No, my aunt has always told
me that the chief thing is politeness." "But I have so
often seen you being impolite." "It's not the same
thing, the lady would be angry with me and would say
nasty things about me to my aunt. I'm pretty well in
her bad books already. She expects me to go and see
her." "But if she's at home every day?" Here Albertine, feeling that she was caught, changed her line of
argument. "So she is at home every day. But to-day
I've made arrangements to meet some other girls there.
It will be less boring that way." "So then, Albertine,
you prefer this lady and your friends to me, since, rather
than miss paying an admittedly boring call, you prefer
to leave me here alone, sick and wretched?" "I don't
care if it is boring. I'm going for their sake. I shall
bring them home in my trap. Otherwise they won't have
any way of getting back." I pointed out to Albertine
that there were trains from Infreville up to ten o'clock at

night. "Quite true, but don't you see, it is possible that
we may be asked to stay to dinner. She is very hospitable." "Very well then, you won't." "I should only
make my aunt angry." "Besides, you can dine with her
and catch the ten o'clock train." "It's cutting it rather
fine." "Then I can never go and dine in town and come
back by train. But listen, Albertine. We are going to
do something quite simple, I feel that the fresh air will do
me good; since you can't give up your lady, I am going to
come with you to Infreville. Don't be alarmed, I shan't
go as far as the Tour Élisabeth" (the lady's villa), "I
shall see neither the lady nor your friends." Albertine
started as though she had received a violent blow. For a
moment, she was unable to speak. She explained that the
sea bathing was not doing her any good. "If you don't
want me to come with you?" "How can you say such
a thing, you know that there's nothing I enjoy more than
going out with you." A sudden change of tactics had
occurred. "Since we are going for a drive together,"
she said to me, "why not go out in the other direction,
we might dine together. It would be so nice. After all,
that side of Balbec is much the prettier. I'm getting
sick of Infreville and all those little spinach-bed places."
"But your aunt's friend will be annoyed if you don't go
and see her." "Very well, let her be." "No, it is wrong
to annoy people." "But she won't even notice that I'm
not there, she has people every day; I can go to-morrow,
the next day, next week, the week after, it's exactly the
same." "And what about your friends?" "Oh, they've
cut me often enough. It's my turn now." "But from
the side you suggest there's no train back after nine."
"Well, what's the matter with that? Nine will do per-

fectly. Besides, one need never think about getting back. We can always find a cart, a bike, if the worse comes to the worst, we have legs." "We can always find, Albertine, how you go on! Out Infreville way, where the villages run into one another, well and good. But the other way, it's a very different matter." "That way too. I promise to bring you back safe and sound." I felt that Albertine was giving up for my sake some plan arranged beforehand of which she refused to tell me, and that there was some one else who would be as unhappy as I was. Seeing that what she had intended to do was out of the question, since I insisted upon accompanying her, she gave it up altogether. She knew that the loss was not irremediable. For, like all women who have a number of irons in the fire, she had one resource that never failed: suspicion and jealousy. Of course she did not seek to arouse them, quite the contrary. But lovers are so suspicious that they instantly scent out falsehood. With the result that Albertine, being no better than anyone else, knew by experience (without for a moment imagining that she owed her experience to jealousy) that she could always be certain of meeting people again after she had failed to keep an appointment. The stranger whom she was deserting for me would be hurt, would love her all the more for that (though Albertine did not know that this was the reason), and, so as not to prolong the agony, would return to her of his own accord, as I should have done. But I had no desire either to give pain to another, or to tire myself, or to enter upon the terrible course of investigation, of multiform, unending vigilance. "No, Albertine, I do not wish to spoil your pleasure, go to your lady at Infreville, or rather to the person you

really mean to see, it is all the same to me. The real
reason why I am not coming with you is that you do not
wish it, the outing you would be taking with me is not
the one you meant to take, which is proved by your
having contradicted yourself at least five times without
noticing it." Poor Albertine was afraid that her contra-
dictions, which she had not noticed, had been more serious than they were. Not knowing exactly what fibs she
had told me: "It is quite on the cards that I did contra-
dict myself. The sea air makes me lose my head altogether. I'm always calling things by the wrong names."
And (what proved to me that she would not, now, require many tender affirmations to make me believe her) I
felt a stab in my heart as I listened to this admission of
what I had but faintly imagined. "Very well, that's settled, I'm off," she said in a tragic tone, not without looking at the time to see whether she was making herself
late for the other person, now that I had provided her
with an excuse for not spending the evening with myself.
"It's too bad of you. I alter all my plans to spend a
nice, long evening with you, and it's you that won't have
it, and you accuse me of telling lies. I've never known
you be so cruel. The sea shall be my tomb. I will
never see you any more." (My heart leaped at these
words, albeit I was certain that she would come again
next day, as she did.) "I shall drown myself, I shall
throw myself into the water." "Like Sappho." "There
you go, insulting me again. You suspect not only what
I say but what I do." "But, my lamb, I didn't mean
anything, I swear to you, you know Sappho flung herself
into the sea." "Yes, yes, you have no faith in me."
She saw that it was twenty minutes to the hour by the

clock; she was afraid of missing her appointment, and choosing the shortest form of farewell (for which as it happened she apologised by coming to see me again next day, the other person presumably not being free then), she dashed from the room, crying: " Good-bye for ever," in a heartbroken tone. And perhaps she was heartbroken. For knowing what she was about at that moment better than I, being at the same time more strict and more indulgent towards herself than I was towards her, she may all the same have had a fear that I might refuse to see her again after the way in which she had left me. And I believe that she was attached to me, so much so that the other person was more jealous than I was.

Some days later, at Balbec, while we were in the ball-room of the casino, there entered Bloch's sister and cousin, who had both turned out quite pretty, but whom I refrained from greeting on account of my girl friends, because the younger one, the cousin, was notoriously living with the actress whose acquaintance she had made during my first visit. Andrée, at a murmured allusion to this scandal, said to me: "Oh! About that sort of thing I'm like Albertine; there's nothing we both loathe so much as that sort of thing." As for Albertine, on sitting down to talk to me upon the sofa, she had turned her back on the disreputable pair. I had noticed, however, that, before she changed her position, at the moment when Mlle. Bloch and her cousin appeared, my friend's eyes had flashed with that sudden, close attention which now and again imparted to the face of this frivolous girl a serious, indeed a grave air, and left her pensive afterwards. But Albertine had at once turned towards myself a gaze which nevertheless remained singularly fixed and meditative. Mlle. Bloch and her cousin having finally left the room after laughing and shouting in a loud and vulgar manner, I asked Albertine whether the little fair one (the one who was so intimate with the actress) was not the girl who had won the prize the day before in the procession of flowers. "I don't know," said Albertine, "is one of them fair? I must confess they don't interest me particularly, I have never looked at them. Is one of them fair?" she asked her three girl friends with a detached air of inquiry. When applied to people whom Albertine passed every day on the front, this ignorance seemed to me too profound to be genuine. "They didn't appear to be looking at us much either," I said to Albertine, perhaps (on the assumption, which I did not however consciously form, that Albertine loved her own sex), to free her from any regret by pointing out to her that she had not attracted the attention of these girls and that, generally speaking, it is not customary even for the most vicious of women to take an interest in girls whom they do not know. "They weren't looking at us," was Albertine's astonished reply. "Why, they did nothing else the whole time." "But you can't possibly tell," I said to her, "you had your back to them." "Very well, and what about that?" she replied, pointing out to me, set in the wall in front of us, a large mirror which I had not noticed and upon which I now realised that my friend, while talking to me, had never ceased to fix her troubled, preoccupied eyes.

Ever since the day when Cottard had accompanied me into the little casino at Incarville, albeit I did not share the opinion that he had expressed, Albertine had seemed to me different; the sight of her made me lose my temper. I myself had changed, quite as much as she had changed in my eyes. I had ceased to bear her any good will; to her face, behind her back when there was a chance of my words' being repeated to her, I spoke of her in the most insulting language. There were, however, intervals of calmer feeling. One day I learned that Albertine and Andrée had both accepted an invitation to Elstir's. Feeling certain that this was in order that they might, on the return journey, amuse themselves like schoolgirls on holiday by imitating the manners of fast young women, and in so doing find an unmaidently pleasure the thought of which wrung my heart, without announcing my intention, to embarrass them and to deprive Albertine of the pleasure on which she was reckoning, I paid an unexpected call at his studio. But I found only Andrée there. Albertine had chosen another day when her aunt was to go there with her. Then I said to myself that Cottard must have been mistaken; the favourable impression that I received from Andrée's presence there without her friend remained with me and made me feel more kindly disposed towards Albertine. But this feeling lasted no longer than the healthy moments of delicate people subject to passing maladies, who are prostrated again by the merest trifle. Albertine incited Andrée to actions which, without going very far, were perhaps not altogether innocent; pained by this suspicion, I managed in the end to repel it. No sooner was I healed of it than it revived under another form. I had just seen Andrée, with one of those graceful gestures that came naturally to her, lay her head coaxingly on Albertine's shoulder, kiss her on the throat, half shutting her eyes;

or else they had exchanged a glance; a remark had been made by somebody who had seen them going down together to bathe: little trifles such as habitually float in the surrounding atmosphere where the majority of people absorb them all day long without injury to their health or alteration of their mood, but which have a morbid effect and breed fresh sufferings in a nature predisposed to receive them. Sometimes even without my having seen Albertine again, without anyone's having spoken to me about her, there would flash from my memory some vision of her with Gisèle in an attitude which had seemed to me innocent at the time; it was enough now to destroy the peace of mind that I had managed to recover, I had no longer any need to go and breathe dangerous germs outside, I had, as Cottard would have said, supplied my own toxin. I thought then of all that I had been told about Swann's love for Odette, of the way in which Swann had been tricked all his life. Indeed, when I come to think of it, the hypothesis that made me gradually build up the whole of Albertine's character and give a painful interpretation to every moment of a life that I could not control in its entirety, was the memory, the rooted idea of Mme. Swann's character, as it had been described to me. These accounts helped my imagination, in after years, to take the line of supposing that Albertine might, instead of being a good girl, have had the same immorality, the same faculty of deception as a reformed prostitute, and I thought of all the sufferings that would in that case have been in store for me had I ever really been her lover.

One day, outside the Grand Hotel, where we were gathered on the front, I had just been addressing Albertine in the harshest, most humiliating language, and Rosemonde was saying: "Oh, how you have changed your mind about her; why, she used to be everything, it was she who ruled the roast, and now she isn't even fit to be thrown to the dogs." I was beginning, in order to make my attitude towards Albertine still more marked, to say all the nicest things I could think of to Andrée, who, if she was tainted with the same vice, seemed to me to have more excuse for it since she was sickly and neurasthenic, when we saw emerging at the steady trot of its pair of horses into the street at right angles to the front, at the corner of which we were standing, Mme. de Cambremer's barouche. The chief magistrate who, at that moment, was advancing towards us, sprang back upon recognising the carriage, in order not to be seen in our company; then, when he thought that the Marquise's eye might catch his, bowed to her with an immense sweep of his hat. But the carriage, instead of continuing, as might have been expected, along the Rue de la Mer, disappeared through the gate of the hotel. It was quite ten minutes later when the lift-boy, out of breath, came to announce to me: "It's the Marquise de Camembert, she's come here to see Monsieur. I've been up to the room, I looked in the reading-room, I couldn't find Monsieur anywhere. Luckily I thought of looking on the beach." He had barely ended this speech when, followed by her daughter-in-law and by an extremely ceremonious gentleman, the Marquise advanced towards me, coming on probably from some afternoon tea-party in the neighbourhood, and bowed down not so much by age as by the mass of costly trinkets with which she felt it more sociable and more befitting her rank to cover herself, in order to appear as "well dressed" as possible to the people whom she went to visit. It was in fact that "landing" of the Cambremers at the hotel which my grandmother had so greatly dreaded long ago when she wanted us not to let Legrandin know that we might perhaps be going to Balbec. Then Mamma used to laugh at these fears inspired by an event which she considered impossible. And here it was actually happening, but by different channels and without Legrandin's having had any part in it. "Do you mind my staying here, if I shan't be in your way?" asked Albertine (in whose eyes there lingered, brought there by the cruel things I had just been saying to her, a pair of tears which I observed without seeming to see them, but not without rejoicing inwardly at the sight), "there is something I want to say to you." A hat with feathers, itself surmounted by a sapphire pin, was perched haphazard upon Mme. de Cambremer's wig, like a badge the display of which was necessary but sufficient, its place immaterial, its elegance conventional and its stability superfluous. Notwithstanding the heat, the good lady had put on a jet cloak, like a dalmatic, over which hung an ermine stole the wearing of which seemed to depend not upon the temperature and season, but upon the nature of the ceremony. And on Mme. de Cambremer's bosom a baronial torse, fastened to a chain, dangled like a pectoral cross. The gentleman was an eminent lawyer from Paris, of noble family, who had come down to spend a few days with the Cambremers. He was one of those men whom their vast professional experience inclines to look down upon their profession, and who say, for instance: "I know that I am a good pleader, so it no longer amuses me to plead," or: "I'm no longer interested in operating, I know that I'm a good operator." Men of intelligence, *artists*, they see themselves in their maturity, richly endowed by success, shining with that intellect, that artistic nature which their professional brethren recognise in them and which confer upon them a kind of taste and discernment. They form a passion for the paintings not of a great artist, but of an artist who nevertheless is highly distinguished, and spend upon the purchase of his work the large sums that their career procures for them. Le Sidaner was the artist chosen by the Cambremers' friend, who incidentally was a delightful person. He talked well about books, but not about the books of the true masters, those who have mastered themselves. The only irritating habit that this amateur displayed was his constant use of certain ready made expressions, such as " for the most part," which gave an air of importance and incompleteness to the matter of which he was speaking. Madame de Cambremer had taken the opportunity, she told me, of a party which some friends of hers had been giving that afternoon in the Balbec direction to come and call upon me, as she had promised Robert de Saint-Loup. " You know he's coming down to these parts quite soon for a few days. His uncle Charlus is staying near here with his sister-in-law, the Duchesse de Luxembourg, and M. de Saint-Loup means to take the opportunity of pay-ing his aunt a visit and going to see his old regiment, where he is very popular, highly respected. We often have visits from officers who are never tired of singing his praises. How nice it would be if you and he would give us the pleasure of coming together to Féterne." I presented Albertine and her friends. Mme. de Cam-bremer introduced us all to her daughter-in-law. The latter, so frigid towards the petty nobility with whom her seclusion at Féterne forced her to associate, so reserved, so afraid of compromising herself, held out her hand to me with a radiant smile, safe as she felt herself and delighted at seeing a friend of Robert de Saint-Loup, whom he, possessing a sharper social intuition than he allowed to appear, had mentioned to her as being a great friend of the Guermantes. So, unlike her mother-in-law, Mme. de Cambremer employed two vastly different forms of politeness. It was at the most the former kind, dry, insupportable, that she would have conceded me had I met her through her brother Legrandin. But for a friend of the Guermantes she had not smiles enough. The most convenient room in the hotel for entertaining visitors was the reading-room, that place once so terrible into which I now went a dozen times every day, emerging freely, my own master, like those mildly afflicted lunatics who have so long been inmates of an asylum that the superintendent trusts them with a latchkey. And so I offered to take Mme. de Cambremer there. And as this room no longer filled me with shyness and no longer held any charm for me, since the faces of things change for us like the faces of people, it was without the slightest emotion that I made this suggestion. But she declined it, preferring to remain out of doors, and we sat down in the open air, on the terrace of the hotel. I found there and rescued a volume of Madame de Sévigné which Mamma had not had time to carry off in her precipitate flight, when she heard that visitors had called for me. No less than my grandmother, she dreaded these invasions of strangers, and, in her fear of being too late to escape if she let herself be seen, would fly from the room with a rapidity which always made my father and me laugh at her. Madame de Cambremer carried in her hand, with the handle of a sunshade, a number of embroidered bags, a hold-all, a gold purse from which there dangled strings of garnets, and a lace handkerchief. I could not help thinking that it would be more convenient for her to deposit them on a chair; but I felt that it would be unbecoming and useless to ask her to lay aside the ornaments of her pastoral visitation and her social priesthood. We gazed at the calm sea upon which, here and there, a few gulls floated like white petals. Because of the "mean level" to which social conversation reduces us and also of our desire to attract not by means of those qualities of which we are ourselves unaware but of those which, we suppose, ought to be appreciated by the people who are with us, I began instinctively to talk to Mme. de Cambremer *née* Legrandin in the strain in which her brother might have talked. "They appear," I said, referring to the gulls, "as motionless and as white as water-lilies." And indeed they did appear to be offering a lifeless object to the little waves which tossed them about, so much so that the waves, by contrast, seemed in their pursuit of them to be animated by a deliberate intention, to have acquired life. The dowager Marquise could not find words enough to do justice to the superb view of the sea that we had from Balbec, or to say how she envied it, she who from la Raspelière (where for that matter she was not living that year) had only such a distant glimpse of the waves. She had two remarkable habits, due at once to her exalted passion for the arts (especially for the art of music), and to her want of teeth. Whenever she talked of aesthetic subjects her salivary glands—like those of certain animals when in rut—became so overcharged that the old lady's edentulous mouth allowed to escape from the corners of her faintly moustached lips a trickle of moisture for which that was not the proper place. Immediately she drew it in again with a deep sigh, like a person recovering his breath. Secondly, if her subject were some piece of music of surpassing beauty, in her enthusiasm she would raise her arms and utter a few decisive opinions, vigorously chewed and at a pinch issuing from her nose. Now it had never occurred to me that the vulgar beach at Balbec could indeed offer a "seascape," and Mme. de Cambremer's simple words changed my ideas in that respect. On the other hand, as I told her, I had always heard people praise the matchless view from la Raspelière, perched on the summit of the hill, where, in a great drawing-room with two fireplaces, one whole row of windows swept the gardens, and, through the branches of the trees, the sea as far as Balbec and beyond it, and the other row the valley. "How nice of you to say so, and how well you put it: the sea through the branches. It is exquisite, one would say . . . a painted fan." And I gathered from a deep breath intended to catch the falling spittle and dry the moustaches, that the compliment was sincere. But the Marquise *née* Legrandin remained cold, to shew her contempt not for my words but for those of her mother-in-law. Besides, she not only despised the other's intellect but deplored her affability, being always afraid that people might not form a sufficiently high idea of the Cambremers. "And how charming the name is," said I. "One would like to know the origin of all those names." "That one I can tell you," the old lady answered modestly. "It is a family place, it came from my grandmother Arrachepel, not an illustrious family, but a decent and very old country stock." "What! Not illustrious!" her daughter-in-law tartly interrupted her. "A whole window in Bayeux cathedral is filled with their arms, and the principal church at Avranches has their tombs. If these old names interest you," she added, "you've come a year too late. We managed to appoint to the living of Criquetot, in spite of all the difficulties about changing from one diocese to another, the parish priest of a place where I myself have some land, a long way from here, Combray, where the worthy cleric felt that he was becoming neurasthenic. Unfortunately, the sea air was no good to him at his age; his neurasthenia grew worse and he has returned to Combray. But he amused himself while he was our neighbour in going about looking up all the old charters, and he compiled quite an interesting little pamphlet on the place names of the district. It has given him a fresh interest, too, for it seems he is spending his last years in writing a great work upon Combray and its surroundings. I shall send you his pamphlet on the surroundings of Féterne. It is worthy of a Benedictine. You will find the most interesting things in it about our old Raspelière, of which my mother-in-law speaks far too modestly." "In any case, this year," replied the dowager Mme. de Cambremer, "la Raspelière is no longer ours and does not belong to me. But I can see that you have a painter's instincts; I am sure you sketch, and I should so like to shew you Féterne, which is far finer than la Raspelière." For as soon as the Cambremers had let this latter residence to the Verdurins, its commanding situation had at once ceased to appear to them as it had appeared for so many years past, that is to say to offer the advantage, without parallel in the neighbourhood, of looking out over both sea and valley, and had on the other hand, suddenly and retrospectively, presented the drawback that one had always to go up or down hill to get to or from it. In short, one might have supposed that if Mme. de Cambremer had let it, it was not so much to add to her income as to spare her horses. And she proclaimed herself delighted at being able at last to have the sea always so close at hand, at Féterne, she who for so many years (forgetting the two months that she spent there) had seen it only from up above and as though in a panorama. " I am discovering it at my age," she said, " and how I enjoy it ! It does me a world of good. I would let la Raspelière for nothing so as to be obliged to live at Féterne."

"To return to more interesting topics," went on Legrandin's sister, who addressed the old Marquise as " Mother," but with the passage of years had come to treat her with insolence, " you mentioned water-lilies : I suppose you know Claude Monet's pictures of them. What a genius ! They interest me particularly because near Combray, that place where I told you I had some land. . . ." But she preferred not to talk too much about Combray. " Why ! That must be the series that Elstir told us about, the greatest painter of this generation," exclaimed Albertine, who had said nothing so far. " Ah ! I can see that this young lady loves the arts," cried Mme. de Cambremer and, drawing a long breath, recaptured a trail of spittle. " You will allow me to put Le Sidaner before him, Mademoiselle," said the lawyer, smiling with the air of an expert. And, as he had enjoyed, or seen people enjoy, years ago, certain " daring "

work by Elstir, he added: " Elstir was gifted, indeed he
was one of the advanced guard, but for some reason or
other he never kept up, he has wasted his life." Mme. de
Cambremer disagreed with the lawyer, so far as Elstir
was concerned, but, greatly to the annoyance of her guest,
bracketed Monet with Le Sidaner. It would be untrue to
say that she was a fool; she was overflowing with a kind
of intelligence that meant nothing to me. As the sun
was beginning to set, the seagulls were now yellow, like
the water-lilies on another canvas of that series by Monet.
I said that I knew it, and (continuing to copy the diction
of her brother, whom I had not yet dared to name) added
that it was a pity that she had not thought of coming a
day earlier, for, at the same hour, there would have been
a Poussin light for her to admire. Had some Norman
squireen, unknown to the Guermantes, told her that she
ought to have come a day earlier, Mme. de Cambremer-
Legrandin would doubtless have drawn herself up with
an offended air. But I might have been far more familiar
still, and she would have been all smiles and sweetness; I
might in the warmth of that fine afternoon devour my fill
of that rich honey cake which Mme. de Cambremer so
rarely was and which took the place of the dish of pastry
that it had not occurred to me to offer my guests. But
the name of Poussin, without altering the amenity of the
society lady, called forth the protests of the connoisseur.
On hearing that name, she produced six times in almost
continuous succession that little smack of the tongue
against the lips which serves to convey to a child who is
misbehaving at once a reproach for having begun and a
warning not to continue. " In heaven's name, after a
painter like Monet, who is an absolute genius, don't go

and mention an old hack without a vestige of talent, like Poussin. I don't mind telling you frankly that I find him the deadliest bore. I mean to say, you can't really call that sort of thing painting. Monet, Degas, Manet, yes, there are painters if you like! It is a curious thing," she went on, fixing a scrutinous and ecstatic gaze upon a vague point in space where she could see what was in her mind, "it is a curious thing, I used at one time to prefer Manet. Nowadays, I still admire Manet, of course, but I believe I like Monet even more. Oh! The *Cathedrals!*" She was as scrupulous as she was condescending in informing me of the evolution of her taste. And one felt that the phases through which that taste had evolved were not, in her eyes, any less important than the different manners of Monet himself. Not that I had any reason to feel flattered by her taking me into her confidence as to her preferences, for even in the presence of the narrowest of provincial ladies she could not remain for five minutes without feeling the need to confess them. When a noble dame of Avranches, who would have been incapable of distinguishing between Mozart and Wagner, said in Mme. de Cambremer's hearing: "We saw nothing of any interest while we were in Paris, we went once to the Opéra-Comique, they were doing *Pelléas et Mélisande,* it's dreadful stuff," Mme. de Cambremer not only boiled with rage but felt obliged to exclaim: "Not at all, it's a little gem," and to "argue the point." It was perhaps a Combray habit which she had picked up from my grandmother's sisters, who called it "fighting in the good cause," and loved the dinner-parties at which they knew all through the week that they would have to defend their idols against the Philistines. Similarly, Mme. de

Cambremer liked to "fly into a passion" and wrangle about art, as other people do about politics. She stood up for Debussy as she would have stood up for a woman friend whose conduct had been criticised. She must however have known very well that when she said: "Not at all, it's a little gem," she could not improvise in the other lady, whom she was putting in her place, the whole progressive development of artistic culture on the completion of which they would come naturally to an agreement without any need of discussion. "I must ask Le Sidaner what he thinks of Poussin," the lawyer remarked to me. "He's a regular recluse, never opens his mouth, but I know how to get things out of him."

"Anyhow," Mme. de Cambremer went on, "I have a horror of sunsets, they're so romantic, so operatic. That is why I can't abide my mother-in-law's house, with its tropical plants. You will see it, it's just like a public garden at Monte-Carlo. That's why I prefer your coast, here. It is more sombre, more sincere; there's a little lane from which one doesn't see the sea. On rainy days, there's nothing but mud, it's a little world apart. It's just the same at Venice, I detest the Grand Canal and I don't know anything so touching as the little alleys. But it's all a question of one's surroundings." "But," I remarked to her, feeling that the only way to rehabilitate Poussin in Mme. de Cambremer's eyes was to inform her that he was once more in fashion, "M. Degas assures us that he knows nothing more beautiful than the Poussins at Chantilly." "Indeed? I don't know the ones at Chantilly," said Mme. de Cambremer who had no wish to differ from Degas, "but I can speak about the ones in the Louvre, which are appalling." "He admires them immensely too." "I must look at them again. My impressions of them are rather distant," she replied after a moment's silence, and as though the favourable opinion which she was certain, before very long, to form of Poussin would depend, not upon the information that I had just communicated to her, but upon the supplementary and, this time, final examination that she intended to make of the Poussins in the Louvre in order to be in a position to change her mind. Contenting myself with what was a first step towards retractation since, if she did not yet admire the Poussins, she was adjourning the matter for further consideration, in order not to keep her on tenterhooks any longer, I told her mother-in-law how much I had heard of the wonderful flowers at Féterne. In modest terms she spoke of the little presbytery garden that she had behind the house, into which in the mornings, by simply pushing open a door, she went in her wrapper to feed her peacocks, hunt for newlaid eggs, and gather the zinnias or roses which, on the sideboard, framing the creamed eggs or fried fish in a border of flowers, reminded her of her garden paths. "It is true, we have a great many roses," she told me, "our rose garden is almost too near the house, there are days when it makes my head ache. It is nicer on the terrace at la Raspelière where the breeze carries the scent of the roses, but it is not so heady." I turned to her daughter-in-law: "It is just like *Pelléas*," I said to her, to gratify her taste for the modern, "that scent of roses wafted up to the terraces. It is so strong in the score that, as I suffer from hay-fever and rose-fever, it sets me sneezing every time I listen to that scene."

"What a marvellous thing *Pelléas* is," cried Mme. de

Cambremer, " I'm mad about it; " and, drawing closer to
me with the gestures of a savage woman seeking to captivate me, using her fingers to pick out imaginary notes,
she began to hum something which, I supposed, represented to her the farewells of Pelléas, and continued with
a vehement persistence as though it had been important
that Mme. de Cambremer should at that moment remind
me of that scene or rather should prove to me that she
herself remembered it. " I think it is even finer than
Parsifal," she added, " because in *Parsifal* the most beautiful things are surrounded with a sort of halo of melodi-
ous phrases, which are bad simply because they are melo-
dious." " I know, you are a great musician, Madame,"
I said to the dowager. " I should so much like to hear
you play." Mme. de Cambremer-Legrandin gazed at the
sea so as not to be drawn into the conversation. Being
of the opinion that what her mother-in-law liked was not
music at all, she regarded the talent, a sham talent according to her, though in reality of the very highest order,
that the other was admitted to possess as a technical
accomplishment devoid of interest. It was true that
Chopin's only surviving pupil declared, and with justice,
that the Master's style of playing, his " feeling " had been
transmitted, through herself, to Mme. de Cambremer
alone, but to play like Chopin was far from being a
recommendation in the eyes of Legrandin's sister, who
despised nobody so much as the Polish composer. " Oh!
They are flying away," exclaimed Albertine, pointing to
the gulls which, casting aside for a moment their flowery
incognito, were rising in a body towards the sun. " Their
giant wings from walking hinder them," quoted Mme. de
Cambremer, confusing the seagull with the albatross. " I

do love them; I used to see them at Amsterdam," said
Albertine. "They smell of the sea, they come and
breathe the salt air through the paving stones even."
"Oh! So you have been in Holland, you know the
Vermeers?" Mme. de Cambremer asked imperiously, in
the tone in which she would have said: "You know the
Guermantes?" for snobbishness in changing its subject
does not change its accent. Albertine replied in the negative, thinking that they were living people. But her
mistake was not apparent. "I should be delighted to
play to you," Mme. de Cambremer said to me. "But
you know I only play things that no longer appeal to your
generation. I was brought up in the worship of Chopin,"
she said in a lowered tone, for she was afraid of her
daughter-in-law, and knew that to the latter, who considered that Chopin was not music, playing him well or
badly were meaningless terms. She admitted that her
mother-in-law had technique, was a finished pianist.
"Nothing will ever make me say that she is a musician,"
was Mme. de Cambremer-Legrandin's conclusion. Because she considered herself "advanced," because (in
matters of art only) "one could never move far enough
to the Left," she said, she maintained not merely that
music progressed, but that it progressed along one
straight line, and that Debussy was in a sense a super-
Wagner, slightly more advanced again than Wagner.
She did not take into account the fact that if Debussy
was not as independent of Wagner as she herself was
to suppose in a few years' time, because we must always
make use of the weapons that we have captured to free
ourselves finally from the foe whom we have for the moment overpowered, he was seeking nevertheless, after the

feeling of satiety that people were beginning to derive from work that was too complete, in which everything was expressed, to satisfy an opposite demand. There were theories of course, to support this reaction for the time being, like those theories which, in politics, come to the support of the laws against religious communities, of wars in the East (unnatural teaching, the Yellow Peril, etc., etc.). People said that an age of speed required rapidity in art, precisely as they might have said that the next war could not last longer than a fortnight, or that the coming of railways would kill the little places beloved of the coaches, which the motor-car, for all that, was to restore to favour. Composers were warned not to strain the attention of their audience, as though we had not at our disposal different degrees of attention, among which it rests precisely with the artist himself to arouse the highest. For the people who yawn with boredom after ten lines of a mediocre article have journeyed year after year to Bayreuth to listen to the *Ring*. Besides, the day was to come when, for a season, Debussy would be pronounced as trivial as Massenet, and the trills of Mélisande degraded to the level of Manon's. For theories and schools, like microbes and corpuscles, devour one another and by their warfare ensure the continuity of existence. But that time was still to come.

As on the Stock Exchange, when a rise occurs, a whole group of securities benefit by it, so a certain number of despised composers were gaining by the reaction, either because they did not deserve such scorn, or simply— which enabled one to be original when one sang their praises—because they had incurred it. And people even went the length of seeking out, in an isolated past, men of independent talent upon whose reputation the present movement did not seem calculated to have any influence, but of whom one of the new masters was understood to have spoken favourably. Often it was because a master, whoever he may be, however exclusive his school, judges in the light of his own untutored instincts, does justice to talent wherever it be found, or rather not so much to talent as to some agreeable inspiration which he has enjoyed in the past, which reminds him of a precious moment in his adolescence. Or, it may be, because certain artists of an earlier generation have in some fragment of their work realised something that resembles what the master has gradually become aware that he himself meant at one time to create. Then he sees the old master as a sort of precursor; he values in him, under a wholly different form, an effort that is momentarily, partially fraternal. There are bits of Turner in the work of Poussin, we find a phrase of Flaubert in Montesquieu. Sometimes, again, this rumoured predilection of the Master was due to an error, starting heaven knows where and circulated through the school. But in that case the name mentioned profited by the auspices under which it was introduced in the nick of time, for if there is an element of free will, some genuine taste expressed in the master's choice, the schools themselves go only by theory. Thus it is that the mind, following its habitual course which advances by digression, inclining first in one direction, then in the other, had brought back into the light of day a number of works to which the need for justice, or for a renewal of standards, or the taste of Debussy, or his caprice, or some remark that he had perhaps never made had added the works of Chopin. Commended by the judges in whom one had entire confidence, profiting by the admiration that was aroused by *Pelléas,* they had acquired a fresh lustre, and even the people who had not heard them again were so anxious to admire them that they did so in spite of themselves, albeit preserving the illusion of free will. But Mme. de Cambremer-Legrandin spent part of the year in the country. Even in Paris, being an invalid, she was largely confined to her own room. It is true that the drawbacks of this mode of existence were noticeable chiefly in her choice of expressions which she supposed to be fashionable and which would have been more appropriate to the written language, a distinction that she did not perceive, for she derived them more from reading than from conversation. The latter is not so necessary for an exact knowledge of current opinion as of the latest expressions. Unfortunately this revival of the *Nocturnes* had not yet been announced by the critics. The news of it had been transmitted only by word of mouth among the "younger" people. It remained unknown to Mme. de Cambremer-Legrandin. I gave myself the pleasure of informing her, but by addressing my remark to her mother-in-law, as when at billiards in order to hit a ball one aims at the cushion, that Chopin, so far from being out of date, was Debussy's favourite composer. "Indeed, that's quaint," said the daughter-in-law with a subtle smile as though it had been merely a deliberate paradox on the part of the composer of *Pelléas.* Nevertheless it was now quite certain that in future she would always listen to Chopin with respect and even pleasure. Moreover my words which had sounded the hour of deliverance for the dowager produced on her face an expression of gratitude to myself and above all of joy.

Her eyes shone like the eyes of Latude in the play entitled *Latude, or Thirty-five Years in Captivity,* and her bosom inhaled the sea air with that dilatation which Beethoven has so well described in *Fidelio,* at the point where his prisoners at last breathe again "this life-giving air." As for the dowager, I thought that she was going to press her hirsute lips to my cheek. "What, you like Chopin? He likes Chopin, he likes Chopin," she cried with a nasal trumpet-tone of passion; she might have been saying: "What, you know Mme. de Franquetot too?" with this difference, that my relations with Mme. de Franquetot would have left her completely indifferent, whereas my knowledge of Chopin plunged her in a sort of artistic delirium. Her salivary super-secretion no longer sufficed. Not having attempted even to understand the part played by Debussy in the rediscovery of Chopin, she felt only that my judgment of him was favourable. Her musical enthusiasm overpowered her. "Elodie! Elodie! He likes Chopin!" her bosom rose and she beat the air with her arms. "Ah! I knew at once that you were a musician," she cried. "I can quite understand an artist such as you are liking him. He's so lovely!" And her voice was as pebbly as if, to express her ardour for Chopin, she had copied Demosthenes and filled her mouth with all the shingle on the beach. Then came the turn of the tide, reaching as far as her veil which she had not time to lift out of harm's way and which was flooded; and lastly the Marquise wiped away with her embroidered handkerchief the tidemark of foam in which the memory of Chopin had steeped her moustaches.

"Good heavens," Mme. de Cambremer-Legrandin remarked to me, "I'm afraid my mother-in-law's cutting it rather fine, she's forgotten that we've got my Uncle de Ch'nouville dining. Besides, Cancan doesn't like to be kept waiting." The word "Cancan" was beyond me, and I supposed that she might perhaps be referring to a dog. But as for the Ch'nouville relatives, the explanation was as follows. With the lapse of time the young Marquise had outgrown the pleasure that she had once found in pronouncing their name in this manner. And yet it was the prospect of enjoying that pleasure that had decided her choice of a husband. In other social circles, when one referred to the Chenouville family, the custom was (whenever, that is to say, the particle was preceded by a word ending in a vowel sound, for otherwise you were obliged to lay stress upon the *de,* the tongue refusing to utter Madam' d'Ch'nonceaux) that it was the mute *e* of the particle that was sacrificed. One said: "Monsieur d'Chenouville." The Cambremer tradition was different, but no less imperious. It was the mute *e* of Chenouville that was suppressed. Whether the name was preceded by *mon cousin* or by *ma cousine,* it was always *de Ch'nouville* and never *de Chenouville.* (Of the father of these Chenouvilles, one said "our Uncle" for they were not sufficiently "smart set" at Féterne to pronounce the word "Unk" like the Guermantes, whose deliberate jargon, suppressing consonants and naturalising foreign words, was as difficult to understand as Old French or a modern dialect). Every newcomer into the family circle at once received, in the matter of the Ch'nouvilles, a lesson which Mme. de Cambremer-Legrandin had not required. When, paying a call one day, she had heard a girl say: "My Aunt d'Uzai," "My Unk de Rouan," she had not at first recognised the illustrious names which she was in the habit of pronouncing: Uzès, and Rohan, she had felt the astonishment, embarrassment and shame of a person who sees before him on the table a recently invented implement of which he does not know the proper use and with which he dares not begin to eat. But during that night and the next day she had rapturously repeated: "My Aunt Uzai," with that suppression of the final *s*, a suppression that had stupefied her the day before, but which it now seemed to her so vulgar not to know that, one of her friends having spoken to her of a bust of the Duchesse d'Uzès, Mlle. Legrandin had answered her crossly, and in an arrogant tone: "You might at least pronounce her name properly: Mame d'Uzai." From that moment she had realised that, by virtue of the transmutation of solid bodies into more and more subtle elements, the considerable and so honourably acquired fortune that she had inherited from her father, the finished education that she had received, her regular attendance at the Sorbonne, whether at Caro's lectures or at Brunetière's, and at the Lamoureux concerts, all this was to be rendered volatile, to find its utmost sublimation in the pleasure of being able one day to say: "My Aunt d'Uzai." This did not exclude the thought that she would continue to associate, in the earlier days, at least, of her married life, not indeed with certain women friends whom she liked and had resigned herself to sacrificing, but with certain others whom she did not like and to whom she looked forward to being able to say (since that, after all was why she was marrying): "I must introduce you to my Aunt d'Uzai," and, when she saw that such an alliance was beyond her reach, "I must introduce you to my Aunt de Ch'nouville," and "I shall ask you to dine to meet the Uzai." Her marriage to M. de Cambremer had procured for Mlle. Legrandin the opportunity to use the former of these phrases but not the latter, the circle in which her parents-in-law moved not being that which she had supposed and of which she continued to dream. After saying to me of Saint-Loup (adopting for the occasion one of his expressions, for if in talking to her I used those expressions of Legrandin, she by a reverse suggestion answered me in Robert's dialect which she did not know to be borrowed from Rachel), bringing her thumb and forefinger together and half-shutting her eyes as though she were gazing at something infinitely delicate which she had succeeded in capturing: " He has a charming quality of mind; " she began to extol him with such warmth that one might have supposed that she was in love with him (it had indeed been alleged that, some time back, when he was at Doncières, Robert had been her lover), in reality simply that I might repeat her words to him, and ended up with: " You are a great friend of the Duchesse de Guermantes. I am an invalid, I never go anywhere, and I know that she sticks to a close circle of chosen friends, which I do think so wise of her, and so I know her very slightly, but I know she is a really remarkable woman." Aware that Mme. de Cambremer barely knew her, and anxious to reduce myself to her level, I avoided the subject and answered the Marquise that the person whom I did know well was her brother, M. Legrandin. At the sound of his name she assumed the same evasive air as myself over the name of Mme. de Guermantes, but combined with it an expression of annoyance, for she supposed that I had said this with the object of humiliating not myself but her. Was she gnawed by despair at having been born a Legrandin? So at least her husband's sisters and sisters-in-law asserted, ladies of the provincial nobility who knew nobody and nothing, and were jealous of Mme. de Cambremer's intelligence, her education, her fortune, the physical attractions that she had possessed before her illness. " She can think of nothing else, that is what is killing her," these slanderers would say whenever they spoke of Mme. de Cambremer to no matter whom, but preferably to a plebeian, whether, were he conceited and stupid, to enhance, by this affirmation of the shamefulness of a plebeian origin, the value of the affability that they were shewing him, of, if he were shy and clever and applied the remark to himself, to give themselves the pleasure, while receiving him hospitably, of insulting him indirectly. But if these ladies thought that they were speaking the truth about their sister-in-law, they were mistaken. She suffered not at all from having been born Legrandin, for she had forgotten the fact altogether. She was annoyed at my reminding her of it, and remained silent as though she had not understood, not thinking it necessary to enlarge upon or even to confirm my statement.

" Our cousins are not the chief reason for our cutting short our visit," said the dowager Mme. de Cambremer, who was probably more satiated than her daughter-in-law with the pleasure to be derived from saying " Ch'nouville." " But, so as not to bother you with too many people, Monsieur," she went on, indicating the lawyer, " was afraid to bring his wife and son to the hotel. They are waiting for us on the beach, and they will be growing impatient." I asked for an exact description of them and hastened in search of them. The wife had a round face

like certain flowers of the ranunculus family, and a large
vegetable growth at the corner of her eye. And as the
generations of mankind preserve their characteristics like
a family of plants, just as on the blemished face of his
mother, an identical mole, which might have helped one
in classifying a variety of the species, protruded below
the eye of the son. The lawyer was touched by my civility to his wife and son. He shewed an interest in the
subject of my stay at Balbec. "You must find yourself
rather out of your element, for the people here are for the
most part foreigners." And he kept his eye on me as he
spoke, for, not caring for foreigners, albeit he had many
foreign clients, he wished to make sure that I was not
hostile to his xenophobia, in which case he would have
beaten a retreat saying: "Of course, Mme. X—— may be
a charming woman. It's a question of principle." As at
that time I had no definite opinion about foreigners, I
shewed no sign of disapproval; he felt himself to be on
safe ground. He went so far as to invite me to come one
day, in Paris, to see his collection of Le Sidaner, and to
bring with me the Cambremers, with whom he evidently
supposed me to be on intimate terms. "I shall invite
you to meet Le Sidaner," he said to me, confident that
from that moment I would live only in expectation of
that happy day. "You shall see what a delightful man
he is. And his pictures will enchant you. Of course, I
can't compete with the great collectors, but I do believe
that I am the one that possesses the greatest number of
his favourite canvases. They will interest you all the
more, coming from Balbec, since they are marine subjects, for the most part, at least." The wife and son,
blessed with a vegetable nature, listened composedly.

One felt that their house in Paris was a sort of temple of Le Sidaner. Temples of this sort are not without their use. When the god has doubts as to his own merits, he can easily stop the cracks in his opinion of himself with the irrefutable testimony of people who have devoted their lives to his work.

At a signal from her daughter-in-law, Mme. de Cambremer prepared to depart, and said to me: " Since you won't come and stay at Féterne, won't you at least come to luncheon, one day this week, to-morrow for instance? " And in her bounty, to make the invitation irresistible, she added: " You will *find* the Comte de Crisenoy," whom I had never lost, for the simple reason that I did not know him. She was beginning to dazzle me with yet further temptations, but stopped short. The chief magistrate who, on returning to the hotel, had been told that she was on the premises had crept about searching for her everywhere, then waited his opportunity, and pretending to have caught sight of her by chance, came up now to greet her. I gathered that Mme. de Cambremer did not mean to extend to him the invitation to luncheon that she had just addressed to me. And yet he had known her far longer than I, having for years past been one of the regular guests at the afternoon parties at Féterne whom I used so to envy during my former visit to Balbec. But old acquaintance is not the only thing that counts in society. And hostesses are more inclined to reserve their luncheons for new acquaintances who still whet their curiosity, especially when they arrive preceded by a glowing and irresistible recommendation like Saint-Loup's of me. Mme. de Cambremer decided that the chief magistrate could not have heard what she was saying to me, but, to calm her guilty conscience, began addressing him in the kindest tone. In the sunlight that flooded, on the horizon, the golden coastline, invisible as a rule, of Rivebelle, we could just make out, barely distinguishible from the luminous azure, rising from the water, rosy, silvery, faint, the little bells that were sounding the angelus round about Féterne. "That is rather *Pelléas,* too," I suggested to Mme. de Cambremer-Legrandin. "You know the scene I mean." "Of course I do!" was what she said; but "I haven't the faintest idea" was the message proclaimed by her voice and features which did not mould themselves to the shape of any recollection and by a smile that floated without support, in the air. The dowager could not get over her astonishment that the sound of the bells should carry so far, and rose, reminded of the time: "But, as a rule," I said, "we never see that part of the coast from Balbec, nor hear it either. The weather must have changed and enlarged the horizon in more ways than one. Unless, that is to say, the bells have come to look for you, since I see that they are making you leave; to you they are a dinner bell." The chief magistrate, little interested in the bells, glanced furtively along the front, on which he was sorry to see so few people that evening. "You are a true poet," said Mme. de Cambremer to me. "One feels you are so responsive, so artistic, come, I will play you Chopin," she went on, raising her arms with an air of ecstasy and pronouncing the words in a raucous voice like the shifting of shingle on the beach. Then came the deglutition of spittle, and the old lady instinctively wiped the stubble of her moustaches with her handkerchief. The chief magistrate did me, unconsciously, a great service by offering the Marquise his arm to escort her to her

carriage, a certain blend of vulgarity, boldness and love
of ostentation prompting him to actions which other people would have hesitated to risk, and which are by no
means unsuccessful in society. He was, moreover, and
had been for years past far more in the habit of these
actions than myself. While blessing him for what he did
I did not venture to copy him, and walked by the side of
Mme. de Cambremer-Legrandin who insisted upon seeing
the book that I had in my hand. The name of Madame
de Sévigné drew a grimace from her; and using a word
which she had seen in certain newspapers, but which,
used in speech and given a feminine form, and applied to
a seventeenth century writer, had an odd effect, she asked
me : " Do you really think her a superman ? " The Marquise gave her footman the address of a pastrycook where
she had to call before taking the road, rosy with the evening haze, through which loomed one beyond another the
dusky walls of cliff. She asked her old coachman whether
one of the horses which was apt to catch cold had been
kept warm enough, whether the other's shoe were not
hurting him. " I shall write to you and make a definite
engagement," she murmured to me. " I heard you talking about literature to my daughter-in-law, she's a dar-
ling," she went on, not that she really thought so, but
she had acquired the habit—and kept it up in her kindness of heart—of saying so, in order that her son might
not appear to have married for money. " Besides," she
added with a final enthusiastic gnashing of her teeth,
" she's so harttissttick ! " With this she stepped into her
carriage, nodding her head, holding the crook of her sunshade aloft like a crozier, and set off through the streets

of Balbec, overloaded with the ornaments of her priest-hood, like an old Bishop on a confirmation tour.

"She has asked you to luncheon," the chief magistrate said to me sternly when the carriage had passed out of sight and I came indoors with the girls. "We're not on the best of terms just now. She feels that I neglect her. Gad, I'm easy enough to get on with. If anybody needs me, I'm always there to say: Adsum! But they tried to force my hand. That, now," he went on with an air of subtlety, holding up his finger as though making and arguing a distinction, "that is a thing I do not allow. It is a threat to the liberty of my holidays. I was obliged to say: Stop! You seem to be in her good books. When you reach my age you will see that society is a very trumpery thing, and you will be sorry you attached so much importance to these trifles. Well, I am going to take a turn before dinner. Good-bye, children," he shouted back at us, as though he were already fifty yards away.

When I had said good-bye to Rosemonde and Gisèle, they saw with astonishment that Albertine was staying behind instead of accompanying them. "Why, Alber-tine, what are you doing, don't you know what time it is?" "Go home," she replied in a tone of authority. "I want to talk to him," she added, indicating myself with a submissive air. Rosemonde and Gisèle stared at me, filled with a new and strange respect. I enjoyed the feeling that, for a moment at least, in the eyes even of Rosemonde and Gisèle, I was to Albertine something more important than the time, than her friends, and might indeed share solemn secrets with her into which it was impossible for them to be admitted. "Shan't we see you again this evening?" "I don't know, it will depend on this person. Anyhow, to-morrow." "Let us go up to my room," I said to her, when her friends had gone. We took the lift; she remained silent in the boy's presence. The habit of being obliged to resort to personal observation and deduction in order to find out the business of their masters, those strange beings who converse among themselves and do not speak to them, develops in "employees" (as the lift-boy styled servants), a stronger power of divination than the "employer" possesses. Our organs become atrophied or grow stronger or more subtle, accordingly as our need of them increases or diminishes. Since railways came into existence, the necessity of not missing the train has taught us to take account of minutes whereas among the ancient Romans, who not only had a more cursory science of astronomy but led less hurried lives, the notion not of minutes but even of fixed hours barely existed. And so the lift-boy had gathered and meant to inform his comrades that Albertine and I were preoccupied. But he talked to us without ceasing because he had no tact. And yet I could see upon his face, in place of the customary expression of friendliness and joy at taking me up in his lift, an air of extraordinary depression and uneasiness. As I knew nothing of the cause of this, in an attempt to distract his thoughts, and albeit I was more preoccupied than Albertine, I told him that the lady who had just left was called the Marquise de Cambremer and not de Camembert. On the landing at which we were pausing at the moment, I saw, carrying a pair of pails, a hideous chambermaid who greeted me with respect, hoping for a tip when I left. I should have liked to know if she were the

one whom I had so ardently desired on the evening of my
first arrival at Balbec, but I could never arrive at any certainty. The lift-boy swore to me with the sincerity of
most false witnesses, but without shedding his expression
of despair, that it was indeed by the name of Camembert
that the Marquise had told him to announce her. And as
a matter of fact it was quite natural that he should have
heard her say a name which he already knew. Besides,
having those very vague ideas of nobility, and of the
names of which titles are composed, which are shared by
many people who are not lift-boys, the name Camembert
had seemed to him all the more probable inasmuch as,
that cheese being universally known, it was not in the
least surprising that people should have acquired a marquisate from so glorious a distinction, unless it were the
marquisate that had bestowed its renown upon the cheese.
Nevertheless as he saw that I refused to admit that I
might be mistaken, and as he knew that masters like to
see their most futile whims obeyed and their most obvious
lies accepted, he promised me like a good servant that in
future he would say Cambremer. It is true that none of
the shopkeepers in the town, none of the peasants in the
district, where the name and persons of the Cambremers
were perfectly familiar, could ever have made the lift-
boy's mistake. But the staff of the "Grand Hotel of
Balbec" were none of them natives. They came direct,
with the furniture and stock, from Biarritz, Nice and
Monte-Carlo, one division having been transferred to
Deauville, another to Dinard and the third reserved for
Balbec.

But the lift-boy's pained anxiety continued to grow.
That he should thus forget to shew his devotion to me by

the customary smiles, some misfortune must have befallen him. Perhaps he had been "missed." I made up my mind in that case to try to secure his reinstatement, the manager having promised to ratify all my wishes with regard to his staff. "You can always do just what you like, I rectify everything in advance." Suddenly, as I stepped out of the lift, I guessed the meaning of the boy's distress, his panic-stricken air. Because Albertine was with me, I had not given him the five francs which I was in the habit of slipping into his hand when I went up. And the idiot, instead of understanding that I did not wish to make a display of generosity in front of a third person, had begun to tremble, supposing that it was all finished, that I would never give him anything again. He imagined that I was "on the rocks" (as the Duc de Guermantes would have said), and the supposition inspired him with no pity for myself but with a terrible selfish disappointment. I told myself that I was less unreasonable than my mother thought when I dared not, one day, refrain from giving the extravagant but feverishly awaited sum that I had given the day before. But at the same time the meaning that I had until then, and without a shadow of doubt, ascribed to his habitual expression of joy, in which I had no hesitation in seeing a sign of devotion, seemed to me to have become less certain. Seeing the lift-boy ready, in his despair, to fling himself down from the fifth floor of the hotel, I asked myself whether, if our respective social stations were to be altered, in consequence let us say of a revolution, instead of politely working his lift for me, the boy, grown independent, would not have flung me down the well, and whether there was not, in certain of the lower orders, more duplicity than in society, where, no doubt, people reserve their offensive remarks until we are out of earshot, but where their attitude towards us would not be insulting if we were reduced to poverty.

One cannot however say that, in the Balbec hotel, the lift-boy was the most commercially minded. From this point of view the staff might be divided into two categories; on the one hand, those who drew distinctions between the visitors, and were more grateful for the modest tip of an old nobleman (who, moreover, was in a position to relieve them from 28 days of military service by saying a word for them to General de Beautreillis) than for the thoughtless liberalities of a cad who by his very profusion revealed a want of practice which only to his face did they call generosity ; on the other hand, those to whom nobility, intellect, fame, position, manners were non-existent, concealed under a cash valuation. For these there was but a single standard, the money one has, or rather the money one bestows. Possibly Aimé himself, albeit pretending, in view of the great number of hotels in which he had served, to a great knowledge of the world, belonged to this latter category. At the most he would give a social turn, shewing that he knew who was who, to this sort of appreciation, as when he said of the Princesse de Luxembourg: "There's a pile of money among that lot?" (the question mark at the end being to ascertain the facts or to check such information as he had already ascertained, before supplying a client with a "chef" for Paris, or promising him a table on the left, by the door, with a view of the sea, at Balbec). In spite of this, and albeit not free from sordid considerations, he would not have displayed them with the fatuous despair of the lift-boy. And yet, the latter's artlessness helped perhaps to simplify things. It is the convenience of a big hotel, of a house such as Rachel used at one time to frequent, that, without any intermediary, the face, frozen stiff until that moment, of a servant or a woman, at the sight of a hundred franc note, still more of one of a thousand, even although it is being given to some one else, will melt in smiles and offers of service. Whereas in the dealings, in the relations between lover and mistress, there are too many things interposed between money and docility. So many things that the very people upon whose faces money finally evokes a smile are often incapable of following the internal process that links them together, believe themselves to be, and indeed are more refined. Besides, it rids polite conversation of such speeches as: "There's only one thing left for me to do, you will find me to-morrow in the mortuary." And so one meets in polite society few novelists, or poets, few of all those sublime creatures who speak of the things that are not to be mentioned.

As soon as we were alone and had moved along the corridor, Albertine began: "What is it, you have got against me?" Had my harsh treatment of her been painful to myself? Had it been merely an unconscious ruse on my part, with the object of bringing my mistress to that attitude of fear and supplication which would enable me to interrogate her, and perhaps to find out which of the alternative hypotheses that I had long since formed about her was correct? However that may be, when I heard her question, I suddenly felt the joy of one who attains to a long desired goal. Before answering her, I escorted her to the door of my room. Opening it, I scattered the roseate light that was flooding the room and turning the white muslin of the curtains drawn for the night to golden damask. I went across to the window; the gulls had settled again upon the waves; but this time they were pink. I drew Albertine's attention to them. "Don't change the subject," she said, "be frank with me." I lied. I declared to her that she must first listen to a confession, that of my passionate admiration, for some time past, of Andrée, and I made her this confession with a simplicity and frankness worthy of the stage, but seldom employed in real life except for a love which people do not feel. Harking back to the fiction I had employed with Gilberte before my first visit to Balbec, but adapting its terms, I went so far (in order to make her more ready to believe me when I told her now that I was not in love with her) as to let fall the admission that at one time I had been on the point of falling in love with her, but that too long an interval had elapsed, that she could be nothing more to me now than a good friend and comrade, and that even if I wished to feel once again a more ardent sentiment for her it would be quite beyond my power. As it happened, in taking my stand thus before Albertine on these protestations of coldness towards her, I was merely—because of a particular circumstance and with a particular object in view—making more perceptible, accentuating more markedly, that dual rhythm which love adopts in all those who have too little confidence in themselves to believe that a woman can ever fall in love with them, and also that they themselves can genuinely fall in love with her. They know themselves well enough to have observed that in the presence of the most divergent types of woman they felt the same hopes, the same agonies, invented the same romances, uttered the same words, to have deduced therefore that their sentiments, their actions bear no close and necessary relation to the woman they love, but pass by her, spatter her, surround her, like the waves that break round upon the rocks, and their sense of their own instability increases still further their misgivings that this woman, by whom they would so fain be loved, is not in love with them. Why should chance have brought it about, when she is simply an accident placed so as to catch the ebullience of our desire, that we should ourself be the object of the desire that is animating her? And so, while we feel the need to pour out before her all those sentiments, so different from the merely human sentiments that our neighbour inspires in us, those so highly specialised sentiments which are a lover's, after we have taken a step forward, in avowing to her whom we love our affection for her, our hopes, overcome at once by the fear of offending her, ashamed too that the speech we have addressed to her was not composed expressly for her, that it has served us already, will serve us again for others, that if she does not love us she cannot understand us and we have spoken in that case with the want of taste, of modesty shewn by the pedant who addresses an ignorant audience in subtle phrases which are not for them, this fear, this shame bring into play the counter-rhythm, the reflux, the need, even by first drawing back, hotly denying the affection we have already confessed, to resume the offensive, and to recapture her esteem, to dominate her; the double rhythm is perceptible in the various periods of a single love affair, in all the corresponding periods of similar love affairs, in all those people whose self-analysis outweighs their self-esteem. If it was however somewhat more vigorously accentuated than usual in this speech which I was now preparing to make to Albertine, that was simply to allow me to pass more speedily and more emphatically to the alternate rhythm which should sound my affection.

As though it must be painful to Albertine to believe what I was saying to her as to the impossibility of my loving her again, after so long an interval, I justified what I called an eccentricity of my nature by examples taken from people with whom I had, by their fault or my own, allowed the time for loving them to pass, and been unable, however keenly I might have desired it, to recapture it. I thus appeared at one and the same time to be apologising to her, as for a want of courtesy, for this inability to begin loving her again, and to be seeking to make her understand the psychological reasons for that incapacity as though they had been peculiar to myself. But by explaining myself in this fashion, by dwelling upon the case of Gilberte, in regard to whom the argument had indeed been strictly true which was becoming so far from true when applied to Albertine, all that I did was to render my assertions as plausible as I pretended to believe that they were not. Feeling that Albertine appreciated what she called my " frank speech " and recognising in my deductions the clarity of the evidence, I apologised for the former by telling her that I knew that the truth was always unpleasant and in this instance must seem to her incomprehensible. She, on the contrary, thanked me for my sincerity and added that so far from being puzzled she understood perfectly a state of mind so frequent and so natural.

This avowal to Albertine of an imaginary sentiment for
Andrée, and, towards herself, an indifference which, that
it might appear altogether sincere and without exaggeration, I assured her incidentally, as though by a scruple of
politeness, must not be taken too literally, enabled me at
length, without any fear of Albertine's suspecting me of
loving her, to speak to her with a tenderness which I had
so long denied myself and which seemed to me exquisite.
I almost caressed my confidant; as I spoke to her of her
friend whom I loved, tears came to my eyes. But, coming at last to the point, I said to her that she knew what
love meant, its susceptibilities, its sufferings, and that perhaps, as the old friend that she now was, she might feel
it in her heart to put a stop to the bitter grief that she was
causing me, not directly, since it was not herself that I
loved, if I might venture to repeat that without offending
her, but indirectly by wounding me in my love for
Andrée. I broke off to admire and point out to Albertine
a great bird, solitary and hastening, which far out in
front of us, lashing the air with the regular beat of its
wings, was passing at full speed over the beach stained
here and there with reflexions like little torn scraps of red
paper, and crossing it from end to end without slackening
its pace, without diverting its attention, without deviating
from its path, like an envoy carrying far afield an urgent
and vital message. "He at least goes straight to the
point!" said Albertine in a tone of reproach. "You say
that because you don't know what it is I was going to
tell you. But it is so difficult that I prefer to give it up; I
am certain that I should make you angry; and then all
that will have happened will be this: I shall be in no way
better off with the girl I really love and I shall have lost

a good friend." "But when I swear to you that I will not be angry." She had so sweet, so wistfully docile an air, as though her whole happiness depended on me, that I could barely restrain myself from kissing—with almost the same kind of pleasure that I should have taken in kissing my mother—this novel face which no longer presented the startled, blushing expression of a rebellious and perverse kitten with its little pink, tip-tilted nose, but seemed, in the fulness of its crushing sorrow, moulded in broad, flattened, drooping slabs of pure goodness. Making an abstraction of my love as of a chronic mania that had no connexion with her, putting myself in her place, I let my heart be melted before this honest girl, accustomed to being treated in a friendly and loyal fashion, whom the good comrade that she might have supposed me had been pursuing for weeks past with persecutions which had at last arrived at their culminating point. It was because I placed myself at a standpoint that was purely human, external to both of us, at which my jealous love dissolved, that I felt for Albertine that profound pity, which would have been less profound if I had not loved her. However, in that rhythmical oscillation which leads from a declaration to a quarrel (the surest, the most certainly perilous way of forming by opposite and successive movements a knot which will not be loosed and attaches us firmly to a person by the strain of the movement of withdrawal which constitutes one of the two elements of the rhythm), of what use is it to analyse farther the refluences of human pity, which, the opposite of love, though springing perhaps unconsciously from the same cause, produces in every case the same effects? When we count up afterwards the total amount of all that we have done for a woman, we often discover that the actions prompted by the desire to shew that we love her, to make her love us, to win her favours, bulk little if any greater than those due to the human need to repair the wrongs that we have done to the creature whom we love, from a mere sense of moral duty, as though we were not in love with her. "But tell me, what on earth have I done?" Albertine asked me. There was a knock at the door; it was the lift-boy; Albertine's aunt, who was passing the hotel in a carriage, had stopped on the chance of finding her there, to take her home. Albertine sent word that she could not come, that they were to begin dinner without her, that she could not say at what time she would return. "But won't your aunt be angry?" "What do you suppose? She will understand all right." And so, at this moment at least, a moment such as might never occur again—a conversation with myself was proved by this incident to be in Albertine's eyes a thing of such self-evident importance that it must be given precedence over everything, a thing to which, referring no doubt instinctively to a family code, enumerating certain crises in which, when the career of M. Bontemps was at stake, a journey had been made without a thought, my friend never doubted that her aunt would think it quite natural to see her sacrifice the dinner-hour. That remote hour which she passed without my company, among her own people, Albertine, having brought it to me, bestowed it on me; I might make what use of it I chose. I ended by making bold to tell her what had been reported to me about her way of living, and that notwithstanding the profound disgust that I felt for women tainted with that vice, I had not given it a thought until I had been told the name of her accomplice, and that she could readily understand, loving Andrée as I did, the grief that the news had caused me. It would have been more tactful perhaps to say that I had been given the names of other women as well, in whom I was not interested. But the sudden and terrible revelation that Cottard had made to me had entered my heart to lacerate it, complete in itself but without accretions. And just as, before that moment, it would never have occurred to me that Albertine was in love with Andrée, or at any rate could find pleasure in caressing her, if Cottard had not drawn my attention to their attitude as they waltzed together, so I had been incapable of passing from that idea to the idea, so different for me, that Albertine might have, with other women than Andrée, relations for which affection could not be pleaded in excuse. Albertine, before even swearing to me that it was not true, shewed, like everyone upon learning that such things are being said about him, anger, concern, and, with regard to the unknown slanderer, a fierce curiosity to know who he was and a desire to be confronted with him so as to be able to confound him. But she assured me that she bore me, at least, no resentment. " If it had been true, I should have told you. But Andrée and I both loathe that sort of thing. We have not lived all these years without seeing women with cropped hair who behave like men and do the things you mean, and nothing revolts us more." Albertine gave me merely her word, a peremptory word unsupported by proof. But this was just what was best calculated to calm me, jealousy belonging to that family of sickly doubts which are better purged by the energy than by the probability of an affirmation. It is moreover the property of love to make us at once more distrustful and more credulous, to make us suspect, more readily than we should suspect anyone else, her whom we love, and be convinced more easily by her denials. We must be in love before we can care that all women are not virtuous, which is to say before we can be aware of the fact, and we must be in love too before we can hope, that is to say assure ourselves that some are. It is human to seek out what hurts us and then at once to seek to get rid of it. The statements that are capable of so relieving us seem quite naturally true, we are not inclined to cavil at a sedative that acts. Besides, however multiform may be the person with whom we are in love, she can in any case offer us two essential personalities accordingly as she appears to us as ours, or as turning her desires in another direction. The former of these personalities possesses the peculiar power which prevents us from believing in the reality of the other, the secret remedy to heal the sufferings that this latter has caused us. The beloved object is successively the malady and the remedy that suspends and aggravates it. No doubt, I had long since been prepared, by the strong impression made on my imagination and my faculty for emotion by the example of Swann, to believe in the truth of what I feared rather than of what I should have wished. And so the comfort brought me by Albertine's affirmations came near to being jeopardised for a moment, because I was reminded of the story of Odette. But I told myself that, if it was only right to allow for the worst, not only when, in order to understand Swann's sufferings, I had tried to put myself in his place, but now, when I myself was concerned, in seeking the truth as though it referred to some one else, still I must not, out of cruelty to myself, a soldier who chooses the post not where he can be of most use but where he is most exposed, end in the mistake of regarding one supposition as more true than the rest, simply because it was more painful. Was there not a vast gulf between Albertine, a girl of good, middle-class parentage, and Odette, a courtesan bartered by her mother in her childhood? There could be no comparison of their respective credibility. Besides, Albertine had in no respect the same interest in lying to me that Odette had had in lying to Swann. Moreover to him Odette had admitted what Albertine had just denied. I should therefore be guilty of an error in reasoning as serious—though in the opposite direction—as that which had inclined me towards a certain hypothesis because it had caused me less pain than the rest, were I not to take into account these material differences in their positions, but to reconstruct the real life of my mistress solely from what I had been told about the life of Odette. I had before me a new Albertine, of whom I had already, it was true, caught more than one glimpse towards the end of my previous visit to Balbec, frank and honest, an Albertine who had, out of affection for myself, forgiven me my suspicions and tried to dispel them. She made me sit down by her side upon my bed. I thanked her for what she had said to me, assured her that our reconciliation was complete, and that I would never be horrid to her again. I suggested to her that she ought, at the same time, to go home to dinner. She asked me whether I was not glad to have her with me. Drawing my head towards her for a caress which she had never before given me and which I owed perhaps to the healing of our rupture, she passed her tongue lightly over my lips which she attempted to force apart. At first I kept them tight shut. "You are a great bear!" she informed me.

I ought to have left the place that evening and never set eyes on her again. I felt even then that in a love which is not reciprocated—I might as well say, in love, for there are people for whom there is no such thing as reciprocated love—we can enjoy only that simulacrum of happiness which had been given me at one of those unique moments in which a woman's good nature, or her caprice, or mere chance, bring to our desires, in perfect coincidence, the same words, the same actions as if we were really loved. The wiser course would have been to consider with curiosity, to possess with delight that little parcel of happiness failing which I should have died without ever suspecting what it could mean to hearts less difficult to please or more highly favoured; to suppose that it formed part of a vast and enduring happiness of which this fragment only was visible to me, and—lest the next day should expose this fiction—not to attempt to ask for any fresh favour after this, which had been due only to the artifice of an exceptional moment. I ought to have left Balbec, to have shut myself up in solitude, to have remained so in harmony with the last vibrations of the voice which I had contrived to render amorous for an instant, and of which I should have asked nothing more than that it might never address another word to me; for fear lest, by an additional word which now could only be different, it might shatter with a discord the sensitive silence in which, as though by the pressure of a pedal, there might long have survived in me the throbbing chord of happiness.

Soothed by my explanation with Albertine, I began once again to live in closer intimacy with my mother. She loved to talk to me gently about the days in which my grandmother had been younger. Fearing that I might reproach myself with the sorrows with which I had perhaps darkened the close of my grandmother's life, she preferred to turn back to the years when the first signs of my dawning intelligence had given my grandmother a satisfaction which until now had always been kept from me. We talked of the old days at Combray. My mother reminded me that there at least I used to read, and that at Balbec I might well do the same, if I was not going to work. I replied that, to surround myself with memories of Combray and of the charming coloured plates, I should like to read again the *Thousand and One Nights*. As, long ago at Combray, when she gave me books for my birthday, so it was in secret, as a surprise for me, that my mother now sent for both the *Thousand and One Nights* of Galland and the *Thousand Nights and a Night* of Mardrus. But, after casting her eye over the two translations, my mother would have preferred that I should stick to Galland's, albeit hesitating to influence me because of the respect that she felt for intellectual liberty, her dread of interfering with my intellectual life and the feeling that, being a woman, on the one hand she lacked, or so she thought, the necessary literary equipment, and on the other hand ought not to condemn because she herself was shocked by it the reading of a young man. Happening upon certain of the tales, she had been revolted by the immorality of the subject and the crudity of the expression. But above all, preserving, like precious relics, not only the brooch, the sunshade, the cloak, the volume of Madame de Sévigné, but also the habits of thought and speech of her own mother, seeking on every occasion the opinion that she would have expressed, my mother could have no doubt of the horror with which my grandmother would have condemned Mardrus's book. She remembered that at Combray while before setting out for a walk, Méséglise way, I was reading Augustin Thierry, my grandmother, glad that I should be reading, and taking walks, was indignant nevertheless at seeing him whose name remained enshrined in the hemistich: "Then reignèd Mérovée" called Merowig, refused to say "Carolingians" for the "Carlovingians" to which she remained loyal. And then I told her what my grandmother had thought of the Greek names which Bloch, following Lecomte de Lisle, gave to the gods of Homer, going so far, in the simplest matters, as to make it a religious duty, in which he supposed literary talent to consist, to adopt a Greek system of spelling. Having occasion, for instance, to mention in a letter that the wine which they drank at his home was real nectar, he would write "real nektar," with a *k*, which enabled him to titter at the mention of Lamartine. And if an *Odyssey* from which the names of Ulysses and Minerva were missing was no longer the *Odyssey* to her, what would she have said upon seeing corrupted even upon the cover the title of her *Thousand and One Nights*, upon no longer finding, exactly transcribed as she had all her life been in the habit of pronouncing them, the immortally familiar names of Scheherazade, of Dinarzade, in which, debaptised also (if one may use the expression of Musulman tales), even the charming Caliph and the powerful Genies were barely recognisable, being renamed, he the " Khalifa " and they the " Gennis." Still, my mother handed over both books to me, and I told her that I would read them on the days when I felt too tired to go out.

These days were not very frequent, however. We used to go out picnicking as before in a band, Albertine, her friends and myself, on the cliff or to the farm called Marie-Antoinette. But there were times when Albertine bestowed on me this great pleasure. She would say to me: " To-day I want to be alone with you for a little, it will be nicer if we are just by ourselves." Then she would give out that she was busy, not that she need furnish any explanation, and so that the others, if they went all the same, without us, for an excursion and picnic, might not be able to find us, we would steal away like a pair of lovers, all by ourselves to Bagatelle or the Cross of Heulan, while the band, who would never think of looking for us there and never went there, waited indefinitely, in the hope of seeing us appear, at Marie-Antoinette. I recall the hot weather that we had then, when from the brow of each of the farm-labourers toiling in the sun a drop of sweat would fall, vertical, regular, intermittent, like the drop of water from a cistern, and alternate with the fall of the ripe fruit dropping from the tree in the adjoining " closes "; they have remained, to this day, with that mystery of a woman's secret, the most substantial part of every love that offers itself to me. A woman who has been mentioned to me and to whom I would not give a moment's thought—I upset all my week's engagements to make her acquaintance, if it is a week of similar weather, and I am to meet her in some isolated farmhouse. It is no good my knowing that this kind of weather, this kind of assignation are not part of her, they are still the bait, which I know all too well, by which I allow myself to be tempted and which is sufficient to hook me. I know that this woman, in cold weather, in a town, I might perhaps have desired, but without the accompaniment of a romantic sentiment, without becoming amorous; my love for her is none the less keen as soon as, by force of circumstances, it has enthralled me—it is only the more melancholy, as in the course of life our sentiments for other people become, in proportion as we become more clearly aware of the ever smaller part that they play in our life and that the new love which we would like to be so permanent, cut short in the same moment as life itself, will be the last.

There were still but a few people at Balbec, hardly any girls. Sometimes I saw some girl resting upon the beach, devoid of charm, and yet apparently identified by various features as one whom I had been in despair at not being able to approach at the moment when she emerged with her friends from the riding school or gymnasium. If it was the same (and I took care not to mention the matter to Albertine), then the girl that I had thought so exciting did not exist. But I could not arrive at any certainty, for the face of any one of these girls did not fill any space upon the beach, did not offer a permanent form, contracted, dilated, transformed as it was by my own observation, the uneasiness of my desire or a sense of comfort that was self-sufficient, by the different clothes that she was wearing, the rapidity of her movements or her immobility. All the same, two or three of them seemed to me adorable. Whenever I saw one of these, I longed to take her away along the Avenue des Tamaris, or among the sandhills, better still upon the cliff. But, albeit into desire, as opposed to indifference, there enters already that audacity which is a first stage, if only unilateral, towards realisation, all the same, between my desire and the action that my request to be allowed to kiss her would have been, there was all the indefinite blank of hesitation, of timidity. Then I went into the pastrycook's bar, I drank, one after another, seven or eight glasses of port wine. At once, instead of the impassable gulf between my desire and action, the effect of the alcohol traced a line that joined them together. No longer was there any room for hesitation or fear. It seemed to me that the girl was about to fly into my arms. I went up to her, the words came spontaneously to my lips: "I should like to go for a walk with you. You wouldn't care to go along the cliff, we shan't be disturbed behind the little wood that keeps the wind off the wooden bungalow that is empty just now?" All the difficulties of life were smoothed away, there was no longer any obstacle to the conjunction of our two bodies. No obstacle for me, at least. For they had not been volatilised for her, who had not been drinking port wine. Had she done so, had the outer world lost some of its reality in her eyes, the long cherished dream that would then have appeared to her to be suddenly realisable might perhaps have been not at all that of falling into my arms.

Not only were the girls few in number but at this season which was not yet "the season" they stayed but a short time. There is one I remember with a reddish skin, green eyes and a pair of ruddy cheeks, whose slight symmetrical face resembled the winged seeds of certain trees. I cannot say what breeze wafted her to Balbec or what other bore her away. So sudden was her removal that for some days afterwards I was haunted by a grief which I made bold to confess to Albertine when I realised that the girl had gone for ever.

I should add that several of them were either girls whom I did not know at all or whom I had not seen for years. Often, before addressing them, I wrote to them. If their answer allowed me to believe in the possibility of love, what joy! We cannot, at the outset of our friendship with a woman, even if that friendship is destined to come to nothing, bear to part from those first letters that we have received from her. We like to have them beside us all the time, like a present of rare flowers, still quite fresh, at which we cease to gaze only to draw them closer to us and smell them. The sentence that we know by heart, it is pleasant to read again, and in those that we have committed less accurately to memory we like to verify the degree of affection in some expression. Did she write: "Your dear letter"? A slight marring of our bliss, which must be ascribed either to our having read too quickly, or to the illegible handwriting of our correspondent; she did not say: "Your dear letter" but "From your letter." But the rest is so tender. Oh, that more such flowers may come to-morrow. Then that is no longer enough, we must with the written words compare the writer's eyes, her face. We make an appointment, and—without her having altered, perhaps—whereas we expected, from the description given us or our personal memory, to meet the fairy Viviane, we encounter Puss-in-Boots. We make an appointment, nevertheless, for the following day, for it is, after all, *she,* and the person we desired is she. And these desires for a woman of whom we have been dreaming do not make beauty of form and feature essential. These desires are only the desire for a certain person; vague as perfumes, as styrax was the desire of Prothyraia, saffron the ethereal desire, aromatic scents the desire of Hera, myrrh the perfume of the Magi, manna the desire of Nike, incense the perfume of the sea. But these perfumes that are sung in the Orphic hymns are far fewer in number than the deities they worship. Myrrh is the perfume of the Magi, but also of Protogonos, Neptune, Nereus, Leto; incense is the perfume of the sea, but also of the fair Dike, of Themis, of Circe, of the Nine Muses, of Eos, of Mnemosyne, of the Day, of Dikaiosyne. As for styrax, manna and aromatic scents, it would be impossible to name all the deities that inhale them, so many are they. Amphietes has all the perfumes except incense, and Gaia rejects only beans and aromatic scents. So was it with these desires for different girls that I felt. Fewer in number than the girls themselves, they changed into disappointments and regrets closely similar one to another. I never wished for myrrh. I reserved it for Jupien and for the Prince de Guermantes, for it is the desire of Protogonos " of twofold sex, who roars like a bull, of countless orgies, memorable, unspeakable, descending, joyous, to the sacrifices of the Orgiophants."

But presently the season was in full swing; every day there was some fresh arrival, and for the sudden increase in the frequency of my outings, which took the place of the charmed perusal of the *Thousand and One Nights,* there was a reason devoid of pleasure which poisoned them all. The beach was now peopled with girls, and, since the idea suggested to me by Cottard had not indeed furnished me with fresh suspicions but had rendered me sensitive and weak in that quarter and careful not to let any suspicion take shape in my mind, as soon as a young woman arrived at Balbec, I began to feel ill at ease, I proposed to Albertine the most distant excursions, in order that she might not make the newcomer's acquaintance, and indeed, if possible, might not set eyes on her. I dreaded naturally even more those women whose dubious ways were remarked or their bad reputation already known; I tried to persuade my mistress that this bad reputation had no foundation, was a slander, perhaps, without admitting it to myself, from a fear, still unconscious, that she might seek to make friends with the depraved woman or regret her inability to do so, because of me, or might conclude from the number of examples that a vice so widespread was not to be condemned. In denying the guilt of each of them, my intention was nothing less than to pretend that sapphism did not exist. Albertine adopted my incredulity as to the viciousness of this one or that. "No, I think it's just a pose, she wants to look the part." But then, I regretted almost that I had pleaded the other's innocence, for it distressed me that Albertine, formerly so severe, could believe that this "part" was a thing so flattering, so advantageous, that a woman innocent of such tastes could seek to "look it." I would have liked to be sure that no more women were coming to Balbec; I trembled when I thought that, as it was almost time for Mme. Putbus to arrive at the Verdurins', her maid, whose tastes Saint-Loup had not concealed from me, might take it into her head to come down to the beach, and, if it were a day on which I was not with Albertine, might seek to corrupt her. I went the length of asking myself whether, as Cottard had made no secret of the fact that the Verdurins thought highly of me and, while not wishing to appear, as he put it, to be running after me, would give a great deal to have me come to their house, I might not, on the strength of promises to bring all the Guermantes in existence to call on them in Paris, induce Mme. Verdurin, upon some pretext or other, to inform Mme. Putbus that it was impossible to keep her there any longer and make her leave the place at once. Notwithstanding these thoughts, and as it was chiefly the presence of Andrée that was disturbing me, the soothing effect that Albertine's words had had upon me still to some extent persisted—I knew moreover that presently I should have less need of it, as Andrée would be leaving the place with Rosemonde and Gisèle just about the time when the crowd began to arrive and would be spending only a few weeks more with Albertine. During these weeks, moreover, Albertine seemed to have planned everything that she did, everything that she said, with a view to destroying my suspicions if any remained, or to preventing their recurrence. She contrived never to be left alone with Andrée, and insisted, when we came back from an excursion, upon my accompanying her to her door, upon my coming to fetch her when we were going anywhere. Andrée meanwhile took just as much trouble on her side, seemed to avoid meeting Albertine. And this apparent understanding between them was not the only indication that Albertine must have informed her friend of our conversation and have asked her to be so kind as to calm my absurd suspicions.

About this time there occurred at the Grand Hotel a scandal which was not calculated to modify the intensity of my torment. Bloch's cousin had for some time past been indulging, with a retired actress, in secret relations which presently ceased to satisfy them. That they should be seen seemed to them to add perversity to their pleasure, they chose to flaunt their perilous sport before the eyes of all the world. They began with caresses, which might, after all, be set down to a friendly intimacy, in the card-room, by the baccarat-table. Then they grew more bold. And finally, one evening, in a corner that was not even dark of the big ball-room, on a sofa, they made no more attempt to conceal what they were doing than if they had been in bed. Two officers who happened to be near, with their wives, complained to the manager. It was thought for a moment that their protest would be effective. But they had this against them that, having come over for the evening from Netteholme, where they were staying, they could not be of any use to the manager. Whereas, without her knowing it even, and whatever re-marks the manager may have made to her, there hovered over Mlle. Bloch the protection of M. Nissim Bernard. I must explain why. M. Nissim Bernard carried to their highest pitch the family virtues. Every year he took a magnificent villa at Balbec for his nephew, and no invita-tion would have dissuaded him from going home to dine at his own table, which was really the others'. But he never took his luncheon at home. Every day at noon he was at the Grand Hotel. The fact of the matter was that he was keeping, as other men keep a chorus-girl from the opera, an embryo waiter of much the same type as the pages of whom we have spoken, and who made us think of the young Israelites in *Esther* and *Athalie*. It is true that the forty years' difference in age between M. Nissim Bernard and the young waiter ought to have preserved

the latter from a contact that was scarcely pleasant.
But, as Racine so wisely observes in those same choruses:

> Great God, with what uncertain tread
> A budding virtue 'mid such perils goes!
> What stumbling-blocks do lie before a soul
> That seeks Thee and would fain be innocent.

The young waiter might indeed have been brought up
" remote from the world " in the Temple-Caravanserai of
Balbec, he had not followed the advice of Joad:

> In riches and in gold put not thy trust.

He had perhaps justified himself by saying: " The
wicked cover the earth." However that might be, and
albeit M. Nissim Bernard had not expected so rapid a
conquest, on the very first day,

> Were't in alarm, or anxious to caress,
> He felt those childish arms about him thrown.

And by the second day, M. Nissim Bernard having
taken the young waiter out,

> The dire assault his innocence destroyed.

From that moment the boy's life was altered. He
might indeed carry bread and salt, as his superior bade
him, his whole face sang:

> From flowers to flowers, from joys to keener joys
> Let our desires now range.
> Uncertain is our tale of fleeting years.
> Haste we then to enjoy this life!
> Honours and fame are the reward
> Of blind and meek obedience.
> For moping innocence
> Who now would raise his voice!

Since that day, M. Nissim Bernard had never failed to come and occupy his seat at the luncheon-table (as a man would occupy his in the stalls who was keeping a dancer, a dancer in this case of a distinct and special type, which still awaits its Degas). It was M. Nissim Bernard's delight to follow over the floor of the restaurant and down the remote vista to where beneath her palm the cashier sat enthroned, the evolutions of the adolescent hurrying in service, in the service of everyone, and, less than anyone, of M. Nissim Bernard, now that the latter was keeping him, whether because the young chorister did not think it necessary to display the same friendliness to a person by whom he supposed himself to be sufficiently well loved, or because that love annoyed him or he feared lest, if discovered, it might make him lose other opportunities. But this very coldness pleased M. Nissim Bernard, because of all that it concealed; whether from Hebraic atavism or from profanation of the Christian spirit, he took a singular pleasure, were it Jewish or Catholic, in the Racinian ceremony. Had it been a real performance of *Esther* or *Athalie,* M. Bernard would have regretted that the gulf of centuries must prevent him from making the acquaintance of the author, Jean Racine, so that he might obtain for his protégé a more substantial part. But as the luncheon ceremony came from no author's pen, he contented himself with being on good terms with the manager and Aimé, so that the " young Israelite " might be promoted to the coveted post of under waiter, or even full waiter to a row of tables. A post in the cellars had been offered him. But M. Bernard made him decline it, for he would no longer have been able to come every day to watch him race about the green dining-room and to be waited upon by him like a stranger. Now this pleasure was so keen that every year M. Bernard returned to Balbec and took his luncheon away from home, habits in which M. Bloch saw, in the former a poetical fancy for the bright sunshine, the sunsets of this coast favoured above all others, in the latter the inveterate mania of an old bachelor.

As a matter of fact, the mistake made by M. Nissim Bernard's relatives, who never suspected the true reason for his annual return to Balbec and for what the pedantic Mme. Bloch called his absentee palate, was really a more profound and secondary truth. For M. Nissim Bernard himself was unaware how much there was of love for the beach at Balbec, for the view one enjoyed from the restaurant over the sea, and of maniacal habits in the fancy that he had for keeping, like a dancing girl of another kind which still lacks a Degas, one of his own servants, who, unfortunately, were all girls. And so M. Nissim Bernard maintained, with the director of this theatre which was the hotel at Balbec, and with the stage-manager and producer Aimé—whose part in all this affair was anything but simple—excellent relations. One day they would intrigue to procure an important part, a place perhaps as headwaiter. In the meantime M. Nissim Bernard's pleasure, poetical and calmly contemplative as it might be, reminded one a little of those women-loving men who always know—Swann, for example, in the past—that if they go out to a party they will meet their mistress. No sooner had M. Nissim Bernard taken his seat than he would see the object of his affections appear on the scene, bearing in his hand fruit or cigars upon a tray. And so every morning, after kissing his niece, bothering my friend

Bloch about his work and feeding his horses with lumps of sugar from the palm of his outstretched hand, he would betray a feverish haste to arrive in time for luncheon at the Grand Hotel. Had the house been on fire, had his niece had a stroke, he would doubtless have started off just the same. So that he dreaded like the plague a cold that would confine him to his bed—for he was a hypochondriac—and would oblige him to ask Aimé to send his young friend across to visit him at home, between luncheon and tea-time.

He loved moreover all the labyrinth of corridors, private offices, reception-rooms, cloakrooms, larders, galleries which composed the hotel at Balbec. With a strain of oriental atavism he loved a seraglio, and when he went out at night might be seen furtively exploring its purlieus.

While, venturing down to the basement and endeavouring at the same time to escape notice and to avoid a scandal, M. Nissim Bernard, in his quest of the young Levites, put one in mind of those lines in *La Juive:*

> O God of our Fathers, come down to us again,
> Our mysteries veil from the eyes of wicked men!

I on the contrary would go up to the room of two sisters who had come to Balbec, as her maids, with an old lady, a foreigner. They were what the language of hotels called two "couriers," and that of Françoise, who imagined that a courier was a person who was there to run his course, two "coursers." The hotels have remained, more nobly, in the period when people sang: "*C'est un courrier de cabinet.*"

Difficult as it was for a visitor to penetrate to the servants' quarters, I had very soon formed a mutual bond of friendship, as strong as it was pure, with these two young persons, Mademoiselle Marie Gineste and Madame Céleste Albaret. Born at the foot of the high mountains in the centre of France, on the banks of rivulets and torrents (the water passed actually under their old home, turning a millwheel, and the house had often been damaged by floods), they seemed to embody the features of that region. Marie Gineste was more regularly rapid and abrupt, Céleste Albaret softer and more languishing, spread out like a lake, but with terrible boiling rages in which her fury suggested the peril of spates and gales that sweep everything before them. They often came in the morning to see me when I was still in bed. I have never known people so deliberately ignorant, who had learned absolutely nothing at school, and yet whose language was somehow so literary that, but for the almost savage naturalness of their tone, one would have thought their speech affected. With a familiarity which I reproduce verbatim, notwithstanding the praises (which I set down here in praise not of myself but of the strange genius of Céleste) and the criticisms, equally unfounded, in which her remarks seem to involve me, while I dipped crescent rolls in my milk, Céleste would say to me: "Oh! Little black devil with hair of jet, O profound wickedness! I don't know what your mother was thinking of when she made you, for you are just like a bird. Look, Marie, wouldn't you say he was preening his feathers, and turning his head right round, so light he looks, you would say he was just learning to fly. Ah! It's fortunate for you that those who bred you brought you into the world to rank and riches; what would ever have become of you, so wasteful as you are.

Look at him throwing away his crescent because it touched the bed. There he goes, now, look, he's spilling his milk, wait till I tie a napkin round you, for you could never do it for yourself, never in my life have I seen anyone so helpless and so clumsy as you." I would then hear the more regular sound of the torrent of Marie Gineste who was furiously reprimanding her sister: "Will you hold your tongue, now, Céleste. Are you mad, talking to Monsieur like that?" Céleste merely smiled; and as I detested having a napkin tied round my neck: "No, Marie, look at him, bang, he's shot straight up on end like a serpent. A proper serpent, I tell you." These were but a few of her zoological similes, for, according to her, it was impossible to tell when I slept, I fluttered about all night like a moth, and in the day time I was as swift as the squirrels. "You know, Marie, the way we see them at home, so nimble that even with your eyes you can't follow them." "But, Céleste, you know he doesn't like having a napkin when he's eating." "It isn't that he doesn't like it, it's so that he can say nobody can make him do anything against his will. He's a grand gentleman and he wants to shew that he is. They can change the sheets ten times over, if they must, but he won't give way. Yesterday's had served their time, but to-day they have only just been put on the bed and they'll have to be changed already. Oh, I was right when I said that he was never meant to be born among the poor. Look, his hair's standing on end, swelling with rage like a bird's feathers. Poor *ploumissou!*" Here it was not only Marie that protested, but myself, for I did not feel in the least like a grand gentleman. But Céleste would never believe in the sincerity of my modesty and cut me short.

343

"Oh! The story-teller! Oh! The flatterer! Oh! The false one! The cunning rogue! Oh! Molière!" (This was the only writer's name that she knew, but she applied it to me, meaning thereby a person who was capable both of writing plays and of acting them.) "Céleste!" came the imperious cry from Marie, who, not knowing the name of Molière, was afraid that it might be some fresh insult. Céleste continued to smile: "Then you haven't seen the photograph of him in his drawer, when he was little. He tried to make us believe that he was always dressed quite simply. And there, with his little cane, he's all furs and laces, such as no Prince ever wore. But that's nothing compared with his tremendous majesty and kindness which is even more profound." "So then," scolded the torrent Marie, "you go rummaging in his drawers now, do you?" To calm Marie's fears I asked her what she thought of M. Nissim Bernard's behaviour. . . . "Ah! Monsieur, there are things I wouldn't have believed could exist. One has to come here to learn." And, for once outrivalling Céleste by an even more profound observation: "Ah! You see, Monsieur, one can never tell what there may be in a person's life." To change the subject, I spoke to her of the life led by my father, who toiled night and day. "Ah! Monsieur, there are people who keep nothing of their life for themselves, not one minute, not one pleasure, the whole thing is a sacrifice for others, they are lives that are *given away*." "Look, Marie, he has only to put his hand on the counterpane and take his crescent, what distinction. He can do the most insignificant things, you would say that the whole nobility of France, from here to the Pyrenees, was stirring in each of his movements."

344

Overpowered by this portrait so far from lifelike, I remained silent; Céleste interpreted my silence as a further instance of guile: "Oh! Brow that looks so pure, and hides so many things, nice, cool cheeks like the inside of an almond, little hands of satin all velvety, nails like claws," and so forth. "There, Marie, look at him sipping his milk with a devoutness that makes me want to say my prayers. What a serious air! They ought really to take his portrait as he is just now. He's just like a child. Is it drinking milk, like them, that has kept you their bright colour? Oh! Youth! Oh! Lovely skin. You will never grow old. You are a lucky one, you will never need to raise your hand against anyone, for you have a pair of eyes that can make their will be done. Look at him now, he's angry. He shoots up, straight as a sign-post."

Françoise did not at all approve of what she called the two "tricksters" coming to talk to me like this. The manager, who made his staff keep watch over everything that went on, even gave me a serious warning that it was not proper for a visitor to talk to servants. I, who found the "tricksters" better company than any visitor in the hotel, merely laughed in his face, convinced that he would not understand my explanations. And the sisters returned. "Look, Marie, at his delicate lines. Oh, perfect miniature, finer than the most precious you could see in a glass case, for he can move, and utters words you could listen to for days and nights."

It was a miracle that a foreign lady could have brought them there, for, without knowing anything of history or geography, they heartily detested the English, the Germans, the Russians, the Italians, all foreign vermin, and

345

cared, with certain exceptions, for French people alone. Their faces had so far preserved the moisture of the pliable clay of their native river beds, that, as soon as one mentioned a foreigner who was staying in the hotel, in order to repeat what he had said, Céleste and Marie imposed upon their faces his face, their mouths became his mouth, their eyes his eyes, one would have liked to preserve these admirable comic masks. Céleste indeed, while pretending merely to be repeating what the manager had said, or one of my friends, would insert in her little narrative fictitious remarks in which were maliciously portrayed all the defects of Bloch, the chief magistrate, etc., while apparently unconscious of doing so. It was, under the form of the delivery of a simple message which she had obligingly undertaken to convey, an inimitable portrait. They never read anything, not even a newspaper. One day, however, they found lying on my bed a book. It was a volume of the admirable but obscure poems of Saint-Léger Léger. Céleste read a few pages and said to me: "But are you quite sure that these are poetry, wouldn't they just be riddles?" Obviously, to a person who had learned in her childhood a single poem: "Down here the lilacs die," there was a gap in evolution. I fancy that their obstinate refusal to learn anything was due in part to the unhealthy climate of their early home. They had nevertheless all the gifts of a poet with more modesty than poets generally shew. For if Céleste had said something noteworthy and, unable to remember it correctly, I asked her to repeat it, she would assure me that she had forgotten. They will never read any books, but neither will they ever write any.

Françoise was considerably impressed when she learned that the two brothers of these humble women had married, one the niece of the Archbishop of Tours, the other a relative of the Bishop of Rodez. To the manager, this would have conveyed nothing. Céleste would sometimes reproach her husband with his failure to understand her, and as for me, I was astonished that he could endure her. For at certain moments, raging, furious, destroying everything, she was detestable. It is said that the salt liquid which is our blood is only an internal survival of the primitive marine element. Similarly, I believe that Céleste, not only in her bursts of fury, but also in her hours of depression preserved the rhythm of her native streams. When she was exhausted, it was after their fashion; she had literally run dry. Nothing could then have revived her. Then all of a sudden the circulation was restored in her large body, splendid and light. The water flowed in the opaline transparence of her bluish skin. She smiled at the sun and became bluer still. At such moments she was truly celestial.

Bloch's family might never have suspected the reason which made their uncle never take his luncheon at home and have accepted it from the first as the mania of an elderly bachelor, due perhaps to the demands of his intimacy with some actress; everything that concerned M. Nissim Bernard was tabu to the manager of the Balbec hotel. And that was why, without even referring to the uncle, he had finally not ventured to find fault with the niece, albeit recommending her to be a little more circumspect. And so the girl and her friend who, for some days, had pictured themselves as excluded from the casino and the Grand Hotel, seeing that everything was settled, were delighted to shew those fathers of families who held aloof from them that they might with impunity take the utmost liberties. No doubt they did not go so far as to repeat the public exhibition which had revolted everybody. But gradually they returned to their old ways. And one evening as I came out of the casino which was half in darkness with Albertine and Bloch whom we had met there, they came towards us, linked together, kissing each other incessantly, and, as they passed us, crowed and laughed, uttering indecent cries. Bloch lowered his eyes, so as to seem not to have recognized his cousin, and as for myself I was tortured by the thought that this occult, appalling language was addressed perhaps to Albertine.

Another incident turned my thoughts even more in the direction of Gomorrah. I had noticed upon the beach a handsome young woman, erect and pale, whose eyes, round their centre, scattered rays so geometrically luminous that one was reminded, on meeting her gaze, of some constellation. I thought how much more beautiful this girl was than Albertine, and that it would be wiser to give up the other. Only, the face of this beautiful young woman had been smoothed by the invisible plane of an utterly low life, of the constant acceptance of vulgar expedients, so much so that her eyes, more noble however than the rest of her face, could radiate nothing but appetites and desires. Well, on the following day, this young woman being seated a long way away from us in the casino, I saw that she never ceased to fasten upon Albertine the recurrent, circling fires of her gaze. One would have said that she was making signals to her from a lighthouse. I dreaded my friend's seeing that she was being so closely observed, I was afraid that these incessantly rekindled glances might have the conventional meaning of an amorous assignation for the morrow. For all I knew, this assignation might not be the first. The young woman with the radiant eyes might have come another year to Balbec? It was perhaps because Albertine had already yielded to her desires, or to those of a friend, that this woman allowed herself to address to her those flashing signals. If so, they did more than demand something for the present, they found a justification in pleasant hours in the past.

This assignation, in that case, must be not the first, but the sequel to adventures shared in past years. And indeed her glance did not say: " Will you? " As soon as the young woman had caught sight of Albertine, she had turned her head and beamed upon her glances charged with recollection, as though she were terribly afraid that my friend might not remember. Albertine, who could see her plainly, remained phlegmatically motionless, with the result that the other, with the same sort of discretion as a man who sees his old mistress with a new lover, ceased to look at her and paid no more attention to her than if she had not existed.

But, a day or two later, I received a proof of this young woman's tendencies, and also of the probability of her having known Albertine in the past. Often, in the hall of the casino, when two girls were smitten with mutual desire, a luminous phenomenon occurred, a sort of phosphorescent train passing from one to the other. Let us note in passing that it is by the aid of such materialisations, even if they be imponderable, by these astral signs that set fire to a whole section of the atmosphere, that the scattered Gomorrah tends, in every town, in every village, to reunite its separated members, to reform the biblical city while everywhere the same efforts are being made, be it in view of but a momentary reconstruction, by the nostalgic, the hypocritical, sometimes by the courageous exiles from Sodom.

Once I saw the stranger whom Albertine had appeared not to recognise, just at the moment when Bloch's cousin was approaching her. The young woman's eyes flashed, but it was quite evident that she did not know the Israelite maiden. She beheld her for the first time, felt a desire, a shadow of doubt, by no means the same certainty as in the case of Albertine, Albertine upon whose comradeship she must so far have reckoned that, in the face of her coldness, she had felt the surprise of a foreigner familiar with Paris but not resident there, who, having returned to spend a few weeks there, on the site of the little theatre where he was in the habit of spending pleasant evenings, sees that they have now built a bank.

Bloch's cousin went and sat down at a table where she turned the pages of a magazine. Presently the young woman came and sat down, with an abstracted air, by her side. But under the table one could presently see their feet wriggling, then their legs and hands, in a confused heap. Words followed, a conversation began, and the young woman's innocent husband, who had been looking everywhere for her, was astonished to find her making plans for that very evening with a girl whom he did not know. His wife introduced Bloch's cousin to him as a friend of her childhood, by an inaudible name, for she had forgotten to ask her what her name was. But the husband's presence made their intimacy advance a stage farther, for they addressed each other as *tu*, having known each other at their convent, an incident at which they laughed heartily later on, as well as at the hood-winked husband, with a gaiety which afforded them an excuse for more caresses.

As for Albertine, I cannot say that anywhere in the casino or on the beach was her behaviour with any girl unduly free. I found in it indeed an excess of coldness and indifference which seemed to be more than good breeding, to be a ruse planned to avert suspicion. When questioned by some girl, she had a quick, icy, decent way of replying in a very loud voice: " Yes, I shall be going to the tennis court about five. I shall bathe to-morrow morning about eight," and of at once turning away from the person to whom she had said this—all of which had a horrible appearance of being meant to put people off the scent, and either to make an assignation, or, the assigna-tion already made in a whisper, to utter this speech, harmless enough in itself, aloud, so as not to attract at-tention. And when later on I saw her mount her bicycle and scorch away into the distance, I could not help think-ing that she was hurrying to overtake the girl to whom she had barely spoken.

Only, when some handsome young woman stepped out of a motor-car at the end of the beach, Albertine could not help turning round. And she at once explained: " I was looking at the new flag they've put up over the bathing place. The old one was pretty moth-eaten. But I really think this one is mouldier still."

On one occasion Albertine was not content with cold indifference, and this made me all the more wretched. She knew that I was annoyed by the possibility of her sometimes meeting a friend of her aunt, who had a " bad

351

style " and came now and again to spend a few days with Mme. Bontemps. Albertine had pleased me by telling me that she would not speak to her again. And when this woman came to Epreville, Albertine said: " By the way, you know she's here. Have they told you? " as though to shew me that she was not seeing her in secret. One day, when she told me this, she added: " Yes, I ran into her on the beach, and knocked against her as I passed, on purpose, to be rude to her." When Albertine told me this, there came back to my mind a remark made by Mme. Bontemps, to which I had never given a second thought, when she had said to Mme. Swann in my presence how brazen her niece Albertine was, as though that were a merit, and told her how Albertine had reminded some official's wife that her father had been employed in a kitchen. But a thing said by her whom we love does not long retain its purity; it withers, it decays. An evening or two later, I thought again of Albertine's remark, and it was no longer the ill breeding of which she was so proud—and which could only make me smile—that it seemed to me to signify, it was something else, to wit that Albertine, perhaps even without any definite object, to irritate this woman's senses, or wantonly to remind her of former proposals, accepted perhaps in the past, had swiftly brushed against her, thought that I had perhaps heard of this as it had been done in public, and had wished to forestall an unfavourable interpretation.

However, the jealousy that was caused me by the women whom Albertine perhaps loved was abruptly to cease.

Printed in Great Britain by R. & R. CLARK, LIMITED, *Edinburgh.*